Darkest Lies

A Gripping Crime Mystery Series

The DI Hogarth Darkest Series 1 & 2

1. The Darkest Lies & 2. The Darkest Grave

Solomon Carter

Great Leap

The Darkest Lies

Prologue

The First Night

Thump. Thump. Thump.
It was a pitch-black night on the edge of the town. A lone man stood outside the only nightclub on Luker Close, his hands stuffed deep in his pockets, his head tilted down toward the street. The relentless noise of the crashing dance tunes pounded through the concrete walls from within Club Smart. A few drunks staggered off the nearby high street. His heart rate spiked as they passed by him, but they all ignored him. Good. He remained anonymous. Just another stranger lurking in the darkness. Around here no one wanted to check out anyone else in case of trouble, especially at night. Alcohol, late nights and the high street were never a good mix, so it paid to be careful. Tonight was going to be a great night to kill. It was going to be a night to celebrate. A night of relief… but for now he had to watch. He had to wait.

Soon enough he saw the man he had been waiting for. The great lummox walked out from the club doors cradling a beer bottle by the neck, like he could break any rule he liked. And maybe for a while he could. But not anymore. The big man was oblivious to being watched from across the other side of the dead-end street. He watched the man walk around the side of Club Smart turning the corner towards the empty square where the old multi-storey car park had been torn down and replaced with the fancy new library. The development had left a neat, barren space between the backs of the high street shops and the great glass library. The library was dark and silent. A couple of drunken girls stood together laughing at the furthest end of the square, sharing some smutty joke. The square was an exposed area. At first glance it was a terrible place to commit murder, but first impressions could be deceptive and he knew the area very well. He had been meticulous. There were always places to do what needed to be done. Even out here in the open. He let the big man walk ahead, keeping his distance. He noticed his target begin to hurry… but why? The watcher knew he hadn't been seen. Now he was curious. The man looked like he was headed nowhere – towards the lines of big red wheelie bins at the back of the shops. Excellent news. Jake Drummond seemed intent on finding the very best place to be killed. And it was fitting. Drummond was the worst kind of human rubbish the watcher had ever known. He watched Jake slow down as he neared the back of the big SavaPenny store and looked around. The watcher stopped, worried he would be seen before his moment came. But it didn't happen. Drummond slowed up and stared ahead of him. There was a wall of bins in front of him now, perfect for what had to be done.

The watcher started to move. He sped up as he aimed across the square, conscious of the CCTV cameras on poles around the library and the college buildings. He knew what to do. He dipped his head down to his shoes but strained his eyes upward to watch Drummond's every move. A scrape of high-heeled shoes echoed across the square. Looking up, he saw the girls tottering around the corner out of sight and a smile crossed his lips. And so his last witnesses were gone. His heart sped up. Adrenaline. Excitement. He knew the feelings well, but everything he'd experienced was nothing like this. *This was exquisite.* In his pocket, his right hand gripped the cool polymer fibre of the pistol he had owned since the old days. No one would ever be able to trace it to him if he used it. He'd gotten it on the black market long ago. The thing had never been fired, at least not by him anyway. But all being well, he wouldn't have to use it. The gun was his backup. His insurance policy. In his left pocket, his hands gripped the sides of a grooved blade handle. He squeezed it, and enjoyed the cool smoothness in his hands. Now there were mere seconds left. He advanced, his eyes on his quarry like a man from a different time. Like an animal. He had always wanted to be more than any normal man. He'd always wanted to be the best. And now he would try it first-hand.

"Hang about! You. What are you doing here?"

What? He was still advancing when he heard the strange disembodied voice. It was familiar but he couldn't see the source of it. The smile faded from his face, and he slowed down. Now his hand gripped the blade handle for comfort instead of intent. Big Drummond stood still, facing the array of bins.

"Come on. You know why I'm here," said Drummond. "I saw you leave. It's bloody obvious what you were up to…" The big man made an obscene laugh. The watcher was angry. His prey so close. He was still tempted to go ahead and take his kill. It had to be done. He moved forward, stalking like a lion, but deep down he knew his moment was disappearing.

As he closed in he saw a second man appear, the man's head rising up from behind the bins like a ghost. The man's hair seemed white in the dark. The second man stood up dead opposite Drummond, his pale face full of shock, his mouth a gaping oval. The watcher gritted his teeth and hid his face. He recognised the man. His heart sank.

"What are you going to do?" said the man with the white hair. His voice was hesitant and timid.

The watcher stopped in his tracks. If the man looked up he would be seen. He lowered his head and made a slow half-turn away, but stood his ground nonetheless. He couldn't bear the thought of giving up so soon.

"Don't play dumb, Mr G. You know what I'm gonna do. Leave. You've had enough for one night…"

The watcher risked another glance towards the bins, and saw a blonde woman with dated cropped hair slowly stand up from behind the bins, pulling down her skirt. A drunken trollop, he thought. She moved close to the man with the white hair, but he didn't move a muscle or say a word.

"You can't do this, Jake…"

"You wish. Now hop it or there'll be consequences."

"What do you mean consequences?"

He watched the big man lean forward as he gave the man with the pale hair something. Something small. The man looked at it for a moment, before Drummond snatched it back.

"Now you know I'm not lying."

He watched it all. The man behind the bins looked at his girlfriend once. Just once. Then he turned his back on her and walked away towards the square.

"Where are you going?" she called. He heard the fear in her voice but the woman got no answer.

"Hey!" she said. Then Drummond stepped passed the boyfriend, and began to close in on her. The boyfriend looked back once more as the girl started to protest, but he kept walking. She wasn't loud for long. Drummond fell upon her, disappearing down behind the bins, smothering the noise to near silence. The watcher had a choice to make. But it wasn't hard. He was no hero. He needed a clean opportunity to do what needed to be done. And with these other fools invading the scene, this wasn't it. Damn them. In his pocket, he stroked the knife handle and turned away, walking towards the high street to blend in with the rest of the late night scum before he could be seen. There would be another night. Jake Drummond would still get what was coming to him. The big man had to die.

Chapter One

Day Four: Monday

The speakers screamed as the music hit a new electronic crescendo, louder even than the last. The youths on the circular dance floor cheered, and jumped up and down like kids on Christmas morning. Most of them looked young enough to be tucked up in bed. PC Rob Dawson folded his arms and supped his pint as he looked out at the youths, feeling dazed and confused for being so out of place. The cop was off duty, dressed down in jeans and a short-sleeved shirt. He was too old for this, and yet he wasn't old at all. Dawson was in his early thirties. But compared to this lot, he was ancient. So why the hell had he agreed to come? Because of Bec Rawlins, that's why. PCSO Bec Rawlins, was a very persuasive and gorgeous young cop who happened to be his girlfriend. She wanted a night out with her friends, she wanted him to come, and so here it was. Pretty much his worst nightmare. He was a trophy boyfriend to be shown around and cast aside as necessary. Trouble was tonight he couldn't even get drunk. Bec was due to be off work next morning, but for Dawson, it was very much a school night. The next morning, he was due to start at eight. But another couple of beers wouldn't hurt. Heck, he'd need something to get through this. Worse, the man standing next to him wasn't exactly his cup of tea. He was a posh nob and didn't have the personality to bridge the gap between them. Andy Cruddas, a man born to money, who as far as Dawson could tell didn't have a proper job, but always seemed to be flush with cash. Until tonight, that was. For some reason Andy hadn't offered to buy him a drink back. And Dawson was buggered if he was going to keep this rich boy in free booze all night. Cruddas was one of Bec's friends. Looking at the man, Dawson guessed Cruddas had only hung around in case Bec became available again. Fat chance of that, he thought. Cruddas tried to make conversation with him every now and then, but his words were empty. He looked anxious, and Rob didn't know the man well enough to inquire why.

"She's a looker, your girl, isn't she?" said Cruddas, sipping his beer like a nervous boy. Dawson saw the man looking left and right as if he was expecting someone.

"I like to think so," said Dawson.

"And so do a few others from the look of it," said Cruddas. Dawson watched a couple of young men in bright shirts closing in on Bec's group of friends. So, far the girls hadn't noticed the dodgy double act moving towards them. Either that or they just didn't care.

"I'm not worried," said Dawson.

Now Cruddas looked at him. "No. I guess not. I kind of envy you, if I'm honest."

"Envy? How do you mean?"

"Oh. It's nothing really. Just that you seem to have it all sorted."

"Don't be silly, Andy. We've all got stuff on our plates."

"Yeah, I suppose," said Cruddas. But he didn't seem convinced. "Listen. I don't suppose you know anybody who wants to buy a decent car at short notice, do you? It's a very nice car. An executive car – at a very cheap price."

"Sorry. The only cars I drive are supplied by the police. I prefer it that way."

Cruddas looked deflated.

"Okay. Go on then," said Dawson almost with a sigh, trying to be heard above the music. "How much is it?"

"It's a Merc C220. Only a few years old. Diesel. Silver. Looks fantastic."

"And? How much?"

"Five grand."

"Five grand! It must be worth a bit more than that."

"It definitely is. It's only got a few miles on the clock. I should really hold out for about twelve grand, but well…"

"Well, why don't you then?"

"Needs must, old bean."

Old bean? Did he really say that? Dawson pondered the car sale, the price, and sipped his pint. His cop brain kicked in and started to process the possibilities. The car wasn't for him. A shoe leather copper driving a top range Merc? The others down the station would rinse him for weeks if he ever bought a car like that. Police banter was about keeping everyone's feet on the ground. No one liked a show off. No the Merc certainly wasn't for him. But Andy Cruddas was making him think.

"You must be in a real hurry to cut the price like that," he said.

"Yes… afraid so. Still. Financial troubles come to us all at some time, so they tell me."

"Hmmmm," said Dawson. If Cruddas was angling for another free drink, he was out of luck. Just in case, Dawson let the conversation dwindle back to a comfortable silence. But Cruddas was fidgety. Dawson watched as he kept looking back to the cloakroom beside the small bar and to the double doors beyond which led to the exit. He watched Cruddas stiffen as two men walked in. One of them was broad and fat, going bald on top with a wispy dark mullet combed back behind him. He wore a bright white shirt, which made his pot belly look big and rock solid. The man looked to be in his mid-forties. Dawson had been a copper for a long time. He recognised people by their types, and this was the moneyed type. Not necessarily rich by honest money either, from the look of him. The smaller, spectacled man at his side looked twitchy. They walked side by side, but there was distance between them. The big man said something, and the smaller man pointed across the club towards Dawson and Cruddas. The men stopped and exchanged a few more words before the big man turned to the smaller guy, and leaned in towards him. He prodded the man in the chest. His spectacles glinted with nightclub light as he pulled back. He looked uncomfortable. Like he was protesting. The scene made Dawson want to walk across and put the big man in his place. But he was off duty and nothing illegal had taken place. After all, the public had to be allowed to act like idiots somewhere. And Club Smart seemed the perfect place for idiots. Dawson noticed Cruddas was watching, the same scene. He was stiffening, straining as if he was about to make a move.

"Friend of yours?" said Dawson.

"What?" said Cruddas with a jump. "Friend? Oh, yes. Excuse me."

"Any time you like," said Dawson, under his breath. Cruddas left his drink on the side and walked away to meet the men by the doors. Dawson thought they made an uncomfortable trio, the big man clearly in charge. He spoke to each of them in turn, prodding the first, before encroaching into Andy Cruddas' personal space. Dawson sipped his pint and got ready to move. Duty was about to call. The men exchanged sharp words, then the big man jabbed a finger at Cruddas and pushed the smaller man away.

Dawson laid his drink aside just as the confrontation stopped. The big man clapped his hands to end the matter and strode off towards the small bar with a serene smile on his face.

Dawson settled back with his drink. He watched Cruddas and the other man talking by the exit. Their exchange looked pretty intense. It was a weird situation, but he couldn't hear a thing because of the music, though he could see they were agitated. He watched them staring at the big man as he walked away to the bar. Then Cruddas pointed at Dawson. *Uh-oh* he thought. *Now they're going to drag me into their trouble. Not tonight, Josephine.*

Cruddas ambled over towards him with the other man at his side. The second guy was smaller than Cruddas, he had curly hair and horn-rim glasses. The smaller man could have been Cruddas' little brother.

"Rob," said Cruddas. "This is my mate. Dan Picton. Dan this is Rob Dawson. He's a policeman."

Dawson smiled and nodded, and got ready for the question. But it didn't come, and that alone had him thinking. *Why bother to make a point of him being a cop?*

"Hiya," said Dawson. "I couldn't help noticing you had some trouble with Bully Beef just now. What was the guy's problem?" Dawson knew he was asking for it. But asking questions were a habit of his career. A habit he couldn't kick.

"Him? Oh, he's nothing," said Cruddas.

Dawson looked at Cruddas, and saw the strained look in his eyes. Cruddas and Picton looked at one another. *Nothing. Yeah, right...*

"You know, I don't feel great. I think I need some air," said Cruddas. Dawson looked at Cruddas but the man averted his eyes.

"What's up with him tonight?" said Dawson.

The smaller man shrugged. "I don't know. I suppose I'd better go and see if he's alright."

Picton made an apologetic face and moved off. Dawson shook his head. Bec's friends were a bunch of weirdos alright. He wondered how she'd managed to turn out so well?

Bec stepped up from the dance floor and laid a hand on Dawson's muscular forearm. She gave him a glowing smile. She'd been dancing a while, and still looked like the most energetic and effervescent person in the room.

"Where has Andy gone?" she said.

"Cruddas? I don't know. The guy's in a weird mood and so's his friend."

"Friend?"

"Some bloke called Dan Picton. Little fella. Do you know him?"

Bec nodded. "Andy's pal. Crikey. You boys need to lighten up. This is a nightclub, not a bloody mausoleum."

"I'm still here, aren't I? It's your male friends who need to lighten up."

"But you haven't even danced yet, Rob" said Bec, with flirtatious eyes.

Dawson raised his pint glass. "I'm just getting loose before I bust a few moves and put you to shame."

"You busting moves? I've seen you bust a few heads, but I've never seen you bust any moves."

"For you, anything," said Dawson with a cheesy grin.

Bec's friend Julie climbed up the steps behind her and tried to pull her back to the dance floor.

"Oh well. It looks like it's over to us girls to show the boys how it's done," said Bec.

Dawson watched Bec step back down to the dance floor. He enjoyed seeing her out, both proud and irritated by the fact that other men clearly wanted her as much as he did. But she was off limits. She was going home with him tonight. He smiled into his pint and glanced at the time on his phone screen. Eleven twenty? Was that all?

There was a sudden shout from the small bar by the club doors and Dawson looked up from his phone. *It was an odd shout.* More like a man screaming. His eyes flicked around on instinct. Down on the dance floor, Bec Rawlins stopped dancing. She spun round to locate the noise. Both of them saw a kerfuffle at the bar. The crowd ordering their drinks blew apart like a flock of birds at the sound of a gun. Another louder shout came from a huddle by the bar. The crowd stepped back, some had covered their mouths with their hands. Others stared. The barmen were staring, wide eyed. The area was filled with noisy chaos. An icy feeling shot down Dawson's spine. He knew it was trouble, bad trouble. He tensed and started to move, but now everything was happening too fast. The people were spilling past him. The surprised, frightened eyes of the barmen and women were fixed on one big figure who stood alone in the centre of the dispersed crowd. The big man stumbled and twisted around and caught Dawson's eye as he approached. He looked utterly confused. Dawson recognised the man as he stumbled forwards. It was Bully Beef, the big man who had entered the club with Dan Picton. He saw the man's eyes were glazed with shock. His mouth was open, a trickle of blood dribbling from the corner of his lip. One fat hand was pressed over his chest, and blood seeped through his fingers. The flashing nightclub lights made the blood look black as ink. Finally, the man's hand fell away as he gave in to gravity. Dawson saw a single dark black hole in the centre of the man's bright white shirt. He slumped down in a heap, head hitting the floor face down, then he rolled still, arms out at his sides. A full second later the screaming started. A door flew open behind the bar and a man in a black polo shirt wearing an ear piece emerged, confused, looking round at the noise. The club manager, Dawson guessed. Now the chaos had started he would soon need the man's help. Dawson ran into the crowd by the body, and pushed a few drunken gawpers away from the victim with a forceful shove. "Police! Move away! PCSO Rawlins!" he shouted. Bec nodded. She was on her way. "Get them to shut off the music and tell the security to lock the doors, sharpish." Bec looked ashen when she reached him. Dawson knelt by the body and pressed his fingers into the side of the big man's neck, hunting for a pulse. But he felt nothing. He looked up at the faces ranged around them, looking for someone half-useful as he hunted for the eyes of the culprit. He scanned them for a few seconds. The truth was it could have been any of them and none of them looked fit to help. One of the bar staff leaned over the bar. He looked like a school kid. "Is he…?"

"Just call an ambulance will you?!" snapped Dawson.
The man nodded and went away to do as he was told.
He tried for the pulse again, but it wasn't there. Dawson looked up at the faces ranged around him. They were waiting for news, eyes appealing to him, like they were watching some bloody crime movie on Webflix. But very soon they would get the news they were waiting for. He would try CPR, but Dawson already knew for certain it would fail. There was no hurry for an ambulance. The bully was dead.

Chapter Two

Detective Sergeant Sue Palmer was far too tired for a late night call-out, but these days, crime in the town wasn't letting up. There were enough cases and names on the CID room incident board to keep them busy for a month of Sundays. And just when she thought she had some time to herself, it had happened again. Lying on her bed, indulging in a chicken chow mein with prawn crackers and an NYPD Blue boxed set for company, the phone call from DI Hogarth was most unwelcome. And with it went all chance of sleep. DS Palmer regretted the Chinese as soon as she put the phone down. Her stomach felt bloated and her mouth was greasy. Not that DI Hogarth would have thought twice about snaffling a quick Kung Po washed down with his favourite whisky before a job, but Sue Palmer was a woman and whatever the blokes said, it was different. At least Hogarth wasn't one of the PC brigade who said there was no glass ceiling. Hogarth was a dark realist with a cynical sense of humour. Lately Palmer had almost gotten used to Hogarth's unintended sexism. It had almost become amusing. And under Hogarth's rough, rotten exterior, she had found a sliver of charm which made her wonder about the distant possibilities… maybe if she was working on the team in the other office, it could have worked. *Maybe.* But then she had seen no signs that he was in the least interested in her. No clear signs, anyway. Oh well. The dating sites would have to wait for another night.

Palmer parked her battered Vauxhall hatchback on the yellow lines on the corner of Luker Close, central Southend.

The close was a dead-end street adjoining the middle of Southend's busy high street. It was lined by a mix of long-closed office blocks, the newish student union bar, and the nightclub, Club Smart. Palmer stepped out of her dented Corsa and tried her best to present a businesslike air to hide her chow mein stomach. As she walked along Luker Close to the door, a homeless guy who lived under the neighbouring shop canopy drifted past and gave her a once-over. At least some men still wanted to look. Palmer shook her head with a weary smile. At thirty-seven years old, Palmer was a single blonde with a few white hairs already showing. And she was a committed career copper with no spare time. It was hardly good material for her dating profile. If nothing happened soon, she'd be eyeing up hobos herself. She marched towards the uniforms guarding the front door. The officers were chatting with the club doormen as if they were on the same team. It showed how naïve they were. In Palmer's experience club doormen were often linked to criminals. It simply went with the territory. The uniforms seemed to feel Palmer's weary gaze fall on them. They instantly shut their chattering and stiffened their backs.

"Any update, Jordan?" she said to the younger of the PCs as she passed him by.

"Nothing yet. No sign of the weapon or the perpetrator, as far as I know."

"No one would tell you anyway, would they, Jordan?" said PC Orton, the bigger and heavier of the men. Orton was a bit of a pillock. Palmer was too tired for the banter. She stepped between the uniforms with a thin smile then walked into the sparkly purple corridor by the cloakroom and ticket desk.

"What's her problem?" said Orton, when she was out of earshot.

"Hogarth, I reckon," said Jordan. "I wouldn't want to work with the man either."
Orton laughed like a drain.

Under the unforgiving strip lights the interior of Club Smart looked like a cave with added flashes of neon. Nightclubs were never supposed to be seen like this. The darkness was how they got away with the low budget décor. Or lack of it. The whole place was dirty and cold, like an industrial warehouse with added sparkle and grime. The club goers had been kept back, still standing about in their short sparkly skirts, smeared mascara and drink-glazed eyes. The men were sweaty and bleary eyed. What a sight. Everyone looked ready for bed. Detective Inspector Joe Hogarth didn't look any better, which brought a mite of comfort. His straggly ginger-brown hair looked shaggier than normal, but it always looked like it needed a cut. And his shirt collar was untidy. He had dressed in a hurry. His favourite navy-blue blazer, tan chinos, and brogues were all in place, but even they looked scruffy. The DI stood in his customary stance with hands in his pockets as he spoke to a small young man in a black polo shirt, while Ivan Marris from the forensic crew and John Dickens from Crime Scene began to unpack their equipment around his feet. Palmer looked down at the place where the body had fallen. Hogarth was so busy asking questions he hadn't yet seen her. Palmer looked around the club until she saw a pair of familiar eyes. The young blonde PCSO Rawlins looked as glamorous as a film star in her little party dress. Looking at the girl was almost depressing. "Rawlins?" said Palmer. The room was quiet, apart from a low chorus of hoarse whispers. DI Hogarth's eyes darted her way.
"What are you doing here, Bec?" she continued.

"Night off. At least it was supposed to be. I was here with PC Dawson."
"Oh, were you now?" said Palmer, with a wry smile.
Rawlins blushed, but she needn't have. Her relationship with Dawson was well known by now. The joke was that they were the royal couple of Southend nick. *Harry and Meghan eat your heart out.*
"Don't worry, Bec. I'm only jealous. I haven't had a night out in years." Or a man, she thought. "I wouldn't know what to do if I did. If you want a life, Bec, please don't join CID."
"CID? I'm not even a WPC yet."
"That'll come soon enough. So, what happened here?"
"It was a stabbing, with no sign of who did it. No one seems to have seen a thing. Rob—I mean PC Dawson said he'd seen the fella throwing his weight around before he was attacked. Sounds like the guy had only been here for a few minutes before he got stabbed."
"And no one saw anything?" said Palmer.
"Not that I know."
"Or are they just too scared to say…?" she said.
"You'd have to speak to DI Hogarth. He's been grilling the people who were at the bar where the man was stabbed. Hogarth has had me and Rob carrying out searches for the knife. But we haven't found a thing."
"You're sure the killer didn't get out?"
"Ninety-five per cent sure. We locked the doors as quick as we could and security helped us hold everyone back."
Palmer saw a tall, shaven-headed man in a black bomber jacket. He was chewing gum and was built like a brick outhouse. "Security being helpful are they?" she said.
"Why? You think security could have been in on it?" said Bec doubtfully.

"At this stage, we don't know a thing. But I wouldn't ever rule them out, that's for sure. But if the place was sealed up in time, that means our killer must still be here…"
"Don't bet on it," said Dawson, appearing at Palmer's shoulder. Palmer looked up at PC Dawson's clean-cut face. She smelt the beer on his breath but the man seemed sober enough.
"Why not?" said Palmer.
PC Dawson looked at Rawlins. "I think a couple of them could have got out just in time…"
Rawlins frowned at him while Palmer waited for an explanation.

"You're telling me the big man was good as gold all the way up until he was attacked?" said Hogarth, with more than a hint of irony. "All sweetness and light, was he?" said DI Hogarth, rubbing his eyes. The young barman in front of him wore one of the standard issue earpieces which made modern people look like a cyborg. Yes, they'd been around for years, but Hogarth still couldn't get used to it.
"Well, I wouldn't say sweetness and light, exactly. Drummie is… I mean, was, built like a beast."
"You called him 'Drummie'?" said Hogarth. "So you knew Jake Drummond then?" he said, his eyes opening a little wider. The young man nodded.
"Yeah. Drummie came here a lot. I still don't know why, though. He never ever danced. He was big and too old for all that. But I think he liked to have a gawp at the young girlies like a few of the older boys who come here do. Look around, you'll see the ones I mean."
Hogarth looked and saw a few haggard faces who were older than him and at forty-five he was far too old for this kind of rubbish. What were they thinking? Hogarth's face crumpled

in disdain. "Might that have upset anyone? The gawping at girls, I mean," said Hogarth, probing his way towards a motive.

"I don't see how. Drummond had only been here five minutes when it happened. I still can't believe it. I've never seen trouble like that in here before… and I've never seen anyone die…"

The kid's eyes drifted away. Hogarth shifted in front of him and forced the kid to look into his eyes. He didn't need help from another shell-shocked bystander. He needed a few answers while things were fresh. Hogarth checked around, keeping his voice low.

"You work behind the bar, so you must hear things, if you know what I mean. Tell me. Do you know if Jake Drummond had any longstanding, enemies, let's say… people with grudges against him… people who may not have liked him too much?"

The man shrugged. "I don't want to get involved in that kind of stuff…"

"You're already involved, son. The man was killed not ten feet in front of you. That's very involved in my book. You could be a key witness."

"Key witness? But I didn't see anything. There was a shout, a scream, whatever, then the man fell down. That's it. That's what I saw."

"I asked you about enemies. Come on. You must know something on that score. Every barman does."

"This is a nightclub, not a pub, Inspector. I don't hear anything they say. They all talk crap when they're drunk, so I shut them out. But look… Drummie was like Marmite. That's for sure. You either loved him or you hated his guts."

"Why?"

The kid looked around, as if suddenly unsure of himself.

"Because he was a bruiser. He threw his weight around. He liked to act the big man. I saw that. But we have plenty of idiots who come in here who are the same. The security boys can spot them a mile off."

"He was a bruiser, was he? So who did he bruise?"

"I don't know. I just heard he was a handful and not always very nice."

"Not very nice. Well, there's a reason to kill a man. Who hated him and why?"

"I can't tell you that…"

"Can't or won't, son? There's a very big difference."

The barman started to wilt under Hogarth's gaze.

"People like him had a rep. I heard about his rep. I don't know the details, but I know I was lucky not to see his rough side."

"Who else might know more about Drummond's friends? Or that rough side of his? Any ideas?"

The kid clammed up before Hogarth's eyes. His mouth turned into a flat line and he shook his head emphatically.

"You'd have to ask around about that. I couldn't tell you."

"What's your name, young man?"

"Gordon Turner. People call me Gordy."

"Thanks, Gordy. You've been a great help," said Hogarth, with a certain emphasis which told the kid he hadn't been much help at all. "I'll be speaking with you again. You can count on it."

Hogarth gave the kid the full-beam snake smile, then watched him go away sullen faced. DS Palmer appeared at his side. She was almost a half foot shorter than him. She was a good cop, and a pretty one too. Her shorter hair wasn't the style he liked most of all, but it suited her well enough. Even so, he could tell the job was already wearing her down. She looked tired and borderline depressed. Hogarth drifted off as he looked at her.

"Penny for them, sir?"

"They're not worth a penny at the moment, Palmer. All we've got is a club full of hear-no-evils and see-no-evils. So far, nobody saw anything apart from Jake Drummond clutching his chest before he dropped down to the floor like a sack of spuds."

"Jake Drummond...? We know the victim then?"

"He's got a good bit of previous from back in the day, a bit of ABH and some extorting with menaces about ten years back. But he's not been on my radar since I landed in town. What about you?"

"Drummond... Jack Drummond?" said Palmer, chewing on the name.

"Known as Drummie to his fan club, apparently," said Hogarth.

Palmer rolled the name around her mind. "No, sir. He's never been one of mine."

"I've heard the man described as a bruiser, and possibly a low level perv, too," said Hogarth. "The kind who hangs around nightclubs to stare at girls and throw his weight around."

"A real charmer then?"

"There are plenty of words for men like that, Palmer, but charmer isn't one of them. To have enemies who wanted him dead, he must have stirred up plenty of trouble. Only it's not on the record. But someone in here must know something. We didn't find much on him. A wallet full of cash, probably all dirty money. His mobile phone. A photograph of a baby in his wallet."

"A baby? So, he wasn't a complete toad then."

"Having children doesn't make a bad man good. It makes him worse in my mind. What example was he setting? From what I've heard Drummond was nothing but a toad."

"What about the murder weapon? Any sign of it yet?"

"I've seen the wound. I'd say we were looking at a narrow blade. The wound was pretty tight – a small puncture wound in the central chest area. He probably died within seconds. I'm pretty certain Quentin will confirm it at the post mortem... what do you think, Marris?" Hogarth looked down at the lanky man hunkered down on the floor below him. The forensic man, Ivan Marris. Marris was already gloved-up and beginning to mark out his territory. He looked irritated, and Dickens had been giving him hard eyes from the moment he arrived. Neither man would be comfortable with so many punters still at the crime scene. They were professionals, and evidence was their business. Every live body presented a threat in terms of contaminating the evidence. Hogarth knew it wouldn't be long before Marris insisted they move everybody out of the club.

Marris looked up at them. "It's not worth me guessing. I've more than enough to be getting on with, what with all these people milling around," he said. Yes, Marris wanted the site clear. But Hogarth was hoping for a collar before he sent them home.

Hogarth shrugged. "I'd still say we're looking at a thin blade, probably no more than six inches in length. Anything else couldn't be hidden too easily."

"That's long enough to kill. The knife must have been seen, then," said Palmer.

"You'd think so, but no... but they're scared. With no weapon and no proper witness as yet, this one's already beginning to look like hard work."

Palmer saw Hogarth looking at her. For a fleeting moment it occurred to her Hogarth was giving her the eye. But she was kidding herself again. Palmer soon dismissed the thought. After all, it was hardly likely, given that some of the team reckoned Hogarth had a secret woman tucked away somewhere. In the next moment Hogarth dispelled any of her illusions.

"You look like I feel, Palmer. Or should that be the other way around?" he said with a grim smile.

"It could be either one, sir. Thanks for the encouragement."

"Sorry, Palmer…" he said with a yawn. "You should know by now I've got a habit of jabbering when I should shut my mouth. Still. At least I'm not as bad as DC Simmons. But we really could have done without this case on top of everything else we've got on."

The weariness in Hogarth's face almost overwhelmed him as he spoke, but then he shook it off. Palmer put on a smile.

"I think Jake Drummond could have done without the case as well, sir," said Palmer.

Hogarth nodded. "I suppose so."

Hogarth scanned the room, looking at the trapped club-goers, taking in details before he was forced to drive the people out. He saw one lively conversation. A man with a craggy, weather-beaten face was talking to a man with bleached blond hair who wore a silver-blue party shirt. The guy in the party shirt looked too old for any such attempts at being fashionable or cool. Hogarth decided he had to be the DJ. The man talking to him had an angular, bird-like face with rough red skin and a big nose. As they were talking, Hogarth turned his ear to tune in.

"…very bloody unlikely, that's all I'm saying," said the man with the bleach-blond hair

"As if I should listen to you. After all you've done, you're no better than vermin! Jake Drummond would have come through with the goods. I told you, we were going to be partners. We would have sorted it out."

"Partners? Leave it out. He would have ripped you off, just like everybody else…"

Hogarth logged as much of what he heard as he could. The conversation could have been nothing, yes, but it could also have been the jackpot. It sounded like the man in the party shirt had known Jake Drummond better than most. It was a chink of light and nothing more. Hogarth knew this case was going to be hard going. And with all their other cases on the go, not to mention the mess of his own private life, Hogarth wasn't convinced he had any more energy to give. But murder was the most serious part of the business. It was his territory, his task, so he would set about it with whatever he had left. He looked once more at the man in the party shirt and his craggy-faced companion. Whether Hogarth liked it or not, the game had already begun.

Chapter Three

"He would have ripped you off, like everybody else," said Hogarth. "That's what you said, Gary. I heard you say it."

"No I didn't," he said. And then, "*Did I?*"

Hogarth had been right. The man with the bleached blond hair and loud shirt was none other than Gary Grayson, known on the club circuit as DJ-GG. Grayson was the man behind Club Smart's *'Wheels of Steel'* three nights per week. Hogarth had taken the man into the back office for questioning. DS Palmer was with them. The back office was a dirty-walled, sweaty pit of a room which smelt of stale beer, cleaning chemicals, and reused air. There were no windows. Hogarth wanted to leave as soon as he arrived, but reminded himself that he had worked in worse circumstances.

"I heard you out there, Gary. You were having a go at some poor old fella who looked like he was upset that his friend had been killed. What a nice time to pick on someone."

"I wasn't picking on anyone!" said Grayson.

Hogarth raised an eyebrow and left it there "Tell me. Who was the man you were arguing with?"

"That silly old sod? Peter Deal, that's who. He's a fool and an old dreamer, that's all. He's nobody."

"But he's worth you arguing with. Come on. Why were you quarrelling with him?" said Hogarth. He picked up the chipped mug of coffee the club manager had given him and sipped it. The hot black brew tasted as foul as it looked, but Hogarth needed some caffeine if he was going to push on for the rest of the night.

"Deal is just an old schmo with too much time and money on his hands. I don't know why you're asking me about him. You could ask him yourself," said Grayson.

"I'm interested in the conversation you had with him, that's why… come on, Gary. Tell me more.

"Whatever. Peter Deal used to own a garage. He was a car mechanic. Then he won some cash on the lottery – not even the jackpot mind – and after that he became a total bore. Kept on telling everyone that he was looking to invest in a new cash-cow business. How stupid is that? Everyone wants an easy life these days, don't they? If you ask me, it's dangerous chasing easy money."

"Dangerous, Gary? Why dangerous?"

Gary Grayson looked confused. DS Palmer stepped in to help.

"What was dangerous about Deal wanting easy money?"

"It's not just dangerous for him, is it? Easy money is dangerous for everyone. It's a pipe dream. Only hard work gets money."

"Hard work? Like spinning discs three nights a week in a cheesy nightclub?" said Hogarth.

"Hey! I work all the hours, I'll have you know," said the DJ. "It looks like a party, but this is graft."

"Good for you, Gary," said Hogarth. "But what about Mr Deal. You told him he would be mugged. Why? He was going to invest in something dodgy, was he? Something with Jake Drummond perhaps?"

The DJ ran a hand through his greasy bleach-blond hair and looked at Hogarth. It seemed he was struggling to answer. "I put two and two together. I heard you talking, remember."

"Yeah, well…" said the man. He pulled his nose between finger and thumb and sniffed. "What happened here tonight saved Deal from losing everything."

Hogarth jangled the loose change and keys in his pockets. Palmer looked at him, sensing the familiar hint of his excitement. The DI smelt something in the air.

"Really now. You seem to know a lot about Jake Drummond, Gary. Or at least, you know most of the bad stuff, shall we say. Care to tell me how you know so much?"

"How? Because I'm a DJ! I get around. I'm the social butterfly type, like most DJs are. Let's just say I met a lot of people who have lived through a few things around here."

"Anyone you'd care to mention? Any specifics?"

"Come on. I'm a DJ, Inspector, not Ask Jeeves. You've asked me some things, and I've told you what I could. Drummond had a rep, and Peter Deal should have known better than to ever get involved with him."

"So you were merely looking out for the man's interests. Very charitable of you, considering what Mr Deal thinks of you."

"What?" said Grayson. But Hogarth had moved on.

"A bad rep. That's what people keep saying. He had a rep. He was a bad man. But people only ever earn their reputations through the things they do. What did Drummond do to make you think that he would rip off Peter Deal."

Gary Grayson shrugged and dragged a hand over his face. "He had form, okay. All I'm saying is that if I had money, I wouldn't have put it near the man. He was bad news and some people will be very happy he's gone."

"Which people, exactly?" said Hogarth. "You maybe?"

The man's mouth was open. His lips glistened with saliva but he didn't say another word.

"Are you one of them, Gary? Did he try anything with you?" said Hogarth. "I must say, you don't seem too devastated that one of your club goers got stabbed to death here tonight."

"I just told you. He was a bad man."

"And what about you, Gary? Are you a bad man? Peter Deal called you vermin. I heard it." Hogarth watched the man squirm as he mentioned the word. "Mr Deal doesn't like you much, does he?"

"It's because of the past. That's got nothing to do with anything."

"How about I be the judge of that?"

"You heard me, Inspector. I've got opinions. Peter doesn't like someone who has opinions and is willing to share them. I'm a man of the world, Inspector. I've worked on the scene for twenty years. I've lived a lot and seen a lot. I speak my mind. I've been in places where punters were shot dead."

"Really now?" said Hogarth. His eyes changed from inquisitor to judge. He let the pressure of his gaze sink beneath the DJ's skin and watched him squirm for a moment until Grayson raised his hands in protest. "I meant I worked in some rough spots, clubs in south London, that's all. I never hurt anyone."

"Never?" said Hogarth.

"That's what I said. Why are you looking at me like that? I told you I didn't like Drummond, I admit that much. Who did like the man? But I would never have picked up a weapon against anyone. I'm a man of peace. Look at me. I'm a pacifist through and through."

"Oh yes, I'm sure. You're Club Smart's very own Dalai Lama and you're coming across as very inspirational, I must say," said Hogarth.

The DJ ran a hand through his hair and gave Hogarth the sternest look he could muster. "I didn't do it. I'm innocent. End of story."

"But what did you see?"
"My decks. That's what I saw. I was deejaying, remember. My job is to keep the party going."
"Let's review your job. You put on a record for three minutes, mix it into another one, say a few cheesy lines over the mic, then drink some more booze until the next one. Hard work, I'll agree. But it still gives you at least two or three spare minutes between every tune you play. More if you can stack some of those records together, or if you play a pre-made mix. That gives you plenty of time to look around, check out the girls, and enjoy the vibe. You must have seen something."
"Enjoy the vibe?" said the DJ, cackling. "Now you're showing your age, Inspector. What vintage are you, eh? Looking at that hair I'd say you were hitting the dance floor in eighty-six."
"I must look rough tonight, Gary. My clubbing days were in the nineties. But I never had much time for dancing. I was too busy nabbing villains. Now come on. What did you see?"
The man's smile fell away as quickly as it had appeared. "Nothing. I heard a noise, saw people scattering away from the bar, and that was it. The big man went down like a felled tree. I was deejaying. Simple as that."
"Simple as that, eh Gary…?" said Hogarth.
The DJ nodded. "Yes. Now, can I go?"
"Yes, but don't go too far, will you now?"
The DJ stood up and nodded at Palmer before he walked out of the room. His eyes stayed on her until he got through the door. Hogarth waited for the man's footsteps to fade away before he said anything else.
"What do you think?" said Palmer.
"He gave you a real once over on his way out. What do I think? I think he's a slimy sod who sees a lot more than he

lets on. It sounds to me like he's had a run-in with Jake Drummond himself. Ask around, see if you can find out if there's any history there. What about the management? You spoke to them. Did you get anything there?"

Palmer shrugged. "Just a few cursory questions. Names, numbers, and addresses, sir. But none of them saw a thing."

"Not very keen-eyed this lot, are they?"

Palmer pulled a notebook from her handbag and squinted at her notes. She started to read.

"The club is owned by John Milford. He manages the place some nights too. I spoke with him, and the door staff, and bar staff."

"I spoke with the bar staff myself," said Hogarth. "None of them saw a thing either. What about CCTV?"

"We've got the club's footage. A quick glance shows the tops of the heads of the people at the bar where the murder took place, but the camera position isn't great and the club uses old kit too, sir. The angle of the shots suggests their main concern is about the dance floor, looking for trouble there. We've got one shot of the small bar taken from behind. It shows lots of people with their backs to camera. I'd say it probably won't show the incident at the bar, but I haven't been through it yet."

"Maybe the camera position was deliberately skewed."

"That would make it an inside job?"

Hogarth shrugged. "Bar staff. DJ. Club manager. Security. Cleaners. Wives and girlfriends of the staff. If you think of all those people alone, it's a good number."

"Someone at that bar must have seen something. It stands to reason. They're our way in to the case, surely," said Palmer. "But a crowd can be easily deceived. We need to go through that CCTV footage. Use another pair of eyes if you need to. What about PC Dawson?"

Poor Dawson always seemed to draw Hogarth's short straw. Palmer recalled what Dawson had said before about the two suspects who could have gotten away. It was the first time she had remembered since. Hogarth needed to be told.
"We might not have all the suspects in the club after all, sir. I wouldn't draw any conclusions yet."
"It's far too early for conclusions, Sue."
He'd used her first name. Occasionally Hogarth slipped between the familiar and formal. Palmer had never been sure what to make of it, whether it meant anything. So she ignored the changes in mode as a quirk of the DI's character. Palmer knew the DI's first name was Joseph, but had never used it. "No conclusions?" Hogarth repeated. "What do you mean?"
"You knew PC Dawson and PCSO Rawlins were here on a night out tonight?"
"Yes. I set them to work right away," said Hogarth with a grin. "The party was over."
"Dawson says two of Rawlins friends left the club soon before Drummond was killed. Right before it happened, as a matter of fact. Sounds interesting, don't you think…?"
"And Rawlins knows them, does she?"
"Yes."
"Then I think we'd best have a word with our PCSO Rawlins, don't you?"
Palmer followed Hogarth out of the office, down the corridor filled with metal beer kegs, and through the double doors into the austere nightclub. The place had turned freezing cold, and some of the girls were shivering in their skimpy dresses.
"Can we let them go now, sir?" said Dawson, approaching as Hogarth reached the bar. "Marris has been on at me about jeopardising the evidence."

Hogarth sighed. "He's got a point. You've got all the names, any statements, and you've had them searched?"

"All done, sir. We didn't find a thing."

"Then let them go before Marris blows up at us. Beside, we don't need anyone dying of hypothermia now, do we? Send them home, Dawson. But before you do, where is your better half?"

Dawson gave Hogarth a look. "Sir?"

"PCSO Rawlins."

"Rawlins is still talking to some of the girls. A couple of them are still in shock from what happened... she's supporting them, sir."

"Yes. Murder is a very shocking thing, Dawson."

Dawson gave him a look. "What do you want with Rawlins, sir?"

"I want to talk to her about those friends of hers you mentioned. The ones who left just before the murder took place."

Dawson looked at Palmer. She nodded.

"Yes, I saw them, sir. One is called Andy Cruddas, that's PCSO Rawlins' friend. The other man is called Dan Picton. He came into the club the same time as the victim. I saw some kind of argy-bargy between them and it was obvious that Jake Drummond had the upper hand. It looked to me as if he was bullying the pair of them."

"Bullying?"

"Yes. It's hard to think of another word to describe it. He prodded the Picton man in the chest and gave him a proper talking to. I couldn't hear what was said because of the music, but I saw it alright."

"And the other man?"

"Andy Cruddas was here with me all night until just before the incident. We were drinking by the dance floor while

PCSO Rawlins and her friends had a dance. As soon as Cruddas' mate Picton turned up, he walked over to greet them, and I saw Jake Drummond give them both some verbal. Then they both came over here, and Drummond went to the bar. Picton and Cruddas left together. Less than a minute later – Jake Drummond dropped down dead."
"You saw all that?"
"I was bored, sir. Cruddas was no company at all. He was very quiet and very tense, and acting very odd."
"Like a murderer before the kill?" said Hogarth.
"I don't know about that. He left before it happened. I don't see how it could be him."
"The timing is remarkable, though. You've said as much yourself. We need to know more about these two. I'll have to have chat with PCSO Rawlins about the company she keeps."
"Not all the company she keeps is bad, sir," said DS Palmer, tilting her head at Dawson.
"*That* is a matter of opinion," said Hogarth. He gave Dawson a breezy smile, and turned away. Palmer rolled her eyes.
"Ignore him. He's tired so he's prickly tonight," said Palmer. "He was only joking."
"You don't have to be his diplomat, DS Palmer. After what I've been through tonight, I couldn't care less what jokes Hogarth concocts."
"Don't take it to heart. He means well."
Dawson sighed. "Really? Now I think *that* is a matter of opinion."
Dawson called one of the other uniforms to his side, then walked to the centre of the nightclub. As Dawson made a loud announcement that the club goers could leave, Palmer moved off in pursuit of DI Hogarth.

"PCSO Rawlins! My my! You do look very fetching tonight. The lady in red," said Hogarth. Rawlins had her hair tied back with a fancy flourish at the back, and the figure-hugging dress she wore sparkled under the harsh lights. The PCSO blushed at Hogarth's words.

"Sir," said Palmer.

"Are we not allowed to pay anyone a compliment these days, Palmer?" said Hogarth. She saw his eyes were full of mischief.

Bec Rawlins changed the subject. "We've spoken to them all."

"Actually, Rawlins, I wanted to talk to you about your two friends. The ones who left just before the main event…"

"Then you've spoken to PC Dawson?" she said with a hint of a frown. "But they couldn't have had anything to do with it, sir. Especially Andy Cruddas. He's a soft little thing."

"Be that as it may, I have to be interested. I need you to tell me all about them."

A look of concern showed on Rawlins' face. Palmer offered her a comforting nod. Slowly, Rawlins did as she was asked. "I've known Andy for years, sir… ever since before the tragedy hit his family…"

"Tragedy, eh…?" said Hogarth. "Do tell…"

Chapter Four

What if? Yes, what if? The man's nerves felt raw as he watched the club doors open and a horde of sad, tired-looking faces trickled out into the darkness. They were silent as they went, walking in twos and threes, peering over their shoulders at the scene around them. Some of them had called cabs. Meanwhile, a small army of parents were parked up along the square by the library, just beyond the edge of the police cordon. He felt their eyes pass over him, as though he was invisible. Omnipotent even. It was a strange feeling to be so detached. He knew why of course. He now knew a power most of them would never have because most people never opted for it. The power to act. To experience a negative feeling, and then to do something about it. Most people lived lives of creeping fear. But for him those awful days had come to an end. Even so, the police had surprised him. They had swooped down onto the club as if it really mattered that some despicable leeching scumbag had been wiped off the map. *As if it mattered!* The man was scum. He had done everyone a favour. Some of them knew it. But the police seemed to be serious, as if they actually wanted to catch the man who had done the job they should have done themselves. It was a mad, twisted world. And it made him angry. Not just angry... upset. Concerned about his future. Maybe he'd been naïve, but he'd never thought the police would try this hard.

Damn them. And what if? What if they had spotted something he had forgotten. A small piece of evidence. A mislaid or forgotten clue. He had been careful, he had thought very hard, but he was only one man after all, and there was no way he could have covered all of the bases by himself. The *what-ifs* plagued him as he stood in the dark beneath the archway of the giant college building on the edge of Luker Close. The what-ifs bothered him even more since the police had tried to lock down the club to contain the danger. They had meant to trap him. If they had tried so hard already, how much harder would they try yet? He thought of high-pressure police interviews and courtrooms and the breath hitched in his chest. He was proud of what he had done. It was nothing less than a brilliant act of justice. But how could he contain his pride when he was put under the microscope? He was sure it would show through, like a flame in a Chinese paper lantern. He was sure they would see his guilt. He was scared of himself.

Even with all his preparation and planning for the kill, there was no way of knowing how good the police would be. Or how they would react. Or even what might come to light. He told himself not to panic, but the truth was he knew there was a need to act. To pre-empt them. He formed a list in his head. The ways forward. The ways to safety.

He could divert them.

Make them look the wrong way.

Make them believe that others were guilty.

And how best to do all that?

Why, it was staring him in the face. It was blindingly obvious. What he had done so well once, he could do again. Think! What was the ultimate diversion? Another murder, of course. A different kind of murder. Yes, that would surely throw the cat amongst the pigeons. He'd send them into confusion alright.

If *absolutely necessary,* he could do it again.

A nervous smile escaped his lips. He was excited at the prospect. But it scared him too. Murder had given him energy, freedom, and a purpose. It would be no problem to kill again… *no problem at all.*

He was surprised. Killing a man had changed him. And there was no going back.

Chapter Five

"How old is the man?" said Hogarth.

"Twenty-nine, sir," said Rawlins.

"Your pal, Andy Cruddas, is twenty-nine years old and he still lives at home with mummy?" said Hogarth.

He looked up at the grand three-storey house, set at the end of a large red-brick driveway. The house had vast leaded-light bay windows. The large antique ornaments and mirrors visible through the glass declared that this was a wealthy home. Chalkwell was one of several patches within the town where the moneyed people lived. New money and old money nestled side by side, some understated and classy, while some flaunted it like dirty underwear. The Cruddas residence was one of the classier homes near the seafront.

"Andy had been starting out with his own insurance business," said Rawlins. Hogarth noticed a sad lilt to her voice. "He was going to be an insurance salesman just like his dad, and it started out well," said Rawlins. The PCSO had barely touched on the tragedy which had befallen the young man's father, and he wanted to know more. "Andy was talking big a few months back. He said he was going to move out and buy himself a nice place in Leigh. Then he went quiet about the idea. I guess the insurance business wasn't as easy as it seemed."

"Living with mummy must be so much easier," said Hogarth. "Well, now that we're here, how about we go and see if Andy wants to come out to play?"

The three of them made an awkward group. DI Palmer had gone back to the station to pore through the CCTV footage

from the club, which left Rawlins, Hogarth, and Dawson standing on the street outside the Cruddas house. Dawson had asked to come along and Hogarth had agreed because the PC had seen Andy Cruddas with Drummond moments before the murder. But Hogarth had also sensed PC Dawson's need to come along, and this time he let it pass. Besides, Hogarth wondered if the presence of two uniforms, including a muscular action-man like PC Dawson might yield unexpected benefits. Their uniforms might add an air of seriousness to proceedings. Hogarth was coming to believe Cruddas was a weak type of man and Dawson's description had done him no favours. If he was guilty, maybe the man would be intimidated and confess. As they peered into the house, a scruffy looking hobo in a green parker coat shuffled by on the other side of the street. His hood was pulled up over his head, and his swarthy face was turned towards them, looking from the side of his hood. Hogarth noticed the man watching. He raised an eyebrow and returned the man's gaze.
"Oi! You," said Hogarth. "Don't be so bloody nosy," he called. Rebuked, the man turned his head and shuffled on.
"You didn't have to be so mean, sir," said Rawlins.
"You forget I worked amongst those types for a long time, Rawlins. They're not all poor lost orphans chucked into the river. Some of them are downright scallywags. We don't need them telling their network about police business." Rawlins didn't look convinced. He sounded too cynical to a young girl like her. But one day she would see the world like he did. A life in the police soon stripped away any green naivety.
"Do you really think he'll be at home?" said Dawson, looking at Rawlins.

"I called Andy's office. The receptionist hadn't seen him yet. It's still early, you know."

"Come on. I'm keen to meet him," said Hogarth.

Hogarth rubbed his hands as he walked up the garden path and pressed the doorbell. A moment later the heavy burgundy-painted door opened with a creak and a woman in late middle age with a waistline to match appeared behind it. She had small eyes and a careful face beneath a mop of curly brown hair. There was a hint of snootiness about her as she appraised them, her eyes eventually fixing on Hogarth as the man in charge.

"Mrs Cruddas?" said Hogarth.

"Yes?"

She pushed the door towards the frame, keeping it open just enough to be civil.

"Detective Inspector Joseph Hogarth and PC Dawson. I believe you might already know PCSO Rawlins here."

"Rebecca!" said the woman with a smile. "I didn't recognise you in uniform." The woman seemed warm for a moment, before she remembered her defensive pose.

"I'm sorry, but what is this about?"

"We need a word with your boy, Mrs Cruddas. Andy."

"Andrew? Why on earth would police need to speak with Andrew?"

Bec Rawlins edged forward.

"He's not at home then, Barbara?"

"No. He isn't."

"Did he come home last night?"

"If he did, I wasn't awake at the time. You're beginning to worry me, Rebecca. What's happened?"

"Do you mind if we come in?" said Bec Rawlins.

Rawlins gave her an earnest look, and the woman slowly shook her head and left the door open for them to follow her inside.

"Go on, then, *Rebecca…*" said Hogarth, pronouncing the name the same way Mrs Cruddas had said it. Bec blushed and walked in. Even Dawson couldn't resist a smile. They walked inside and shut out the world behind them.

The front room was very fancy. Hogarth and the others looked around at the fine armchairs, tables, and sofa, and the antiques ranged around the mantelpiece. Each of them looked for a place which they wouldn't soil by their presence. When the woman sat down in an armchair and gave them no invitation, Hogarth didn't linger. He sat down and positioned himself opposite her. He leaned forwards and knitted his hands together.

"Did you hear what happened last night, Mrs Cruddas?"

"You mean that awful murder? Yes, I did. It's terrible what's happening to this town. I mean, the place has always had its problems, but now it's going to hell in a handcart."

Hogarth nodded and moved on. He knew the town all too well.

"The attack took place at a nightclub called Club Smart, a venue on Luker Close."

He waited for recognition on the woman's face. There was none.

"Your son, Andy, was there last night – with these two as a matter of fact."

The woman looked at Dawson, confused. Then at Rawlins. The girl coughed into her fist and removed her police hat. She sat down on another chair.

"We were on a night out together," said Rawlins. "We'd arranged it a long while back. Just a fun night out. But then

this attack happened – the murder – and right after that…
we think… well, it's hard to say but…"
Hogarth watched Rawlins struggle. She was a friend of the
family and she was being too careful to make much sense.
Hogarth didn't want the woman to miss the central point.
"Your son was there until just moments before the attack
took place," he said. "It's almost as if he knew something
was going to happen."
The woman turned pale before she regained the power of
speech. "Then he must be safe, at least."
"We have no reason to believe that your son has been
harmed, Mrs Cruddas…"
"Then why are you here?"
"Because if we have our timings correct, your son's
departure from the club could well be linked to the murder."
"But I'm sure it's not," said Bec, hastily. Hogarth jumped.
"At this stage," said Hogarth, "we can be sure of nothing.
All we know is that we need to speak to your son. Do you
know where he might be?"
"Of course. It's a weekday. He'll be at work."
"We've tried his office. He isn't there yet," said Rawlins.
"Well… it's early. Maybe he's gone somewhere for
breakfast."
"But he's not answering his phone, Mrs Cruddas," said
Rawlins. "Is that normal?"
The woman blanched again. "Not for Andrew, no.
Something must be wrong. Maybe he's unwell."
"You didn't see him last night…" said Hogarth. "Did you
see him this morning – before he left?"
"No. I assumed he'd left for work before I got up. I've been
having trouble sleeping at night lately…"
Hogarth nodded. "So… you really couldn't be sure if he
came home at all last night?"

"Not certain… but he usually does…"

"I'm sorry, but would you mind checking in his room? There must be signs whether he's been home or not. A bed not slept in. The shower not used. That kind of thing…"

The woman nodded and gave Bec a fraught glance. Rawlins smiled and the woman walked away.

"He didn't come home," said Hogarth, when the woman was out of earshot.

"We don't know that," said Rawlins.

"I know he's your friend, Rawlins," said Hogarth. The look on Dawson's face matched Hogarth's. A moment later they heard the woman padding down the wooden staircase. She walked into the room wringing her hands.

"No. He didn't come home. His bed wasn't slept in, as you said. What's happened to him, Rebecca…?"

"We have no reason to believe anything has happened," said Hogarth. "But we do need to speak to him as soon as possible. He was seen talking with the victim shortly before he was killed. They argued. We need to know the substance of that argument."

The woman nodded.

"What do you know about Jake Drummond, Mrs Cruddas?"

"Jake who?" she said.

"Jake Drummond. Your son knew him. Dan Picton knew him as well."

"Daniel too?"

"Dan Picton was at the club. He arrived there with Drummond. They were already arguing before he started on your son," said PC Dawson.

The woman turned ashen. She shook her head. "I'm sorry. I can't help you. I wish I could. I want to know where Andrew is. I need to know that he's alright."

"We want to know where he is too, Mrs Cruddas. If your son has chosen to disappear immediately after a man is killed, well, it doesn't reflect too well upon him, does it? If you see him, tell him to think about that. And tell him to get in touch."

"Of course. But Andrew couldn't have done it. You said he left before it happened…"

"He left in a hurry, just moments before the murder. It suggests at the very least that he might have known something about it, Mrs Cruddas. Have you any idea where he might be? Any idea at all?"

"Well, Rebecca mentioned Daniel Picton. Have you tried Daniel's house? Maybe he stayed there?"

"I don't know Dan very well, Barbara," said Rawlins. "Do you know where he lives?"

"Yes. He lives in Leigh…"

The woman picked up an old-fashioned flower-printed address book from a side table and started to flick through the peach coloured pages. "Here it is." She gave them the address and Rawlins copied it down into her notebook.

"If you find Andrew there, tell him to come home. I need to see him. I need to know he's safe."

Hogarth stood up and nodded. "Of course. Don't you worry, Mrs Cruddas. We'll track him down, I'm sure." He left the woman with a hint of threat in his words, just in case the mother wasn't clear. But her frown said the message had been well and truly received.

When they left the house. Hogarth felt his mobile phone buzzing in his blazer pocket. He had an inkling that it wasn't the DCI. When they reached the street, Hogarth glanced at the screen. Without another word, he turned away from

Dawson and Rawlins and walked away by himself. They watched him put the phone to his ear.

"Lately, he's a proper man of mystery…" said Dawson.

"What's it about, I wonder," said Rawlins.

"If that's his girlfriend on the other end then I feel sorry for her," said Dawson.

They left Hogarth to it, walking back towards his car to wait for a lift back to the station.

"Ali?! What is it? What's wrong?" said Hogarth. He wondered if Ali's husband had finally cottoned on to their *involvement*. Not an affair. It was far too early to call it that. Too early, with too few private moments to call it much more. There had been a kiss, and a wonderful afternoon where things had gone too far. And back then, right after it happened, they had spoken about calling it off. Avoiding one another on a permanent basis. But Ali Hartigan was in trouble, and she needed his help. There was no way he would abandon her. The woman was in a dire situation. Ali was married to the local MP, James Hartigan, but was twice as smart as the man, which was how she'd found out about his affair with his parliamentary secretary. If that had been the sum of Ali Hartigan's troubles Hogarth would have still left her alone. But her situation was much worse than that.

"Joe… I think I saw him again."

"The stalker?"

"Who else?" she said.

"Sorry, Ali. I'm working a new case. My mind's elsewhere."

"Yes," she said. "Sorry. I heard about the nightclub murder."

"Don't worry about that. Where did you see him?"

"This time I was out shopping. I thought I saw him outside the supermarket, but told myself I was being paranoid. Then when he walked right past me in the grocery aisle. He didn't look at me directly, but he stayed around. He wanted me to know he was there."

"Tell James. You've got to. He's an MP, for God's sake! He's got to be good for something," said Hogarth. He looked back across his shoulder and saw Rawlins watching him as she walked away. Hogarth nodded and ran a stressed hand through his hair.

"Come on, Joe. You know where my husband's priorities lie."

In his secretary, of course, thought Hogarth.

"Even so, he must still care about you enough to do something."

"He says the stalker must be in my imagination. Or it's just a political thing, as if that's any better. Everyone knows what happened to that poor Labour MP last year. Maybe he wants the same to happen to me."

Hogarth didn't need to try and remember. He couldn't forget. It was all over the news. A caring and proactive local MP was slain by a fanatical extremist for no good reason.

"Don't even say it, Ali. So, he didn't listen to you this time?"

"Face facts, Joe. I already have. He doesn't care about me at all. Which is why I wish things were simpler. I know I should be with you."

Breath caught in Hogarth's throat. He was finally hearing her say it. He wanted to be with her too. But his life had always been more complicated than he had wanted it to be. Hogarth had always been a specialist in making things difficult. "I want that too, but you don't need the scandal, Ali. I don't want to be the one to cause you hurt. Your husband deserves that, not you."

"I shouldn't think it would help your career much if the police knew, either…?"

"My career got switched off the moment I transferred out of the Met. I'm a grass-roots copper now. I'll probably stay at this grade, or maybe I'll reach the next, until they pension me off. Don't worry about my reputation. I haven't got one to worry about."

"I'm sure that's not true."

It was true alright.

"Look, Ali. Meet me for a coffee. Just a coffee. And don't tell anyone. Meet me, but try and make it easy for this sicko to follow you. If he does, I'll have a polite little word with him, ID him, and make his life difficult until he leaves you alone."

"A coffee? That's all?"

He paused and swallowed.

"I'd like it to be more, but I'm thinking of you. It'll have to do for now, won't it. Keep your eyes peeled, Ali, and keep those doors locked. Promise?"

"Promise."

"Coffee… how about tomorrow afternoon?"

"Fine," said Ali. "Where?"

"Café Seven One Seven, Southchurch Road. It's quiet. Discreet. And gives your scumbag ample chances to follow. Two pm. Can you make it?"

"Yes. I'll be there, I promise."

"Bye, Ali. Be safe." The words seemed so inadequate. Half formed things hiding his true sentiments, but some things couldn't yet be said. Hogarth wasn't sure if they ever would be.

He slowly returned to Rawlins and Dawson who were standing close by his car, looking down to the strip of seafront at the end of the wealthy road. Dawson looked at Hogarth and noticed something in his eyes. Hogarth stared back a moment too long. He wondered if Dawson had seen something he would have rather stayed hidden.

"Trouble?" Dawson said, referring to Hogarth's call.

"No more than usual," said Hogarth.

The trio nodded at each other, knowing there were secrets. They were quiet as they drove, staring at the sea. Rawlins looked at the street and frowned.

"You're going the wrong way," said Rawlins. "Don't you want to find Picton?"

"Ah, yes. I'm just a little distracted and tired, that's all," said Hogarth. "Never mind. Let's get you two back to the station. I'll borrow Palmer to help me hunt for Picton."

But Hogarth hadn't just been distracted by thoughts of Ali. Rawlins was too involved with the Cruddas family for it to go well. She wanted them to be innocent. It was a conflict of interest which looked set to become more difficult unless Hogarth nipped it in the bud.

***

Picton's apartment was situated above a fancy artisan bakery on Leigh Road, at the only slightly less fancy end of Leigh. Hogarth spent a good minute sniffing the tantalising smells of fresh baked bread while appreciating the rustic-style commercial artwork above the shop. Even though the bakery prices were exorbitant, he still wondered if they sold the kind of bread Ali liked. As Hogarth rung the bell on the door beside the bakery he pushed thoughts of bread aside.

"It's amazing how much people can charge once they've slapped the word 'artisan' on it," he said while they waited for the door.

Palmer nodded, and pressed the doorbell. No reply. They spent another minute knocking and ringing before they turned away.

"That's it. Picton's off the radar too," said Palmer.

"Do we know where Picton works?" Hogarth said.

"No, but I'll look into it."

Hogarth nodded. "It looks like these boys are shaping up to be our main suspects."

"But they can't really have done it, can they? We know they were away before Drummond was hurt."

"They mightn't have pulled the trigger, but they're not in the clear by any means."

Hogarth and Palmer turned away. Out of habit, Hogarth looked up to see if the net curtains twitched on the first floor. But there was no movement. All was still. Picton wasn't at home. But even if Cruddas and Picton weren't the killers, Hogarth was sure something was going on with them. They had to be found.

Chapter Six

Day Five: Tuesday

"No joy, guv," said Palmer. Hogarth's team was safely nestled in the scrappy mess of the main CID room. Calling it the main room made it sound grander than it really was. The name came from the fact that the team who worked the east district had an even smaller cupboard to call their home. The police station had been grandly refurbed not more than ten months back but Hogarth's CID room looked as bad as any other he could recall in his career. The incident board was stacked with crimes and there was paperwork everywhere. Every desk in the office was overflowing with paperwork and case files from cases past and present. The walls were closing in. In short, it felt like home.

"No joy?" said Hogarth. DC Simmons looked round. DC Simmons with his slicked-back hair was known across the station as a young slacker and a sycophant. His reputation wasn't entirely fair but there were moments when it seemed to fit well enough. Hogarth had inherited Simmons when he joined the Southend outfit from London as part of the new order to try and clean up a station tainted by corruption. There was no corruption anymore, Hogarth was pretty sure of that. But Simmons was still a brown-nose, and Hogarth pretended not to notice. But Palmer was good. She was staunch, though Hogarth made sure he paid only fleeting compliments about Palmer's quality as he didn't want it going to her head. Give her too much praise and she might fly the nest to another station with a bigger office and better coffee. Hogarth needed someone like her to stick around.

"Dan Picton used to work at Southend Airport," said Palmer. "He was an apprentice aviation engineer for Essex Air Works. But they haven't seen him in months. They've hired someone else."

"And he's had no other job since?"

"If he has, we can't find it."

"Then what's he been living on?" said Hogarth. "Is he claiming benefits?"

"I haven't checked with the dole office yet."

"Hmmmm. So Picton really has done a flit? My, my… that doesn't look good now, does it? That marks these boys out from the rest of the suspects. From now on, finding them is a priority. Any ideas? Simmons?"

Simmons' hair looked particularly gel-slicked this morning. He rubbed a hand across his head as if it helped him think, but his face stayed blank.

"Thanks for the input, Simmons."

The man blushed. "Sir, I was thinking their disappearance could be unconnected to the murder, that's all. They left the club right before Drummond died, but so what?"

"Unconnected to the murder? You're not the first one to say it. But these two disappeared five seconds before Jake Drummond dropped down dead. And we know Drummond gave them a hard time just before he was killed. There's something in that. I can't rule it out until we've looked at it thoroughly."

"It's still possible, I suppose. But the timing could have been a coincidence," said Simmons.

"Everything is possible. But I think it's likely they knew what was coming. They're a priority. Palmer, any ideas where they might have gone?"

"We need to know more about them before we could say," said Palmer.

"Okay. What do we know already?" said Hogarth. "We know Picton and Cruddas had a problem with Jake Drummond. Or Jake Drummond had a problem with them. We know Drummond had good form for violence and extortion... and plenty of the people we spoke to at the club seemed to know about it."

"There's the finer details too. PC Dawson says Cruddas offered him a twelve grand Mercedes for just five grand."

"A Merc? Sounds like a bargain," said Hogarth.

"He was definitely in urgent need of cash," said Palmer.

Hogarth nodded. "That money could have been to pay off Drummond, right? The blackmail game must be a high-paying business. So then? What dirt did he have on those boys? Or was it simple good old-fashioned bullying. The *pay me or I'll punch your lights out* method...? There's no real way of knowing until we find them. Get the uniforms out there looking for these two on their rounds. It's far too early in the game to make any public appeal for information. The chief will only want us to use the media as a last resort and he'll want to vet any briefing himself. Which means we'll have to put the feelers out through our own sources..."

"Our own sources?" said Simmons.

"Come on, DC Simmons. You've made it this far in the detective game. Get your thinking cap on. We need to get out there and start asking some questions."

Simmons nodded and made a note on his notepad. Hogarth wondered if what he'd written was a meaningless squiggle, but chose not to humiliate the man any further. Not today anyway.

"What about the CCTV?"

"Nothing much," said Palmer. "I scoured the club camera footage, and it backs up the witness statements. Drummond was surrounded by people the moment he was stabbed, and it was dark. It's hard to even locate the moment he was stabbed. It's a flurry of movement at the bar which tells us close to nothing. The crowd parts and Drummond drops down clutching his chest. That part is on camera. There are a few familiar faces around at the time. Peter Deal is in the pack there. Gary Grayson is queuing for another drink. The club manager, John Milford, is on the scene, the barman you spoke to, Gordy Turner, and some shadows passing the lens…"

"Shadows?"

"Sir, the footage is naff, believe me. No matter where I look, I don't get a killer, and I don't see the weapon."

"This was a knife attack. Our killer *was* there. He got close enough to stick the knife in. We need to keep looking at that footage until we see something."

"You want me to try again?"

"No, Palmer. Get some of the uniforms on it. I need your brain out there, looking at the angles. We need to find these two pronto. Where do you want to start?"

"With the witnesses, I'd say. Someone must have seen Cruddas and Picton leave Club Smart," said Palmer. "We can try the cab firms too. Maybe they got some fast food on the high street. Someone will have seen them."

"All worth a try. Okay, I'll leave you two to try those angles." Hogarth stood up and pulled on his blazer. "As for me… I'm going to see if I can take a shortcut," said Hogarth.

"A shortcut?" said Simmons. "I thought shortcuts were a bad idea."

"But not all shortcuts are the same, Simmons. Leave me to work my magic, and one day, I might even explain how you can work some yourself," said Hogarth with a wink.

"When?"

"In the memoirs, dear boy. In the memoirs. Okay, let's hit the street. We'll meet up later on."

As Palmer waited for Simmons to get his stuff together, Hogarth lingered in the CID room door. He called her name. Palmer followed Hogarth out of the door into the corridor.

"Sir?"

"Use Dawson and Rawlins as much as you need to. They were on the scene first. And I know those two have got their heads screwed on. Screwed on a lot tighter than Simmons, anyway."

Palmer nodded. "Understood. So where exactly are you going to weave this magic of yours?"

"Trade secrets, I'm afraid, DS Palmer. I've been sworn to secrecy by the Magic Circle."

"Right. If you say so…" said Palmer. Hogarth wondered if he detected a trace of irritation in Palmer's voice. Then he told himself it didn't matter if he did. He had a lot more to worry about than Palmer's happiness. Hogarth checked his blazer pocket for his car keys and set off. It was time to catch up with some old faces.

The Sutland Arms. The dingiest pub in town. Always a chore, never a pleasure. The Sutland was situated on a corner halfway down the rough, raw, and very urban part of Southchurch Road, which spilled off the top of Southend High Street. DI Hogarth had spent twenty years of his police career swooping the London streets before accepting his transfer to sort out Southend's problems. He had expected an easier ride, a more sedate atmosphere, but central Southend was nothing of the kind. Southchurch Road symbolised the town's problems. The place reminded Hogarth of South London with its dilapidated buildings, graffiti, constant exhaust fumes, and hordes of drunks and junkies. The place would have fitted right into one of the South London boroughs. And some of the problems around the town were London in origin. Such as the young drug mules who travelled the Fenchurch Street line to do their London dealers' dirty work. And the international gangs who groomed the local junkies and turned their flats into temporary drug factories. He'd seen it all before. Southend was home from home.

Hogarth walked through the saloon-bar doors of the ramshackle pub and found his brogues sticking to the dark wooden floor as he walked. It was early, but that was why he was here. There was a chance his informant would still be sober. And the pub would presumably be at the peak of cleanliness before the punters came in and ruined it all. Evidently the cleaning standards were not high at any time of day. The smell of stale beer and disinfectant dominated the dark interior. But even those smells were much better than old Vic Norton. As expected, Norton was there at his favourite back table. Norton was thin, with a face shaped like an arrowhead. He was gaunt, with grey stubble all over his chin. His hair was grey, overgrown, and straggly with a widow's peak at the front. As usual, he was wearing a garish shell suit. Hogarth couldn't work out where he got them all from. There was a pint of a dark brown beer in front of him and a copy of The Gambler's Life newspaper folded beside it.

"Oh dear… look who's turned up," said Norton in his raspy old voice.

"Shut it, Vic, or I'll search you for contraband tobacco. I know I'll find it too, won't I?"

"You lot use the law as you like it," said Norton.

"And you lot break it as you like it. It's like a game of chess, Vic. Except with you it's more like tiddlywinks."

The man looked at Hogarth with his yellowing eyes. Hogarth wondered if the drink was finally catching up with him. There were a few coppers he knew who weren't far off, either.

"Right, Vic. The nightclub murder. What do you know?"

"That it was murder, same as you."

"And the rest. What do you know about Big Jake Drummond?"

"Not much. I've heard about him like everyone has."

"Like everyone else. See no evil, hear no evil, speak no evil," said Hogarth. "But you always hear more, Vic. Don't you?"

"Oh, I heard about him alright. A dark, selfish specimen of a human being. Not afraid of using his fists on anyone, men or women."

Hogarth nodded. "Is that why someone topped him? Because he'd been cruel?"

Vic Norton's eyes sparkled and he took his time to sip his pint.

"Maybe."

Hogarth sighed and took out his wallet. "I need information, Vic, not fairy stories."

"You know I don't do fairy stories. And Drummond is no fairy."

Hogarth laid a crisp new tenner on the table. Norton looked at it, blinked, and looked up. Hogarth peeled off another tenner, and laid it on top of the first.

"Okay…" said Vic. "That's better. He's dead, and that's the only reason I can say anything."

"Go on then."

"He was back in the old routine is what I heard. Coercion. And he was going for it left, right, and centre. Forcing people to pay him. He'd bully people, he'd use blackmail, anything which would make people pay up."

"Blackmail? I knew he'd been in bother for extortion with menaces, but out and out blackmail?"

"So… he must have learned it was another way to earn a living. They say you have to diversify to succeed, don't they?"

Hogarth nodded. "So they say. Who was he blackmailing, Vic?"

"I don't know the details, but pretty much everyone he knew."

"Details, Vic. That's twenty quid I just gave you."

"Twenty quid well spent, I'd say. You didn't know about the blackmail. But I can't tell you anything else. Least not about that."

"Eh?"

Vic Norton sipped his pint again. A conspiratorial glint flickered in his eyes. "I heard a little rumour. Tell me. Is it true?"

Hogarth squinted and scratched his cheek. Then he leaned forward over the table. "Is what true?"

Norton's eyes sparkled like dark stars. "I heard a certain MP's wife is getting knocked off by a certain hard-faced copper."

"You heard what?" said Hogarth, horrified.

Norton stared at him and slowly nodded once. Just once. Hogarth tensed, reached out for the man's scrawny neck, and Norton shrank back. Hogarth's fingers fluttered loose in the air. He drew them back, but his voice was filled with tension. He was always disgusted by Vic Norton, but now he wanted to punch him hard in the face. He wanted to break his teeth.

"So, it's true then…" said Vic.

"No, Vic. It's not true. It's not true in the least."

Norton's eyes said he didn't believe Hogarth's words.

"Don't worry, your secret's safe with me."

Hogarth's voice turned sharp and quiet. "Listen here you vicious old codger. I know you haven't got a decent bone in that withered old body. The only thing you care about is yourself. So pay attention. This is about consequences for *you*. No one else. *You*. If you so much as breathe those awful lies to anyone else… if The Record newspaper hear about it… if anyone else hears at all, I'll know where it came from. And I'll hold you personally responsible. If you think you know what I'm capable of, Vic, you're wrong. Do you hear?"

Norton blinked. His smile was gone.

"Where did you hear that? Tell me!" snapped Hogarth.

Norton looked shocked and afraid.

He shook his head.

"The person who told you… what did the man look like? Come on! Have you had dealings with him before?"

"Calm down, Hogarth. It was just a rumour. I didn't know you'd take it so personal."

"You watch your mouth. And if you hear anything else about that woman, anything at all, you call me first. Are we clear?"

Hogarth stood up and walked away. Behind him Norton's face turned into a sneering smile. He sipped his pint and left a moustache of froth on his lip.

"Crystal," said Norton.

By now Hogarth was hardly in the mood for pleasantries, but the job called for a social call. By the time he arrived at the private investigators' office, Hogarth was strung out with questions about how Norton came to know about Ali Hartigan. But he needed to put it aside. He would see her tomorrow. He needed to park it until then. He walked to the window of the shop-cum-office and peered through the glass. The PIs were in. Dan Bradley, a thirty-something likely-lad raised a coffee mug from the back-room kitchen, while the brains of the outfit, Eva Roberts was hard at work on her laptop. Eva wasn't just brains, she was beauty too, a gorgeous red-head with a detective's inquisitive mind. But she was off limits and a good five or ten years too young for him. Besides, their swords had crossed too many times for that. But at least he had shared enough information with them to call in a favour of his own.

The old-fashioned shop-door chimed as Hogarth walked in.

"To what do we owe this unexpected pleasure?" said Dan Bradley, grandstanding as usual.

"As if you didn't know," replied Hogarth.

Eva Roberts looked up and Hogarth couldn't help but appreciate those green eyes. "The nightclub murder," she said.

"Club Smart, yes. A big bully called Jake Drummond got topped. Either of you heard of him before?"

Eva leaned back in her chair. "No, it doesn't ring any bells." Eva looked back at Dan. Dan shook his head as he sipped his coffee.

"Any suspects yet?" said Dan.

"It's not clear cut, but I have at least two people in mind. Two men who may have been bullied or blackmailed by the victim. They disappeared from Club Smart just before Jake Drummond was killed. And it seems they've done a moonlight flit. I need to track them down. I know you're pretty good at missing persons."

"But there's usually a fee involved," said Dan with a smirk.
"Usually maybe," said Hogarth.
"What are their names?" said Eva.
"Andy Cruddas is one. He's a rich mummy's boy who dabbled at selling insurance. And another lightweight by the name of Dan Picton. Picton lives in Leigh above the posh bakers on Leonard Road. You know it?"
Eva nodded. "The pricey place."
"That's the one. Andy Cruddas lived at home with mummy in Chalkwell."
"You think they disappeared together?" she said.
"They might have, that's as far as I can go."
Eva Roberts put the end of a biro between her teeth while she thought about it. "We can look into it for you, but I can't make any promises."
"You don't have to make promises, Miss Roberts. This is a murder investigation and we're up against it. If you could do anything it would help."
"Okay. Leave it with us. I'll call you if we find anything."
Hogarth nodded in thanks. For a moment he considered sharing his private matter. Having someone like Eva Roberts on side to help Ali Hartigan would have taken a load off his mind. But that meant sharing, and DI Hogarth knew he couldn't risk it. It was madness to even think it.
"Is there something else?" said Eva, as he hesitated in the doorway.
"No. Nothing else. Cheers for your help."
Hogarth steered himself out of the door and smoothed down his hair as he sped up the walk towards his car. He got into his Insignia and rubbed his forehead. His phone started to ring. This time it was Palmer. "The post mortem on Jake Drummond is at one o'clock."
"Just after lunch. Nice timing on Quentin's behalf."

"You want me there?"

"To share the pleasure, Palmer. Of course."

"Fine," she said. The call ended and DI Hogarth started the engine.

Chapter Seven

The pathology lab was at the back of Southend Hospital beside the chapel of rest. Hogarth had been there many times by now, and had a love hate relationship with the tubby pathologist, Dr Ed Quentin. Quentin was a stiff-mannered type, sometimes officious and stuffy, and at other times surprisingly funny. It was like there were two different Quentins and Hogarth never knew which he was going to get. The thought added an extra tension to his thinking. Hogarth walked into the reception area where DS Palmer was standing looking at a large and dour still life painting of a vase of flowers in a gilt frame. The rest of the room was plain and clinical, and lined with information posters, hand gel dispensers, and little else.

"Have you seen him yet?" said Hogarth.

Palmer shook her head. "Did your magic pay off?"

"Not much. I've asked around. I might hear back later. What about you?"

"A little. They were seen leaving the club. Both men left Luker Close on foot and headed through the residential streets towards Westcliff. After that, we don't know."

Hogarth was more than frustrated. A set of double doors opened, and Dr Quentin appeared. He was decked out in his white coat, blue gloves, and blue shoe covers.

"Are you ready?" he said, raising his eyebrow.

"Always," said Hogarth. "You first, Palmer." He added with an animated smile.

They gloved up and put on the masks as directed by Palmer then walked into the lab. The young pathologist's technician was tinkering with equipment at the back. Hogarth met his eye and nodded at him, but he didn't quite trust him for some reason. His gut told him the man was slippery. The man offered the slightest nod back. They were an odd breed, pathologists. Odd but extremely necessary.

"Here we are…" said Quentin. The naked body of Jake Drummond lay facing up on the slab under the bright lights. The bulk of his body was like a range of white and blue fleshy hills, with the mountain of his stomach reaching highest of all. His dead skin was pale blue-white. His eyes were open and glassy. Hogarth looked at the puncture wound in the man's chest as Quentin's gloved fingers probed around the wounds. He pointed at them with a ballpoint pen, though it did not touch the dead man's skin. "I think the wound would have been instantly fatal, but we can check now. Quentin picked up a scalpel and pressed it to the top of Drummond's mountainous gut. Hogarth and Palmer looked at one another. There was no need to stare at the gory detail. All they needed were the facts. Little by little, Quentin slopped guts and organs into an enormous steel bowl at his side. Soon, he located the heart. "Here. There it is. The blade punctured the heart muscle and on exit cut the left ventricle. He was virtually dead on the spot."

Hogarth swallowed and tried not to think about the blood and guts. Even after all these years it was hard work.

"What do you think did it?" Hogarth looked at Palmer. She looked pale, but these days she generally did.

"A blade of between five and six centimetres long, and a relatively narrow one. Something like a stiletto. If it wasn't for the cut of the ventricle, I would have even said a tool like a beadle. But it had to be serrated, which means a knife. But we're not talking a hunting knife here. We're talking a typical modern knife, like the youth gangs regularly use these days. Easy to conceal, and easy to use. The incision suggests this blade was particularly sharp. It went in like a knife through butter."

"Any indications about the killer?" said Hogarth. "Does the angle suggest the killer's height, strength, gender, anything?"

"The cut is very direct – almost a straight line into the heart. The killer intended to do maximum damage. They were aiming for the heart and they got it. This was a very intentional kill."

Hogarth nodded. It wasn't just an angry, vengeful act. It was a determined kill.

"What about the killer?"

"Probably of a similar height to the victim., just under six foot. The killer might have held the blade like this." The pathologist balled his fist and held it up with the bottom of his fist facing Hogarth. "The blade could have protruded from the fist, and the killer could have hammered through the chest wall. It would have given the force needed, and if they wanted to be quick and unseen, they could have hidden the blade very quickly after the stabbing action. That way the blade would have been concealed from people even relatively close by.

"That would have meant the killer was close to the victim. Very close."

Quentin nodded.

"Maybe they were close enough to embrace…"

"You think it was a woman, Dr Quentin?" said Palmer.

"It's not my sphere, DS Palmer," said Quentin.

"But an embrace would have been easy to pick up. The CCTV doesn't show anything like that."

"But the CCTV is dark and inconclusive," said Hogarth. "We need to keep checking. This wound suggests the victim knew the killer, then?"

Quentin nodded. "It's very likely, given the necessary proximity for the kill. It certainly doesn't seem as though Drummond defended himself. I'd say he could have known the killer."

"Then we can rule out a psycho… which is good. The local rag must have been praying they'd land a serial killer. They sell papers like hot cakes."

"What about forensics? Have they given you any pointers?" asked Quentin.

"Not so far. I didn't hold out much hope to be honest," said Hogarth. "The scene was packed with punters. It was like a stampede when he was attacked. Any evidence would have been messed up long before we got there."

"Shame. But at least you now know the kind of knife you're looking for. The weapon always turns up in the end."

Hogarth nodded. "Sooner the better."

"So, who are we looking at?" said Palmer.

"Everyone. Especially everyone who knew the man well enough to get close. A little dickie bird told me Drummond had progressed from extortion to out and out blackmail. We need to find out all those he was blackmailing and bullying, list them, and work through it, one by one. If we do that, we can find our knife and our killer… good job, Dr Quentin. Thank you."

The big man nodded and pulled the sheet back over Simmons' body.

Hogarth walked out of the mortuary with DS Palmer, both of them taking lungsful of fresh air like deep-sea divers just reaching the surface.

"It feels like we're getting somewhere, but much too slowly," said Hogarth. "We should be further than this. If our killer can strike and disappear like this, then we need him off the streets. This is a balls-up."

"What?" said Palmer.

"That's what Melford will say, and he'll be right," said Hogarth.

"Why?" said Palmer.

"The knife must have been there at the club. It had to be. The doors were shut right after the man dropped down dead. Even if Picton and Cruddas didn't kill him; whoever did – had to be there with the knife. The critical piece which forensics could have nailed for us. But we didn't find the knife. By now it could be anywhere…"

Chapter Eight

It was Palmer's turn to drive. Hogarth said his head was starting to hurt. It was easy to see why. They dropped his Insignia back at the station and Palmer took up driving duty in her less than regal Corsa. Trouble was, without the steering wheel in Hogarth hands, he fidgeted in the front passenger seat like a child. Palmer tried not to notice him bouncing his knee up and down like someone with ADHD. She stayed quiet about it. Hogarth was distracted, and probably in a bad mood, chewing over the missing murder weapon. It was a real problem. Hogarth's mobile phone broke the silence. He answered it keenly.

"Dawson?" he said. Palmer kept her eyes on the road and tuned in as best she could. Dawson worked harder than most, and showed far more promise than some of his more senior colleagues.

"And you're sure about that? Who told you?" said Hogarth, his voice suddenly energized and excited.

Palmer gripped the wheel tighter and tried to listen in, but she couldn't hear Dawson's words at the other end.

"I don't believe it," said Hogarth. "And you know why that happened? Because Cruddas was born with a bloody silver spoon in his mouth. We should have known this was coming right back at the start. Still, at least we know now. Well done, PC Dawson. Now, listen, we still need to find that knife. I want you to go back to Club Smart and run a thorough check over the toilets and the cloakroom. I want you to check anywhere the killer could have stashed a weapon. You couldn't find it before, so go back and check again. Provided you did your job well enough there's got to be another reason we didn't find that knife. Go over the whole place with a fine toothcomb. And if you don't find it in the public areas, insist on getting into the staff areas. You never know. Good. See you later then."

Hogarth ended the call and Palmer gave him a look.

"What was that about?" she said.

"Dawson has found out that Andy Cruddas has some secret previous."

"Previous? But his record is squeaky clean. I checked it myself."

"That's because it was secret. It turns out that Cruddas was involved in a ruckus at Ryan's Bar just around the corner from Club Smart only six months back."

"So, if it was off the record how come we know about it?"

"Because PC Jordan had a quiet word with Dawson in the canteen. PC Orton was the man who swept up after the ruck at Ryan's Bar. Jordan said Andy Cruddas was blind drunk, swearing and swinging his fists like a wild man but for some reason PC Orton kept him out of trouble. He didn't even issue a caution. I wonder why, don't you?" Hogarth gave Palmer a deadpan look, and raised an eyebrow.

"Orton is a bit of a beast," said Palmer, "but he's not corrupt."

"Corruption is a very emotive word in Southend, Palmer. It's more likely he thinks of it as a spot of beer money. I'm only surmising, by the way. I could be wrong, but Orton strikes me as a loafer. What matters is that Jordan shared what he knew, which gives us much more to go on concerning Cruddas."

"Such as?"

"He's got form for violence, that's what. It won't help the CPS form the prosecution one bit, but it helps us see who

we're dealing with. Who knows how he could have pulled off this murder, but I think he really could be our man."
Hogarth frowned and chewed his lip.
"We've got to find him, Palmer."
A second later his phone was back in hand. Hogarth dialled and put the phone to his ear. He glanced at Palmer from the corner of his eyes as he spoke.
"Yeah, hi… this is DI Hogarth again. Did you manage to find anything on Cruddas or Picton?"
Hogarth tapped the dashboard in front of Palmer and pinched his fingers to ask for a pen. Palmer delved a hand into a messy dashboard pocket and handed him a broken biro.
"*You did?* Brilliant. Where? Okay. Very useful. Yes, of course. What goes around comes around. Come on! Do I really need to promise? Thanks again."
Hogarth dropped the phone onto his lap and scribbled some notes on a tiny pad from his jacket. Palmer couldn't read his spidery scrawls at all, so she would have to wait for him to explain.
"Okay. We're heading for the Grange Estate, around the back of town. Do you know it?"
"The dilapidated place near The Greyhound?"
"That's it."
"Why there? It's half empty and virtually derelict."
"Virtually. But not quite. It turns out our man Picton was spotted there only a little while ago."
"Dan Picton? But who spotted him."
"Outsourcing, Palmer. I asked some other brains to join the hunt. They checked Picton's contacts and it turns out he knows people in the car trade. They have a garage on that estate. If someone wants to disappear in this town, where

better than a decrepit industrial estate like the Grange? You never know, Cruddas might even be there with him…"
Hogarth clearly wasn't going to reveal his sources and Palmer decided not to push it. She didn't want Hogarth venting at her because of one question too many. She hoped the Grange Industrial Estate would reveal all the answers by itself.

Chapter Nine

To Hogarth's eye, the Grange Industrial Estate was a very odd looking-place. It was tucked away in the labyrinthine guts of Southend, a relic of the past just about repurposed for the present. He walked around with his hands in his trouser pockets, and looked at the flaking whitewash on the concrete buildings, and the weeds breaking through ancient concrete wherever he looked. The whole place was built out of concrete and asbestos, but held together by no more than spit and wishful thinking. "What a wreck…" said Hogarth.
"It used to be a train station, apparently."
"In the steam age? These buildings look bloody dangerous to me."
"But the tenants pay a pittance, which keeps their overheads low."
"What tenants?" said Hogarth, eyeing the grey, dusty windows of the nearest buildings.
"The garage is round here. Come on."
"You know the area, do you?"
"I think I used it to fix my Corsa once. It was so cheap I wondered if they'd actually done the work but was too afraid to ask."
"Looks like your Corsa needs a spot of work again."
Palmer winced. She was happy with her car. It was reliable and cheap and on a police salary she was hardly likely to upgrade any time soon. Cheeky sod. Palmer huffed and led Hogarth along the second back lane of the Grange Estate. Halfway down she could see the largest building of the estate. The garage was big enough to drive a bus inside. But

something was amiss, the big steel roller shutter was closed, pulled all the way down, and there was none of the usual radio music or banter to be heard.

"They're shut," said Palmer. "That's odd. You're sure your information was sound, sir?"

Palmer looked up at the huge shutter and stood back slowly, reading the faded paint sign above it. Her eyes widened as she read the business name.

Hogarth grunted. "Usually, yes. They said Picton was around here, so he will be. The garage is a detached building, right?"

"Sir…" said Palmer.

"What?"

"Look. It's called Deal's Garage. Didn't Grayson say Peter Deal was a mechanic…?"

"Yes, he did. Well I never… small world, eh?"

"Small indeed," said Palmer. She could see the spark of excitement in Hogarth's eyes.

"It is detached, yes. And I think there's a mini junkyard on the other side. As I remember, it's filled with all kinds of rubbish someone should have taken down the tip…"

"Righto," said Palmer. "You go round the back of the building, I'll take the front. Look out for any hiding places, and use your ears too. If Picton's seen us – if he's got a guilty conscience, he'll be ready to run."

Hogarth watched as Palmer stepped into the urban undergrowth of weeds and gravel at the left side of the building. She picked her way through the mess with her arms splayed at her sides as if she was afraid of losing balance and falling over. Hogarth shook his head. If Picton made a run for it, Palmer wasn't going to be much use in a chase.

Hogarth cut past the front of the big garage. He took a hand out of his pocket, and poked at the letterbox slot. He bent down and peered into the cold, dusty interior. There was a large mechanical contraption in the centre of the empty space – a machine for lifting vehicles for inspection. Beside it was a workstation with business stickers all over it. There was grease, dust, and dirt everywhere, and no sign of a car. Hogarth glanced down to the floor immediately behind the door. There was a stack of letters, bills, and junk-mail spilling wide in all directions. He heard something. A scratching sound and it came from inside the garage. Hogarth narrowed his eyes and searched for it. Maybe a rat or a pigeon had snuck in to die. He saw a huddle of cardboard boxes at the back of the garage. Nope. Hogarth turned his head to peer left and looked up to a strip window high up on the wall. A shadow was raking at the window from outside. Hogarth's eyes flashed, and a thin grin spread over his face. He saw a long ladder set against the inside wall beneath the window. He'd thought nothing of it until he'd seen the movement outside. Hogarth stood up and edged along the shutter door. He kept his tan brogues quiet, shuffling along until he felt safe to lean out, past the corner of the wall. Just as Palmer had described, he saw a junkyard chock full of broken fence panels, rotting fence posts, empty paint pots, car engine grilles, rusting signage, and engine parts from another era. Some of the old parts were stacked against the garage wall to form a rough slope. And scrambling up at the top was a slight man in a grey fleece top and blue jeans.

"In you go," muttered Hogarth, under his breath. Palmer appeared through the fence on the other side of the junkyard. He saw her mouth open to speak. Hogarth quickly put a finger to his lips, and nodded to the top of the pile. Palmer saw the man and stayed quiet. They tucked themselves out of the way as the trespasser climbed through the window and disappeared inside. Hogarth darted back to the shutter letterbox and watched the man climb down. He got down the ladder and shot across the concrete floor towards the stack of boxes at the back. The little man was instantly busy, in a verminous, scurrying way. He moved most of them aside, and kicked another pile of mess out of his way to get at what he wanted. He crouched low and started to prize some boxes open. It was time to intervene. Hogarth moved quickly toward the junkyard and scaled the flimsy fence, hefting himself up and throwing himself down without any grace. He climbed the mountain. "Keep an eye on him from the front, will you…" he called to Palmer in a hoarse whisper. She nodded and took up position at the letterbox.

Now in his mid-forties, Hogarth was not at his limber best, but he wrenched the window wide open and thrust his torso through with a heave. The small man below him froze and looked up. The bespectacled man's eyes met his and his mouth dropped open.

"Dan Picton?" growled Hogarth.

The man didn't answer, but his expression was a response in itself.

"Stay exactly where you are. You're in deep trouble, so don't go making it any worse."

Hogarth peered back over his shoulder as he climbed down the tall ladder. He watched Picton drop something from his hands and it landed behind his feet. Then he kicked it away with a back heel.

"He tried to get rid of something – on the floor," called Palmer. Her voice echoed into the garage and made Picton jump. Hogarth grinned as he reached the floor and straightened out his jacket.

"Was that the sound of your conscience, Mr Picton?" said Hogarth. He walked calmly across the garage.

"So, what exactly have you got to hide, Mr Picton?"

"How did you even know I was here?" said the man, in an impish voice.

Hogarth shrugged, but he saw understanding dawn on the man's face.

"It was the bloody caretaker, wasn't it? He saw me."

The caretaker. So, he was the PI's source.

"Let's just say a little bird told me," said Hogarth. "So, out with it. Where is Andy Cruddas? And why exactly have you been avoiding everyone?"

The man shook his head. "I'm not avoiding anyone at all."

"Just the police then," said Hogarth.

He stepped past Picton, and kicked at a manila envelope left on the floor behind him. "My colleague saw you drop this. It'll have your fingerprints all over it. Care to tell me what it is?"

"It's nothing. It's not mine. I don't even know what it is."

"You don't look like an idiot, Mr Picton, but you certainly act like one," said Hogarth.

The window rattled as DS Palmer's backside slid through and her flat heels scuffed the top rungs of the ladder. "DS Palmer. I think you're distracting this man with your posterior," said Hogarth with an air of levity.

DS Palmer tutted as she climbed down.

But Picton wasn't smiling. The man looked deeply fraught.

"What are you doing skulking around on this estate, breaking into old garages? It doesn't look good. Especially after you disappeared moments before a man you dislike got stabbed to death."

"What?" said Picton.

Hogarth waited and watched the manclosely. There was a flurry of confusion on his face, but Hogarth knew it could have been faked.

"Don't tell me you don't know, Picton. Jake Drummond. Maybe you call him Drummie, as some idiots do. You did know him, didn't you?"

Picton turned pale by degrees.

"We know you did. We know he was picking on you at Club Smart. You were seen entering the nightclub at the same time as him, at his side. He had a go at you, didn't he? What did he want from you? What was the issue between you?"

"Nothing. He's dead, is he? That man was a selfish piece of crap, always exploiting people. He tried it with me, but it didn't work."

"No?" Hogarth walked past Picton and picked up the envelope with delicate fingers, trying not to contaminate it with his own fingerprints. He peered inside and saw some small flimsy cardboard cartons with bright logos and colours. He recognised the type of thing. A couple of years back the local 'head shops' had been able to get away with selling all kinds of toxic legal highs. But then people started dying all over the country. It wasn't an epidemic. Just the next batch of poisons exploiting a loophole because the substances had not yet been banned. Stuff like 'Spice'. Now there was nothing legal about them.

"Well, well, well? Did dear Jake know about this? That you had a little side business on the go? Or maybe Jake Drummond wanted you to sell this crap for him. Maybe he was blackmailing you because he found out about it."

"No. You're wrong…"

Hogarth's eyes narrowed. "Am I? Fine. So, tell me how it worked, Daniel. I'm all ears."

He watched the man's hand press against his belly, and heard something slide beneath the smooth fleece material. "What you got under there?!" snapped Hogarth. "Tell me now."

Hogarth clicked his fingers and. the man seemed to wilt.

Picton pulled up his jumper and revealed another envelope. This one looked stiff and flat as if filled with card.

"It's not what you think."

"Oh, it never is, son," said Hogarth. He clicked his fingers again and Picton gave him the card-backed envelope. Hogarth stuffed the first one in his pocket and opened the second. At first it seemed there was nothing inside, but then at the bottom he saw a little green book. The thing looked creased and worn from use. Hogarth pulled it out and flipped through the handwritten pages. There was a list of numbers, amounts, and a good few names, many of which repeated as the pages flicked by. It was amateur-hour stuff. Hogarth grinned. He had Picton by the short and curlies. Not only him but Cruddas too. Andy Cruddas' name went through the cash book like a stick of rock.

"So, you're a big cheese then, Daniel. You're in the import, export business, you and Andy. You get it all from Holland, right? Where? From the Hook to Harwich, maybe. Then one of you drives it in and then what? You knock it out at clubs like Club Smart? Maybe the local bars too? I bet I could work it out just from reading this." Hogarth waved the book in the air. "You know this crap kills people, don't you? That's why they banned it, Dan. And to be honest, you don't look like the kind of man who could handle a death on his conscience… but then again, appearances can be so deceiving."

Picton's head dropped.

"Jake Drummond knew about your business, didn't he?"

Picton's mouth formed a word, but then his brain seemed to kick in. "No comment."

"You killed Drummond, didn't you? Because he threatened to expose your business."

"No!" said Picton out loud. Hogarth looked into his small eyes. The outcry seemed genuine.

"Then why did you run?"

"From the club? But we didn't run. We just didn't want to be there anymore."

"People to see, places to go?" said Hogarth, waving the cash book.

Picton's Adam's apple bobbed up and down in his throat.

"If you didn't run, then why is Andy Cruddas missing? Even his dear old mum doesn't seem to know where he is. You wouldn't want to make his mother upset, would you?"

"Andy is missing?"

Hogarth waited then nodded. "Don't try to blag me, Daniel. You're not very good at it."

"But I don't know where he is. *Are you sure?*"

"You're telling me you really don't know where he's hiding?" said Hogarth.

"I don't. I swear. I called him, and he hasn't replied."

"So why did you come here today? Why now, the day after the murder…?"

"Because I was worried. I thought you might have found out that Drummond knew Peter Deal. If you did, you would have come right here."

Hogarth frowned.

"Peter Deal?"

"He owns the garage here…"

"We worked that part out, thanks, Daniel. Now, I think you'd better tell me everything you know because if you don't, the magistrate isn't going to like you one little bit. And if Andy Cruddas is still on the run, it's beginning to look like he's our prime suspect for the murder."

"He didn't do it."

"Then why did you both act so guilty and why is he on the run?"

"He didn't. I swear. But you need to find him quick. He could be in danger."

"You're coming with us."

"But I didn't do it."

"We'll see about that. Daniel Picton, I'm arresting you on suspicion of importing controlled substances, and possession with intent to supply…" Hogarth quoted the man his rights, and Palmer gave him a set of handcuffs. It was their first collar. It wouldn't be their last.

Chapter Ten

He sat in the darkness with the curtains drawn, because he was a man well used to the dark. It was a way of life. He turned on the stereo with the remote control and flicked to the local radio station. He had never liked local radio. It was too provincial. Too trivial. It was all about parish council announcements, seasonal food recipes, jumble sales, ancient cheesy music, and local events. But these days he couldn't get enough of it. He was keen to listen just in case he got another mention. In case his handiwork got a mention. He'd had plenty of airtime already. The phone-in DJs said a disaster had befallen the town. "What was the world coming to?" All those call-in DJs made him smile. But now the news was beginning to dry up too early and he didn't like it. He'd seen photographs of the detective in charge of the case. They were all over The Record. A DI Hogarth. He'd seen that knackered old copper on the first night. The man looked like a rock 'n' roller with his hair and his blazer. Paul Weller with a police car. Yes, he looked like someone with an ego. Which was good, because the man in the dark liked to do battle with people like that. He liked to measure himself. Which was part of the reason he'd had to take down Jake Drummond. That and the fact the man was trying to screw him for money. But now Drummond was gone and so the tension which had kept him planning and waiting for months was gone. He was empty, and it made him twitchy. Who would have ever thought that killing a man would have made him feel so clean and empty? He felt a strange mix of power and boredom after such a high. After all the highs he'd tried in his life, he'd finally found the undisputed best.

Murder. The heady mix of adrenaline and fear and commitment to the act was one part of it. Then delivering the final fatal contact itself was like a sexual climax. There was no other way to describe it. It was the best rush ever. The man grinned to himself, nodding because it was the most apt description he could muster.

It was only day one, but even so, the police had slackened up considerably since their lockdown at the nightclub. As far as he knew there had been no arrests. He had already heard they had gone back to the club, searching for a weapon they would never find. He'd seen them. Pathetic. Their aggressive start had scared him, but today he wasn't impressed.

The local radio station started playing something by The Carpenters, and he hit the off button. The police were useless. For all his obvious ego, this DI Hogarth didn't seem to be up to much. Which was interesting. Maybe there was room for a little fun. Was it time yet to set up another kill? The idea set him tingling with anticipation. Then the police really wouldn't have a clue, would they? He had enjoyed the thrill of the kill so much, he wanted to do it again. He had never known that murder could be so damn moreish. His face formed a wide grin. He lifted the greasy empty pizza box from his coffee table, and saw the faithful knife glinting at him from the table top. He had cleaned, disinfected, and polished it. It shone like precious metal.

"What do you think? Shall we try again?" he whispered in excitement. "Okay. Just a little bit longer. First, let's throw him something else to think about."

The man looked up from his knife to the special something he'd saved back. The value of his planning was becoming more evident with every day that passed. It was an emergency object he'd saved for just such a rainy day. If that didn't stir things up nicely, then he would all too gladly give in to his urge…

Chapter Eleven

Hogarth's team was gathered in the cramped confines of the main CID room. PC Dawson hung by the doorway at the back under the resentful gaze of DC Simmons.
"What's Dawson doing here again? He shouldn't be a part of this. He's uniform."
"While I understand PC Dawson may not be everyone's cup of tea," said Hogarth, "he has played a full part in this case already, so he stays. That is, unless you think there should be a show of hands, Simmons?". Everyone in the room knew the vote idea was pure sarcasm. No one raised a hand, not even Simmons.
"Good. So here we are. As you know, the Jake Drummond case is priority number one. Today we picked up one of our runaways in the form of one Daniel Picton. Picton is bum-chums with Andy Cruddas. Both men went missing from Club Smart just moments before Jake Drummond was killed. Want to chip in, DS Palmer?"
The DS nodded and took over the reins. "We've looked at the CCTV footage and found it inconclusive. It doesn't show any detail pointing to a specific killer or a weapon, though it does show several persons of interest, including Peter Deal and Gary Grayson."
"We'll be interviewing them," said Hogarth. "The pathologist believes the weapon to be a narrow-bladed knife. Unfortunately, the knife remains missing, even after PC Dawson's second go-over at the club today. The killer, whoever he or she is, must have taken the knife with them. Shame. By now it could have been disposed of anywhere. The timing of Cruddas and Picton leaving the club suggests they could be innocent of murder, but thinking from another

angle, it would be a great way to create an alibi. Even if they weren't physically responsible for the murder, it has to be highly likely that Andy Cruddas was involved. For now, we're holding Picton on drugs charges. That might lure Cruddas out of hiding. Picton denies any knowledge of a plot to kill Drummond. But Picton isn't one of life's tough cookies. I think he'll crack if we apply a bit of pressure."

"You think he did it, sir?" said DC Simmons.

"My view? I think Cruddas is the more likely candidate. He's still missing. Picton has all but admitted his guilt in terms of drug trafficking, and the cash book we found him taking from the garage proves that he and Cruddas were selling banned drugs. The CPS will have them for that. I asked Picton if Jake Drummond knew about their drug racket and he didn't deny it."

"Then that's virtually a confession," said Simmons.

"Not quite," said Hogarth. "Now we know Picton is more or less a nobody. But Andy Cruddas comes from money. And by the look of things – from his attempt to offload his Mercedes onto Dawson on the cheap, through to his involvement in a high-risk drug business – we can assume Cruddas was broke. But how did that happen? Was he bled dry by Drummond? Could be. As you can see, we've still got plenty of questions."

"Forensics give you anything?" said Dawson.

"Nothing from Marris, I'm afraid," said Hogarth. "The murder scene was so busy what could we expect? Forensics will have to make way for old-fashioned police work on this one. Most of our questions could be answered if we had Andy Cruddas."

"How come Picton was hiding his cash book and drugs at Grange Road?" asked Dawson.

It was a question which DC Simmons should have asked, but the DC's brain still seemed out of gear. Hogarth's eyes passed over Simmons before he looked at Dawson. Simmons seemed oblivious.

"Peter Deal owns the garage there, but it's not in use. Picton says that Peter Deal had his own relationship with Jake Drummond. But we knew that much already from Gary Grayson. I heard the DJ mocking Deal about a business partnership with Drummond. But Picton still hasn't given any good reason why he was using the garage to store drugs. It could be unrelated – that he just found a useful empty space – or maybe Drummond knew about the drugs there. But for now, the priority has to be the murder."

Hogarth looked at Palmer, Simmons, and Dawson. As he looked at Dawson by the door, Hogarth thought he caught sight of a flash of blonde lingering outside.

"Open the door, PC Dawson. I think someone else is attending our meeting."

Dawson turned his shoulder and yanked the door open. Right beside the door and walking away quickly was PCSO Rawlins.

"Bec!" said Dawson. PCSO Rawlins looked at Dawson and her face flushed pink.

"Come in, come in, then."

Sheepishly, Rawlins walked into the office. Dawson shut the door behind her.

"Sir?" she said.

"If you're going to eavesdrop you may as well help us. Do you recall anyone mentioning anything suspect to you about Peter Deal at Club Smart?"

Rawlins took her time. "Not that I remember. He was at the club. One of the older types, same age group as Jake

Drummond, mid-to-late fifties. Quite a curious looking man."

"I saw him and Grayson arguing. Did you talk to Grayson at all?"

Rawlins shook her head.

Hogarth nodded. "I asked Grayson about the argument and he told me Peter Deal had had a minor lottery win and wanted to invest in a new business. It seems he was intent on the mechanic game…"

"And he wanted to invest money in Jake Drummond?" said Dawson. "Sounds like a very bad idea to me."

"I think Grayson was right," said Hogarth. "Deal was about to get ripped off in a big way," said Hogarth. "The killer did save him from getting shafted."

"Did Deal know Picton and Cruddas were storing illegal substances in his garage?" said Simmons.

"Who knows? It wouldn't surprise me either way," said Hogarth. "It doesn't sound like Peter Deal is the brightest spark does it? But the more we push, the more the dots are beginning to join up. Drummond was about to rip off Peter Deal. Cruddas and Picton were under serious pressure from Drummond. Picton stored drugs at Deal's garage. It's even possible Deal was in on the murder. The dots are joining up, but we're still missing the biggest dot of them all. Andy Cruddas. Why is he still missing? If he didn't do it, he needs to clear his name."

"And where is he hiding?" said Palmer.

Hogarth shrugged. "Mummy's boy, Cruddas, has all the abilities of a Harry Houdini…"

"Sir," said Bec Rawlins with a hint of reproach in her voice.

Hogarth met the young Rawlins' gaze. She looked hesitant, like she was holding back.

"Speak your mind, Rawlins."

"Andy Cruddas is not who you think he is."

"Or maybe he's not who you think, Rawlins. We now know the man is a drug dealer, for one."

"But drug dealing and murder are very different things."

"That's a matter of opinion too, I'm afraid. Both kill," said Hogarth.

Rawlins nodded, taking Hogarth's point.

"Even so, I'm sure whatever he's done wrong stems from depression, sir. Andy Cruddas might have been born into a moneyed family, but he's had a very hard life. I mentioned his family tragedy…"

"You mentioned it in passing, yes…"

"His father died a couple of years back – in a car crash. His family has had a lot of trouble. He's got a kind heart, sir. He really couldn't have killed Jake Drummond, even if the man was doing him harm."

"So you say…" As Hogarth spoke, a thought drifted over his face, clouding his eyes. "Trouble you say…? His father was killed in a car crash. When?"

"Two years back. Yes, they've had a lot of trouble since."

"Trouble…" said Hogarth, chewing on the word.

Rawlins took a deep breath as if she was about to explain a complicated story. Hogarth raised a palm to stop her in her tracks.

"It wouldn't be *financial* trouble, by any chance?"

Bec Rawlins nodded. "That was what it resulted in, sir. For a while at least. Andy's father, was very well paid. But when he died, the family ended up broke for a long time."

"Very interesting, Rawlins. I must say this Cruddas lot sound very unlucky."

Hogarth kept his own counsel, but the look on his face spoke volumes of a new idea, and a hint of mischief to boot.

There was a knock at the office door. "Come in," called Hogarth. It was DS Burton, one of Jobson's team from the other office. "Yes?"

"DI Hogarth – the cleaner at Club Smart has found something of interest. I think you might want a look before forensics get hold of it."

Hogarth's serene smile faded, and he got up out of his chair as Burton closed the door.

"Let's hope it's good news, eh?" said Hogarth. He walked out of the CID room in search of the news, good or bad.

Chapter Twelve

Later.

"Are these yours, Daniel?" said Hogarth.
Hogarth dropped the clear plastic clip-lock bag on the table of interview room one. Picton pushed his spectacles up his nose and shuffled in his seat. He cleared his throat to speak. DI Hogarth and DS Palmer watched his responses.
"They look like a pair of my glasses. Another pair I own. Spares."
"If we checked these against your usual prescription I'd say there's a very good chance they'd be the same, wouldn't you?"
Picton stayed silent.
"In fact, if I called your optician, do you think he would confirm that he issued these glasses? He might even have the date he issued them in his big log book. A little bit like your log book, I suppose. What do you think, Daniel?"
"I want to speak to my solicitor."
"Yes, of course you do. But just to settle my mind, are these yours?"
"They could be."
"Interesting. Because if you look a little closer, just here, in that corner, what do you think that blemish might be?"
"They're glasses. Glasses often get dirty. I'm always cleaning them."
"I think that might be a bit more than a typical bit of smearing." Hogarth leaned forward in his seat. "Some of my colleagues think that could be blood. Now, I'm no expert, but I know some people who are. These spectacles are going

to go to forensics. They have a lab. They can run tests on things like that. And just in case you didn't know, if that blood turns out to belong to Jake Drummond, I might need to revise the charges you're being held under. Do you understand what I'm saying, Daniel?"

Picton hammered the table with his fist.

"You can't do this! I've read about things like this! This is a frame-up. A fit-up!"

"You need to think carefully before you throw around accusations like that here, son. You're beginning to sound like every guilty bugger I've ever nicked."

"But I wasn't there! You know I left the club before he was killed."

"For the record, I don't know that for certain. Witnesses thought they saw you leave, and that's different. But those witnesses were in the nightclub, not the cloakroom corridor. You may not have left the building at all. A good killer is a smart killer, Mr Picton. But a bad killer leaves clues. Did you drop these glasses when you hurried out of Club Smart on Monday night?"

"But I wasn't even wearing those glasses! I haven't seen them for days, weeks even…"

Hogarth nodded and leaned back in his chair. "You had plenty of motive to want this man dead. And with clues like this popping up, it's beginning to look like you could be our man."

"That clue didn't just pop up," said Picton. "Where did you find them?"

"In the club. The cleaner says they were found under a table not far from where Drummond was stabbed. They could have been knocked off your face in the chaos after you stabbed him. Then they were kicked under the table when you were trying to make your getaway."

"I told you, I didn't do it. You're trying to frame me."
Hogarth shook his head. "Not me, Mr Picton. I'm just following the crumbs and I've got to say, this is a big one. I'd think about that if I were you. Call your solicitor if you like, but we're finished here. You can go back to your cell now."
Picton looked more drained than ever. "What about Andy? Have you heard from him? Do you know where he is?"
"I don't think he wants us to find him. So, the answer is no. Things are getting worse for him every moment he stays off the radar. But if Andy Cruddas has information which could prove you innocent, you'd better get your thinking cap on. We need to find him. With your help, maybe we could."
"I don't know where he is."
"That's not good enough. Do you really want us to find him?"
"Yes. To prove he didn't do it either."
"If he's not guilty why would he run?"
"Because you'll think he killed the man, it's obvious."
Picton's face was turning dark with fluster and emotion. Hogarth saw it and dropped another question laced with innuendo.
"But why would I ever think that?"
"Because Andy couldn't pay him anymore, that's why!" Picton snapped, and sat back in his chair, emptied of his emotion.
Hogarth glanced at DS Palmer. When he looked back at Daniel Picton, the man was looking down at the interview room table.
"That's what we call progress, Daniel. And it also shows you were lying to us before. So, I think it's time for a change of heart, don't you? You scratch our backs and we might even scratch yours. If you're going to talk, the time is now."

Picton stared at the spectacles in the plastic bag, then he met Hogarth's eyes. He looked up and nodded slowly.

"I'll talk. But the only thing I can tell you is about the background. I don't know how Jake Drummond died. Now, I'm not sorry he's gone. Nobody who knew him could ever miss the man."

"No more shilly-shally. Start talking."

Picton gulped, knitted his eyes tight shut then started talking. The flow of words started to pour forth.

"Drummond knew that Andy's insurance business wasn't working out. Not long back, when Andy started out in the game, he was stupid. You might say he was even a little boastful. He used to tell people how much he was going to make from this sale or that sale. When we were drinking, Andy used to say he was going to make a killing in insurance. He was always speaking about getting one of those big houses on the seafront at Thorpe Bay. I mean, it was actually a little ridiculous. It was the drink talking. How many insurance brokers do you know who live on millionaire's row?"

"I don't know any millionaires at all, Mr Picton. On with the story."

"My point is, I think Jake Drummond heard those stories at the club – when Jake was giving it the big one."

"Bad news. So how did Drummond make his approach?"

"It wasn't that hard, really. Drummond already knew Andy in a roundabout way. The first time we both met him, he even seemed like a good man. He was helping Barbara, Andy's mum, through her bereavement after she lost Andy's dad in the accident."

Hogarth felt DS Palmer's eyes latch onto his. But he ignored her and stayed in the moment.

"And how did Jake Drummond help Andy's mum exactly?"

"It didn't look like anything more than tea and sympathy. I guessed he was after marrying into her money, like some people do, but I never mentioned my thinking to Andy. But later, when we met the real Jake Drummond, I'm sure he must have figured it out. Wherever the man saw cash, he went for it, no matter who he hurt in the process."

"So, Drummond got into Andy. How did he turn the screws?"

"The usual way these scumbags do. Threats of violence, which eventually turned into a beating. Once Andy gave him as good as he got. Just once."

"In Ryan's Bar by any chance?"

Picton was wrong footed. "How do you know about that. We thought it had been dealt with?"

"It has been. Forget it. What happened after that?"

"The next time we met Drummond, the big man battered Andy good and proper. I got hurt too just for being around. We were scared of him after that. We made sure we paid him on time. I paid him from my salary, Andy from his insurance earnings. But soon after that his business started to dry up. I blame Drummond. Without confidence a man can't sell. Drummond broke Andy's confidence. He couldn't operate as a salesman anymore."

"But then you came up with the bright idea of importing ex-legal highs?" said Hogarth.

Picton shook his head. "How would people like me and Andy come up with an idea like that? It was all Drummond's idea. It was his idea that we pay the mules to bring it in, his idea that we stash it and then distribute it at the clubs and bars. It was all his idea, so he could watch us do the dangerous part while he took all the cream of the cash."

"He must have left you something for yourselves?"

Picton's eyes turned away. "A little compensation maybe. But it wasn't worth the stress. I quit my job, just so I could keep an eye on it. I was forever terrified we'd be caught."

"How would good people like you and Andy ever end up doing something like that, eh? Let me tell you, in case you haven't figured it out. People like you might think you're the victims. But you make other victims too to save your skin. You're actually not much better than Drummond, are you?"

"We never hurt anyone."

"Wrong. You just don't know who you hurt. That's the only difference. Is that why Andy Cruddas ran and left you to take the flak? He didn't want to face the rap for the drugs game?"

Picton blinked. "I don't know. I'd like to see him. To see if he's okay. What if the person who killed Drummond hurt him too?"

"People like you and Andy Cruddas strike me as the type who always prioritise their own survival above anything else. When we find him, we'll let you know. Eventually. You got anything else to say, Daniel? No idea where he's hiding?"

The young man shook his head and averted his eyes.

"Then thanks for your cooperation."

Hogarth opened the interview room door and called PC Jordan to take the man back to his cell. When Hogarth walked into the corridor, Palmer was keen to join him.

"You got that, didn't you?" said Hogarth.

"It sounded genuine."

"And it had the ring of truth. He just exposed Old Mother Cruddas as a liar."

"She said she didn't know Jake Drummond."

"Mr Tea and Sympathy, eh? Well, I know people have all kinds of hidden facets to their personality, but Jake Drummond strikes me as man who wouldn't have given a rat's backside for a woman's grief. He wanted something from her. And I wonder if he got it. As for her, if she can lie about that, maybe she could lie about any number of things."

PCSO Rawlins had been loitering in the corridor near the interview room. Now the interview was finished, she approached Hogarth carefully.

"Well, if it's not our intrepid PCSO, Rebecca Rawlins." Rawlins tried for a smile.

"Did Picton tell you anything about Andy?"

"As a matter of fact, yes. The good, the bad, and the ugly. You can have the edited and abridged version, Rawlins," said Hogarth. "Andy Cruddas and Picton were importing and dealing so-called legal highs around Southend, maybe for months."

Rawlins' smile faltered. "No. That can't be right."

"It isn't right, but that's what they were doing. He blames Drummond. Says Jake Drummond set them up in the business, so he could continue to extract money from them."

"I can believe that. Andy wouldn't have harmed anyone through choice."

"But he *was* harming people, Rawlins. Dealing that stuff, deceiving you, now evading the police to save his own skin while his pal, Picton, is hung out to dry. And now we've found out his dear old mum has her share of secrets too."

"What?" said Rawlins.

"Keep all this under your hat, Rawlins," said Hogarth. "Right now, nothing these people do would surprise me. Come on, Palmer. Let's go and pay another little visit to Mother Cruddas. It'll be nice to hear what those cosy chats with Uncle Jake were all about."

Hogarth stuffed his hands in his pockets and breezed through the new open plan office where the uniforms and the PCSOs had their desks.

"That man is a cynical old grouch," said Rawlins.

"Actually, this is the happiest I've seen him all day," said Palmer.

"Dawson reckons he's got some kind of woman trouble. Like a girlfriend holed up somewhere."

"Someone he doesn't want to tell people about? That would be a strange kind of girlfriend," said Palmer. She looked away in case Rawlins saw something in her eyes.

"With his mood swings it's got to be love trouble. Either that or he's hit the menopause."

Palmer rolled her eyes. "Actually, I think it's the job, Bec. Just you wait. One day you'll wonder why you ever wanted into the force." Palmer turned away and started walking after Hogarth.

"Some days, I still do…" whispered Rawlins, but Palmer was already gone.

Chapter Thirteen

When Barbara Cruddas opened her big burgundy front door, she tried hard to hide her displeasure. But she didn't hide it quite well enough. Her polite smile wavered and her eyes turned stony. "Oh. You again. Have you heard anything about Andrew?"

"As yet, no, Mrs Cruddas. Then you've heard nothing yourself?" said Hogarth.

"No. I'm beginning to get very worried," she said. "What are you people going to do about it?"

"The same as we're doing now, Mrs Cruddas. Investigating, leaving no stone unturned, as they say. Do you mind if we come in?"

This time the woman stayed blocking the door. "I don't see how you'll find him by coming back here so soon."

"Life throws up all kinds of surprises, Mrs Cruddas. Now, can we come in? Or do we have to conduct a private conversation out here?"

The woman's face tightened. "You must come in, of course." She let go of the door and shuffled away in her big skirt towards the living room. Hogarth grinned at Palmer as they followed after her.

Hogarth sat down without waiting for an invitation. The woman had lost the right to professional deference. She was the lying kind. She looked displeased at his lack of good manners.

"Mrs Cruddas," said Hogarth. "It appears there must have been a mistake."

"A mistake?" she said, her cheeks quivering.

"Yes. You see, last time we were here you told us that you didn't know Jake Drummond. I'll remind you that Jake Drummond is the man who was stabbed to death at Club Smart the other night."

The woman met his eyes fleetingly, then placed her hands on her knee, one over the other. The woman's posture reminded him of the queen posing for her royal portrait. The woman seemed stiff and awkward.

"A mistake, you say?" she said, guardedly.

"Yes. You see, Daniel Picton recalls that for a time after your husband's tragic accident, Jake Drummond used to come to see you."

"Then Daniel is mistaken."

"Is he now? He seemed pretty certain to me, didn't he DS Palmer?"

"Yes, he did."

"He even recalled the nature of the visits. He gave the impression that when he saw Jake Drummond here, which was before Picton and your son properly knew the man, that he was here as a listening ear, someone to give you a little tea and sympathy in your time of grief. It must have been a very difficult time for you. Drummond must have been a great help."

The woman nodded slowly. "Yes, yes, it was a difficult time."

"Yes… I hear that bereavement like that can cause deep shock. Shock can cause people to forget all kinds of things. How did your husband die exactly?"

"Must we talk about this now? At the very point when you don't even know what's happened to my son."

"No, Mrs Cruddas. We don't have to talk about it now. But it *would* help us better understand Mr Drummond, which could help us locate your son. And if you have information which would help us, now really would be the time to share it."

"What do you think I can tell you, exactly?"

"That, Mrs Cruddas, is for you to say. Let's start with your husband, may we?"

The woman nodded "If we must… my husband, Wilbur, worked in insurance. He was a high-flyer. He served a portfolio of high-net-worth clients. They trusted him immensely. He used to make recommendations to them, and they would simply buy whatever he suggested. His job was the foundation of everything we had. But then we lost him in his prime. He was just fifty-five when he died in that awful car crash on the M25."

"Terrible. When did it happen, Mrs Cruddas?"

"Two years back. Can it really be that long?"

"Daniel tells me your family has struggled since then. Financially, speaking."

The woman's face flushed. Her eyes filled with defiance. "My financial affairs are not for public consumption. I've never flaunted our wealth, and I have never sought a penny from anyone to cover any misfortune."

Hogarth felt Palmer's eyes running over the fine china ornaments, the chandelier, and the antique wooden furniture.

"So, there was misfortune, as you put it?"

"Misfortune, yes. But does it look like we have struggled?"

Hogarth looked around. "To be honest, madam, no. I don't see much flat-pack Ikea furniture in this room. But appearances can be deceiving and in my line of work they often are…"

As intended, Hogarth's words hit a raw nerve. The woman stiffened again.

"The reason I'm asking you about your finances... the reason I'm asking you about Jake Drummond, is because we know Drummond had a background in extortion. It looks like he made a career out of it, leaving plenty of people around who weren't too sad about him being killed. It's likely that someone who was being coerced by Drummond was the person who killed him."

"Well you surely can't suspect me! I wasn't in that awful nightclub. I've never been to such a place."

"No. But your son was there frequently, and he had good reason to dislike Jake Drummond. I wondered if you felt the same."

"Why would my son have any reason to dislike the man? He didn't know him!"

"Why would you think that, Mrs Cruddas? Maybe you're beginning to recall a little the times he spent with you."

The women met his eyes. "Daniel Picton had no obvious reason to lie to us. Jake Drummond visited you here after your husband's death, didn't he?"

The woman hesitated. She settled her hands on her lap. "Tell me. Do I need a solicitor?"

"Not at present, no."

The woman sighed, and the stiffness sank out of her body. She leaned back and looked up at the ceiling.

"Jake Drummond was once, for a while, a client of my husband. He was supposedly high-net-worth too, though Wilbur confessed to me once he didn't know where the man ever got it all from. Wilbur believed in client confidentiality, but he told me about this one, because he seemed odd. He said Drummond had a string of businesses with rather odd modes of making money. Wilbur even guessed Drummond was laundering money, but only after he helped the man organise his insurances. But later, we both knew Wilbur had been wrong. Because Jake Drummond started visiting Wilbur while he was at work."

"Jake Drummond targeted your husband first?" said Hogarth.

"Yes. When my Wilbur was at his peak, Jake Drummond started appearing. Wilbur even believed the man was following him around."

"Following…?" said Hogarth. He shifted in his chair.

"Like a stalker," she added. Hogarth's face flickered with discomfort. He tried to hide it but DS Palmer's eyes glanced his way.

"What did he have on your husband, Mrs Cruddas?"

Mrs Cruddas struggled.

"Do we really have to do this, Detective?"

"I'm afraid so."

"Very well. My husband was having an affair. But worse than that, he was having an affair with two women at the same time. One of them was a friend of mine, a good friend. Lois and I led the local Women's Institute together. I remember working with her during the time she must have been sleeping with my husband. We made jam together, can you believe it? We organised jumble sales for the needy… we shared a glass of wine. And she was sleeping with Wilbur the whole damn time."

"And the other woman?" said Hogarth.

"One of his clients, of course. A high-net-worth harlot. I'm afraid the secretary was a little ordinary for his tastes."

"And you didn't know about these affairs at the time? This was how Drummond was able to blackmail your husband."

"Yes, and later when Wilbur confessed I began to understand why our living standards had declined. The holidays were gone. The long weekend breaks. The house started to deteriorate, and our relationship came next. We had arguments, and I asked him if he was pouring our money into an affair. Wilbur was relieved – can you believe it? Relieved, when I found out he was sleeping with Lois. His ordeal was finally over. But mine had just began."

Hogarth nodded. "But after that Drummond couldn't blackmail you anymore."

"He couldn't blackmail Wilbur. But the harm had already been done. Wilbur was a wreck., his business was in tatters, and when I got hold of our bank statements, I saw we were sinking fast. It was only a matter of time until he lost the lot."

"And yet, here we are, Mrs Cruddas, surrounded by finery of all kinds."

"I only asked does it look like we suffered, Detective. But suffer we did."

Sharing her pain had made the woman look drawn and unwell.

"Mrs Cruddas. Have you got anything more to tell us?"

She met Hogarth's eyes. He saw something of a haunted look. There was more, but the woman shook her head.

"Wilbur wasn't thinking straight anymore. He was a mess. It was only a matter of time, I suppose until he gave up the ghost. In the end, my poor Wilbur wasted his life, didn't he?"

"Forgive me if this sounds crass, Mrs Cruddas… but you make it sound like your husband just gave up the ghost or died from an illness. But he didn't, did he? He died in a car crash. Are you saying you blame Jake Drummond for that?"

"Yes. Most definitely. If not for Jake Drummond, Wilbur would still be with us. As it stands, I'm a woman growing old alone, at my wit's end…"

Hogarth sensed there was much more to come, but he wouldn't get it by pushing today. The woman's big face had become impassive, immovable, like a brick wall.

"Please, find my son…" she said. "He wanted so desperately to live up to his father's high hopes. Maybe the burden of expectation has been too much. If only he knew he was already a better man than his father ever was. Find him so I can tell him that, will you…?"

"Oh, we're looking for him, Mrs Cruddas. Don't you worry. And we won't stop until we find him."

Hogarth stood up and slowly navigated his way towards the front door. He opened it and looked back down the grand hallway. As expected, prim Mrs Cruddas was standing there, arms folded in front of her waist as she waited for them to leave.

"And should you remember anything you've forgotten to tell us, Mrs Cruddas… if anything else has slipped your mind and you recall it later… do give us a call. It could save an awful lot of trouble later on…"

Hogarth let his words sink in. Palmer nodded at the woman and closed the door behind them.

"What do you think?" said Palmer.

"She's lied once. She could do it again. She's up to something."

"Like what? You think she could have been involved in Drummond's murder?"

"Not likely. But she's up to something. I'd bet your car on it…" said Hogarth with a faint grin.

Chapter Fourteen

Peter Deal, the mechanic with the lottery win was on the list. While Hogarth went to catch up with Marris and do some more digging into the Cruddas family, DS Palmer was left to catch up with the curious Mr Deal. Palmer had already formed a picture of a man who was something of a simpleton. An easy mark for a man like Drummond. The man had been given a cash windfall and wanted to get out of the grease-monkey business to find something easy and profitable. People like that had to be fodder for every scam going. Palmer wondered about the closed down garage. And she wondered about the stashed drugs. What did Deal know and what didn't he know?

Peter Deal lived in the low-rise block of private flats at the end of Princess Avenue, the very end of the busiest road in Southend. Further on, the four-lane road turned into the A127, one of the two main roads into London. Deal's address was hardly millionaire territory. DS Palmer parked her dented Vauxhall Corsa in the front car park and walked into the stairwell of the flats.

***

"So, how much did you win, if you don't mind me asking?" said Palmer.

"Strange question for a police lady to ask, isn't it?"

Police lady. That was a term Palmer didn't hear very often. Peter Deal was a craggy-faced man with red skin and prematurely grey hair. He looked to be in his fifties, but the hair made him seem older. He wore a grey shirt with an unfashionable granddad collar, and sat leaning forward over his knees. His fingers were covered with gold rings, but none of them looked either expensive or recent buys. Deal had an out-of-town accent. He was either a Norfolk yokel or a man from the West Country. Palmer couldn't tell the difference.

"It could prove relevant to the investigation, Mr Deal."

The man nodded. "Well… okay. I got five numbers one week, but you don't get a lot for that these days. Then the next week I won something on the smaller game. The raffle. I won more on that than I did with the lottery game, can you believe it? I picked up four hundred and fifty thousand all in all. Not too shabby for a few random numbers, eh?"

Four hundred thousand quid. Palmer thought about the money for a few seconds. If she had won it, the police force wouldn't have seen her for dust. In fact, Palmer wondered how little money it would have taken to prise her away from her career. A hundred grand maybe? Enough to start again. *Fifty?* Palmer shook the thought off and noted down the four-fifty k figure in her notebook.

Looking around the flat, Palmer wondered if he'd spent any of his winnings at all. But Deal wasn't as stupid as he seemed. The man read Palmer's inquisitive gaze, and answered her thoughts.

"It's all in the bank at present. I draw a little to live from, just a little mind, and the rest is waiting for my next venture. I was glad to get out of the garage business. That place, that estate, was very downmarket. I always wanted to do something more. Hang on a minute. You brought your car in to my garage, didn't you?"

Palmer felt awkward at the reminder of her dented Corsa. Had Peter Deal been there when she dropped it in. Surely, she would have remembered a face like that.

"That's right," she said, hesitantly.

"Trouble with the alternator, as I recall"

"Spot on. You have a very good memory, Mr Deal."

"Sometimes. I remember a pretty lady is all I'll say."

DS Palmer hadn't been referred to as a pretty lady for a long time. It was just a shame the compliment came from a man like Deal.

"Do you know why I've come here today, Mr Deal?"

"Because of Jake Drummond being killed."

Palmer nodded. "Pretty much. Though there are some other things we'll need to discuss."

The man frowned.

"Oh? You know I never had anything to do with his death. Me and Jake were about to embark on something. A joint venture. He was going to stump up half the cash and so was I."

"Doing what exactly?" said Palmer.

"Buying and selling stuff on the internet. It was a no-brainer, the way Jake explained it. I had a huge empty garage, perfect for a storage and distribution centre. All we needed to do was set up the branding and pick our stock."

Recalling Picton's boxes, Palmer wondered about that stock. "What stock were you looking at, exactly?"

"Chinese. Anything Chinese, you name it. They sell the stuff for cheaper than it can be made! Anything you name they make it. Not only that, you buy their stuff in bulk and they give it away! We were going to flog it all on that auction site, EBay or whatever, but with a fixed price. No mucking around that way. I was going to look into hiring a lad to help us, someone with half a brain, then everything else would have been had as profit. It was a great idea. People today want those rock bottom prices, but no one wants to wait for delivery from China, see. Instead, we would do that, and they'd buy direct from us. We'd mark it up and sell it on. Sounds good, eh?"

"It sounds like a great idea but there must be plenty of competition out there."

"Jake didn't seem to think so. He showed me how it stacked up. He showed me the business plan. We talked about it for weeks. He was in no rush, that's why I trusted him on it."

Palmer nodded. "Was this your idea?"

"No. It was Jake's. But it was sound. We were going to make a killing… what do I call you by the way? Detective? Officer? Madam?"

"DS Palmer will do just fine."

The man nodded, but stiffly. Was he hoping for a first name, Palmer wondered. Well he wasn't going to get one from her. She made a note. "Jake Drummond had the idea. And how much were you going to have to put in to get this business off the ground?"

"Two hundred and fifty grand, with another hundred to follow."

Palmer winced. Peter Deal shrugged.

"The numbers stacked up, miss. I'd seen the plan, and Jake had convinced me. He was going to invest the same, even stevens all the way."

"How did you know it was fifty-fifty?"

"Drummond showed me his finances. He was in a better position than I was. I had nothing to worry about on that score."

There was something defensive, something false about Deal's explanations. But as yet it didn't feel like deceit. Not yet. So Palmer wondered what it was.

"The finances. In what form did he show you them?"

"Bank statements mostly. They were in his business plan."

Palmer nodded. "Bank statements can be easily forged you know."
"It was a good plan and it was ready to go. There's no point disparaging the man now. He's dead. It's disrespectful."
Palmer decided to change tack.
"The night Drummond died, DJ Gary Grayson was overheard telling you that you'd been kidding yourself about being business partners with Drummond. What did you think about that?"
"That fella is nothing but hot air. He's a bloody waster, content to let others pick up his mess. He spends half his life drunk. Why would anyone listen to a word he says?"
"Mess? What mess?"
Deal shook his head. "You've seen the man. Draw your own conclusions."
Idle gossip was no use to Palmer. She moved on.
"So, you didn't hear about Drummond's reputation for taking other people's money? Not a thing?"
Deal shrugged. "I tend to make up my own mind."
"How much did you pay him – before he was killed?"
"A little."
"How much?"
"Ten grand. Just enough to order a selection of stock from China. For a test run."
"And did you actually see any of the stock you paid for?"
"They send it in a container ship, miss. It takes weeks. I knew I wasn't going to see that for a long while."
"But how long ago was the order made? When did you part with your money?"
"About a month back."
"Mr Deal, don't you suspect the order was never placed? I'm sorry to say you could have lost ten grand to a con man…"

"No. You don't know, that's just talk. But what of it, anyway. The business is scotched now anyway. Even if the goods turn up, I wouldn't be able to run it by myself. Not unless the lad Drummond recommended is willing to stay and help…"

"Excuse me? Drummond chose you an assistant, did he?"

"Yeah. It was a good offer," he said, nodding, "The guy would run the warehouse on near enough minimum wages. Looked like he had a brain in his head too."

"Did you meet him then?"

"Once. Bookish looking lad. Ideal for the job."

"Let me guess," said Palmer. "He's not called Daniel Picton by any chance?"

"Dan? Yep. That's him. Worked in aviation before apparently, but Drummond said he'd given it all up and was looking for a new thing. Dan was a pushy little bugger though. Kept calling me to see if he could get access to the garage before we started receiving the stock. He said he wanted to clear up and get it ready. As far as I was concerned it was empty enough, bar the shouting."

Palmer smiled. Deal smiled back, not knowing the context. Peter Deal was indeed a simple man. He seemed ready to forget a ten grand loss because the man he gave it to showed him some bank statements. He didn't wonder why Drummond recommended Picton for the job either. Picton had needed the garage for his drug business, and when Deal had denied him access, he'd taken matters into his own hands. Palmer reckoned the man was too simple to be involved with the drugs. But in the eyes of the law, ignorance wasn't a good enough defence, though Deal's innocent mind might just have gotten him off the biggest hook of all. Murder.

"Mr Deal. Do you really believe Jake Drummond intended to set up a business with you?"

The man stroked his stubbly chin and looked away.

"You keep pushing don't you. Look. In the end I did have a few doubts. But not the way you're thinking. I liked his business idea. It made sense to me and I wanted in. I had doubts because I saw his head get turned by another business opportunity quite late into our dealings. He denied it, but I knew what I saw. I'd seen him with her. That's the only reason why that bloody DJ was poking his nose in at the club. If he knew what was good for him, he'd have left me alone."

"Sorry, I don't follow you, Mr Deal?" Palmer had been ready to leave but now she took out her notepad and gel ink pen once more. Deal saw the pen poised above the pad and hesitated.

"Go on. You'd seen Drummond with someone?"

"It was Gary Grayson's latest girlfriend. The one he spends most of his time with, at least. I heard the woman was in the double-glazing business with her husband. She left him and took him to the cleaners, so I knew she had some money going and a head for business too."

"You saw Drummond with her?"

"Yes. And I'd heard her yapping about wanting to set up a new business just a few weeks back. I was out with Jake talking about our business, and there was this girl sitting there with Gary Grayson. It was early – before he started working the club that night. The woman was half drunk and yapping so loud about her plans, half the town must have heard. I thought it was the drink talking, but it caught Jake's interest. I knew he was listening. It didn't bother me right then, mind. It only bothered me when I saw them drinking coffee together at one of those posh coffee houses in the town."

"But what made you think it was about business rather than pleasure?"

"It was obvious. For one, Jake was no looker. And I saw Jake had his leather case with him. I saw it on their table. The only time I'd seen that case with him was when he was talking about business. There was paperwork on the table too, just like what he did with me when he told me about the business. Then I got worried. But I didn't speak to him about it, because I didn't want to cause friction. So I left it. But that woman, and Grayson, they're bloody loudmouths. They're the kind of people who would have stitched me up to get a piece of that deal. Drummond was one of the sharpest people I've met. I didn't want him getting poached by someone else…"

"Oh, I don't know about that, Mr Deal. I'm learning a lot about Jake Drummond on this case. I'm pretty certain he would have stayed with you until the bitter end."

Peter Deal nodded. He seemed pleased with Palmer's words.

"I wouldn't have been too chuffed if he had dumped me for them, I can tell you. You hear about people getting done over all the time in business, don't you?"

"You certainly do, Mr Deal. You certainly do," said Palmer. "Now, do you mind fleshing out a couple of things you said…"

"Of course. Such as?"

"You suggested Gary Grayson had more than one girlfriend on the go?"

"Him? He's what I call a shagabond, if you catch my drift…"

"A womanizer?" said Palmer.

"Absolutely. Alison Craw, that's his girlfriend, she's the one with the money. The poor woman seems to think he's a good bet. If only she knew…"

"Knew what, Mr Deal?"

"He gets through women as quick as he gets through his beer."

Palmer put her pen to her mouth. Visiting Deal had been worth it. Palmer looked at her notes. She had collected news on Grayson and Alison Craw. Drummond's web of activity and range of scams were impressive. And the more she found, the more motives for murder seemed to pop up. But looking at Peter Deal, DS Palmer couldn't help feel a shred of pity.

"We may need to speak to you again, Mr Deal. Until then, all the best with your business."

"Yes. I think I'll keep that Daniel on. He's pushy, but I'll need someone if this is ever going to work. Jake's gone, but that Chinese stock will be here soon."

"Yes," said Palmer, standing up from the couch. "It's very good that you're so positive, Mr Deal."

Deal grinned at the compliment. DS Palmer sensed another flirtation coming, so hurried out politely and closed the door on the man with a thin but firm smile, and walked down the stairs. Deal was a benign idiot who had been fleeced for ten grand. In the grand scheme of things, he'd gotten off lightly. He was almost certainly innocent of the crimes Picton and Cruddas had committed on his property, but he was still on a sticky wicket with them being on his premises. But as motives for murder radiated in every area of life Drummond had ever touched, it seemed as good a time as any to go back to the scene of the crime. That was where the scumbags gathered. The club seemed to be the centre of the web and it sounded like Gary Grayson and his girlfriend Alison Craw had a few questions to answer.

Chapter Fifteen

Day Six: Wednesday

Almost recharged by a full night's sleep, DI Hogarth and Palmer left the station with the address of Gary Grayson's girlfriend, Alison Craw. Hogarth felt almost bright eyed. He'd chosen to skip the extra nightcap and settled on just the three drams of whisky in front of the news channel. These days drinking was compulsory to get through the news. The world was going to pot and in a big way. Hogarth only watched the news to remind him that a world existed beyond the confines of Southend's shores but after a half hour's viewing, the news channel made Southend look like a kibbutz. Even so, Hogarth wasn't tired or depressed. The killer was still very much on the loose, and there was a chance he would kill again. There was still the conundrum about the blood on Picton's spectacles to solve, and the fact that Picton and Cruddas had left the club before he died. And the murder weapon was still missing, as was Cruddas. The case was a mess. But it couldn't dampen his mood or the faint but growing belief they were getting close. Palmer and Hogarth had already swapped stories about Peter Deal and Barbara Cruddas. Somewhere between these names and their murky stories, the killer was lurking, hiding just out of reach. The case was still up in the air and the killer on the loose, but he felt buoyant. But there was a reason for that. At 2pm he was set to meet his own Alison, the gorgeous Ali Hartigan. He could barely wait. He still needed to work out a decent excuse to cover an hour's absence from the case, but he'd blag it somehow. Until then he needed to focus his mind on the job. So, it was time to visit a new name in this mess. Another Alison –Mrs Alison Craw. Each time they looked at the case again a new layer appeared. Hogarth wondered what they would discover next.

Alison Craw lived in a street of semi-detached houses in Hadleigh, five miles out from Southend. Some of the houses still wore their eighties pebble-dash like a shabby suit. But not this one. Mrs Craw's house had been done up in a fashionable white, with trendy period-grey doors. The windows, he noted, were fully double glazed. "You reckon she got him to do those windows before the divorce?"

"What?" said Palmer.

"Her ex. The double-glazing man. This must have been his work. Looks like she's taken him to the window cleaners," said Hogarth with a grin.

"You don't know anything about their marriage. He probably deserved it."

"From what I see of divorces, it's the blokes who usually get rinsed and the women get the lot. Makes me glad I never got married."

"And not being married makes you happy, does it?" said Palmer.

Hogarth sensed he needed to tread carefully with what he said next. Palmer was a woman. They were sentimental about marriage. Like they were about horses.

"It doesn't make me happy, but it makes me less unhappy than it would if I was in that double-glazing man's boots. Enough gender politics for one morning, eh? Before I cause an uproar."

Hogarth walked up the path and rang the doorbell. The bell made a deep chime which echoed in the hall. When the door

opened, a sleepy-eyed Gary Grayson answered. The DJ was wearing only a pink terry towelling dressing gown which finished high on his hairy legs. Grayson blinked at them, yawned, and dragged a hand through his scruffy bleached-blond hair before he stepped behind the door for dignity's sake. Palmer grimaced. She'd seen too much already.
"Look it's DJ GG. Well I never. Pink suits you,"
"Eh?"
"The dressing gown. Very new man. I think DS Palmer would approve."
"What do you want?" said Gary Grayson.
"Not you, Gary. Not yet. Though I might want a word afterwards. I came here to see your good lady, Mrs Craw."
"Alison? Why? What's she got to do with Jake Drummond."
Hogarth grinned. He put his hands in his pockets and gave Gary Grayson a glare which said it was none of his business. Hogarth gave Grayson a testing look, to see if the man was blagging. But Grayson's morning eyes were so small and beady they were impossible to read.
"Deejaying last night, Gary? Or just on the razz for the sake of it? I heard you have a liking for the bottle. *Amongst other things.*"
"What's that supposed to mean?" he said.
"Nothing Gary. I was just making small talk. Now, if you don't mind I'd like to speak with Mrs Craw."
They heard feet advance along the hallway before a well-presented woman appeared. She had long, thick dark hair. It was tight and curly, almost as if it had been permed and there was a hint of red in it. The woman had a wide face and big serious brown eyes. Hogarth might have described her as thickset or fuller-figured, but she wasn't fat in the least. She looked strong. And those eyes looked nothing less than bolshie.

"Alison Craw?" he said.

The woman was dressed in a brown business suit, with a white blouse. "Yes?"

"Off to work, are you?" said Hogarth.

"No. I don't have a job at present. But I've got some business meetings. Why? Who are you?"

"Detective Inspector Hogarth and this is Detective Sargent Palmer, Southend CID. We'd like to talk to you about a certain matter, if you can spare the time…"

Palmer wondered why Hogarth was being so deferential, then she realised he was filling time as he waited for Gary Grayson to disappear. Grayson lingered by the stairs. Alison Craw followed Hogarth's eyes.

"Do us all a favour, Gary," said Mrs Craw. "Go and have a shower and put some clothes on. You look a right state."

"Charming. Just don't let these coppers do a job on you, Alison. Coppers are always on an angle," he said, as he started to climb the stairs.

"Nothing like you, eh, Gary? You've got nothing to hide."

The DJ looked back at Hogarth but said nothing. Then he carried on his way.

"You'd better come in then," said the woman. "But I can't spare long."

"No one ever can. Thanks, Mrs Craw. I do call you Mrs, do I?"

"Unfortunately, I can't undo what's been done. Yes, it's Mrs Craw."

She led them down a neat modern hallway with a wooden floor into a mocha-walled lounge.

"Sit down," she said. The woman made a point of shutting the heavy living room door while Hogarth and Palmer took their seats. Hogarth studied the woman's manner. She closed the door firmly, checking it was sealed. It was as if she was making a point of shutting Gary Grayson out. Hogarth wondered what she was about to say.

She sat down on a deep brown leather chair opposite their perch on the sofa.

"You and Gary are quite a couple," said Hogarth, with typical bluntness.

"What do you mean?" said the woman. Alison Craw seemed pretty blunt in her own right.

"Nothing. It's just that… you're very different, shall we say," he said.

"Gary's nothing like my ex," said Alison. "But after him different is good. Besides, we've been together two years now., so it must work. So," she said, her voice changing tone. "What's this about?"

"I have a feeling you might already know," said Hogarth. The woman gave him a steely look with her wide brown eyes, but she gave nothing away.

"Jake Drummond," said Palmer, to break the silence.

"Part time blackmailer and extortioner," said Hogarth. "You knew him, didn't you, Mrs Craw?"

"You mean the man who was killed at Club Smart?"

Hogarth ignored the question. He kept his gaze on hers. "You knew Jake Drummond well enough to have one-to-one meetings with him in local coffee shops, so I'm told."

The woman blushed. She batted her eyelids until she regained control of her face.

"It's a small town," said Hogarth. "People get spotted doing all kinds of things they thought hadn't been seen. Don't fret it."

"I don't like the tone, or the implication of the way you're speaking, Inspector."

"Maybe not. But I'd still like you to acknowledge the question. Did you know Jake Drummond?"

Hogarth said the name louder and the woman flinched.
"Keep it down, will you... yes, I knew him."
"What is it? Doesn't Gary know that you had dealings with the man? My, my, Mrs Craw... Whatever did Jake Drummond have on you?"
"Excuse me?" said the woman. She frowned.
"You had meetings with him in coffee shops. From what I hear Drummond wasn't the best kind of company. Not exactly a raconteur or a cuddly friend. More of a chiselling scoundrel. The kind who only bothered with you if he thought he could get something out of it. From the look on your face, I'd say I'm right..."
"What happened to Jake Drummond had nothing to do with me."
"This is an investigation, Mrs Craw. We push every door, turn every stone and we don't jump to any rash conclusions. Right now, we're gathering information."
The woman let this sink in and nodded. The tension evident in her bunched shoulders melted just a little.
"Then what do you want to know?"
"The nature of your meetings with Drummond."
"I don't see how that could be relevant."
"Let me be the judge of that."
"But it's not the kind of thing that's easy to discuss." Craw's eyes flicked towards DS Palmer. Palmer and Hogarth shared a glance, and the DS shifted in her seat.
"Did the man put you under some kind of pressure... to do something?" said Palmer.
"I'm not the kind of woman people can mess with easily. You may have gathered that already," she said. "The trouble was Jake Drummond didn't come at me like that otherwise I would have dealt with him. I thought I recognised him from the club, but I wasn't sure, because I only went there once.

It's a place for kids, not grown-ups. But I remembered that later, after our first meeting."

"The meeting. How did it come about?"

"He called me about a business proposition. I was sceptical, but intrigued. I agreed to meet him to look at his proposal. At this point, I was neutral to cold on the idea, but I was being polite. I owed it to myself to make sure that I didn't knock back a golden goose. But as soon as he took out his paperwork, I knew the idea was a dud."

"So? What was his pitch?" said Hogarth.

"Essentially he was offering a business as a re-seller of cheap Chinese tech. But there were so many holes in his plan I didn't know where to start. Cheap Chinese tech is a liability. It breaks easily. It can get lost in transit or never arrives even after you've paid for it because it didn't exist in the first place. It was a badly flawed business plan built on lots of risky assumptions."

"Did you tell Drummond that?"

"I skirted around it, but tried to let him know what I thought *politely.*"

"How did he respond?"

"He turned stony-faced and said he had another idea. I tried to tell him *no thanks, another time*. But he said I needed to hear it now."

"And?"

The woman looked at Hogarth. He saw her struggle, and then she turned away to face Palmer.

"He brought out some photographs. They were copies of very personal photographs. I don't know where he got them. They depicted things I did with my ex, Andrew, when we first got together. Private things. Things I now regret."

Hogarth stayed silent. Palmer nodded. Craw took a deep breath.

"To cut a long story short, we briefly became friends with some wealthy couples. It turned out this set were into some extreme sex games. We went along with it because my husband wanted us to become like them. Rich, cool, all of that. I supposed I did too at the beginning. But it went too far. We went back once after the first time, before I said never again."

"Can you elaborate…?" said Palmer, carefully.

"It was basically a swingers set, but with a few scary add-ons. They liked BDSM stuff. To be honest, I don't really want to talk about it. The bottom line is, I was a mother with two children in my early thirties and I ended up in a situation I didn't want to be in. I was drunk. There were two grown men, supposedly respectable men, who should have known better. I don't remember the photographs being taken, but there they were. Seeing them made me feel sick. I tried to reach for them, then Drummond put his great fat slimy hand on mine. That's how it started. I have two kids in their teens… I have a daughter. I don't *ever* want her to know what I did. I don't ever want her to end up like that. Can you understand?"

Palmer nodded. "Yes, Mrs Craw. I think I can."

The three of them turned as they heard a subtle, slow creeping sound come down the stairs. The room fell silent as the footsteps approached. Then the door swung open. Gary Grayson appeared in the doorway, his hair damp, his eyes suspicious. Hogarth, Palmer and Alison Craw stared right back. He wore a turquoise surfing T-shirt which showed his beer belly. The shower had made him clean, but it didn't do much to hide the signs of his wastrel lifestyle.

"What do you want with Alison here?" said Grayson. "She hasn't done anything. Has she?" Grayson didn't sound too sure. He studied Hogarth and Palmer for clues. Hogarth stared right back.

"Besides…" said Grayson. "I thought you had Dan Picton down for this already."

Alison Craw's story had gnawed at Hogarth. And now this idiot was badgering him, Hogarth felt himself start to lose his temper.

"And how in the world would you know about that, Gary, eh?"

Grayson's eyes flicked left and right as he tried to invent a decent response.

"It's common knowledge that you've taken him in."

"Common amongst who? I didn't know you were in his circle of friends."

"I'm not but I hear things. I'm a DJ, remember. People talk to me."

"That's the second time you've invoked the DJ line. Funny thing is I want to talk to you too," said Hogarth. "Give us one more minute. Don't go anywhere, okay?"

Grayson eyed Alison Craw. "What's all this about Alison? Why are they talking to you?"

"What's the matter, Gary?" said Hogarth. "Have you something to hide?"

Alison Craw had stared at her hands since Grayson entered the room. Now she looked up. "Just wait out there, will you. I'll explain everything once they've gone."

"Something fishy's going on here…" said Grayson.

"That's probably just your aftershave," said Hogarth.

Grayson grunted and shut the door. They waited and listened until Grayson's feet faded away, then Hogarth started again, but quietly enough to ensure they wouldn't be heard.

"So, he got the photographs. What did he want from you?"

"Can't you guess?"

"It was usually money…" said Hogarth, words soon failing him. "I guess this was something else."

"Oh no, it was money too. But when I needed to keep a little back for my kids – when I couldn't pay the full sum – then he insisted on sex. And sex with Jake Drummond was worse than what happened the first time. But at least there aren't any photographs to prove it happened."

Hogarth settled back in his seat. After a moment's thought, he looked at Alison Craw with new eyes. "What?" she said. "Just a thought. With Drummond gone, at least you won't have that particular sword hanging over you any longer, will you? And you won't have to sleep with the beast either."

"No, no…" said Mrs Craw. A streak of defiance returned to her eyes. "You're not pinning that on me. I'm a mother. I did what I did with Drummond only to avoid trouble. I wouldn't do anything to make my children's life any worse…"

"But you've got to admit, Mrs Craw, you'd have a very strong reason to want him dead."

"Jake Drummond was an odious piece of crap… but I didn't kill him. I wasn't at the club that night. You can ask Gary about that. I only ever went there once. It's not my scene at all."

Hogarth and Palmer exchanged a brief glance. He saw Palmer had reached the same conclusion. The woman had motive, but that was all.

"If you need any help… you know… because of what has happened to you…" said Palmer.

"The only help I need is to make it go away. Permanently."

"Then I'd say your fairy godmother has already answered that one, Mrs Craw. Wouldn't you?"

"Not unless those photographs died with him…"

Hogarth stood up. "I'd like that word with Gary now, Mrs Craw."

"You won't mention any of this to him, will you? He doesn't know a thing about it. And he doesn't need to either. This is my business. *All of it.*"

Hogarth nodded. "Of course. I'm not here to cause trouble, Mrs Craw. I've come here to sort it."

The woman sniffed, and stood up. "Okay. Can I go now? I need to clear my head before my meeting."

"Yes, of course."

They left the living room together and watched Mrs Craw depart. Gary Grayson caught up with her at the front door, and Hogarth watched them share a brief but tender kiss before she walked out. Hogarth wondered what a strong woman like Alison Craw saw in an idiot like DJ GG. Hogarth hadn't enjoyed a kiss like that since, well, for a week or two at least. He shrugged off his daydream. The door closed, and Grayson faced them.

"You wanted to talk to me?"

"Yes, Gary. I heard you have a few secrets of your own. Like your various girlfriends."

"What?"

"Normally, another man's complicated love life wouldn't be my domain. But seeing as you manage to maintain a full-time relationship with Mrs Craw here, and a full-time job deejaying, I wondered how you fit it all in."

"You're right, Inspector. My love life is none of your business. But if you need some pointers…" said the man with a mocking smile.

"Your love life is indicative of your character, Gary. And your character – your tendencies – they are my business. I'm looking for a very untrustworthy person. A man or woman who has likely hidden his true nature from people close to him. A person who likely seems affable and friendly, but feels enough hate inside to kill someone in cold blood. You don't strike me as a killer, Gary, but I'm beginning to think you could be a very adept liar."

"How dare you?!"

"The affairs. The other women. Were any of them connected to Jake Drummond?"

Gary Grayson blinked at Hogarth. It was a shot in the dark question, a question to sound him out. But like sonar picking up a blip in the darkness, he saw a flicker of feedback appear on the DJ's face. Hogarth had struck something without even trying.

"Out with it, Gary. Come on. Who?"

"You're barking up the wrong tree, Inspector. I have girlfriends, yeah. In my job, it goes with the territory. Temptation is always there. I know I'm only a nightclub DJ, but on the night when those girls come out to play, some of them get a drink in them and they think you're a star. In a way, you are. In a small way. So, they flirt with you. And some of them want more."

"You're a true stud, Gary."

"I know it's not me. It's the decks and the mic. You become a character for them... I can't help it if I sometimes get a bit frisky."

"Mrs Craw doesn't know, does she?"

Grayson shook his head. "You're not going to tell her, are you? I love the woman."

"The tangled webs we weave, Gary. All I care about is finding that killer. And I *will* find him, Gary. Just now, when I asked if any of your girlfriends had dealings with Drummond, it seemed to me like you knew something. Come on."

"You're wrong… you just had me on the back foot, that was all."

"Really now?" Hogarth narrowed his eyes. "You've got an answer for everything, haven't you? I'll be watching you from now on. You'd better not be lying to me, because if you are, I might let slip what a greasy little liar you are. Who knows. It might even happen when I next see Mrs Craw. It'd be an accident, of course."

"Leave her out of it. She isn't involved in this at all. Is she?"

"The tangled web, Gary. Maybe you should tell me if those girls knew Drummond."

"I've answered you already, DI Hogarth. You know, maybe you should leave, instead."

"Only too glad to oblige, Gary. Remember what I said. All of it."

Hogarth opened the door and stepped out onto the drive. He left the DJ brooding after them before he slammed the door on him. Hogarth strode away, head high, a bounce in his stride. The case wasn't yet going his way. But his hopes were high.

"Well, guv?" said Palmer.

"Grayson stinks, Palmer. He's in it up to his neck and I'm not going to let him off the hook. Not until this case is history."

Chapter Sixteen

Palmer noticed Hogarth's eyes flick towards the office clock. He'd been at it ever since they got back to the station and the longer they were back, the quieter he became.
"You okay, sir?"
"Yes, yes. We've just got a lot to process, that's all," said Hogarth, almost too quickly. "I'm thinking it over. We've got enough suspects to fill a bloody phone book and motives coming out of our ears. We need to narrow it down. I'll call Marris. Maybe forensics have managed to dredge up something after all."
Palmer's brow furrowed. What was up with him now? Palmer was considering Hogarth's off behaviour when she noticed something else through the glass of the CID room door. Out in the open office she saw PC Dawson was engaged in an intense discussion with PCSO Rawlins. Palmer guessed it was a lover's tiff. They could happen anywhere. Palmer looked away, about to delve into the notes she'd made from the recent interviews, when Dawson glanced up and met her eye. Rawlins and Dawson weren't arguing. They were discussing something. She looked again and saw they were poring over something on Dawson's desk. Palmer offered Dawson a quizzical frown, and the PC's face changed.
Dawson stood up, picked up a paper from his desk and started walking towards the CID room. Bec Rawlins didn't look comfortable in the least. Beside Palmer, Hogarth hung up the phone.

"Marris isn't much help at all lately," he said, sounding irritated. "He says the sheer volume of footprints in the blood is enough to mask the killer's prints and movements. That and no weapon leaves forensics clutching at straws. Well, we may as well give up there. If we're going to get anything it'll have to come from putting our suspects under pressure…"

"Or until something else comes up," said Palmer.

"Something else? Things don't just come up, Palmer. In this trade you have to work bloody hard for everything you get. You know that by now…" As Hogarth finished speaking PC Dawson appeared at the door. "Come in," he called.

Hogarth frowned and lounged back in his chair. He glanced at the clock once more before his eyes rolled Dawson's way. "The dynamic duo. What can we do for you?"

"I think you should see this, sir," said Dawson.

There was a serious yet excited look on Dawson's face. Hogarth took notice.

"What have you got there?" he said, holding out his hand.

"This is Bec's doing, sir, she's like a dog with a bone."

"Your man's a real charmer, Rawlins."

Rawlins gave a weak smile at Hogarth's quip.

Dawson ignored it. "She wondered about the club, sir… so she started looking at its history. That's how she found this."

Dawson handed Hogarth a printout of an internet news article. It was an old clip from The Record. The article was over a year old, a simple review of the nightclub after a recent refurb and relaunch. Hogarth scanned the article, and narrowed his eyes.

"What exactly am I looking for here?"

"It's the photograph, sir," said Dawson.

"It could be nothing," said Rawlins. "I could be wrong."

"Spit it out, come on."

"Look at the man standing at the edge of the photograph there, by the club doors. Just look at him."
Hogarth blinked at the grainy image and squinted. He looked at the figure on the edge of the image. The figure was broad shouldered, big and wide, and had an arrogant face.
"Jake Drummond?"
"Yes," said Dawson.
"But we already know Drummond frequented the dive. Club Smart was a small pond for that big fat fish."
"But there's something else, sir. To his left, there's a man beside him but you can only see his profile. Do you see?"
Yes, Hogarth saw him. A tall man in a hat and coat. The picture wasn't clear. The hat could have been one of those cheap straw fedoras the fashion shops sold for the summer holidays. Or it could have been something more substantial. The face beneath it was thin and had a big, long nose. Some would have called it a Roman nose. The man didn't look like the nightclubbing type.
"I see him."
"I could be wrong, but I don't think I am." Rawlins was hesitant.
Hogarth nodded. "Go on."
"I think that's George Cruddas. I'm almost sure of it."
"George Cruddas? What? Andy had a brother?"
"No, sir. George is *Andy's father.*"
Hogarth blinked at the image as the implications seeped in. He remembered his sense of suspicion as he sat in front of Barbara Cruddas. *So there had been more under the surface...*
"That article was dated more than six months after Andy's father was killed in that car crash," said Rawlins.
"You're saying Andy's father is alive?"

"When that picture was taken, he must have been. He couldn't have died in a car crash, sir. It looks like his death was fabricated."

Hogarth's eyes moved past Palmer as he turned in his chair. "Well, well, well," he said. "Now why would a man fake his own death during a time of financial crisis and high pressures… an insurance salesman too. Let me guess…" said Hogarth. He turned to face Rawlins and Dawson.

"You know this family well, Rawlins. This can't have been a very easy discovery for you."

Rawlins nodded in agreement. "Sir."

"Well done. You kept on looking and you found something. This could yet prove a very important discovery. Convictions will almost certainly follow."

Rawlins winced.

"Why the long face? You did your duty, Rawlins. You did good. But seeing as you're so committed, I want you to go and do even better. Andy Cruddas is your friend, so I need you to have a good long think. Brainstorm this one with Dawson. I want you to think of all the places Andy could be. And his father too, for that matter. Is it possible they're in cahoots? Andy and his old man hiding out together?"

"No sir, not at all," said Rawlins. "That's what's so troubling about this. Andy was absolutely devastated by his father's death. He adored the man. He was in total shock when his father died. I don't know how he's going to cope when he finds out about this."

"Okay. Then get to work. See what you can come up with and update me later on,"

"Yes, sir," said Dawson. Hogarth and Palmer watched the uniforms leave the room.

"Rawlins is far too good to be left as a PCSO," said Palmer.

"I agree, the girl's got potential. But that's a matter for the future. But this is gold, Palmer. Gold. If this old bugger is alive, then *he* could be the man we're after."
"So now you think he killed Jake Drummond?"
"It doesn't take much of a leap to read the man's motives… Jake Drummond visited the wife after his death. What if Cruddas knew she'd been blackmailed?"
Palmer nodded. That kind of motive would have been weight indeed.
"We'll need to speak to Barbara Cruddas again," said Palmer.
"Undoubtedly," said Hogarth. "But we must save it for the right time. You only get one chance with dynamite like this. Let's make sure we use it well."
Hogarth stood up, and straightened out his crumpled trousers. Palmer watched him drag a hand through his uncouth hair.
"What?" he said, looking back at her
"You've been watching the clock all morning, sir. What's the matter?"
Hogarth gave her a careful look and shook his head.
"Nothing, Sue. I'm having a hungry day, that's all. I can't wait to eat something. Famished. I think I might go and grab something from the high street. I'll bring you something back if you like…"
Hogarth's answer wrong-footed her. "No, thanks, I'm fine. I'll get something from the canteen and keep digging around here. Who knows what else we'll find…"
Hogarth nodded. "That's the spirit. I'll be about an hour."
Palmer watched the man leave. Since when had Hogarth ever offered to buy her lunch? Maybe he was softening on her after all. But she doubted that very much. Still, he had her more than intrigued.

Dawson and Rawlins watched Hogarth leave the station. Dawson shook his head. They had given him gold, and now he wanted diamonds as well. But Rawlins was busy. While Dawson looked away, Rawlins ran a quick web search for Club Smart's website. She checked for updates and opening times, then she scan-read to the bottom of the page. There it was. The club was already back open after the murder. She suspected as much. And DJ GG was playing tonight. Rawlins wondered…

"Look at them. Open again already. Those people don't have any respect for the dead, do they?" said Dawson.

Rawlins only murmured in agreement because she was busy making other plans.

Chapter Seventeen

Café Seven One Seven. Not really a place for Hogarth, but more a place for ladies who lunched. If the pastel-pink wood-cladded walls didn't give it away, then the posy of ribbon-tied flowers on each table should have done the trick. Each table wore a pink gingham table cloth. Seven One Seven served elderflower cordial at three pounds a bottle. No, the place wasn't for him. Hogarth preferred whisky, rough-cut wooden tables, and ancient leather chairs. But for Ali he was willing to make all kinds of concessions.

The door shuddered open and Ali walked in. Without missing a beat, Hogarth stood up, passing by the other lady punters drinking their dainty flat whites with their ciabatta sandwiches. He squeezed Ali's soft cold hand briefly. He watched her look around to make sure their contact hadn't looked too informal. *Too intimate.* Hogarth moved to the café window, staying behind the net curtain. His eyes flicked out onto the street. Cars passed. People walked by. He took the measure of them all, but didn't see anyone acting odd. No one stopped to look inside. Hogarth waited by the window and counted time. It was almost a full twenty seconds before he turned back towards Ali.

"It's good to see you," he said. His eyes had shaken off their usual sleepiness. They gleamed. But they gleamed because they were looking at her. Ali Hartigan was five years his junior, but to look at her, it could have been ten. She had long blonde hair with a soft pretty face. There was always a singular line of determination about her, but he liked it. For Hogarth, Ali was the most attractive woman he'd ever known. She even had her own Cindy Crawford beauty spot. Yes, she was distinctive. Which was another reason he had to be very careful. They took their seats and he glanced over her shoulder to the window. Still, nothing. Hogarth was elated simply to be in her presence. He watched her eyes flicking around the coffee shop as she settled in. Finally, when she was saw no one was watching, she relaxed and found Hogarth's eyes on her.

"You're looking at me like you haven't seen me in years," she said.

"Feels like it. I've missed you," said Hogarth. Romantic words felt extremely awkward in his mouth. They rolled around like cracked rocks. But the sentiments were real. He had to control himself. Being the gushing sort didn't suit him, nor Ali for that matter.

"I've missed you too," she said. For a moment there was a deep warmth between them, and he wanted to reach out and kiss her. Dear God, he wanted much more than that. Instead he coughed and picked up a menu.

"Do you think he followed you?"

"No. I was careful. I kept checking along the way. I never saw a sign of anyone. He can't be around."

"Or he could be very smart. Villains are smart. They have to be."

"Who says he's a villain? Yes, he's a weirdo. He might have a mental illness or something. That doesn't mean he's a villain."

"The Nazi psycho who killed that MP last year had a condition too. Anyone can get a condition. The doctors give 'em out to anyone who asks. That doesn't make him any less a villain."

The woman blushed. He had gone too far, speaking if he was lecturing Dawson, Simmons, or Palmer.

"I'm sorry, Ali," said Hogarth. "I worry about you, that's all."

"It's okay. I get it."

"I wish your husband gave a damn. He should have his own people on this. The best kind of people."

"We've been through that, Joe. James doesn't care about me. He's sleeping with his parliamentary secretary. He doesn't even make much effort to hide it these days."

"I still don't know how he could do that to a woman like you."

He watched a glisten of tears mist Ali's eyes. She blinked and looked away. When she looked up they were gone.

"It's over between me and him. I know that. But there's no process underway yet. Nothing. That's why I have to be careful. I don't want him to make it out our troubles are my fault come the divorce."

Divorce? Hogarth felt a burst of hope. She had used the *D word*. Not him, but her.

They ordered a ciabatta and a coffee each and looked at one another while they waited.

"You could find proof on him, Ali," said Hogarth. "That would seal it. He wouldn't be able to blame you for anything then"

"What?" she said.

"Proof? How would I get that, exactly?"

"I know two private investigators. They're very good at what they do. Dogged. Persistent."

"I can't spend money on things like that. He'll see it in our accounts."

"But I could. I wouldn't mind paying for a month or so."

"No, Joe. Then he'd soon know that we were… that there was something between us."

"He'll know one day."

"When the timing suits us, and he can't wrong-foot me."
Hogarth nodded. It was time to back off. But the idea of using the PI services still stayed in mind. It was a useful option for proving grounds for divorce, and maybe they could solve other problems too. Stalkers for instance. But Hogarth held his tongue. He wanted to enjoy the moment.
"I should pop round now and then. Just to see if the stalker is there. I'd soon spot him."
"But then you'll be playing into James's hands. What if he already has someone watching me?"
"Like the stalker, you mean? That's a bit extreme, Ali."
"Not the stalker. I'm sure he's genuine. I mean an investigator."
"I need to make sure you're safe…" said Hogarth.
Ali reached out and laid a soft hand on the back of his. She stroked his skin a few times before she drew her hand away.
"I know. You can drive past the house. You can look then. But for both our sakes, please don't stop and visit. You know how much I want to see you… but…"
Hogarth nodded.
"The last time we were together…" he muttered.
Ali nodded. "I know. I want that too."
Hogarth sighed and finished his sandwich.
"This isn't enough, Ali. I'm sorry. I don't mean to be ungrateful, but seeing you like this isn't enough."
"What are you saying?"
"Nothing dramatic. I'm not saying anything like that. I'll always be here, but I need more."
Ali nodded. "It's the same for me." She checked her bangle watch. "I best go. I told James that I was meeting my friend Amanda. We always meet for an hour for lunch. I should keep to the same pattern."

Hogarth nodded reluctantly and threw down his napkin Her heard the café door chime, but his mind was full of yearning and regret and confusion. Only when no one entered did he look up. As Hogarth looked through the glass, the man who had been holding the door open turned abruptly and walked away. The door clunked shut and the traffic noise faded. But Hogarth was alert. He blinked and stood up. He peered through the glass, and saw a figure rushing away. Hogarth had hardly seen the man. He had no description to count on, but adrenaline was bursting through his body.

"What is it, Joe?"

"That man. He stopped, he opened the door, he looked in, and now he's gone…"

Hogarth peeled a twenty pound note from his wallet and laid it on the table.

"Pay the bill with this. But you stay here a minute. Wait for me, promise?"

Ali Hartigan nodded. Hogarth strode out of the coffee shop and looked left to see a shoe heel disappear around the nearby corner onto a side street. Hogarth scowled and broke into a jog. He ran past the shops until he came to the charity shop on the corner. There, walking away down Turner Drive was a thin man with a smart raincoat flapping around him like a cloak. He was walking away quickly.

"Got you," muttered Hogarth. He kept his feet light and jogged on. When he was close enough, the man in the raincoat must have heard him coming. The man turned around and looked at Hogarth's menacing face with big frightened eyes. The man was slight and dark haired. There was something Latino about his eyes. Portuguese maybe. Hogarth reached out and grabbed the man's coat.

"You… what were you doing at the coffee shop just now?"

"What?" said the man. Hogarth detected a faintly Scottish accent.

"You heard. What were you doing?"

"At a coffee shop? I wasn't at a coffee shop. I've been at work all morning. Get your hands off me!"

Hogarth's fingers loosened with doubt. Then they tensed again.

"I know your game, pal. You're a sicko. Twisted. I'm warning you – leave her alone. Do you hear me?"

"How dare you!" said the man. "I don't know what you're talking about. Let go of me at once, or I'll call the police, and have you arrested for assault!"

I am the police, thought Hogarth. But wisdom prevented him from saying the words.

"Work? Where do you work?"

"Lattigan and Davis. The solicitors. Happy now?"

Hogarth knew the firm, but never had any dealings with them. He knew they had an office down Southchurch Road. He looked at the man's smart clothes, his clean-shaven, college-educated appearance. His soft-bellied fear. A solicitor made sense.

Hogarth let him go. "Touch me again, you lunatic, and I'll call the police. Do you hear me?"

Hogarth nodded, and the man turned away. He looked back over his shoulder as he walked off. Hogarth scratched his head and looked to the sky. A man *had* been at the coffee shop door. He knew that much. But he had lost him before he even left the door. He grunted at his own inadequacy and turned away. If the solicitor did call the police, he would have been in trouble with the chief at a time he couldn't afford. It was a near miss. But poor Ali still had to live with the consequences. He started walking back to Southchurch Road and saw Ali turn the corner. There she was in her

plush winter coat and scarf, her long blonde hair and brown eyes. Just to look at her near bowled him over. He stopped.
"Are you okay?" she said.
"It wasn't him."
"I told you. He didn't follow me today. The trouble is I don't know when he will and when he won't."
Hogarth nodded. They approached one another at the side of the charity shop passing out of sight from the shop windows.
"What are we going to do, Ali?"
"We are going to carry on, aren't we?"
Hogarth nodded slowly. "As we are, I suppose. Well, there's no other choice."
"Joe…" she said, softly. She leaned close to him, resting her forehead on his chin. He kissed her skin.
"This is so difficult, isn't it?" she said.
"This? Meeting you is the highlight of my fortnight."
The woman laughed at that. Then she turned her face to his, and their lips reached for each other. The kiss was sweet and warm. Ali Hartigan's hands wrapped around him and she gently steered him willingly around the corner behind the shop, into a gravel and weed strewn back alley. There they kissed, and pressed their bodies close. Eventually, the kiss ended and they slipped away from one another.
"Correction," said Hogarth. "This is the highlight of my entire month."
Ali put a hand to her lips. "Same here, Joe. But I've got to go."
He nodded and watched her turn the corner walking back towards the main street. Then Hogarth looked around. He checked the doors and the lanes opposite. He checked the whole area and he saw no one worth seeing. With a long

deep sigh, and the broad smile of some well-stoked hopes, Joe Hogarth walked away.

Hogarth couldn't have known it.

But he was watched the entire way.

Chapter Eighteen

Bec Rawlins and Rob Dawson had reached the point where they spent almost every night together bar the odd one. But PCSO Rawlins was careful to prepare the ground for a night off, by telling Dawson that she was unwell long in advance of the evening. Her illness came on from the moment she decided to take matters into her own hands. Of course, Dawson offered to look after her, but Rawlins wouldn't hear of it. Hogarth had appreciated her efforts and she felt encouraged. Rawlins wanted to progress from her lowly rank to become a proper police constable. But this particular decision was not about progressing her career. This was about doing what was right.

There would be risks involved, like being recognised by the club goers from the night of the murder. But to mitigate against the risks, there were always things a woman could do. Firstly, Bec changed her look. A change of hairstyle, a different dress and new make-up would help. No matter what needed to be done, she was going to do it. Andy needed help badly. He was a good man in a deep fix. He was sensitive and thoughtful. Being involved in a drug racket was no good thing, but he was being accused of a murder he didn't commit. Rawlins knew there were plenty of potential killers still in the frame. And the way she saw it, all of them seemed to be in the orbit of Club Smart. And the photographs showed that even George Cruddas had been there once. Club Smart was at the centre of it all. And who was at the centre of Club Smart? Who knew everything there was to know? The one and only Gary Grayson. DJ GG.

He'd been there the night of the kill. She'd seen him acting as if he had more than a few beers in his system. She had never spoken to him directly. The DJ had been busy gossiping while she and Dawson had been corralling people and running their searches. Which gave Rawlins enough hope that her plan might work.

Rawlins got out of the taxi outside Club Smart, pulling the hem of her shiny gold dress down over her thighs. It was cold out and it was late. She had styled her blonde hair differently, fringe pulled low over her eyes with swishy little flicks at the sides and back. Her make-up was bolder too. A bit tarty, even, but the main purpose was for disguise. There was another purpose too.

It was just after ten pm and as she walked towards the queue, and her gait picked up pace as she got near. She recognised the two security guards from the other night. The brutes gave her a look-over, and the biggest one offered a predatory grin. Rawlins got ready for him to say he remembered her. But tonight, he didn't seem interested in her face. In fact, his eyes went everywhere but.

"Ello, darling," said the tallest doorman. "Where's your boyfriend, eh?" he said with a wink. For a moment Bec thought he meant Rob Dawson, then she realised he hadn't recognised her at all. It was a chat-up.

"Oh. He's in there already," she said.

"Lucky man," said the other guy. "When you get bored of him, you know where we are…"

The bouncer took away the boundary rope and nodded for Bec to go inside. The few girls and boys held queueing at the other side tutted and complained, but Rawlins didn't grumble. She was in. She smiled and nodded in thanks, and walked right inside. As soon as she hit the crazy noise, darkness, and air-conditioned chill of the nightclub, her heart started thudding faster than ever. Now she had to follow through on her plan.

Bec peered across the dance floor and found it surprisingly busy for a weeknight. Even more surprising considering a man had been killed there just days before. But she saw none of those older faces. And there was no sign of Andy Cruddas. Of course not. And Picton was still in a cell pending remand. Rawlins took a breath and told herself to look at ease, like she was enjoying herself. She walked to the little bar near the exit, the one where Drummond had been stabbed and looked around. It was as if nothing had happened. There was noise and drunkenness, laughter and unwanted eye contact. It was just like any other night at Club Smart. Bec got the attention of the little barman and asked for a bottle of Vodka Ice. The guy made eyes at her, but didn't show any sign of knowing her. Make-up was a wonderful invention. Bec swigged from her bottle and surveyed the room behind her. A couple of men tried to make eye contact, evaluating her availability, but she ignored them. Tonight, Bec Rawlins was a one-man woman. Shame the man in question was nothing like up to her usual standards. DJ GG was in his booth at the top of the dance floor. Bec fixed her target in mind, and weaved her way to the dance floor. She kept her eyes on DJ GG, as he moved around between the decks and record boxes in his booth. She watched him take out another record. DJ GG still used vinyl. He was a man of the old school. She reached the dance floor, sipped her drink, and started to dance, doing her best to overcome her sobriety, ignoring the people around her. Rawlins enjoyed dancing. And throwing herself into the music meant she was better able to ignore the predatory eyes vying for her attention. Halfway through her second record, Bec looked up and saw the DJ watching her. He looked at her, raised a pint glass and grinned, nodding his head to the music.

A minute later he was still looking. Rawlins gave him a smile. Grayson waved at her from his booth. As she came near, he leaned down over the edge of his decks towards the dance floor. He was wearing a bad Hawaiian shirt, and he stank of alcohol and too much aftershave.

"Hello, sweetheart. You got any special requests? Any tune you love to dance to?"

Bec smiled up at him and took her time to answer. She needed to know if he remembered her. Her sparkling eyes tested him. She saw a flickering moment when his face changed.

"Do I know you?" he said.

"You could have seen me before," said Bec, with a flirty grin. "I've been in here a few times. Mostly with my mates…"

Gary Grayson thought about it, nodding. Then he smiled. "Where are your mates tonight then?"

"Being boring. I didn't want to be boring. Not tonight…"

Gary smiled and sipped his beer as he looked at her. Rawlins could almost feel his rising excitement. Like an angler reeling in his catch.

"Well we can't have you dancing down there all alone, can we?" He leaned down further. "You ever done any deejaying?" he called.

Bec shook her head. "No. Never." She cupped a hand to his ear, egging him on.

"Fancy having a go?"

Bec gave him a beaming smile.

"Why not?"

Bingo. It seemed Gary Grayson was keen to keep up the habit of a lifetime. And to a very limited extent, Bec was happy to oblige. She climbed the few steps to the DJ booth, and Grayson opened the gate to invite her in. He locked the gate behind her then gave her a big leery grin.

"Welcome to the cockpit," he said. "This is where the magic happens."

There was precious little space in the booth, between the stacked boxes of records, music-mixing decks and record decks and Gary Grayson took full advantage of it. He leaned past Bec, his shoulder brushing her chest twice as he picked up an unopened bottle of white wine.

"Can I get you a drink?" he said, flashing a grin.

"Oh, go on then. Just a small one," said Rawlins. When the drink arrived, she saw he had poured at least a third of a bottle.

"No girl ever wants a small one really, do they?" Grayson winked. Bec worked very hard to smile back.

Rawlins played along for twenty minutes, smiling on cue, pretending to drink, pouring some away when the man wasn't looking and not complaining when he brushed against her. But after a while he couldn't hold back. She saw him staring at her between his cheesy lines. She knew it was coming.

"Want to come out back with me?" he said. She saw his mouth twitch. He made her feel sick.

"Where?" she said, with a laugh. "What for?"

"For a giggle. You know."

Bec didn't want to things to go too far. What she wanted was a chance to quiz the man. To catch him unawares, but there was also a chance that things could go badly wrong. She found herself hoping he wasn't the killer. Damn it. She'd never even considered it until now!"

"But you're deejaying. You can't go anywhere."

"I can get cover for twenty minutes. Come on, girl. Live dangerously."

She smiled thinly. Live dangerously? Bec Rawlins had given herself no choice on that score. She nodded, and Gary Grayson called over one of the younger barmen. He whispered in the guy's ear and the youth looked at Bec, laughed, and nodded, taking Grayson's place while the music was still playing.

"Come on then, sweetheart. Tonight, darling, it's access all areas…"

The young barman liked that one. He even laughed out loud. Bec cringed, but walked away with Grayson. She stayed just out of range as his hand reached for her backside. They walked out into the austere white corridor, and she saw what a mess he looked. Bloodshot eyes, sweating booze, the man was a sorry state.

"Look at you," he said. "What a beauty…"

"You said you were going to show me something…"

He laughed. "Ha. Yeah. Soon enough. Come on then. Come and see my special little room."

"You have a room?" said Bec.

"When I'm running the show, they let me do anything I like."

"Why?" said Bec, keeping in character.

"Because I'm DJ GG. I spin the wheels and get the punters coming in. I'm the star of the show, honey."

He opened the door into the office. Bec was less than impressed. It was a poky place that smelled of beer, cleaning chemicals, and damp. The room was cold and dingy. It was hardly a film star's dressing room. GG made a show of sprawling back over the black leather couch. The thing had seen much better days. He left enough room for her to sit beside him, but Bec intended to play hard to get. *Very hard to get*. She noticed a leather jacket had been dumped on the back of the office chair and that contents had spilled from the pockets. Grayson reached for the jacket, rolled it into a bundle and tossed it on the desk, giving her another leery smile, but Rawlins' eyes were on a small square piece of card which tumbled to the floor. The thing seemed to have fallen from the jacket. The card landed face up. It was a photograph showing two round little faces – two young children – seated on a woman's knees. The picture was distant, but Bec made it out clearly enough. Odd. She didn't remember that Grayson had children. Maybe they were his sister's or something. As far as Rawlins was concerned, DJ GG was far too selfish to have any feelings for anyone beside himself.

"Come and sit down beside me. Tell me about you," he said. He patted the sofa next to him, but Rawlins stayed where she was and perched herself on the edge of the functional black office chair.

"First, tell me about you…" she said.

"Why?" he said.

"Because I want to know all about Southend's most famous star DJ…"

For a moment he'd looked spurned, but Rawlins' reply disarmed him.,

"What can I say? It's a very good life. You can see that, right? What more is there to tell, sweetheart?"

"Oh… but you must see all the things that go on from the other side, don't you? You see the things we don't."

"True," he said, nodding. "I get a real inside view of this game. What do you want to know? What celebs I've met? I've met Bobby Andre. Freddie Nelson. You name them, I've met them."

"I bet," said Bec. "And then there's the other side of it all. Like there was that horrible thing that happened here a few nights back."

Grayson stiffened and reached for his drink.

"That was a bad business. You really don't want to go there."

"But it happened, didn't it?"

"It's not exactly fun to talk about, hun. The bugger deserved what was coming to him, but nobody wants to see that. Not on a night out."

"You say he deserved it? Why?"

"Because he was a nasty piece of work. Honestly, a really vile piece of work."

"How come?"

Gary Grayson scratched his head through his thinning bleach-blond hair.

"Because he liked to bully and blackmail and upset people. There. Is that enough gossip for you?" he snapped.

Bec tried for a meek and mild face.

"Sorry, hun. It wasn't a nice thing. I told you."

"But you knew the man then?"

"I knew he was scum. I'd seen it first-hand. In fact, I saw it just a few nights before he was topped." Grayson's eyes glazed, and he gulped his beer. Rawlins' eyes flashed with intrigue before she could mask it. Grayson's eyes narrowed. "Hey! We didn't come in here to talk about this crap. We came in here for some fun. Come over here and keep me company. Let me give you a little hug to keep you warm…"

"But there's no hurry," said Rawlins. "Can I have a drink?"

Grayson thought about it before he nodded. "Sure." He picked up an open bottle from the desk and poured a large measure of wine into an office mug. He gave it to her and swigged some himself from the bottle.

"How did you know him?"

Grayson snorted. "What is this? Twenty questions. Come on! Killers turn you on, do they? Is that it? I've seen it all in my time, sweetheart, believe me."

Rawlins did believe him. In her brief time with the police she'd seen it all too.

"No. I'm just curious. You said you'd seen him being nasty. You knew him. Why someone would want to kill him?"

"You what?" he said quietly. Grayson looked at her carefully.

"I wondered if you knew why someone would want to kill him? That's all."

"Because let me tell you, *that man* hurt people for fun…"

"Even so… who would want a man dead so much that they'd actually go and do it?"

Grayson stood up. He strode the short distance towards Bec, and leaned down into her space. The man's wild eyes were close to hers. His hot, sour, beer breath washed over her face. She saw the veins and sinews protrude in tight pulled cords all over his neck. For the very first time, Gary Grayson wasn't a pathetic joke. The man was menacing. Rawlins worked hard to keep her cool.

"You! I remember you!" said Grayson. "You were here that night – wearing your little red dress. You're a copper! Look at you! Tarted yourself up. What is this, a bloody honeytrap? You think I'm guilty, do you? I told your boss, I didn't kill the man. I wouldn't do it. None of it. This is harassment! It's a sting." Grayson turned away from her and flung the door open.

"You better get out of here before I do something I'll regret. Do you hear me?"

Rawlins face was hot and red. But she was as angry as she was embarrassed.

"You know everybody, Grayson, don't you? You watch it all. I bet you know who killed him, don't you? Eh?"
"I heard it was Dan Picton. Maybe his buddy, Cruddas, too."
Rawlins shook her head. "You know that's not true. You know, don't you? Or you think you know…"
"Now you're just clutching at straws."
Bec Rawlins forced herself to be brave. She stepped into Grayson's space and stared at the darkness in his bleary eyes. She saw the emptiness and wondered just how deep it went.
"To be honest with you, Mr Grayson, I really don't think I am."
He backed away from her. "Get out! Get out now!"
"Gladly. Say hello to your girlfriend for me, won't you, Gary?"
Her eyes flicked to the photograph of the kids on the floor before she turned away. Rawlins moved fast, in case she had just made a very bad move. What if she had just riled a killer? With her heart pounding, Bec Rawlins walked out of Club Smart certain Grayson knew something. But she couldn't prove it. She walked away down cold Luker Close with propositions from the bouncers ringing in her ears. She walked quickly with her arms folded over her chest, until she reached the local taxi rank and then she waited. For some reason she felt a low level, rising panic. She looked around the street but didn't see anyone. When the first taxi finally appeared, Rawlins was only too glad to climb inside. She looked at the cab's licence number, ID badge, and meter, and felt relieved to see it was kosher. What was up with her.
"Where to love?" said the cabbie.
The taxi made a U-turn across the street and pulled away. When the taillight s faded by the roundabout, the man who had been watching stepped out of the shadows.

Chapter Nineteen

Day Seven: Thursday

"That's it. We've got confirmation from the technical boys," said Hogarth. "The photograph Rawlins found in The Record is almost certainly an image of George Cruddas, almost six months after his supposed demise in the M25 pile-up. It's him. Which means we've opened yet another can of worms in this case…" said Hogarth.
"But the photograph was from a while back," said Rawlins. Hogarth was about to reply, when he noticed how rough Rawlins looked. And she'd been more quiet than usual. Sheepish even. Maybe the lovers had had a barney. But if so, Dawson didn't seem to be suffering.
"Who confirmed it?"
"I asked the Met E-fit boys to run their face recognition software. They had a ninety-five per cent hit that he's our man. That's enough for me."
"And me," said Palmer.
"So where does that leave us?" said Dawson.
"The truth?" said Hogarth. He began to count the case's problems off on his fingers one by one. "We've got no weapon, because it vanished into thin air. We've got no forensic evidence, and we've got a list of possible suspects as long as your arm, with my odds-on favourite missing in action. And now we've got a resurrected George Cruddas who is also still missing. Like father like son, eh? You really couldn't make this up."

"But why would George Cruddas have faked his own death?" said Rawlins. "Poor Andy will be devastated."
"Forget poor little Andy, Rawlins. That M25 pile-up killed four other people. If that was all faked, George Cruddas has more blood on his hands than Andy."
"Andy may not have any blood on his hands at all," said Rawlins
"Come on then, *Detective* Rawlins. Who is your money on?"
Bec stiffened under the pressure. DC Simmons, who had been perched on a desk at the back of the room let out a snicker.
"You could do a lot worse than take another look at that DJ, you know," said Rawlins.
"Oh? And why him?" said Hogarth.
"He just reeks of trouble."
"Don't worry. I haven't given up on him. DC Simmons? Palmer?"
"We have to consider that father and son could be working this together," said Palmer. "We know Andy Cruddas was bullied for money by Drummond, and we know that he was forced into the drug business. Picton told us that much."
"If Picton wasn't lying," said Simmons.
"Granted," said Palmer. "But assuming it is true, George Cruddas also knew Jake Drummond What if the man had something on both of them? Or what if Cruddas came back to stop Drummond harming his son?"
"Drummond liked to play hardball," said Hogarth. "It was his business. He was never going to give up any blackmail. People like him, if you beg them to spare you, they only hurt you more. I've seen plenty of them in my time. We still need Andy Cruddas. He's the key to this. Did you manage to get anything on him? Rawlins?"
Rawlins tamely shook her head.

"Nothing new, so far."
"You know Picton pretty well, don't you?" said Hogarth.
"I know him, that's all. But we weren't close. We're acquaintances, that's all."
"But you have a mutual friend in Cruddas. Pee Wee Picton acts upset, like he hasn't got a clue where Cruddas might be, and while that may be true, I know he's still hiding something from us."
"Why not forget Picton and Andy Cruddas? Cut out the middle man and go straight for the mother," said DC Simmons. "She's lied to you more than once, hasn't she?"
"It's the ace up my sleeve, Simmons," said Hogarth. "I only want to play that card when I can put maximum pressure on her. When she talks I want her to tell me everything."
"Well she hasn't done so far."
"We need to set things up first. Set them up just right and she'll talk all right."
"The evidence on Picton…," said Palmer, turning to Simmons. "The spectacles with the blood spatter on them…?"
Simmons nodded. "Yes. The blood does belong to Jake Drummond. Marris says it's a match."
"But those spectacles were found more than a day after the murder in the club. If that went to court, defence would tear it to shreds," said Hogarth. "The CPS will steer clear of using that as evidence. That blood went everywhere."
"From what I saw, Picton didn't lose his glasses that night," said Dawson. "He wasn't in the club long enough to lose a thing. I watched him leave. He walked out with a pair of specs on."
Hogarth's eyes glazed, and he tapped his bottom lip. "Where did the specs come from then…?" he muttered. "Picton was

hardly likely to bring a spare set of specs to the club just so he could dump them in blood and incriminate himself."

"To me it sounds like someone is trying to cast the blame elsewhere," said Palmer. "A diversion."

"Agreed. But if we believe that, then who would have access to the man's spectacle collection? And, who could have access to the club in order to set up fake evidence?"

"I don't know about the access to Picton's glasses. You need to speak to Picton about that," said Rawlins. "But if the DJ was in the frame, he could easily have set up that evidence. He's there all the time."

"You don't like DJ GG one bit, do you, Rawlins?"

"The man's a sleaze, through and through."

"But does that make him a killer?" said Hogarth.

"That depends on what Jake Drummond had on him," said Dawson, on her behalf.

"Right. We need to find out about those glasses. And we need Picton to tell us about all the places where his old pal could be hiding. Rawlins… I'm beginning to think we need you in the interview room."

"Me, sir?"

"Yes. He knows you. Come on, I'll square it with the DCI first, but you're in."

Rawlins sighed and gave a nod.

"And Bec?" said Hogarth.

"Yes, sir?" she said.

"Don't fluff it up," said Hogarth. "We badly need to move this case forward. So far this has all hallmarks of a revenge killing. But If we're wrong the bugger could strike again."

Hogarth walked out of the room to get clearance from the DCI.

"No pressure then," said Simmons, with a laugh. But no one else joined in.

Picton looked pale and pathetic in the interview room. He was a shadow of the man Rawlins remembered, and Picton hadn't been much then either. He looked up at her from across the table, and nodded with a glum smile. Next, he looked at Hogarth, sitting beside her.

"Hello Bec," said Picton.

"Hello, Dan."

Hogarth leaned forward. "Have you any idea why I might have brought PCSO Bec Rawlins in here today, Picton?"

Picton shook his head. "I'll spell it out for you. Your friend Andy is in deep doo-doo. It's getting deeper by the second. If you cared about the man, you'd be interested in helping us find him, so we can clear his name. Do you understand?"

"I understand, but I still can't help you."

"But I think you can. Tell you what. I'm going to give you two a little chance to catch up, just like old times" said Hogarth. "Why don't you use those two minutes to have a serious think about what you're going to do, eh? Would you like a cup of water, Bec?"

"No, thanks, sir."

Hogarth got up and walked out of the room. He had clearance from DCI Melford for Rawlins to sit in on the interview, but not for her to conduct it. But then, everyone needed a cup of water now and then, didn't they? Hogarth closed the door and looked back through the porthole window into interview room one. But Picton's mouth stayed shut, so Hogarth walked away.

"Where is Andy?" said Rawlins.

"I don't know. I told you," said Picton.

"That's not going to wash with anyone here. And it's not helping you either. If we find him, we could prove that you were put under duress by Drummond to do what you did. Who knows, it could get your sentence reduced…"

"What we did?" said Picton, making a face.

"I meant the drugs, not the murder…" said Rawlins. "If we find him, you can coordinate your stories better. Make it work. As it stands, if you go down separately, it looks bad for each of you. Your excuses look exactly that. They'll throw the book at you, I know it."

"So Bec, are you a friend, or a cop?"

"I'm both, so you'd better hear me, Dan. In this place I'm the only friend you'll ever have. Those glasses of yours. How did they end up in the club?"

"I don't know, exactly. I thought it was you lot, trying to set me up."

Bec shook her head. "Hogarth's an old fox, but he would never do that. None of us would. But we think someone could have tried that… someone who had access to those glasses."

"Honestly, it could have been anyone, Bec. They were my spares. My old glasses. I took them out sometimes because I was worried I'd lose my only good ones. It looks like I lost the spares instead. I must have dropped them in the club at some point."

"And you didn't notice?"

"I'm long-sighted, Bec. Sometimes, if I'm feeling brave, or if I see a girl I like the look of, I take the glasses off. I can get by without them. I've done that a few nights at Club Smart. I guess I must have dropped them one night after a few bevvies."

"And you didn't ever notice they were missing?"

"Not really. I knew I couldn't find them, but so what? Half the time I can't find my car keys and they always turn up. I was sure they'd turn up again. But not like that."

Bec Rawlins nodded and offered him a smile. "Okay, Dan. That makes sense."

He seemed encouraged.

"Now," she said. "You've got to tell me all the places where Andy could be."

"I've got to, have I?"

"Stop it, Dan. This is me. It looks like I'm the only friend you've got. I can help you, but only if you help yourself…"

Picton looked at her for a long moment before he started talking.

"Okay. I think I know a couple of places. But I'm just guessing, Bec. I don't know…"

"That's a start."

A minute later, Hogarth walked in carrying a plastic cup of water.

He looked at Picton, then at Rawlins. The PCSO turned her head.

"Have a nice little chat, did we?" said Hogarth.

"Yes, we did. And I think I know where we need to go."

A gleam appeared in Hogarth's eyes. He nodded at Rawlins.

"Good work. Come on then, Rawlins. Let's shake a leg."

Chapter Twenty

The first address Picton supplied belonged to Andy Cruddas's girlfriend, Amy Carlton. But when they arrived, they soon found that Amy had since shacked up with a new man with tattoos all over his bare arms. He looked like a Hells Angel on his day off, and as though he could have eaten Andy Cruddas as a mid-morning snack.
"We broke up a while back," said the girl. "How long would you say?" she asked, looking back at her tattooed boyfriend. "Weeks," said the guy with the tattoos. The monosyllabic response looked about as much as the man could handle. And it seemed Amy had gone off the Cruddas type in a big way.

The next address was Cruddas's business address. They hadn't tried it yet, which was a definite flaw in the investigation so far, but Hogarth knew why. When they'd called his office, the receptionist where Cruddas worked had said she hadn't seen him for days. They had taken the response at face value, but they couldn't do so any longer. Simmons called the estate agent and found that the office keys had been handed in back when Cruddas's new insurance business started to fail. But when they arrived outside the blue corrugated shell of the shared-occupancy business hub in Shoebury, Hogarth, Rawlins, and Palmer noticed that some other units were empty too. There were plenty of big TO LET signs hoisted up on timbers in the car park.

"Andy Cruddas's office was in here then. You ever been here before, Rawlins?" said Hogarth.
"No. We were only pals outside of work. I never had any reason to be here."
Hogarth studied the layout of the building. It was shaped like a back-garden bomb shelter. With a horseshoe domed roof.
"Well, if he's in there I doubt he'll see us coming until we're inside. Let's go."
They walked in and found a stout woman standing behind a reception desk. She was flicking through some papers, and looked up as they approached.
"DI Hogarth, DS Palmer from Southend CID. Do you mind if I ask you a few questions? About one of your ex-tenants here…"
"Ex-tenants?"
"Yes, specifically Andy Cruddas. The young insurance salesman."
"Him? Oh. He wasn't with us long He lasted about six months I think."
"And you've not seen him lately?"
"Nope. Not at all."
"What about his office? Have you re-let it to someone else?"
"Not yet. We haven't had many enquiries lately, to be honest. They say businesses are holding back on their commitments, what with this Brexit business…"
Hogarth wasn't in the mood for small talk.
"Would you mind if we looked at his old office?"
"Why? What has Andy done?"
"Maybe nothing. That's what we're here to look at. If you don't mind…" Hogarth opened his hand for the key but the big woman picked a key off a wall rack and kept it in her own hand.
"It's okay. I'll take you there myself. Come through…"

The woman walked them upstairs and through a set of narrow corridors until they reached a small dead-ended corridor, built with flimsy looking partition walls and wooden doors.

"This is it. Room 16a. It used to be one room, but they split 16 into two so the smaller businesses could afford the rent…"

She was still speaking as she opened the door into a dim windowless office. Hogarth peered inside and forced his way through.

"He's not here, as you can see," said the receptionist. Hogarth didn't respond. His eyes poked around the dim browns and shadowy creams of the interior. There was still furniture in the room, mostly kicked across to one end. A wall unit. A desk turned up on its side. A chair with wheels, and a cheese plant that hadn't been watered for weeks.

"Wait a second…" said Hogarth. He looked at Palmer and Rawlins, and put a finger to his lips. His eyes trailed back towards the mound of furniture at the back of the room. There was something sticking out from behind the plant pot and the wall unit. Hogarth almost didn't notice, and even when he did, the shape might well have been a piece of office equipment, shiny and black. Or it could have been a shoe.

"What are you doing?" said the woman from reception, as Hogarth advanced quietly. He feared the worst, wondering if he was going to find a body. But when he got very close, the figure of a man sprang up from the floor. Andy Cruddas got ready to charge past Hogarth like a fleeing rabbit.

"Mr Cruddas!" said the woman, shocked. She jumped back and away from him as he charged at her. Palmer put herself into the doorway. Hogarth reached out, seized the man by his arm and dragged him back into the centre of the room.

He came face to face with the man. Curly-haired, wild-eyed, and thin. His breath smelt like he hadn't seen a toothbrush in days.

"Calm yourself, Andy Pandy. We've been looking for you."

He struggled, and Hogarth added a little force into his grip.

"Andy! You need to calm down," said Bec.

"Listen to her, son. None of this is helping you, believe me…"

Cruddas stopped squirming, but Hogarth kept a tight grip. He didn't trust the man not to make another run. And now that he had him, he wasn't going to lose him again. With Andy Cruddas found, things were just beginning to get interesting…

Chapter Twenty-one

Hogarth didn't arrest Andy Cruddas on the spot, even though protocol and common sense said he should have. If he'd played it by the book, he would have nicked the fella every time. But Hogarth was aiming to pack his dynamite in just the right way. And in his career, he'd learned that an occasional gamble could pay off handsomely. With Andy Cruddas in his hand, he felt it was the right time to make a play. But he needed to get rid of Rawlins first. PCSO Rawlins had helped him catch the man, granted – but her raw emotions were a risk again. Hogarth drove Rawlins back to the centre of town and dropped her on Victoria Avenue not far from the police station. She got out and realised Hogarth had no intention of sending Cruddas with her.
"Sir? Where are you taking him?" she asked as she got out of the car.
"Don't you worry. I'll bring Mr Cruddas here back for tea and biccies by three o'clock. Then we can all get cosy together."
"Sir?" Hogarth closed the electric window of his Insignia and looked at the young man's big eyes in the rear-view mirror. The doors were locked. Cruddas was secure enough. Palmer sat in the front passenger seat at Hogarth's side.
"You're not going to arrest me?" said Cruddas.
"All in good time, dear boy," said Hogarth. He glanced across at Palmer and saw she seemed unperturbed by his break with protocol. Either she'd already worked out his next move, or was getting dangerously familiar with his errant ways.

Cruddas hissed and yanked at the door when the saloon rolled up beside the grand driveway of his family home.
"What's the matter, Andy? You and mummy had a falling out?"
"Of course not. But you shouldn't do this to her. She's been through enough."
"I'm sure she has. In fact, I'm convinced of it. But just think. Won't it be a relief to see her little boy home safe. Come on, Andy. Let's make your mother happy. But I'm warning you, try and run on me, I won't go easy when I get hold of you again."
Hogarth pulled the man out of the backseat and gripped his wrist, steering him towards the garden path of his family home. Cruddas slackened and became compliant.
"How did you manage to stash yourself in that building without being seen?" said Palmer as they walked.
"Doreen…" said Cruddas. "The woman on reception. She's lazy. Very lazy. She opens up the doors at eight and then drifts about downstairs all day, drinking tea. I was almost able to come and go as I pleased." He spoke with a hint of juvenile pride.
"You had a spare key cut for your office door, right?" said Hogarth.
Cruddas shrugged.
"I still don't get it…" said Cruddas, as Hogarth pressed the doorbell and the deep chime sounded through the house. "Why are we here?"
They watched through the glass as the wide shape of Mrs Cruddas came shuffling towards the front door. When she opened it, her mouth dropped wide open. She looked at Hogarth, Palmer, and her son, before tears welled up from her eyes and slid down her cheeks.

"Andrew. My dear Andrew. Are you well…?"
The young man stiffened as his mother lashed her hefty arms around his neck.
"Go on, Andy! She's your mother. Hug her back," said Hogarth, shaking his head. He waited for the hysteria to die down, then the woman parted from her son, wiped her eyes and regarded Hogarth with a more restrained air. "Thank you for finding my son… but is there anything more we have to discuss?" she said.
"Oh, yes, Mrs Cruddas. We have much, much more. May we come in?"
The woman's face turned stiff, and her eyes flicked away.
"If you think it's necessary…"
"Oh, it's necessary alright" said Hogarth.

"Can I get you a cup of tea?" said the woman.
Hogarth shook his head.
"Do you know why we're here, Mrs Cruddas?"
"You brought me my son. That has to be the reason."
"It's one good reason. But there is something else. Can you think what it might be?"
The woman and the son met each other's eyes. Hogarth studied their gaze. He picked at it. There was something weighty in the woman's eyes. But Cruddas just looked like a frightened young man. A man who knew he was in deep trouble.
"Last time we came here, you confessed something to us," he said
The woman's face flushed.
"Inspector, do you really feel the need to humiliate me in front of my son?"

"I'm afraid when we're in pursuit of justice, we're not at liberty to keep secrets, madam. Especially when those secrets could be connected to a murder.

"Secrets? *Murder?*" said Cruddas, frowning. He knitted his hands in his lap, clamping them between his knees like a schoolchild.

"Connected to a murder! Come on!" said the woman. "You must see by now that neither Andrew nor myself could have any connection to the murder of Jake Drummond…"

The son's eyes snapped towards his mother in surprise.

"The truth, Mrs Cruddas, is I know no such thing. And that's exactly why I came here today. To establish the facts around your dealings with Jake Drummond."

"Jake Drummond?" said Andy Cruddas, with a tone of disbelief. "What dealings could my mother have ever had with him?"

"You remember him, don't you, dear? He came here to the house after your father died."

"I never realised that Dad even knew such crooks… I remember now, he lingered around here for a little while before I got to know him. Then he stopped coming."

Hogarth watched the woman squirming. She avoided his eyes.

"Your father had to deal with all kinds of people, in his business. Even people like Jake Drummond."

"I remember him here," said Cruddas, drifting through his memories. "He was always quiet back then. I thought he was a friend of yours. Until I met him elsewhere, but he had stopped visiting you by then. If I had known what he was like, I would have warned you to keep away from him. That man was evil. Mum, you really don't know what a lucky escape you had."

The woman stayed silent, but now she met Hogarth's eyes. Hogarth nodded for her to go on.
"Andrew..." she said., slowly, like her throat hurt. "If I had known that you had been dealing with him..." she said, struggling, *"I would have been the one to warn you."*
"What?" said Andy.
The woman's face contorted with pity and shame. Her face turned red as beetroot.
"He never came here as my friend, Andrew. I know you must have believed he was trying to woo me. Trying to jump into your father's shoes. But that wasn't the case, either."
"What then? Oh no. Don't tell me he was bullying you, too? Blackmailing you? The bastard just couldn't help himself. They think I killed him, didn't they, that's why I stayed away. I didn't do it, but I'm glad he's dead. But what could he have possibly had on you? A bereaved widow..."
"Yes, Andy. I must say that part intrigued me, too..." said Hogarth.
"You're a very cruel man, Inspector Hogarth."
"It's nothing to do with being cruel, Mrs Cruddas. I want the complete truth, the full story from both of you. And this might be the only way to get it."
Andy Cruddas looked tense and fragile.
"Mother? You know what we did, don't you?" said Andy.
Tears filled the woman's eyes "He broke you. He broke your business and forced you into the drug trade..."
"It sounds so foolish when you say it like that, doesn't it? So pathetic. But it's true. We were scared. He promised to let us alone if we did it. And he made it all sound so simple. But once we were doing it, he even used the business against us. The business he forced us to set up, he bled every penny from it while we took the risks...

"He did the very same thing to your father…" she said, quietly.

"What?" said Andy Cruddas again.

"He broke your father's business, and once that was done, your father took the only route left available to him. It was the only way he could see that would finish it permanently. But Drummond turned even that into the ultimate blackmail."

"Mum… what are you saying?"

Andy Cruddas looked at Hogarth and Palmer for help as his mother stayed silent. They looked back at her.

"Mum, please… are you saying Jake Drummond was responsible for Dad dying? I never knew the business was failing… why? Because Jake Drummond was blackmailing him! I don't believe it. Blackmailing him over what?!"

"I'm sorry, Andrew. I never wanted you to be hurt like this."

"Hurt like what? I don't understand what you're saying. Please, just say it… Say it! What did Drummond do to dad? What did he have on him?"

"I'm sorry… But your father strayed from me. He had an affair, Andrew. In fact, he had more than one."

Andy Cruddas sat in wide-eyed silence. "No… I don't believe he'd do that… he just wouldn't."

The woman met her son's eyes.

"Yes, Andrew. He did. And for a while, your father kept the awful man quiet by paying him off. I only learned of it when the money began to dry up. That's when it all came out."

"When?"

"Just over two years ago."

"*Drummond?!* Drummond is the one responsible for Dad's death? He broke him. He killed him!"

"No," said Hogarth. "That's not it at all, is it, Mrs Cruddas?"

"Like I said, you're a cruel man."

"A case of pot and kettle, Mrs Cruddas…" said Hogarth.
"What's he on about?" said Andy. "My father was killed in a car crash on the M25, two years ago. It was in the news. It was horrific, how dare you use that against us!"
"Yes. It was deeply horrific. Your father's car was burnt to a cinder, and they found no remains. It went up like napalm, so they said. But they found the remains of others alright. The poor buggers caught up in that crash when the car spun out of control."
"How dare you!" said Andy Cruddas.
"Andrew…" came his mother's frail voice. "Andrew, listen to me. The truth is coming out, so you have to hear it from me. Just promise you'll forgive us, will you. We did it all for you."
"What? What did you do?"
"Your father didn't die in that crash. I'm sorry…"
Silence reigned along with the tick of the clock on the mantelpiece.
"What?"
"We were almost bankrupt. Your father felt guilty for everything he'd done. He felt he was responsible, so he decided it was the only way left to provide for us. But it only made things worse. Drummond saw through it, of course he did. He knew why your father had done it. That was why he started with his visits. He started blackmailing me because he knew. He guessed."
"Dad isn't dead…?"
There was another long silence.
"No, he isn't. You did it for the insurance payout, didn't you?
"No."
"Didn't you?!"

"I'm sorry. I'm sorry he ever thought of the idea. I'm sorry I didn't try hard enough to stop him. I'm sorry Jake Drummond ever entered our lives."

"You… faked his death too. Don't put all the blame on him. You kept the lie real for me. Not just for the insurance companies. But for me too…"

"We had to keep it a secret, you must see that. He couldn't be alive. He couldn't ever visit family or be a part of our lives like he had before. After what he'd done our family life was over… he knew that."

"But he was my dad. My father! He's still my father. How dare you?! Both of you! I'll never ever forgive you for this."

"We both wanted you to have an inheritance. It's what you deserved as our son. It was yours."

"Bullshit! You wanted an easy life. Where's my inheritance now, eh?"

"Jake Drummond took it all."

"Because you still wanted an easy life all the way to the end. This is your fault as much as his."

"Don't say that. Please…!

"I'll say what I like from now on… so, where is he? Where is my father? You at least owe me that."

"I can't tell you, Andrew. I made a promise."

"The time for any such promise is over, Mrs Cruddas," said Hogarth. "Your husband had very serious dealings with Jake Drummond and we'll need to speak to him as part of our investigation into the murder and, of course, there's his own situation to discuss – it'll have to be dealt with. He will be found, Mrs Cruddas."

The woman grimaced.

"Tell me," said Andy Cruddas. He was shaking as he spoke. "Where is my father. I have a right to know. Tell me or I swear I'll hunt him down," said Andy Cruddas. The young man surged towards his mother. Hogarth slapped a firm hand on his shoulder to restrain him.

"He was up in the north last time we spoke…" she said, her voice faint. "He moved around, working different jobs. He didn't tell me too much, and I didn't ask."

"Where?" snapped Andy.

"Last time I heard he was in Stockton-on-Tees…"

"You're evil. Selfish, that's what you are. I would never have done this to you." Hogarth dragged Andy Cruddas away from her.

"Come on, Andy. I think it's time we had a nice, frank chat, don't you?" Hogarth stood up and steered the young man towards the door.

"Where are you taking him?" said Mrs Cruddas.

"I think it's best he didn't stay here, for all concerned, don't you?"

Hogarth felt Cruddas shaking as he led him towards the front door. "I think there's a few things you could tell me, Andy," said Hogarth. "But it's a two-way street. There's something I could tell you too… about your father…"

Andy Cruddas looked him in the eye. Hogarth nodded, and Cruddas stopped struggling. As Hogarth opened the front door, the old woman's voice rang out down the hallway.

"You've destroyed my life, Inspector. I hope you're happy with yourself."

"I think I'll sleep at night, Mrs Cruddas. But I do wonder how you've managed for so long. Palmer, you deal with Mrs Cruddas here. She'll need to be taken in. Call in for help from the station. We don't want her to do anything rash now, do we?"

"Shall I arrest her?"

Hogarth nodded. "Yes. We've got a confession. It's time to put this one to bed."

"Yes, sir," said Palmer.
He left Palmer in the house with the old woman, to arrange her own lift back to the station.

Hogarth ducked Andy Cruddas into the back of his car and made sure the doors were locked before he set off for the station. He drove slowly. Hogarth intended to use the time to get acquainted with the man. His wide solemn eyes, his troubled face.
"Did you do it, Andy?"
"What?"
"You know what. Did you kill Jake Drummond?"
"Of course, I didn't."
Hogarth let his brooding eyes stay on Cruddas.
"I said no, and I meant it. Lord knows I had enough reason, but I couldn't kill anyone."
"How did he get you into that drug racket. I've heard Picton's version, but it doesn't give me the full story. What did he have on you? Picton says he was bullied, pure and simple. And he looks the type to me. But you, you have some dignity about you. I honestly think you would have preferred a beating to doing what Drummond said."
"No, he didn't bully me. But I was still as much of a fool as my damn mother was. Drummond seduced me with the idea of wealth. I was starting out in the same line of work as my father. In the old days, Dad made it look easy. I believed it was easy money. I didn't know Drummond, but when I met him he was flash with his money. He told me I could end up flush just like he was – from the insurance game. All I had to do was write up a few policies for the IDs he would supply me. I knew it sounded wrong. But I wanted to be rich.

That's all anyone in my family ever wanted. I wanted to be successful…"

"And you were willing to do anything to get there?"

Andy Cruddas averted his big dark eyes. "I was listening to the wrong voice, wasn't I? As soon as Drummond's dodgy policies started paying out, he was into me for most of the cash. He told me he'd dob me in to the FCA and to the police, and that it would all be on me. I'd go to prison. It snowballed from there. He had me by the balls…"

"Greed had you, Andy. That's what I hear. All of this stems from greed. Sounds like a virus of greed, passed from Drummond, to your father, to your mother, to Picton… Drummond had you all infected with it. I feel sorry for you, but I can't save you from the law. You'll have to face what's coming."

"I don't want saving. Drummond's dead. That's enough for me. I'll take what's coming. That and I want to see my father… I must see him…"

"Funny you should mention that. I have more than a sneaking suspicion that he didn't stay up in Stockton," said Hogarth.

Hogarth took the folded A4 printout from his blazer pocket and handed it to the man in the back seat. Andy Cruddas unfolded the sheet and stared at the shadowy image and the article below.

"Club Smart. This was the reopening last year…"

"Yes, that's it. Recognise anyone in that picture?"

Hogarth watched as Cruddas scanned the picture. It took a few moments before he saw the young man's eyes widen. Cruddas looked up.

"My dad! He was there?! He came back!"

"Any idea why?"

"He's standing next to Jake Drummond in this picture. Drummond was bleeding my family dry. My father must have come back to stop him…"

"If so, he would have soon learned that Drummond wouldn't ever stop. Maybe this time your father came back to kill him…"

Andy Cruddas's face contorted with revulsion. "My father would never do that."

"Andy, snap out of it son. Four people are already dead because of the choices your father made. You might not want to think about it, I get that, but look at what your father's done already. To you, your mother. Those people on the M25…"

"No. That's not what he's like. I need to see him. I need to confront him."

"Good, Andy. Because I'm relying on you to help me find him. We know your father is alive, and he's up to his neck in this mess, just like you are."

"I'm not guilty of killing Drummond and neither is he. I know it."

"Then it's time for you to prove it. Help me find him, then one way or another I can solve this murder."

"But he's in hiding," said Cruddas. "He could be up north again. He could be bloody anywhere."

Hogarth shook his head. "No. You've had plenty of problems lately, Andy, wouldn't you say? Some of those problems weren't all your making. Your parents share some responsibility. I've got a feeling your father is closer than we think…"

Chapter Twenty-two

He sat in his dark apartment with the laptop open on the coffee table. The curtains were drawn tight. On the leather couch beside him were copies of the two local free papers, and a new copy of The Record. The news in the free papers was always out of date. Those free rags weren't even good enough for chip wrappers. But he had expected better from The Record. Even their nasty little journo, Alice Perry, the blonde flirt who covered most of their juicier news hadn't squeezed the story to its maximum potential. Her articles were absorbed with the council's latest sleaze crisis. Did political sleaze really outweigh murder? Surely not. Murder won hands down. Didn't they get it? He was news.
But at least he was safe. Safe but bored. He should have felt pleased that the comments from Southend's police chief were all clichés. *The police are pursuing all avenues. We are working day and night. Public safety is our number one concern.* But safety wasn't good enough anymore. It didn't give any comfort. And if he was being honest, safety didn't give him the buzz he was craving. Drummond had had to be killed, pure and simple. But since the killing he was a changed man. He had crossed the Rubicon. He had done what many wanted, but only *he* had the guts to do it. So where was his applause? Didn't Drummond deserve to die? Of course, he did! So why wasn't The Record covering what a monstrous lying bastard he was? Why didn't they consider that the killer might even be a hero? And while the paper squandered his story, the stupid police dithered. At first, he had wanted to

feel safe from their investigation, so he had thrown them Dan Picton's bloody spectacles. It was a neat trick, and a sweet piece of misdirection. But the press hadn't even mentioned it. And as far as he could tell, the police hadn't responded by charging Picton with the murder as he'd wanted. That would have been something, wouldn't it? That would have showed him that they had taken the killing seriously. Because it was serious. And he was just as serious about getting away with it scot-free. But not at the price of his success being ignored altogether. And as he had shown once already, he could do anything he liked.

If they were going to pretend he didn't exist…If they were going to ignore his smart moves which put the other fools in the frame…

Then what good were the police or the journalists? He'd seen that little police tart stalking around at Club Smart, fishing for information. But what could she do? She was only a lowly PCSO. She had no authority. No clout. *It wasn't good enough.*

He shook his head and picked up his laptop. He scrolled through Alice Perry's article from the day after the kill. There was the sour-faced detective inspector in the blazer and chinos, lording it up and hogging the spotlight. But what had he done to deserve it?

Nothing.

As far as he could tell, they had ignored his ploy to pin the murder on Picton. So how else could he influence the game? He smiled and folded his arms as he stared at the little image of the pompous DI Hogarth. He stared down at the man's face and planned his next move.

If they were going to ignore him while they blundered through their investigation, he still had other ideas about how he could change things up again. Some of his ideas involved risk. But since experiencing the power of snuffing out another man's life, he was up for it. Those dangers brought a reward he had never dreamed of and he was keen for more. And he intended to twist the police inside out. If they couldn't handle one simple murder case, even when he was dropping the evidence right into their laps, how would they handle two?

He would have to give up on applause if he killed again. But all those other benefits lay in wait. The high.

The adrenaline kick like no other.

The sense of infinite power.

The knife gleamed at him from the mantelpiece and the man smiled back.

Chapter Twenty-three

Palmer sat in the CID room. The small room was empty which was how she liked it best. Simmons was upstairs going over the club CCTV footage for the third time. She doubted anything else would come to light now. And if it did, it wouldn't come from Simmons. Palmer sipped a mug of tea as she waded through the paperwork on her desk. There was the file on Jake Drummond, and the collection of notes she'd made about the missing weapon, and her notes on the main suspects. It was all there but she knew she wasn't seeing the whole picture. Maybe Hogarth's confidence was misplaced and that bothered her in more ways than one. Hogarth was frosty and hard to know, but for all his faults Palmer was coming to like him, and wanted to strip away some of his mystery. She was angry with him for being distracted in the middle of a serious case but Palmer knew she was in danger of becoming a hypocrite. Fascination with DI Joe Hogarth was becoming her own distraction. A knock at the door disturbed her. Another distraction had arrived. This time Palmer was glad of it.

"Come in…"

PCSO Rawlins walked into the room. Palmer smiled at her, but Rawlins looked furtive and uncertain. The young woman closed the door behind her and the polite smile on Palmer's face wavered.

"What's the matter, Bec?"

"Nothing's the matter. At least, it shouldn't be, but if you don't mind me saying I think DI Hogarth has got this one wrong."

"Got what wrong?"

"I honestly don't think Andy Cruddas could have killed Jake Drummond."
"No. But we've got his mother in the cells on a host of charges relating to fraud and deception and she could end up implicated for murder in those M25 deaths. If she knew in advance about George Cruddas faking his death, the very least she'll be looking at is manslaughter… then look at George Cruddas himself. He's not a saint, I think it's fair to say. We already know Andy Cruddas was involved in dealing banned substances. He's not a saint either, Bec, no matter how much you want him to be…"
"I know all that, Sue. But he's not a killer."
"Do you still think you know him well enough to say so?" said Palmer. "Because Andy Cruddas is still right here on my list of suspects. Look, I get it. DI Hogarth is a very tough customer, but he won't see Andy arrested for any crime until he's sure. That's what he's doing right now. Making sure."
"He told you that, did he?"
"No, Bec. But by now, I know what the man is like."
"I wish I had your faith in him."
Palmer offered a thin smile and averted her eyes. Until recently she'd made a very good show of being a Hogarth sceptic. It wouldn't do any good to change her opinion too quickly. Tongues were always wagging at Southend nick.
Then Rawlins took her by surprise.
"I went out to Club Smart last night."
"What?" said Palmer. She looked up at the PCSO, and Palmer saw the girl was struggling to keep her composure. "Why did you do that? When?"
"After work last night. I didn't tell anyone. I didn't even tell Rob. I knew Rob would have gone absolutely ballistic."
"And rightly so, Bec! The Drummond murder looks like a revenge murder, but even so. Someone is dead. You go

poking your nose in by yourself, who knows what could have happened to you."

"Yeah. But there's more to this, Sue. Somebody at that club knows what happened, I'm sure of it. If we could find that person it would put Andy Cruddas in the clear."

"You're not even a WPC yet, and you want to play detective? Don't let Hogarth's praise go to your head, Bec."

"That's not it. I just want to help.

"Okay. So, you went there and you're not going to do anything like that again. Are you …?" Palmer gave Rawlins a stare until the PCSO nodded back. "Good. But, did you learn anything?"

"Only that Gary Grayson is after any girl he can get his filthy hands on. I thought he'd got a partner, hasn't he?"

"Yes, he has. And she's not stupid, either. I don't know what she sees in the man."

"Totally. He's awful. Has his partner got any kids at all?"

"Yes, so I heard. By her ex-husband. Nothing to do with Grayson. Why do you ask, Bec?"

Rawlins frowned in thought. "I tried to do a bit of undercover questioning. I got close to Gary Grayson. I let him think I was interested in him, if you know what I mean…"

"Bec! And he didn't recognise you from the first night?"

"He had his beer goggles on. If I'd let him have his way, I don't think he would have cared if he did."

"You're right about Dawson. He would have gone mental," said Palmer.

"It's a secret, Sue. I took the risks. It's on me."

"Of course. But you asked him questions? What questions?"

"About Drummond. About his relationship with the man. I asked him who he thought had motive to kill the man."

"So, you think Gary Grayson killed him? Grayson's a flaky old soak, and a bit of an idiot, but I wouldn't have him down as the killer…"
"I saw another side to him in that office at Club Smart last night. Honestly, Sue. He almost totally lost it. I thought he was going to attack me."
Palmer nodded. "I think he's an alcoholic, Bec. Those types can turn just like that. You shouldn't have taken the risk."
"No. It wasn't just the booze. I saw something in his eyes. The man's dark, Sue. I mean it."
"Why did you ask about the kids?"
"When he was trying it on with me, he dropped a photograph from his jacket. The photograph was of two podgy little toddlers sitting on a woman's knee."
Palmer frowned and looked at her notes.
"What?" said Rawlins. Palmer flicked through the pages. She'd made entries of basic facts and details as well as the bigger matters. There it was. Her notes from the meeting with Alison Craw.
Two children, one daughter. Older teenagers…
"No, Bec. Grayson's live-in girlfriend, Alison Craw, doesn't have young children. She's older than me. Her kids are teenagers. And from what I've seen, Alison probably wouldn't let Gary Grayson near them. He wouldn't have their photographs. That doesn't fit at all."
Now it was Bec Rawlins who was frowning. "But I know what I saw… a photo of kids. Little kids. I wondered if they belonged to his sister or something… but I thought about it. People don't keep photos of their sister's family in their wallet. Not usually. Not unless they're odd."
"I don't think the man has any brothers or sisters anyway…" said Palmer.
"Then why would he have a photo like that?" said Rawlins.

"You know the man better than I do by now and I've got a fair idea why he's got that photograph, haven't you?"
"You mean the kids are his?!"
"Sounds like it… how old were they?"
"Young infants. Could be a touch older than that, but the photograph didn't look that old."
"Dear me. Gary Grayson just doesn't know when to stop, does he?"
Palmer looked at her notes and flicked to Gary Grayson's pages. She scribbled a new note and underlined it. *Two young children? By who?*
"But Alison Craw said Grayson had been with her for at least two years. Oh dear. That poor woman. I wonder if she knew…"
"What if she didn't know? I don't think he gives a toss what any girl thinks."
"But he has a good life with Alison Craw. They live in a decent house and she seems like a responsible woman. Gary Grayson landed on his feet with her. If she found out about that, I'm pretty sure his life on easy street would have been over…" said Palmer.
"What?" said Rawlins with a smirk. "You're thinking about letting her know?"
"No. I was thinking about Jake Drummond. If Drummond knew about those kids, that would have given him plenty of blackmail material."
Rawlins nodded. "Which would have given Grayson plenty of motive to kill…"
"Absolutely," said Palmer.

Chapter Twenty-four

DS Palmer returned to the CID room ready for action. By now DC Simmons should have been ready too but Palmer found him standing in the middle of the CID room studying his phone like a teenager hanging about on the high street.
"Aren't you ready yet?" said Palmer.
"Course I am," said Simmons, but he stayed where he was, scanning his phone screen just a little faster. Palmer tutted. Bec Rawlins had thrown them another line of enquiry and it seemed hotter than the others. The more Palmer thought through the implications of the photograph, the more she felt there was something to it. Gary Grayson *did* have something to hide – if Alison Craw knew about his secret children, there was no way a woman like her would have continued with him in her life. She had enough problems already, shielding her children from the legacies of her past. And if Drummond knew about the secret children, Grayson might have been desperate enough to stop Jake from blabbing. Up to now Palmer had assumed Gary Grayson was using Alison Craw as his guarantee of a comfortable future. The man was knocking on a bit, and from the looks of it had drunk away any life savings. The DJ was a man with no future, but Alison Craw offered him one. Palmer looked at it from another angle too. Drummond had met with Alison Craw because he had known about her money from the double-glazing game. Grayson would have known about that too. One last leap of logic took Palmer to a darker place. What if Grayson had discovered that Drummond had been blackmailing her for cash and favours – sucking away the money he believed would one day be his? If an angry man with an alcohol problem found out about something like

that, there was no telling what he might do. It was time to have another discussion with Gary Grayson, to dig deeper and see what he was made of. If they dug carefully enough, Palmer wondered if she would find the critical detail that would lead to his arrest. "Come on, Simmons. Put the phone away. You can send your girlfriend a text as we go. We're working a murder case, remember…"

Simmons looked up. "I'm not sending a text. I was checking the weather."

Palmer's eyebrows arched up, as if to say *'seriously?'*.

Simmons shrugged. "I'm supposed to be kite surfing this weekend. No wind means no surfing and that sport costs a bloody fortune, I need to know."

"Then find a different sport and stop mucking about," said Palmer. "Let's go."

He glanced up at her and nodded towards her desk.

"You should check your phone first. You missed a call when you went out."

Palmer sighed and picked her phone up from the desk. She'd taken a one-minute toilet break and ended up missing a call. DI Hogarth had called her. There was a voicemail. She clicked on the voicemail icon and stuck her phone to her ear.

"Palmer, it's me," said the voicemail. Hogarth's voice sounded even rougher on the recording. Rough but quiet. "Don't bother to call me back. I'll be driving. I hope the arrest of Babs Cruddas went well. You'll have to apologise to her ladyship about the lack of fine china when she gets her tea. Anyway. I'm with Andy Cruddas here. We're going out on a little expedition together, hunting for his old man. I'll be a few hours, so do your best to motivate DC Simmons. And if Melford asks where I am, tell him I'm hard at it, nose to the grindstone and all that. Seriously, make a decent excuse for me. If this little jaunt comes off, we'll crack this whole bloody case wide open, Wish me luck, Sue."

"And if it doesn't come off, then the DCI will probably crack you wide open instead…" said Palmer, muttering to herself.

"What?" said Simmons, looking up.

"Nothing," said Palmer.

Palmer. Sue. Sue. Palmer. Hogarth couldn't decide whether DS Palmer was a subordinate or a confidant, but at least there were a few hints of some good feeling there. For now, that would have to do. If anyone asked, she would make an excuse for Hogarth and that anyone included DC Simmons.

"Who was it?" said Simmons.

"Just the bank again. They wanted to know if I wanted to take on another loan."

"And do you," said Simmons with a grin, slipping his phone away.

"No thanks. I've got enough liabilities in my life right now as it is."

Simmons smiled for a second before his face wavered. But Palmer's smiled stayed firmly where it was as she led the way out of the station.

Thankfully, Alison Craw was home. The woman opened the front door for them as they approached. She was on the phone, and from the tone of the conversation Palmer reckoned it had to be Gary Grayson or her ex.

She rolled her eyes at Palmer and turned away from the front door to let them know they were welcome to come inside.

"No. No, that's not what I said! I never said anything like it. You can promise what you like to those kids, but if you're going to make promises, you're bloody well going to keep them, and you'll be the one to pay for them too!"

There was a long pause. Alison Craw fussed around with some pot pourri in the hallway while she listened.
"No. You said they could go on that trip – so they can go. But you'll foot the bill. End of story. Look, I've got to go, Ron. I said I've got to go!" Alison Craw ended the call and turned to face them. She was smartly dressed but her face bore all the hallmarks of an argument. Her eyes were severe, her mouth tight.
"Excuse me if I am little brusque with you, but I have my reasons as you'll have heard."
"Man trouble is it?" said DC Simmons, in the words of a fool. Palmer tried not to wince too hard.
"It's always man trouble. From the sound of it, you're probably trouble for some other poor lady. My ex-husband has promised my son and daughter they can go on a post-school holiday with their friends next year. Unsupervised! Can you believe that? She's seventeen. He's fifteen. Now you tell me. How in hell is that responsible parenting?"
"It doesn't sound good," said Palmer. In some ways she was relieved she had by-passed parenthood.
"It isn't good at all. And he wants me to pay for it. He says I fleeced him in the divorce. He doesn't know the half of it." Mrs Craw took a breath. "So, what is it now, if you don't mind?"
"Don't worry," said Palmer. "We won't keep you very long. We just need to know a bit more about Gary…"
The woman rolled her eyes and sighed. "Okay. What is it?"
"We already know about your situation with Jake Drummond. Now we want to speak to Gary Grayson about his dealings with Drummond."
"Dealings?" Craw replied.
"Is Gary here….?" Palmer looked at the empty staircase. There was no noise upstairs and no sign of the man.

"No, he isn't," said the woman, firmly and she didn't sound pleased about it either.

"Oh." Palmer wanted to ask why, but postponed the question. "Then maybe you'd know something about it."

"About Gary and Drummond? No. I know Drummond was a toad. And I knew he went down that club to letch at the girls. Why do you think I never went there? It wasn't just that I felt too old. It was Jake Drummond's second home. I didn't want to be near the man."

"Of course," said Palmer. "I don't think many people did…"

Alison Craw shifted on her feet, revealing a hint of impatience. Palmer needed to move things forward, but she had to tread carefully.

"Do you think Drummond might have any leverage for blackmailing Gary?"

"Leverage?" said Alison. "What are you getting at?"

"Do you think there was anything Drummond could have used against Gary to extort money from him?"

"Money? From Gary? All his money goes on those stupid bloody shirts and his boozing. I'm actually supposed to be glad when he gives me twenty quid towards the shopping bill."

"Why do you put up with him?" said Simmons. It was another classic Simmons statement. This time Palmer had to intervene.

"Those aren't the sort of questions we should be asking, Simmons…"

"But he's right though, isn't he? I wonder that myself sometimes. Some dumb part of me must love him, I suppose. Look. I'm sure Gary probably has a pile of sordid little secrets from his years' deejaying in those dirty little holes. But the truth is he doesn't tell me any of them, and I wouldn't want to hear about it if he did. You know that I've got my secrets. All I want to do is focus on the present. Jake Drummond's dead and I want to get on with my life, and want Gary to shape up. That's it."

Palmer blinked, searching for another way to ask the question. Alison Craw seemed to read her mind.

"What could Drummond have had on Gary? Gary's not your killer, detective. I mean it."

"Then I want to clear his name," said Palmer. "Did you ever hear about Gary's past? His other relationships?"

"No. I didn't ask, and he didn't say. Like I said, I want to live in the present. What exactly are you getting at here?"

"I have to ask all kinds of questions, Mrs Craw. Any idea where Gary might be? Maybe it's best I speak to him."

"No, I don't. But when you see him, please pass him a message for me. If he stayed out last night because he's been messing about with other women, tell him not to bother coming back. Can you do that for me?"

Palmer nodded. "I'll see what I can do…"

As they walked out of the house Palmer gave Simmons a hard look. When the door was firmly shut behind them, she added some words of advice.

"Get your brain in gear, Simmons. It needs to join up with your mouth. Any more foot-in-mouth gaffes like that and next time I'll leave you at the station to read your weather reports."

DC Simmons sulked but Palmer didn't much care.

***

Gary Grayson's flat wasn't as billed. The address sounded something alright. It was listed as Thorpe Bay, the wealthier end of the seafront where the millionaire mansions faced out to sea. But the address was far closer to the notorious Talbot Estate, a quartet of low-rise blocks surrounded by a high brick wall which even the residents knew as Alcatraz.

Grayson's home was in a more upmarket estate tucked behind the seafront in a gated estate. The old signage – no more than five or ten years old, declared the place was a luxury apartment estate. Who were they kidding? Alcatraz was within five minutes' walk – seconds if you wanted to scale the walls. Palmer parked up and buzzed the intercom, but there was no answer. She tried again then buzzed a couple of neighbours. A woman answered.
"Yes?"
"Hello. This is Detective Sergeant Sue Palmer from Southend Police. We're looking for Gary Grayson – the man who lives next door to you. Have you seen him? Or heard him at all?"
"What? Him? The noisy oaf with the ridiculous hair? I've called you people about him so many times. Are you really going to do something about him?"
"What about?"
"The noise. The hellish noise. He's up all hours playing that ghastly music."
"Was he loud last night?" said Simmons.
"No, not last night. That's something I suppose. But any other night you care to mention, he'll be in there, music pounding… nobody can stand him around here."
Palmer raised an eyebrow and looked at Simmons. For once the slick-haired DC seemed to be paying attention. "Club Smart?" he asked.
Palmer nodded. "Okay, madam. Thanks for your help," said Palmer over the intercom.
"What help? Are you going to do something about that noise or not?"
"That's not our department. But don't worry. I'm sure it's all in hand." Palmer and Simmons walked away while the intercom squawked at their backs.

***

It was still too early for most staff to show up for the evening shift at Club Smart but Palmer found the main entrance door ajar. She looked at Simmons then she walked inside. Simmons walked in behind her. Their footsteps echoed in the dim corridor. The place was dark and cold as a fridge.

"Hello?" said Palmer.

Her voice echoed. No one replied.

"Bloody spooky in here, don't you think?" said Simmons.

Palmer didn't reply, but the truth was she did feel more than a hint of chill.

"They surely wouldn't just leave the door open like that. Someone's got to be in here," said Palmer, trying to convince herself. Opening the double doors into the nightclub room itself was like peering into an abyss. There was no light at all, just a feeling of limitless black space, abetted by a chill draught coming from unseen crevices and vents beyond.

"What's going on here?" said Simmons.

"I don't know…" said Palmer. She walked in, listening to the acute echo of her heels clicking on the hard floor. "Wish I knew where the bloody light switch was."

"Hang on or we're going to end up stacking it in here…" Simmons fumbled until the coloured light of his phone screen appeared beside her face. A moment later, a bright torch beam cut into the blackness. His phone torch illuminated a short cone of space ahead of them. Sparkling walls and neon baubles reflected at them wherever the light fell. Soon enough Simmons picked out the distant doors by the larger of the two bars.

"Over there," said Palmer. She saw a hint of light coming from underneath the doors. She walked eagerly towards it, her feet getting louder. Palmer reached the door and pushed it open and cold white light poured over them. They saw the back of a man in overalls, his face hidden because he was looking into a big cupboard.

"Excuse me," said Palmer but the man didn't react.

"Excuse me, sir…" Still nothing. "Police!" she called. The man jumped round, and she saw the wireless of the stereo plugged into his ears. The little bald man's eyes were wide open. He looked in shock.

"The door was open to the street," Palmer explained. The man put a hand to his chest, and pulled two little white earphones from his ears.

"You gave me a bloody fright there, I can tell you."

"It's okay. We're the police," said Simmons.

"But you could have been that killer, couldn't you…"

"Maybe next time you should try closing the door." Simmons was as blunt as a sledgehammer.

The old man nodded. "I'm starting my shift. I'm cleaning up before the punters come in and make it messy again."

"Are you the only one here, Mr….?" said Palmer.

"Mr Henry. Tom Henry. Yes. The only one at present. Some of the others will be in later."

"So, Gary Grayson's not here?" said Simmons.

"DJ GG? I shouldn't think so. The whole place was dark when I got in. But I haven't checked the back office. Try in there if you like."

Henry pointed a finger to a door further down the corridor. Palmer stayed where she was, but Simmons nodded and walked down the hall. He pushed open the door, flicked on the light, then looked back at Palmer. He shook his head.

"So, where is he?" said Palmer.

"What? DJ GG?" said the cleaner, chuckling to himself.

"Why are you laughing, Mr Henry? I don't get the joke."

"Oh, if you knew him like I do, you would. That one needs a cleaner walking behind him permanently."

"Why?" said Simmons, returning to the conversation.

"Because he can't keep it in his pants, can he? I've caught him myself, more than once."

"We've already heard Mr Grayson likes to sleep around," said Simmons.

"Hah. I don't think there's much sleep involved to be honest. He doesn't waste much time with them. Wham, bam and no time for a thank-you ma'am. That's just the usual girls. I know he's mucked a few about worse than that. Gets in their heads and such. Probably told a few lies to get what he was after. That's worse, I suppose."

"Lies? What lies?" said Simmons.

The bald man's lips pursed up. "I'm not one for gossip… but… I've heard him tell a couple of those girls that he loves them. Those are the ones who come back for more. I suppose he uses that line just to keep 'em ready and willing. I don't know, do I? That kind of life was never for me. Messing about with women's feelings only ever causes trouble – for all concerned."

"Sage advice," said Simmons.

Palmer gave him a steely eye.

"None of that was on the record, was it? I was just making conversation, that's all. I don't see too many people in here."

"Oh, we don't mind a little chat now and then, do we Simmons?" said Palmer. "These girls… the ones he says he loves… do you know many there might be?"

"I don't count them, exactly. But I know he got with some of them a few times…"

"And do you think it went further than a bit of fun with any of these girls?"

"What, like wedding bells, you mean? Don't be daft."

"Like children, Mr Henry."

Henry blinked. He looked away and pursed his lips. Then he looked up again. "It's not my business. But let's just say it might have. I'm not certain, but I do remember him consoling some little madam a while back. Got to be a while back now. For them young girls, having unwanted kids can ruin their lives, I suppose…"

"Especially if the father is a good for nothing liar," said Simmons.

This time Palmer didn't rebuke Simmons. It was true.

The phone started ringing in Palmer's jacket pocket. She moved away and answered the call without checking the screen. She hoped for an update from Hogarth, but the voice she heard instead made her stiffen up.

"DS Palmer. Any idea where DI Hogarth is? I can't get hold of him."

"Sir, I believe he's dealing with an important lead relating to Andy Cruddas."

"Cruddas? Has he found the man? His mother's rambling suggests you already know his whereabouts."

Palmer frowned. The DCI already knew. "Yes, Hogarth has found him. I think he's about to bring him in, sir."

The DCI turned quiet. Something in her tone must have caused suspicion.

"Well, Palmer. I'd rather have told Hogarth, but since he's ignoring his phone… it seems that Cruddas and Picton are off the hook."

"Sir?" said Palmer. She looked round at Simmons. He gave her a furrowed brow and tried to listen in.

"It's not good news, Palmer. Where are you?"

"Club Smart, sir. Luker Close.

"Excellent. At least someone's on the job. You're just around the corner."

"From what?"

"There's another body, Palmer. A shop worker phoned it in just now. From the description of the wound on the chest, it sounds like our killer has struck again. They found the body by the wheelie bins around the back of the SavaPenny Store. I want you to go straight around the back of the store to where the body is. Secure the area and look around. Uniforms have been dispatched."

"Righto, sir. We're on the way."

"And, Palmer?"

"Sir?"

"Your team need to get your ruddy finger out. This looks terrible. The national press will be on this one. I need progress. And tell Hogarth to call me, asap."

"Yes, sir."

Palmer turned away and started moving for the door. "DS Palmer!" said Simmons.

"There's another body, Simmons," she said, without looking back.

"Another one? Where?"

"Just follow me…"

They left the cleaner where they'd found him and ran out through the darkness of the nightclub. As they bundled through another set of doors, they almost bumped into three tall men. Palmer recognised two of them as security, but the first man looked different. He was shaven-headed like the rest, but smarter.

"Whoa!" he said. "Who are you and where are you going?"

Palmer looked at him, but kept moving.

"Police," she replied. "And who are you?" she said, as she backed out of the doors.

"John Milford. I only bloody own the place."

Milford? She hadn't spoken to him yet, but she and Simmons kept on running. If the evidence was fresh, there was a chance they could keep it fresh and secure for Marris and the forensics. But with the public around, there were no guarantees.

"That was the DCI?" said Simmons.

"Yeah," said Palmer, panting as they rounded the corner towards the library.

"Where's Hogarth then?"

"How am I supposed to know?" said Palmer.

Out of breath, Palmer felt herself flagging, but out of sheer bloody mindedness would not allow Simmons to overtake her. A group of students had already gathered outside the library, and were pointing their snacks towards the noise and kerfuffle at the back of the shops. A moment later Palmer drew to a halt. She found a middle-aged woman in a cheap black suit kneeling beside a man lying still on his side. A dark puddle of blood had spilled either side of him. His eyes stared ahead, his mouth open as if frozen in shock. His matted bleach-blond hair looked wet. But the worst part was the man's lower body. Gary Grayson's trousers had been yanked down by his feet, and were gathered into folds around his ankles.

"With his pants round his ankles…" said Simmons.

"I can see for myself, Simmons…" said Palmer. "Madam?" she said, addressing the woman by the body in the cheap black suit. The woman looked up. She was fortyish, wearing glasses and had short hair. She looked like the shop manager. "Please move away from the body."

"It's the killer, isn't it… he's struck again. Here. Right outside my shop. Why here?" Her face spoke of shock. The other staff lingered, a hushed pack by the back door of the shop.

"Have you touched the body?" said Palmer.

The woman shook her head.

"Good. I'm Detective Sergeant Palmer and this is Detective Constable Simmons, Southend CID.

The sound of sirens punctuated the air, rising over the noise of the high street.

"I only touched his neck and his wrist. I was trying to find a pulse… to see if I could help him. But he's gone., isn't he?"

"At least you tried."

"Oh, and there's something else we need to talk to you about," said the shop manager as she backed away.

Palmer looked at her. "What?"

"It's probably nothing, but we think there were some people messing around out here a few nights back."

Palmer's eyes narrowed. "How do you mean?"

"One of my staff, Alexandra, says the bins were all moved around. And now this happened in the same spot."

Palmer chewed it over when she noticed a camera flash in the corner of her eye. She turned and saw the distant students aiming their mobile phone cameras towards the crime scene.

"Thanks for letting me know. Okay, now can you please wait by the door, and tell your staff to stay back. Simmons, can you deal with those students by the library. Keep them out of the way."

"How?"

"Come on. You used to be in uniform once. Stand tall and tell them to keep back. We don't want the whole bloody town getting their eyes on this."

Gary Grayson was dead. And the body didn't yet look cold. Surely, somebody must have seen something. And for his own sake, if nothing else, Hogarth needed to get his arse in gear. Palmer took her phone from her handbag. If Hogarth wasn't taking calls, she hoped he would at least read a text message from her.

Chapter Twenty-five

Hogarth marched up the winding ramp between the three huge tower blocks of the Kingsmere Estate. Andy Cruddas stayed right by his side. There was no way the lad would risk doing a runner here. Criminal or not, Andy Cruddas reeked of having a pampered, gilt-edged life. Left alone, he would have been easy meat for the locals.
"Why are we here?" said Cruddas.
"Because the soup kitchen's open. That's why."
Andy Cruddas shook his head.
"What's the matter? Don't you like soup?" said Hogarth.
"I don't get it. Shouldn't you be taking me to the police station by now?"
"If I were you I wouldn't be in such a hurry, lad," said Hogarth. "The grub in here is going to be haute cuisine compared to what they serve at Southend nick."
At the centre of the platform was the bright-coloured single-storey brick building of the homeless centre known as The Refuge. The Refuge was a foodbank and a soup kitchen and acted as a night shelter once a week. Hogarth hoped he had found them on the right night. Opposite each end of the building was a small square area, edged by a low concrete wall. One square housed a play park for kids which was often littered with discarded syringes. At the other end, the square was empty. In the absence of any other use, its low wall had become a street bench for the troublemakers, street drinkers, and hobos. A few people wearing overfilled backpacks were making use of the bench, necking booze

from their cans as day tilted towards evening. They turned and looked at Hogarth and Cruddas the way a cat looks at a dog. Hogarth didn't fancy dealing with that bunch yet. No, he would try The Refuge first. He looked at Cruddas as they approached the centre and saw the panic in his eyes.

"Ever been to a place like this before, Andy?"

"Never," he said.

"Then think of this as an education."

"Why? What's the point?"

"The point is I'm following a hunch."

"You said you would find my father."

"I made you no promises."

"My father wouldn't be seen *dead* in a place like this…"

"But your father is already dead, remember…"

Hogarth pushed open the door before Andy Cruddas had time to reply.

Inside, a bearded man in fingerless gloves sat by the door looking at a chunky old desktop computer. He wore an overcoat with his coat collar pulled high about his neck. Hogarth couldn't tell whether the man was a hobo or a helper. The steam coming from the man's mug of tea was as thick as smoke from a bonfire.

"Do you work here?"

"Yeah. I help run the night shelter. Can I help you at all?"

Hogarth smiled. He'd picked the right night. During the winter the local churches and The Refuge clubbed together to run an extra night shelter for the homeless who the council couldn't provide for. The man with the beard called down the hall and the centre manager arrived at the door, rubbing his hands. "Yes. How can I help?" The manager looked dressed only marginally better than the man on the door. He looked at Hogarth with fascination. Then he looked at Cruddas with a different reaction. Curiosity.

"Detective Inspector Hogarth, Southend Police," said Hogarth. He didn't bother to introduce Cruddas. If this little mission turned into a disaster, he didn't intend to leave a trail of witnesses saying he took a criminal on a Southend tour before making the arrest.

"We're looking for a homeless gentleman in his late fifties, but he could look older than that. He wears a big parka jacket. A green one with a big fur-lined hood."

Hogarth felt Cruddas watching him at his side.

"Who exactly are you describing here?" said Cruddas.

"You just wait a minute…" said Hogarth. "Well? Does he sound familiar?"

The centre manager shrugged. "Come winter a good few of them wear coats like that, and they all begin to look a bit old when they've been out on the street for a while. It ages them."

Hogarth frowned. "Could we ask around inside?"

"Sure. But it's only the volunteers in there at present."

"But they will know some of the homeless people, won't they?"

"Yeah. Some of them used to be homeless themselves. Help yourself. The volunteers are in the hall." The manager pointed down a blue-carpeted corridor which stretched along the centre of the building towards a wooden-framed security door. Beyond the door was a pale coloured hall. The room was busy with people noisily shifting tables and positioning airbeds on the floor. Steam poured from a kitchen doorway on the right. The thick steam carried smells of curry spices on the air. They passed the door and looked in. A stick-thin figure was stirring two vast steel vats of hot food on the hob. Hogarth's mouth started to water. "Excuse me, chef. We're looking for a homeless guy in his fifties or sixties. He wears a parka coat. A green one."

The stick man looked back at them as he stirred. He was a youngster, maybe as old as Cruddas, but he dressed like a teen.

"That describes about half of the people we get in here," he said. There was an unfortunate arrogance in the guy's tone.

"This is pointless," said Cruddas.

"Until further notice will you just keep shtum," said Hogarth. "You're just lucky you're not in a cell."

The kitchen guy smirked at them like they were good entertainment. Hogarth's face darkened and the youth stopped smiling.

"Look. I only volunteer here twice a month. You need to ask him instead. Steve, the tall guy. If anyone knows who you're talking about, Steve will."

Hogarth peered through the serving hatch into the hall. His eyes found the tallest man in the room, a chap who looked like a total scallywag, shaven-headed and stoop-shouldered, with nasty gold rings all over his hands. Hogarth could tell the man had served time. But volunteering in a homeless centre suggested a reformed character.

Hogarth led Cruddas into the main hall and the eyes of the busy volunteers turned their way.

"Steve-o!" said a chunky man with a goatee beard. "Looks like you've got visitors."

"Oh, have I now?" said the man called Steve. When the big man saw DI Hogarth his eyes turned flinty, before a polite smile slowly dawned. Yes, he looked like a lag alright. The type who knew a copper when he saw one.

"How can I help you gents?"

"We're looking for a homeless man. He's an older type. Wears a green parka. Tall kind of chap as I remember. Does that ring any bells?"

"We have a few like that. Got any other details?"

Hogarth looked at Andy Cruddas. There was no pointing giving the man's real name. George Cruddas would have been an idiot to have used that. So, what else was there? He snapped his fingers. "He'll be well spoken. And if you talk to him, you might get the impression he had money once upon a time."

"There's a few with hard luck stories, to be sure. But well spoken? Posh, you mean? That's a hard one. You know, I can only think of one fella who fits that description. He's not easy to know either. He hasn't bothered with the night shelters since one of the others had a pop at him last year."

"Last year?" said Hogarth. His heart sank. They were talking about the wrong man.

"Yep. He's called Wilbur, but we call him Free Willy, because he only comes here for sandwiches in the daytime. He doesn't bother with any of the rest of the help he could get from us. All he wants is his sandwiches."

"Hmmmm," said Hogarth.

Free Willy. He remembered the homeless man who had been watching them outside the Cruddas house. All of a sudden the man seemed important. But Hogarth felt he was at risk with losing touch with the heart of the case. The further he investigated, the further away from the murder case he seemed to travel. And he couldn't risk another wild goose chase. He was trying to solve a murder. But here it was. His instinct was trying to drag him away yet again. "Do you know where we can find him?"

The tall man looked to his volunteers. "Does anyone know where Free Willy is hanging out these days?" His words were followed by a din of dirty laughter.

"I didn't know you were in the market, Steve!" said one of the jokers.

"I know where he is," said one of the volunteers, who put down the table he was carrying and wiped his brow. "He's started hanging around underneath the canopy by the side of the old JV Sports shop. A few of the guys hang around there, but Willy's a bit different to them. Willy always keeps to himself."

"By JV Sports, you say?" said Hogarth.

"Yeah," said Steve. "The side on Luker Close. Just off the high street. You know it?"

"Yes, I know it," said Hogarth. He looked at Andy Cruddas. Cruddas looked in his eyes with confusion. "What?" said Cruddas. Hogarth didn't reply.

"Thank you, Steve. You've been a great help. Keep up the good work." Hogarth pumped the tall man's hand, then turned for the door. "Come on, Andy. Don't hang about. We've got an urgent appointment with Free Willy…"

"This is absurd. You know my father is hiding up north," said Cruddas, trying to keep up.

"Absurd? Of course, it's absurd," said Hogarth. He walked into the cold air and closed the homeless shelter door behind them. "Everything your father has done is absurd. But we already know he came back to Southend once. What's to say he ever left? He could have invented the gone-up-north idea to keep your mother quiet. Or maybe she made it up herself."

"There's no way my father could handle being homeless He wouldn't lower himself."

"Wouldn't he now?" said Hogarth, stopping and turning around to face Cruddas. "He certainly lowered himself enough to set up a car crash that killed four other people on the M25. And what about you? You lowered yourself to knock out drugs just to save your own skin. No. You Cruddas types wouldn't lower yourselves for anything, would you? Don't make me laugh. See those guys sitting over there?"

Hogarth jabbed a finger towards the homeless men sitting on the wall. By now they were little more than silhouettes holding beer cans.

"Those men have got more integrity than you Cruddas types will ever have."

"And I'm supposed to listen to *you*?" said Cruddas.

"Yes, son, you should – and you will. Because you've got no bloody choice." Hogarth stomped off towards the ramp. A moment later Cruddas chased off after him.

Luker Close, eh? The same little road which housed a nightclub called Club Smart. Maybe it was a coincidence, but Hogarth was a detective by trade. He found it hard to believe in things like coincidence. And, coincidence or not, Hogarth was going to pursue this particular rabbit hole to the very end. Until then Sue Palmer would rub along just fine by herself. After all, nothing much could have happened in the last couple of hours, could it?

Chapter Twenty-six

It was almost four pm when Hogarth and Cruddas reached the middle of the high street. Pure habit made Hogarth's eyes focus on the faces in the high street as he passed them by. It was a rogues' gallery. Between every anonymous face Hogarth caught sight of countless disreputables he'd encountered through the job. He'd almost forgotten what it was like not to see other people as a mess of problems, threats, and danger. And somewhere among them lurked Ali's stalker, another problem blending in with all the rest. The thought made him feel queasy. But Hogarth forced his mind back to the issue at hand, determinedly scanning the streets for one particular homeless man instead of an unknown stalker.

"He's not here," said Cruddas. "I told you that already."

"But what you tell me doesn't count for much," said Hogarth. "The guy in the homeless shelter gave us a steer in the right direction."

"He said the man was called Wilbur. And that helps us *how*?"

"He said the man was seen on Luker Close. Can you remember what else is down Luker Close, Andy?"

He blinked. "Club Smart. But what does that mean?"

"At the moment, nothing. But it soon might…"

They passed a string of stores on the high street. There was some kind of hysteria going on inside the SavaPenny store, but then nothing was unusual in Southend. He'd have to leave that one to the uniforms. They soon reached the big Coffee Italia coffee shop on the corner of Luker Close. Hogarth felt a twinge of anxiousness and excitement. Coffee

Italia's edifice retreated at the side, giving way to the canopy over the side of JV Sports. Pressed low against the window was a scruffy set of well-flattened cardboard boxes, and squashed and torn winter coats with their white linings exposed. The coats had been crushed into pillows, and there was a mess of crushed beer cans and rag-tag belongings left at their side. Hogarth counted three deserted homeless plots. Further ahead and just out of sight was the doorway of Club Smart. Hogarth looked around and wondered about that night. Had he seen Free Willy there that night? It was possible, but he'd been tired and stretched. These days he barely saw the homeless. They were so much a part of the scenery that they faded into the background.

"There's no one here," said Andy.

"Well done, mastermind," said Hogarth. He paced around, checking both ends of the street before he walked to the little kiosk positioned in the middle of Luker Close where it joined the high street. The guy inside looked like a typical, shady market trader. When their eyes met it was like magnetic forces repelling one another, but Hogarth asked his question anyway.

"Do you know where those homeless fellas have gone?"

"What for? You lot gonna bully them again?"

"No one's getting bullied here, pal. I'm trying to reunite father and son."

The kiosk man scratched his balding head.

"I dunno. They go drinking in Warrior Square park sometimes. Could be there."

"Oh..." said Hogarth. But that didn't sound right. Free Willy wasn't a social person. The kiosk man stepped out of his booth.

"Hang about..." he said, looking into the coffee shop window. "One of them is in there. Is that your man?"

The guy pointed through the window of Coffee Italia. A tall man wearing a scruffy green parka was at the front of the queue, ordering his coffee. The hood was down, and he wore a beanie hat underneath. But they couldn't see his face.
"He's homeless. How can he afford those prices?" said Cruddas.
"That place gives the homeless free coffee. And he's always in there, that one. It's like he's their pet or something."
Hogarth walked to the side window, eyes wide, waiting. He watched as the man took his coffee and turned to the side, taking a stirring stick from the condiment counter. Hogarth studied the man's profile. He was ruddy faced, but gaunt. His cheeks were sunken, and his face lined. There was no way he would have picked the man as Andy Cruddas's father… and yet his large eyes, and prominent cheekbones said there was a resemblance. Hogarth stared on. The man turned to pick a seat. Their eyes met through the glass and the man froze in shock. It was the same man who had been outside the Cruddas house. Hogarth didn't need any further confirmation. He moved like lightning, forgetting Andy Cruddas altogether.
"Hey!" said Andy. The young man's eyes landed on the man behind the glass. His mouth fell open and he froze. Andy Cruddas walked slowly into the coffee shop to face a man who should have been dead.

Chapter Twenty-seven

The haggard man in the parka watched as they entered. He stood rooted to the spot, his hands shaking so much that a tongue of black coffee slopped over the side of his white mug. The spillage seemed to wake him up. His eyes flicked across the busy coffee shop towards the doorway in the back. Hogarth read his intentions.

"Mr Cruddas!" said Hogarth, in warning. But he didn't listen. The hobo plonked his mug down on the condiment shelf. He ran past the tables. Heads turned as he buffeted past them.

"What's he done wrong?" called one the coffee drinkers. Another woman called out. "Why don't you leave him alone!"

Hogarth grimaced. These people didn't have a clue. Once again good old human nature was getting in his way.

"Stop running, Cruddas. We need to talk to you," said Hogarth.

"Dad…" called Andy Cruddas. "Dad?!"

The hobo reached the back door first, but Hogarth followed, pursuing him into a dark wooden panelled corridor. The man stopped by a fire exit door looking out onto Luker Close. He put a grubby hand on the fire exit door, ready to push it open but Hogarth was almost upon him, and his lip trembled.

"I'm sorry…" he muttered.

"But it's not me you need to apologise to, is it, George?" he said. "It's all those others."

The old man pushed the door open into the street. As he stepped out, Hogarth wrapped a hand under his arm and dragged him back inside.

"You're not disappearing this time, George. You're coming with me."

"I can't! You don't get it, do you?" said the man, his eyes fearful, his stubbly chin quivering. "Oh, I think I get it, alright," said Hogarth. "But it still ends here." Suddenly the fight went out of him. Hogarth looked back over his shoulder, following the old man's gaze. He found Andy Cruddas staring. There was no denying it now. They were father and son.

"Why don't you come back and finish your coffee, Mr Cruddas? We don't need to make more of a scene than we did already, do we?" Slack-shouldered, the man did as he was bid.

They sat down on one of the tan leather sofas at the very back of the coffee house, getting furtive glances from some of the coffee shop staff and coffee drinkers. Hogarth turned their gazes away with a few choice looks. George Cruddas wilted under his son's unrelenting gaze. He scratched his chin, shuffled in the chair and looked at Hogarth. It was easier to stare at the hard eyes of a seasoned cop than it was to face his own son.

"You know, Andy, don't you?" said the older man. His voice was a whisper.

Hogarth kept quiet. If he played his cards right, there was a chance of a full confession without pushing. "Know what, Dad? Know that you ran out on me? On your family? That you let us think you were dead. Yeah. I know all that right." The older man leaned forward. "But I only did all that for you... so you could continue to enjoy the life you'd become accustomed to. The life you and your mother deserved before I went and ruined it all."

"Don't you dare! Don't you dare play the self-pity card. You walked out. You pretended you were dead. Did you ever think I would thank you for that?"

"Thank me? No. I sincerely hoped you would never see me again."

"But then you came back."

"But I didn't come back for this. I didn't come back to see you in trouble…"

"Then what did you come back for, eh? To watch us? Like we were on some bloody reality TV show where you didn't have to get involved?"

George Cruddas dipped his head.

"No. I came back because I didn't have any choice."

Hogarth tensed, ready to seize upon the words he wanted to hear.

"Choice?" said Andy. "You're the only one had any choice! Seeing you now, knowing what you did to Mum… that the accident was a fake – and about those poor people who died out there in that crash, how the hell can you live with that? Those people were killed because of what you did. You've hurt everyone you touched."

"It was the law of unintended consequences, Andy. I'll have that on my conscience for the rest of my life."

"Seeing you now… I almost wish you were dead."

The old man sighed.

"I know… but this has been worse, believe me."

He had an admission of guilt for the M25 deaths. But Hogarth needed more. He needed the confession for Jake Drummond. Hogarth couldn't hold back any longer.

"You said you had no choice but to come back, George. But you did have a choice. You were invisible. Everyone thought you were dead. You'd won. You could have stayed away and it would have all been hunky dory. But when you showed up at Club Smart a year back you were caught on camera. You blew your cover apart. I don't get it, George. Why did you do it? And a year later you're still here risking your skin, hanging around outside the family home. Tell me, George. Was it a sense of guilt? Or did you come back for revenge, George? Was that it?"

George Cruddas looked at Hogarth with watery eyes and shook his head.

"He found me, didn't he?

"Who?"

"Come on. Who do you think?"

"Jake Drummond?" said Hogarth. George nodded.

"How?"

"Because he was smarter than I ever gave him credit for. He had a true crook's mind. By the time I died in that crash, Jake Drummond had drained me dry. I literally had nothing left to give him, but he still wouldn't stop coming after me. I was afraid he would turn on Barbara. In the last few meetings I had with Drummond, I was already working on my exit-plan. I was jittery. It must have shown. I don't even remember what we talked about. By then I'd confessed all to Barbara and I was suffering in all kinds of ways. I think I started blabbing something to him about an away trip. I mentioned Stockton because it was easy to say. My family lived there when I was young. By then we had a strange kind of relationship. It had even become polite. I hated him, but we still had to talk. Maybe I told him my family hailed from Stockton before, or I let it slip somehow. Either way, a few months passed after I disappeared. I thought I had gotten away with it. Then I saw a notice in the local paper saying a man called Jake Drummond was looking for his long-lost brother. George Drummond. It was a threat, pure and simple. I was terrified because I was sure he would expose me to the police. But that wasn't what he was after, was it? Drummond saw me as a prospect for a better blackmail. He had more leverage on me than ever. The moment I responded to his newspaper ad, I was done for. He told me to send him more money and I did, just once, even though I was skint. I robbed a corner shop to make that payment. But I couldn't go on like that. I came back. I told him it was over… but he wouldn't have it. He made me stay in contact with him, made me send him the pittance I could afford, because that way I was still his. *He owned me.* But if he kept my secret I didn't care. I came back last year because he was threatening to expose me again. I asked him to stop, and he went quiet. But I stayed because I was afraid. I had to keep him calm. How was I to know he was bleeding Barbara dry of the life insurance payout?!

Hogarth leaned forward.

"And how exactly would you know about that, George?" Hogarth scented blood.

"The life insurance? Because I got curious. I wanted to see if all my suffering had been worth it. I used my old pin numbers to look at the online accounts. They worked. I needed to know the money was there. But when I saw what was left, I was devastated. I saw money had been transferred out on a regular basis. Before I even checked where the money had gone, I knew. The money was going to Drummond every month without fail. He'd taken my whole life, and now he was taking the last thing I could ever give my family."

Hogarth leaned forward, lowering her voice. "And that must have driven you mad… this man who had driven you to commit fraud, to fake your own death, to kill others… all you did for your family… then you learned he'd even stolen that. If I was in your shoes, I don't think I could have handled that – not without taking some measure of retribution."

Light glimmered in Hogarth's eyes.

"But it was far worse finding out what he had done to Andy… I begged him to stop blackmailing Barbara… and I stayed close because he wouldn't listen. I kept begging him to stop week after week. It was all I could do. I hoped against hope he would give in, seeing he had taken enough…"

"Was it really all you could do, George?" said Hogarth. "Come on. You spent your time dressed as one of the tramps outside JV Sports, living on scraps, sleeping on pavements just to watch a cruel man siphon your family's money? Is that all you did? Or maybe you were there, biding your time, waiting for the perfect opportunity to end Drummond's blackmails once and for all…?"

George Drummond's eyes flared.

"Drummond knew I was in town, but I was careful. He didn't know I was living on the streets. It was my last advantage. I was able to hide from him in public places… because no one really looks at a homeless person. And I worked out that if kept away from giving my name to the homeless services, I could stay hidden for good. So that's how I did it. I watched Drummond from near and far… and I begged him to stop. But he sneered and carried right on."

Hogarth nodded, urging the man forward with his confession.

"I might have coped with that. But when I saw him driving around with Andy… I couldn't do anything. I couldn't even warn you, Andy. I wanted to, but it would have exposed everything. It would have ruined your mother's life…"

"What?!" said Andy. "You saw Drummond with me? You knew he was pressuring me? And you still didn't even try to help me?"

"Yes, of course I tried. I pleaded with him to leave you alone. I offered him money I didn't have. But he just laughed in my face…"

"That must have been the ultimate insult, George… that must have been the moment when you could take no more. How did you do it, George? Tell me."

The old man looked at Hogarth. He looked empty and spent.

"I know what you want from me detective. But I'm sorry, I can't give it to you."

Hogarth grimaced.

"The lies have to end, George. I've got the shadow of a killer on CCTV, and I want to put a name to that killer. Tell me what you did…"

"I didn't kill Jake Drummond."

"But George… you knew where he was. You knew how he operated… you were in the area. That's motive. You know how to hide, how to get into a sleazy club like Club Smart under the radar. And you'd killed before. The taboo was gone…" said Hogarth, whispering. "Blood was already on your hands. It must have been so easy to cross that line. All you needed to do was slink into that club and hide and wait. You'd become an expert at skulking, hadn't you?"

"I wanted to do it, yes, damn it, of course I did. But I couldn't."

Hogarth blinked. A sinking feeling was taking hold of his gut.

"Where's the knife, George? What did you do with it?"

"It wasn't me. I wasn't even there."

Hogarth shut his mouth tight and gritted his teeth. He leaned back in his seat.
Andy Cruddas shook his head.
"I really don't care if you put my father in jail for the rest of his life. It's what he deserves. But no matter what motive we may have had to hurt Drummond, I wasn't there when that man died and neither was he," Andy nodded at his father. "You thought we worked it together, didn't you?"
The wind had been taken from Hogarth's sails. Both men were guilty of terrible crimes, but they hadn't killed Jake Drummond. He was getting nowhere fast. And a killer was still at large.
"Sorry to disappoint you, detective," said Andy.
"Maybe you didn't kill the man, but I think you may still know who that killer is."
"What? Of course I don't know who it is," said George Cruddas.
Andy Cruddas shrugged. "If I did, then this farce would be over. You're clutching at straws."
"No, I don't think I am. You both know Club Smart very well. And so does the killer. He knew exactly where to find Drummond, he knew where best to attack him. The killer knew how to get away unseen. He knew how to hide his face from the CCTV. I think it's very possible that the killer is someone you know very well. My advice to you, gentlemen, is that you'd better start thinking if anyone you know could fit that bill. Because right now, even without a confession, you two are still my best fit for the kill."
Hogarth sighed and stood up. "I think it's time I gave you both a tour of the station."

He steered them through the doors onto the busy high street and as soon as he got outside, he heard the loud wail of police sirens. They were close. They stopped nearby, just out of sight. Car doors slammed and he heard the sound of running feet. A jab of panic hit Hogarth in the chest. He plucked his phone from his pocket and saw the missed message from Palmer. There was another body. *Damn it! Another one!* And it was just around the corner. Hogarth felt as if he'd been punched in the guts. He looked at the Cruddases, unable to speak. He worked hard to snap himself out of it. "You two. Come with me. Come on! *Now!*" Hogarth pushed both men away from the high street, turning them back onto Luker Close. With Gary Grayson's death Hogarth's theories had come apart at the seams. Another suspect was dead and he was nowhere near solving the case. Halfway down Luker Close, Hogarth saw two police cars parked by the bollard outside Club Smart. He recognised one of the uniforms by the cars as PC Jordan.

"Jordan!" said Hogarth, waving as he approached.

Jordan ran over towards him.

"Sir?" said Jordan.

"Jordan, I need you to put these two gents in the back of a car. Make sure they get taken to the station."

"Sir?" said the cop, confused. Hogarth shook his head. He was in such a panic, he'd almost forgotten. He didn't have time for this, but it had to be done. He gritted his teeth and spoke quickly. "George Cruddas, I am arresting you on suspicion of fraud, obtaining life insurance money by deception and on suspicion of murder."

"Murder?!" said the older Cruddas.

"Murder, George. Remember the four people who died on the M25, George? That's murder in my book. And Andrew Cruddas, I am arresting you on suspicion of possession of controlled substances with intent to supply. Jordan, read them their rights and take them in…"

"Yes, sir."

Hogarth started walking while Jordan took hold of the men. Hogarth stopped and turned back.

"And Jordan – where's the body?" said Hogarth.

"Straight ahead, sir, across the square…behind the SavaPenny, sir."

Hogarth scanned the square until he saw the uniforms gathered by the line of red wheelie bins then he broke into a jog, as a cold sweat formed on his forehead. The case had gone south and he needed a result before another person died and before Melford could steamroller what was left of his career.

Chapter Twenty-eight

"Gary Grayson died with his trousers round his ankles." said DCI Melford. "While you were caught napping."
The antique clock on the wall above DCI Melford's head ticked like a big grandfather clock. Hogarth was sure Melford had only had the clock installed to intimidate coppers during their rollickings.
"Napping? Not quite, sir. I was pursuing another line of enquiry. You'll have heard about the arrests?"
"I know about those, but I want to talk about the Grayson murder. It was broad daylight when Grayson was killed," said Melford. "He was killed in a busy precinct. CCTV or witnesses must have given you something." Melford stared at Hogarth. Melford was a tall, moustachioed cop of the old school. His dark-eyes always seemed to pose an unfathomable question. Most often Melford's gaze made Hogarth feel like he was doing extremely badly at his job.
"We've checked the cameras, sir. CCTV shows Grayson walking towards the wheelie bins behind the SavaPenny – he was alone. Around the same time, we also see a man in a dark jacket and hood walking around the vicinity before the killing and afterwards. We know he's probably a white European, because we glimpse his hands. But his face was hidden. Other than that, there's nothing except that the man is of average build."
"And we have no footage or witnesses for the murder itself?" said Melford.
"No, sir."
"He's white European? That's all we've got?"

Hogarth nodded.

"Well, at least that cuts it down to this continent! What fantastic progress, DI Hogarth! I'll be sure to share your expert insight at the next press conference. Come on! You must have learned something."

"We looked at the CCTV camera footage taken from the library cameras. If we zoom in on the footage, we lose the quality of the picture in pixellation. But even if it wasn't the footage quality, the man is still covered up and he's hiding his face the whole time. He knows those cameras are there, just like he knew about the ones in the club. The killer knows this area well, sir. He's done his homework and he's smart."

"Smarter than all of us, evidently," said Melford. "So, the suspect, Hogarth. Who could it be?"

"There's only a few names left in the hat."

Under the heat of Melford's gaze, Hogarth resisted the urge to tug at his shirt collar.

"A *few*?" said Melford.

"A few, sir."

"And you're convinced the killer is among them?"

Hogarth tried to look certain. He gave an emphatic nod.

"Then work harder and work faster. We need a result, pronto. This man in black. Did you see which way he went?"

"He was walking away from Luker Close, Towards Queens Street, sir. But there was no sign of him on Queens Street CCTV."

"How is that even possible?"

Hogarth shrugged. "The man could have taken off the jacket and hood in the alley before he reached Queens Street. The CCTV just isn't as useful as we want it to be."

"But neither was forensics."

"Not in the Club Smart murder, no. But Marris shouldn't have the same issues with Grayson. The crime scene can't have been compromised like it was at the club – far less footfall there."

"Let's hope so. And what of your disappearance earlier? It's not good enough. You swan off on some rogue mission while the killer strikes again!"

"Sir, I was working flat out to bring this killer in."

"No. You spent this afternoon chasing shadows."

"With respect sir, we've made arrests on charges including fraud, possession, deception and murder, sir. None of it was wasted time."

"But the man killed again, Hogarth. *The man killed again.*"

Hogarth paused and looked away.

"There is something else, sir," said Hogarth. He wondered whether the detail was even worth sharing. In this mood, Melford would likely throw it back in his face.

"What?" said Melford.

"One of the SavaPenny shop workers told DS Palmer that something must have happened at the back of the store a few nights back. She said their wheelie bins had been moved around. It could be nothing, but it's the very same area as the murder. We asked to look at the store's CCTV footage in case it reveals anything."

"And? Have you heard anything back yet?"

"No. We're waiting on it, sir."

"And what about Grayson's murder itself? Were there no witnesses at all?"

"PCs Orton and Dawson asked around the precinct, but no one saw anything. We'll put out an appeal of course."

"Which will make it sound like we're desperate. Which is what we bloody well are! The Record is going to have a field day with us. Not to mention the national bloody tabloids.

They've started calling. I need something to tell them, Hogarth. We need to deliver on this case *now.*"

"We're still following a number of leads, sir…"

"Don't feed me the press lines, Hogarth. I can do those well enough myself."

"Yes, sir."

"DI Hogarth, let me make it plain. *This is on you.* You can't afford any more botch-ups."

"Yes, sir."

Melford leaned back in his chair and fixed Hogarth with his eyes.

"I don't tend to believe everything I hear. I always try to use my experience. But I have been informed by people who know you well that you can be a little *slack and slovenly.* When you transferred here you came in with a decent reputation and that's the copper we need to see right now. Is that clear?"

Slack and slovenly? Who the hell had called him that? Hogarth's face flushed and his eyes turned brooding. Melford must have seen it all.

"Compose yourself, DI Hogarth."

"Sir, with respect, I was pursuing another—

"—line of inquiry. Yes, you said that. But those deaths are ancient history."

"They are two years old, sir, and they were serious crimes," said Hogarth.

"But look at what's become of George Cruddas, since then. He's hardly been living it up in Rio. He's been homeless all this time. The defence will plead diminished responsibility on the grounds of mental health and they'll almost certainly get it. It'll be downgraded to manslaughter. The only murders I care about are the current ones. *I want this killer off the streets.* Now, tell me. Do you think you can handle that? Or should I look for help from elsewhere?"

"We've almost got him. I know it."

"Last chance, do you understand? No more slacking. No more disappearing. No more *anything* except doing your damnedest to bring this killer in. I've got to face the press and I've got nothing to give them but excuses. I'll handle it. But on the very next press conference, I want to tell those bloody hacks that we've taken this killer off the streets. Are we clear?"

"Yes, sir. We're clear."

"Don't let this killer make a fool of you, Hogarth."

"I don't intend to. But I think he's already tried that more than once, sir."

"How, exactly?"

"We found a set of glasses, with blood on them. The glasses belonged to Dan Picton. Marris confirmed the blood belonged to Jake Drummond… but it shouldn't have been there."

"Why?"

"The glasses were found days after the kill. They should have been found before, but the cleaner called in as soon as he found them. I'm almost certain the glasses were planted by the killer. They belonged to Picton, suggesting he was the killer. But we already know it wasn't him."

"Did Marris find any prints?"

"Nothing useful."

Melford snapped his fingers. "The cleaner found them. So, you think it's the cleaner?"

"It's possible but Palmer made him sound like a moron. I don't think our killer is a moron."

"Don't let your assumptions get in the way here."

"There's no chance of that. We'll look at the cleaner too."

"And if not the cleaner, then who?"
Faces and names flicked through Hogarth's mind. Peter Deal. The cleaner. Gordy the barman. But none of them had the same clear motives as Andy and George Cruddas. A new thought took hold in his mind and Hogarth frowned.
"What is it?" said Melford.
"It's motive, sir. Drummond had sworn enemies in all directions. Everyone the man knew had motive to want him gone. But Gary Grayson was a nothing but a cheap lothario. The only people he wound up were women, sir."
"Women can kill too. Maybe woman is the killer, after all. The man in black could be another dead end. What about Grayson's partner?"
"Alison Craw? She has motive, but not the means or the opportunity. She wasn't there. It's not her."
Hogarth looked away, his eyes narrowed.
"Out with it," said Melford. "You've got something on your mind."
"Gary Grayson, sir. His murder just doesn't fit."
"Why not?"
"The trousers pulled down like that. It's a cheap and nasty stunt A comment on his personality. There was no such gimmick with the Drummond murder. The man was stabbed to death and that was it. The kill was very minimal and efficient. This murder is showy, excessive."
"Go on," said Melford.
"I think it's like the glasses, sir. I'm beginning to think Gary Grayson was another diversion. The killer is trying to tell us that this murder is a very obvious punishment killing. An eye for an eye, and all that. I think he could be trying to muddy the waters, to mess with how we're reading his motive."
"He wants us to misread his motives?"

"It's possible. Grayson's murder could be another attempt at deception. He wants us to consider the Drummond killing and the Grayson killing as part of a pattern. Like he's punishing them for their sins. I don't buy it. Drummond was killed because he was ruining someone, sir. It was revenge. It was a way out. The killer is trying to take our eyes off that with the second kill."

"A murder as a diversion? That's a very dangerous assumption. Don't stake your career on it, DI Hogarth. Or mine."

"No sir.

"Get me the killer. And make sure it's the right one." Melford looked away, and Hogarth knew the meeting was over.

"Sir," said Hogarth. He stood up, nodded, and retreated from Melford's office. Slack and slovenly, eh? But whatever Melford thought of him, Hogarth knew he was onto something. Grayson's death didn't fit with the first kill, though it was clearly the same killer. The killer was smart, but not as smart as he believed. He wasn't subtle about his misdirection. The glasses had been clumsy and obvious. In its own way, the showy Grayson killing was even worse. Hogarth chewed on Melford's warning. Yes, it was risky to draw conclusions about a killer from one kill, but wasn't it more dangerous also to be misled?

Hogarth walked into the CID room to find Palmer poring over the files, while Simmons stared at a computer screen showing the shadowy image of the Club Smart bar.

"Seen anything new Simmons?"

"Just the same things," said Simmons, shaking his head. Hogarth decided to take a fresh look for himself."

"Tell me again. Who do you see?"

Simmons shrugged and rewound the footage and set it to play again.

"Okay. Here goes. I can see Peter Deal in the crowd there. Drummond obviously. Gary Grayson is there at one point but not for long. He is given a drink then leaves the scene."

"Anyone else we know?"

"Not really," said Simmons. "We see the club owner, Milford, moving around behind the bar, giving orders to the barmen. Then he's gone out back. We see Peter Deal at the bar for a while. Then he's gone too Then there's just this shadow passing the camera a moment after Drummond is hit and the crowd disperses as he falls."

"The shadow. Can we get a better look at it?" said Hogarth, staring at the blur.

"No chance, sir," said Simmons. "Look at it. It's a blur. That's all it is."

Hogarth watched the shadowy blur pass the lens. The blurred head seemed to look away just as it came past.

"He knew where that camera was, the blighter. Look at him dip his head!" said Hogarth. "I swear he knew where the camera was when he topped Grayson today."

"Guv?" said Palmer, looking up from her files.

"The man is a strategist. Not a great one, but he's an expert in the cameras, that's for sure. The killer knows we're used to using CCTV and he's worked bloody hard to avoid getting caught by it. The man in black who walked away from that murder today. Did we get any more on him – any witnesses?"

"Dawson interviewed plenty of people," said Palmer. "But no one remembered much about him, or where he went."

Hogarth chewed on an idea, but it felt risky. It was too early, too fresh, too raw. He shook his head. He couldn't take a risk like that. Not yet. Because Melford had it in for him, they needed to play it by the book.

"Our man knows these cameras. Palmer, what do you think?"

"You're on to something. He is cautious. He's CCTV savvy. So why the open air kill today?"

"To show us he's boss? For a bit of drama? Or to send us a message."

"What message?"

"That's the thing," said Hogarth, dropping his backside into a chair. His eyes drifted to the image of the blur on the screen.

"I think this was another piece of his strategy. Like the glasses with the blood, this is another misdirection. Our killer wants us to believe something which leads us away from the truth. Where's he trying to lead us?"

"To the idea of a serial killer maybe?" said Palmer. "With Grayson he looks like a killer who punishes people for their sins."

"Yes, an avenger type. But that's not what I got at the first kill. Did you?"

Simmons kept quiet. Palmer thought it over.

"No," said Palmer. "Drummond was an evil bastard. But he wasn't killed for some vague grand sin. He was an out and out threat to lots of specific people. He was killed because someone wanted and needed him gone. It was personal."

"Which is why we chased Cruddas and Picton for so long," said Hogarth. "We weren't wrong, about the motive, not in the least. We just had the wrong person."

"Then who is it? You've got an idea, I can see it."

"I'm working on it, Palmer. But we can't mess up because of one of my misguided hunches this time. From here on in, we go by the book. Bring them in one by one. There's only a few names left. Let's give them a going over and see what we get. You know, if Grayson wasn't dead, he'd be my very next man in the hot seat."

"So, who do we pull in, sir?"

"Start with the obvious. Alison Craw. The cleaner. Peter Deal. Bring in the club owner, Milford, too Anyone else we've spoken to. Bring them in. It's one of them. And if we find the motive we'll find the killer. Start with Alison Craw."

Hogarth turned away to leave the room.

"Where are you going now, sir?" said Simmons.

"What's the matter, detective? You think I might be off *slacking* somewhere do you?"

"Um. No," Simmons blushed. "Just wondered… that's all."

"Keep your eyes on that CCTV. The truth is out there somewhere, Simmons."

Hogarth walked out into the open plan office. He wasn't surprised to see PCSO Rawlins perched on the edge of Dawson's desk. Despite the neighbourhood sergeant's constant efforts to steer PCSO Rawlins away from him, the girl was always there. Hogarth mused that the force might as well have bought them a double desk to match the double bed at home. When she saw him approach, Rawlins slid off the desk and stood tall.

"Don't mind me, Rawlins," said Hogarth.

"Sir," said Rawlins.

Dawson looked up. "Yes, sir?"

"Much as it obviously pains me to say, you two have done some good stuff on this case. There's a lot riding on this one. If you could spare the time I could do with your help again."

"Help with what?" said Dawson.

"Why do you think our killer chose the back of SavaPenny to stage his kill?"

"What?"

"Don't worry. That's a question I'm chewing over. But there must be a reason. We've asked the store if we can look at their CCTV footage. I'm going to get Palmer on it, but you two have got ears close to the ground. We heard there was a whisper of a disturbance there a few nights back. I'm wondering if that was the same night as when Drummond was killed…"

"If DS Palmer is on it, what can we do?" said Rawlins.

"Rumours come from people, Rawlins. And you bobbies mingle with enough of the rabble to get something. Have a word with the people on the street. See what you can find, will you?"

Hogarth had given them a rough ride on occasion. But now he needed their help. He gave them a nod of thanks, stuck his hands in his pockets and went on his way.

"DI Hogarth asking for a favour?" said Dawson. "Melford must have put a proper rocket up his backside this time…"

Chapter Twenty-nine

The first murder got attention, but the second murder was off the scale. Killing Jake Drummond had been fodder for the local rags. But the national media had given it no more than a mention. But putting an end to DJ GG worked out even better than he'd hoped. From luring the man to his death, to the epic coverage. The local news interviewed distraught club-goers, friends, and hangers-on who were in tears. They were people who never gave a damn about him in real life. People who actively didn't like him, and their crocodile tears made him angry. He liked the coverage and the attention, but those liars made him furious. They made him so angry that his eyes passed over the blade on the mantelpiece more than once.

He'd never been a killer before Drummond… and after Drummond he'd never intended to kill again. But Grayson had been a useful kill – and pulling the man's trousers down by his ankles had been another nice touch. Yes, he could be smart when he wanted to be. But deep down he also knew he was kidding himself. He was becoming hooked. Smart people got addicted too.

The killing had become fun.

The hiding. The sport. Just like the thrills of old, when simple pleasures were all he needed. But after the release of removing Drummond, he'd needed to get another high. So, he'd planned it well. But it turned out Grayson had already done most of the plotting for him. Why did he take that slut behind the bins that night? Because Grayson knew the street cameras and knew the bins would hide his exploits. Grayson was another kind of addict and he had made it his business to get away with philandering on an epic scale. And because Grayson was an expert in choosing the best secluded sites to have his way, he had known the place was perfect for the kill. It was so easy to arrange. A handwritten note from an unknown girlfriend left where he would find it. A sex-junkie with a chance of getting some cheap thrills behind the shops. Even when he was sober, even on a cold grey day, Gary Grayson was always up for it. Easy. He'd taken the note back from the body, so it had never existed. Easy. The killing added a layer of confusion and misdirection he was proud of. Yes, proud.

But he didn't like the sense of need in him returning so soon.

He couldn't become an out-and-out killer. He had too much to do. He was a businessman. A smart man. He wasn't a psycho. So why was the urge coming to him again, so soon? But as a smart man, he already knew. It was all about the highs. The adrenaline. He had always loved his highs, and this one had taken him as high as he could get. *The thrill of the kill.* The words brought a smile to his lips, but now he felt as much fear as he did joy. And the fear was what he was capable of. Once the taboo had gone, what was left to stop him from doing it again? He was becoming a big game hunter, beginning to get a taste for hunting the biggest game of all. But he was scared of being caught. It fuelled his study of the media, and made him analyse every single word.

He flicked the channel to the local news to watch the police press conference. A tall, thickset man with receding brown hair and an old-school police moustache sat at a desk holding some stapled sheets in his big hands. He looked up at his audience with a glassy eye. As the cameras flashed and the journalists coughed in the audience, the policeman's words came out slow and heavy with police authority.

"Today police discovered the body of a local man dumped behind one of our high street shops here in Southend. We can confirm another man has been murdered. The victim, Mr Gary Grayson, was a local nightclub DJ, a man well known in the town, and well loved by people in the local club scene and friends and family alike. Police are now investigating the time and circumstances of his death and we wish to communicate to the public in the strongest terms that we will stop at nothing until the man who killed Gary Grayson is brought to justice. Initial reports suggest that this second killing was very probably carried out by the same person who killed Jake Drummond just a few days ago at a local nightclub. These murders are very local to each other. Within a couple of hundred yards and the same method was used for the killing. It is possible these victims knew one another. Today, we have a very simple and very clear message to the person carrying out these heinous crimes. You may think you are being clever. You may think you are getting away with it. But you should be aware that with every act you are providing us with information that is leading us to you. We have reports of a man in a dark hood walking away at pace across the square towards the high street around the time of the murder between 3pm and 4pm yesterday afternoon."

The warnings had bothered him. What had he done that he hadn't considered? Someone had seen him walking away from the scene, but no matter. He had been well disguised. No one would have *really* seen him. But what about the forensic evidence? He recounted the scene. There had been no struggle. Just a chat. A cosy little chat – and then the knife went in, and he had taken back his note. Grayson's face appeared in mind. More shocked than pained. Then then man fell down, and it was over. Fingerprints? None. He was sure of it. He had been careful. Blood on his clothes? Not possible. They had been cleaned and washed and tumble dried. So, what else? Nothing. The police were bluffing. They would never find his knife. So why did the senior cop seem so confident?

He couldn't kill again. He saw it now. They were triangulating the murders. They were drawing inferences from the locations. If he did kill again, it would have to be somewhere far away. No! No more killing. The proximity of the killings had given them hope, and given them ideas. But that was all they had. Which meant they had nothing. But the fear was rising in him. He thought about killing. *Maybe another kill would do it? To lure them away?*

No. He was becoming addicted. The addiction was misguiding him, and he needed to resist. The man got up from his seat, and scratched around the dark living room for a pad and pen. He sat down, and began to think. Then he started making notes of the things – and the people – who he needed to be prepared for. The curveballs he couldn't control. One by one they surfaced in his mind. He started to list them and with each one he felt an idiotic spike of fear. Damn him, he'd not been thorough enough. But at least he could be thorough now. He wrote their names. He rated the risks. Thank God, he was smart and streetwise. Yes, he was still ahead of them. And he would make sure that he stayed ahead all the way. Because if he didn't stay ahead, there would be hell to pay. And he wouldn't be the only one to pay it.

Chapter Thirty

Alison Craw was pale faced and drawn. Gone was the look of the modern day Boadicea. The fire had gone out of her eyes. The moment Palmer brought her into the interview room, Hogarth saw there was hardly any point interviewing her. But she was a busy woman and he respected her. She had older children. She was trying to set up a business. Hogarth didn't want to confirm he had wasted her time by sending her home too soon. "How are you?" said Hogarth.
"How do you think?" said Alison Craw.
"Fair point," said Hogarth.
"Why am I here?" she said, as she sat down at the interview room table. "You still can't think I'm a suspect?"
"It's part of the process, Mrs Craw. We've got a man who's killed more than once. He could kill again unless we get hold of him. We have to be thorough."
"You should have caught him before this," the woman snapped. "It's too late now, isn't it?! Whoever did it has ruined what was left of my life."
Hogarth nodded. "I understand how you feel, Mrs Craw, but I still need your help."
"My help? What help can I possibly give you now?"
"I need you to think about who Gary knew well. Who he knew best of all. People he liked and people he didn't like."
The woman shook her head and offered a bitter smile. "Why would any of that help anyone? You should be out there looking for him, not in here interviewing the people left behind."

Hogarth frowned as he thought about how to say it. Palmer was with him. Shame she couldn't read his mind. Hogarth had no choice but to say it himself.

"Look, Mrs Craw. People have many reasons to commit murder. I don't believe the motives in this instance were the same as the killing of Jake Drummond."

"Of course they weren't. Drummond was a blackmailing bastard. The only thing Gary was ever guilty of was being a drunken idiot."

Hogarth sighed and got ready to say it. His eyes settled on the glint of light he saw there.

"They found Gary with his trousers round his ankles, didn't they?" she said.

"Yes... but how did you know about that?" said Hogarth.

"I watched the press conference with your DCI Melford on TV. One of the journalists asking questions said they'd heard about it. She wouldn't leave it alone. Forget the fact he'd been killed, it was his bloody trousers she was interested in..."

Hogarth knew who that was. Alice Perry from The Record, it had to be.

"It hurt, but not any more than losing him. I knew Gary was a louse. I knew he was a stupid, cheating sod but somehow I managed to pretend to myself that it wasn't happening." The woman looked at DS Palmer sat beside him.

"Now you think I'm the stupid one, don't you? But for all his many, many faults... he was my idiot. I loved him."

"Please, Mrs Craw," said Hogarth, "we need your help. Tell us about the people in his circle. Who did he tell you about? And who did he hate most of all?"

Alison Craw sniffed and covered her mouth with a hand before she composed herself.

"Gary liked to impress people. He was friends with everyone. The bouncers, the bartenders, the cleaners… you name them, he was friends with them."

Hogarth nodded for her to go on. "He got on well with the other DJs, and the club owner John Milford."

"Milford," said Hogarth, looking at Palmer. "We should speak to him, Palmer. Make a note. And the security too."

Palmer made some quick jottings at his side.

"The only person apart from Jake Drummond – the only person I remember he didn't like was Peter Deal."

"Peter Deal?" said Palmer, looking up from her pad. "But why? He seems harmless enough."

"Does he? Well seems harmless and being harmless are two very different things."

"Can you explain?" said Hogarth.

"Peter Deal was always trying to make an earner here or there, never satisfied with his lot. I don't know the ins and outs, but the man was always on at him about some past business they had together. Something that went wrong between them. I never knew what, but from what I heard about Peter Deal, it's likely to be with one of his previous wheeling and dealing operations."

"Mr Deal has a history of starting new businesses then, does he?" said Hogarth, catching Palmer's eye.

"I met Peter on the only night I went to that awful club. He was there, talking about how he was going to get rich. Gary told me that the man was always talking like that. That he was an idiot and it would amount to nothing. Later on that night, I saw them having words. It looked heated alright. I asked Gary about it later and he told me it was about one of his past ventures. I guess Gary had to have been involved somehow…"

Hogarth nodded and narrowed his eyes. "Thank you, Mrs Craw. That's been most helpful. Is there anything else you can think of, before we let you go?"

The woman shook her head. "I don't know why he killed Gary, but believe me, it had nothing to do with an affair. The trousers round his ankles was more of an insult to me than anything else."

"An insult to you?" said Hogarth.

"Not to me directly. They did it to shame him and because of that, they shamed me. You should start with Peter Deal. He's the only man I know who didn't like Gary."

"Peter Deal. We know they didn't get on, Mrs Craw, but do you really think Deal had any reason to kill Jake Drummond?" said Hogarth.

"Come on. Who didn't?" said Alison Craw. Soon after that, they let her go, but Hogarth and Palmer stayed talking at the interview room table.

"What do you make of that?" said Hogarth.

"Peter Deal couldn't have done it," said Palmer. The man's a fool. He would have left clues all over the place."

"A wise man can appear a fool when he needs to," said Hogarth. "Which could mean DC Simmons is a genius in disguise."

Palmer smiled.

"But back to Peter Deal…" said Hogarth. "Alison Craw suggests the man is a serial entrepreneur. That's certainly a new take on the man. But if so, this arrangement with Drummond could have just been his latest gambit. Deal paints himself as a mechanic who struck lucky, not a late-blooming Alan Sugar. Whatever his problem with Gary Grayson, it clearly didn't play out well. If Peter Deal had learned that Jake Drummond was taking his money with no prospect of return, Deal would have had plenty of reason for doing in Drummond. But Grayson? That sounds extreme to me, even if they didn't get on. But Deal was caught on the CCTV footage at the bar. Not in the act of murder, but he was right there when it happened."

"If Deal isn't a simpleton, he certainly had me convinced," said Palmer.

"Maybe he is. But what if his latest business venture included Picton's drugs business? Drummond could have been blackmailing him about that, too. How's that for motive?"

"But you heard Grayson mocking Deal's arrangement with Drummond back at the start… that doesn't sound to me like Deal and Drummond had a falling out. As far as Deal was concerned the Drummond business was going ahead."

"Agreed. Okay, so Deal didn't want the man dead. But we still have this bad blood thing between Peter Deal and Grayson," said Hogarth. "Alison Craw knew about it, but we need to know more. Grayson had a past with Deal. We need to know what it was. We need to get Deal brought in here pronto. I bet you could get him in here. The way you described his reaction to you last time, I dare say he'd follow you anywhere…"

"You've become expert in flattery, I see," said Palmer.

"A silver tongue saved for the right moment. Okay. Go and bring in Peter Deal. And take Simmons with you. I think his brain could do with an airing."

"Yes, guv…"

Hogarth lingered in the interview room after Palmer had left. He paced the room with his hands planted deep in his pockets, his thoughts drifting between the murders. The differences and the similarities. The location was still a big factor binding them close together. Forensic evidence had been thin on the ground, and as yet, the SavaPenny people hadn't provided the CCTV. If one of those things came in, there was a chance the culprit would be unmasked. Until then it was back to interviews and pressure on the suspects. The killer was playing them, disguising himself by sending them in all directions. The bastard was enjoying himself and getting cocky too. Hogarth had the feeling either another kill or some evidence would soon come to light, but there was no knowing which would come first. Either way, he knew his career depended on it. If the case went against them, Melford was ready to hang him out to dry.

Even so, Hogarth found his mind drifting to Ali Hartigan. Her soft face and her lovely brown eyes. Ali was vulnerable and alone while her stalker was somewhere out there with dark intentions unknown. A stalker who might yet kill. Hogarth stopped pacing the room and grabbed up his blazer from the chair. Maybe a drive would make things clearer. Yes, a drive would sort him out. Then he could check in on Ali on the way. Hogarth moved fast hoping to avoid Melford as he left the station.

***

James Hartigan MP lived in one of the big houses on the road winding up from the Thorpe Bay seafront to North Shoebury. As he drove, Hogarth looked out over the roofline of the beach huts towards the wide silver Thames, before he took the left turn up the slope of large houses towards North Shoebury. Hogarth knew the man would be in London. With his government's narrow majority, James Hartigan would certainly be in Westminster, earning brownie points with the Prime Minister. Or he would be busy humping his secretary. Either way, it gave Hogarth the licence to act. He slowed as he passed the fancy house with the topiary and manicured lawn. He saw they had installed net curtains. They were new. Ali was not exactly a net curtains kind of girl, but at least they would give her some protection from being snooped on. Hogarth doubled back down the road for a last drive-by on his way back to the office. As he glanced at the house he caught a glimpse of movement within. A shadowy jerking movement which disappeared as fast as he had seen it. Hogarth frowned. He slowed the car, pulled over sharply and took a breath. His eyes flicked to the street around him. There were plenty of cars around, but very few pedestrians. He considered leaving it there and driving away. Ali didn't want him to come knocking like this – in fact, she had warned him against it. But what if she was in danger? What if she was struggling with the stalker while he dallied at the roadside? His worrying was down to the case, of course. It had sullied his mind with thoughts of risk, blood, and danger, but Hogarth still couldn't risk it. Ali was in his care. Hogarth blinked at himself in the mirror then got out of the car and took another look around. One man was walking up the hill passing Ali's house. But the man passed it by without looking. There was no one else in sight. Hogarth double-checked the driveway for signs of the husband but his Jaguar wasn't on the drive or parked on the street.

He heard some loud music coming from the house. Ali didn't like stuff like that. She was a thinker, a romantic, and an introvert. She liked peace and harmony. Hogarth sped up. Reaching the house, he moved to the edge of the big cinematic front window. He peered in through the net curtain, but saw nothing. There was a loud *thud-thud-thud* from inside. Hogarth knocked loudly on the door. "Ali! Ali!" He rang the doorbell. But there was no answer. Lastly, he moved to the side gate. Reaching over the top, he slid the sliding bolt and pulled the gate open and moved around the back patio. There was the kitchen window and the back door. He plunged the handle, once and then again. It didn't budge. It was locked. Hogarth considered breaking the glass, but decided to knock once more. He knocked. Once. Twice. Three times. Still no answer. He stepped back into the garden, considering where best to strike the door to make sure it gave way. His eyes fixed on the door handle area and took aim. How the hell was he going to explain this one to Melford? And who bloody cared anyway? Hogarth started his short run up. In the very moment before he kicked the door in, he heard a window open and a female voice came to him from above.

"Joe!" He looked up to see Ali. Her hair was tied back. Her cheeks were pink and glowing. "What are you doing here?" Like a guilty schoolboy caught in the act, Hogarth looked up at her without an explanation.

"Just wait there," she said. Don't move." She closed the window and disappeared.

A minute later Ali appeared at the back door. She opened the door and looked at him. He took in her attire. She was in a black and pink Lycra leotard over a black body suit. He'd never seen her dressed like that, but Hogarth was the one who felt ridiculous."

"You really need to lock your gate, Ali…"

"And you came here to tell me that?" she said.

Hogarth shook his head and Ali smiled. Her eyes sparkled. "You came here to check up on me."

Hogarth nodded. "I saw movement inside. I heard loud music. Then banging. I thought the stalker had got in."

"I was doing my Bodyfit DVD."

"Oh, I see. That explains the, ah, the um, outfit, then."

"You weren't supposed to see me in this," said Ali. "Not ever," she added with a grin.

"Well. It's very snug, isn't it?" said Hogarth.

Ali shook her head at him. "You shouldn't' have come here. James might even have the neighbours watching me."
"And now here I am watching you too."
"You? You watching I wouldn't mind so much… "Ali stayed inside the doorway but beckoned Hogarth towards her with a grin. She stayed where she was just inside the doorway and when Hogarth came near she gently steered his face towards hers and they kissed. The kiss lasted long enough to tempt him further, but Ali seemed to sense it and broke away.
"That's because I know you care. But you mustn't come back here like this. We can only meet away from here. If you want to check on me, please just drive by."
"I did drive by. I couldn't see anything, thought something had happened…"
"Please Joe, I'm fine. You'd better go."
Hogarth nodded. "Call me. Let's organise something soon."
Ali gave him a smile which warmed his whole body and she squeezed his hand.
"Fine. Now go…"
She closed the door and waved at him from behind the glass. Hogarth lingered on the patio as she withdrew inside. He sensed movement somewhere nearby, and he glanced up and caught something in the window of the house next door. By the time he looked, all sign of movement was gone. The window was empty. Hogarth shook his head and walked away, closing and locking the gate behind him. He walked out to the street and looked around and saw nothing.
When Hogarth got back in the car his eyes tracked over the front passenger seat. He saw his mobile phone lay on the seat, begging for a thief to take it. He saw the screen was bright with another missed call. Melford's face filled his mind and he grabbed the phone. The call was from the nick,

but there was no telling who from. As he looked at the number, the phone rang again.

"I missed your call," said Hogarth with a careful, cagey voice.

"Sir. It's Dawson. You wanted us to do a spot of digging about the incident at the SavaPenny store?"

"Yes?" said Hogarth.

"We've got something. I think you'll want to hear this for yourself."

Something had come in. *Hogarth prayed it was something good.*

Chapter Thirty-one

"Where did you find her?" said Hogarth, the heels of his brogues thudding on the tiles as he walked past the reception desk at the station.

"We were asking questions out front of the SavaPenny store," said Dawson, walking at his side. "The store was closed of course, what with Marris and forensics being out back. But PCSO Rawlins knows plenty of the local characters from the communities around the Kingsmere and Talbot Estates. But to be honest, sir, we didn't really find her… she came to us."

Hogarth could barely wait to reach the interview room. They had found a crack in the shell of the case which had threatened to never break. But with the national media spotlight now upon them there was still a chance the woman wasn't who she claimed to be. Hogarth had needed to keep his feet on the ground. He could not afford another mistake with Melford scrutinising his every step

"And do you know her?" said Hogarth.

"No, sir. But Rawlins recognises her from night patrol on the seafront. Says she's seen her face in the pubs."

Hogarth nodded. "Okay. Let's see what we can make of this. Could you tell DS Palmer where I am. I'll need her with me in there…"

Dawson nodded and made off through the main office. Hogarth walked into interview room 1. He found a woman with shor,t peroxide-blonde hair drumming her fingers on the table. When she saw Hogarth come in, she didn't stop. Instead she scratched at the table with her finger nail.

Hogarth watched her for a moment, wondering if she knew he was there. She glanced up at him.

"Don't worry. I'm not damaging anything. Someone's marked it. I'm trying to scratch it off. It's like paint or something."

"Very considerate. Most people who come in here would prefer to wrap that table around our heads."

"But I came to see you…"

"Apparently so. Davina. That's your name, right?"

"Davina Brooks. Yes."

"Hello Davina. I'm Detective Inspector Hogarth…"

The door creaked open behind him and DS Palmer nodded as she entered the room.

"And this is Detective Sergeant Sue Palmer. DS Palmer this is Davina Brooks. Apparently, she's got something she'd like to tell us. You saw our officers outside the SavaPenny store this afternoon, didn't you, Davina?" Hogarth pulled out a chair and sat himself down. Palmer followed suit.

"That's right. They were asking people if they knew anything about what happened there. The murder and all that. I walked past at first, because I knew something… but not about what happened when he was killed. I really didn't know anything about that…"

"Then what do you know about?" said Hogarth.

The woman carried on picking at the table. She spoke hesitantly. "I didn't want to stop. I wasn't sure I was ready for all that."

"Ready for what exactly?" said Hogarth.

"Ready to talk about what happened between me and Gary, the DJ."

Now the woman had his attention. Hogarth watched and waited.

"What happened, Davina?"

Hogarth watched the woman's eyes tear up. She blinked and looked away. "

"Davina. Miss Brooks," said Hogarth. "Whatever you came here to say, please, now is the time to say it. Our resources are stretched, and we are working against the clock to prevent another killing. If there is something you know, you need to tell me now so that I can do something with it. Now please… what do you know?"

"I was there last Friday."

"Where, Davina? The SavaPenny?"

"No. Club Smart," she said, lifting her eyes to his. "And I was there again on Monday night."

"The night Jake Drummond was killed."

"The bastard…"

"I don't get it. What's your relationship with Drummond? Was he blackmailing you too?"

"No. I never met the man until last Friday night. And I never wanted to meet him ever again after that."

Hogarth nodded for her to go on.

"I'd been talking with Gary Grayson, that night. We'd had a right laugh. He invited me up into the DJ booth with him and he even let me spin a couple of tunes. We had a few drinks. After that, he invited me behind the scenes. We had a good time. To cut a long story short, I let things go a bit further than they should have. He asked me to come with him for a walk."

"A walk," said Hogarth. But he knew what she meant.

The girl nodded. "I was drunk, so I went with him. We walked around the corner from the club and we got as far as the back of the shops when we started kissing. Which was okay, but then he was all over me like a rash."

"Gary Grayson?"

"Yeah. And I should have stopped then, but I felt like I'd led him on. So, I felt obliged to go a little bit further. Before I know it, we're… you know. We laid down behind the dustbins at SavaPenny…"

Hogarth looked towards Palmer and she got the message. The interview was going into a sensitive area. Hogarth shifted back in his seat, and Palmer leaned close to take the mantle. "Davina, would you be more comfortable if we continued our chat without DI Hogarth in the room."

"It doesn't bother me. He's the one leading this thing, isn't he?"

"That's right," said Palmer.

"Then he might as well stay. He needs to hear this."

"We were in the middle of it all when I heard someone coming towards us across the square. It put me right off. I tensed up and told Gary to stop, but he wouldn't listen. He was drunk, and he was a bloke and he was too far gone. He told me I was imagining it, but I knew I wasn't. Gary only stopped when the guy appeared behind him and called him out. The bloke called him, and Gary leapt off me and pulled his trousers up. I covered myself as best I could and crawled back to the bins, but everything happened so fast and I was drunk. But as soon as I saw the man I knew there was something dark about him. The way he looked at me, it wasn't right."

"Who was it, Davina?" said Palmer.

"It was the man who got killed before Gary did. The big sweaty, horrible monster of a man. Balding, yet hairy. Smelt of bad cologne and curry."

"You're saying this man was Jake Drummond?" said Hogarth.

"Yeah. That's his name. I knew his ugly mug from the club that night, but only from a distance. Gary told him where to go, but he didn't try too hard to chase him off. In fact, Gary looked scared of him. He threatened Gary, like a veiled threat. But Gary wasn't having it at first. He argued back. But then the big man showed him something – I didn't know what it was at first – but after that Gary changed. He didn't argue any more. When Drummond snatched it back I saw it was a little white card. I don't know for sure, but it was the shape and size of a photograph."

Hogarth glanced across at Palmer. She gave him the slightest nod of recognition. The photograph of the child found on Drummond's body. So, it wasn't his child after all. It was one of Grayson's. Of course it was. The only photograph of a child Drummond was ever likely to carry was one he could use for blackmail.

"Did you have any idea of what the photograph might have depicted?" said Palmer.

"No. I've no idea."

"Then what?" said Hogarth.

"Gary turned cold and he started walking away. I mean, he didn't look back. He just walked away, and then this awful, sweaty, great big lumbering horror of a man came at me. I was cold and scared and half naked already. I had no chance. I tried to scream but he covered my mouth with his hand until he was done with me. I should have bit him, I should have fought back, but I was in pieces…"

"To be clear, Miss Brooks. You were raped by Jake Drummond?" said Palmer.

The woman nodded as tears ran down her cheeks.

"I'm glad that man is dead."

"Did you ever see Gary after that? Did he ever mention wanting to get even with Drummond after that?" said Hogarth.

"Oh, I saw him alright. But he wouldn't look me in the eye. He knew what he'd abandoned me to."

"If Grayson was alive at this moment, I'd be utterly convinced that he killed Jake Drummond," said Hogarth wearily.

"But it wasn't him," said Davina Brooks. Hogarth shifted in his seat and looked at Palmer.

"What? How do you know?" Hogarth's heart started to race.

"Drummond had covered my mouth… he had my head pressed to the floor, but I was awake and alert. I lived through every bloody second of what that man did to me. He pressed my face to the floor, so I had a good view of freedom. I could see through the gaps between the wheelie bins. I saw people walking past on the other side, drunk, shouting, happy and ignorant. They were all going about their business, but I saw one man wasn't moving like the others. I saw him when it started, standing in the middle of the square. He was watching as Gary was walking away. He wore dark trousers, dark jumper, a hat or a hood, I wasn't sure, but the radio said you were looking for a man like that and I knew it was him. He was looking my way that night. He couldn't have seen what was happening, but he knew all right, and he did nothing either. I swear he knew what was going on. Just after Gary walked away so did he. He was after Gary then, I swear. That man… *that man is your killer.*"

Hogarth stared at the woman, checking her face for lies. But her eyes backed it up.

"And did you see him go?"

"Eventually, I think he moved off, back towards the college and the high street I think."

"Towards Luker Close?" said Hogarth. "Where he went is important, Miss Brooks. It gives us a chance to work out where he came from."

"Yes… he went back towards Luker Close."
"Was he old or young, tall or short?"
"I couldn't say, detective. Tallish maybe. I was a little bit distracted at the time."
"Yes, of course you were. Can you think of anything else about the man? Anything at all?"
"He was a white man. And he was looking straight towards us through those wheelie bins. Isn't that enough?"
"A tallish man…" Hogarth's mind began to flip through the suspects in his head. Several faces came and went, but one lingered more than all the rest. "*Tall…*" said Hogarth. "Yes, that might just be enough… DS Palmer. Would you take the rest of Miss Brooks' statement? There's something I must attend to very urgently…"
"Sir?" Palmer gave him a quizzical look, but Hogarth ignored it. He bolted up out of his seat and moved for the door. He paced back to the CID room. Simmons looked up at him from the CCTV images as he came in.
"Where's the file on the Drummond murder?" said Hogarth.
"On Palmer's desk. She's been through it ten times over. Like I have with this."
Hogarth ignored Simmons, but Simmons kept talking. "There's nothing new here. Nothing we haven't seen before." Hogarth rifled through the open files on Palmer's desk until he found what he wanted. There between the notes, witness statements and reports from forensics and pathology, was the little white card they'd found on Drummond's body. There was the child, small and pudgy with a little mole on its chin. It was held in a veiny white hand with a ring on the finger. Back then they had thought the hand belonged to Drummond. But they had been too quick to make assumptions. The hand was too thin, too hairless to belong to Drummond. And, as if a man like him

could have ever loved a child! The villain was utterly self-centred to the last.

"But I did notice one thing."

"Oh," said Hogarth, almost absent-mindedly as he studied the photograph. He looked at the hand.

"The shadow which crosses the screen… there's like a little bit of light around the edge of it. Just at the back," said Simmons.

"Hmmmm," said Hogarth. The ring. Now the photograph was important he needed to know about the ring. He should have recognised it. *Had Grayson ever worn a ring like that?*

"The more I look at that shadow, the more convinced I am that his head is reflecting light from the bar… if I'm right, sir, that guy would have to be bald or shaven-headed."

Hogarth looked up from the photograph.

"What?" he said.

"Sir?" said Simmons, taking note of the determined energy on Hogarth's face as he studied the image. "I think the man in the image here is bald. The shadow we've been looking at all this time. If he's the killer, our man is shaven-headed or bald."

"You're sure?" said Hogarth.

"After staring at this screen, I'm not sure of anything anymore. But I'd wager I'm right."

Hogarth's eyes flicked left and right. Yes, it fitted with his latest thinking. Tall. Bald or shaven-headed… but something didn't fit. What about the photographs? The children. Hogarth couldn't afford to be wrong again. "Good work, Simmons. Check again. I want you to be doubly sure about this."

"Yes, sir."

"We're close, Simmons, very close. PCSO Rawlins met with Gary Grayson shortly before he died. Rawlins said she saw a photograph of a woman with children lying on his office floor. It fell out of his jacket in the office at the club. We need to find that photograph, Simmons. Do we have Grayson's belongings or are they with forensics?"

"Marris and forensics still have them, sir."

"Call Marris. Ask him if there was a photograph of a girl and some children in with Gary Grayson's belongings. And ask him about a ring too. Was there a ring on Grayson's little finger?"

"Yes, sir."

"Tell him we're closing in on the killer. I need to know these details right away."

"I could call him now. You don't want to wait?"

"No. If the killer realises there is any value in that photograph, it could disappear. I'm hoping it's still there. I'll go now. Just let me know what he says, okay?"

"Of course." Simmons picked up the phone as Hogarth made his way out.

Two minutes later, Hogarth was in his Insignia, heading for the cold black hole that was Club Smart.

***

The main entrance doors of Club Smart were ajar, and Hogarth walked inside. He pushed open the inner doors of the nightclub and found the little old cleaning man pushing a noisy cleaning machine around the dance floor. The room was as ugly, garish, and bright as on the night of the murder. The cleaner looked up at Hogarth as he passed him by, heading towards the double doors at the back.

"Excuse me, mister," said the cleaner "But the club is closed."

"You don't say," said Hogarth. "Where is Gary Grayson's office?"

"Gary's dead," said the old man.

"I'm with the police," said Hogarth. "Grayson's office please."

The old cleaner nodded. "Turn left out there. It's the last door on the left. But it wasn't just Gary's office. It was used by everyone."

"Has anyone else used it since Gary Grayson?" said Hogarth.

"The acts and the DJs use it. But no, Gary was the last one to use it…"

Hogarth moved on without a word. He stomped down the corridor and found the last room down the hallway. He tried the door handle but found it was locked.

"He could have bloody told me it was locked," muttered Hogarth under his breath.

"Can I help you?" said a voice. Hogarth nearly jumped out of his skin but did his best to disguise it. He looked round and recognised the man from the night of the murder. Tall, shaven-headed like one of the bouncers, but without the meat and muscle, the club owner, Milford, was leaning out of another door into the corridor. Hogarth's eyes glinted as he saw the man. He noticed the glow of a strip light reflecting from the top of the man's head.

"Detective Inspector Hogarth," said Hogarth. "I wondered if I could take a quick look around this office. To see if there was anything Gary Grayson left behind. You don't mind, do you?"

"I doubt it," said the man. "It's a shared office. I let the entertainment use it – whoever's in. GG was only here three nights a week. He usually took it all with him."

Hogarth nodded. "But do you mind – just in case?"

The tall man shrugged and pulled a set of keys from his belt.

"Do you know who this bastard killer is going to target next?" asked the man, as he unlocked the door.

"Not yet, sir. You're the owner, aren't you?"

"John Milford, yes. I own Club Smart."
No, Mr Milford. We don't know who the killer is. But we're definitely closing in. In fact, we could probably do with you answering a few questions later on."

Milford pushed the door open. "Okay. Whenever you like. There you go. All yours. What sort of questions do you have in mind?"

"At this moment, Mr Milford, I couldn't tell you. But it really feels like this case is starting to progress."

"Good," said Milford "It's bad for business apart from anything else."

"I'm sure," said Hogarth.

Hogarth moved into the room and walked to the desk, recalling what he had already heard about the photograph. He should have brought Rawlins with him. Without her here he would have to scratch around until he found it. He dropped to his haunches and started to prod around the dirty carpet, staring into the corners of the dingy room. But he didn't see anything of use. He stood up and pulled at the desk drawers. Old nightclub flyers, a screwed-up penalty parking notice, chewing gum, and a couple of unused condoms still neat in their foil wrappers. Hogarth flicked the worst mess out of the way, but found nothing in the first drawer. He slammed it shut and opened the second one, before he realised John Milford was still in the doorway watching him.

"Don't let me keep you, Mr Milford. You must have plenty of other work to do…"

"It's a terrible business," said Milford.

"Murder always is," said Hogarth. Beneath some cigarette papers and scrapings of tobacco he found a smooth piece of white card. He flipped it over and found the image he'd been looking for. Two young children bouncing on the knee of a

young woman who seemed both pretty and yet hollow eyed and world weary. Her smile seemed strained. Children could do that to people. As could being Grayson's other woman.
"But every now and then we get a little closer, Mr Milford and then hope appears," said Hogarth.
"Hope?" said Milford. His eyes flicked to the photograph. "What about that gives you hope?"
Hogarth slid the photograph in his pocket, hoping Milford hadn't seen it. "You knew Grayson well, didn't you, Mr Milford?"
"As well as most. He had his secrets. Looks like you've just found one of them."
"Maybe," said Hogarth. "You never know."
Milford nodded. "What, the kids in the picture there. You think they were Gary's? Poor kids." Hogarth's face darkened. "I think they could be. But that's just a theory at present, Mr Milford. I'll have to take it for the investigation. That okay with you?"
"Of course," said Milford, as Hogarth moved out of the room. "And there's nothing else you need?"
"Not until later. But keep your phone on, Mr Milford. *Just in case.*"
The big man nodded and locked the door as he watched Hogarth go.
Hogarth's phone rang as he past the cleaner. The strange old man gave him a look as he walked by. Hogarth returned the look as he answered the phone.
"I found it, Simmons…" said Hogarth, speaking again before Simmons could answer. "… and tell Palmer to get ready. I'll pick her up. I'm taking her to meet someone special."
"Oh, really?" said Simmons, getting excited at the gossip. "Any news?"

"Yes, sir. Marris didn't have the photograph, but he did say something about a ring. He'd logged it, but said he hasn't got the thing. Pathology still have it at the moment."

"Damn it. I need to know."

"I took the liberty of calling Doctor Ed's office. I got through to the technician."

"And? Don't keep me in suspense, Simmons…"

"They have a small ring which was worn on Grayon's little finger!"

Hogarth gritted his teeth in grim smile of victory. "Yes. It's Grayson. The photo in Drummond's pocket was of one of his children."

"And that's good because?"

"It closes down one part of the mystery. Drummond's leverage for blackmailing Grayson was his children."

"What about the killer, sir?"

"It's part and parcel, Simmons. We're closing in. Tell Palmer to get ready."

He could smell the arrest. They were almost there. But they still weren't close enough.

Chapter Thirty-two

Hogarth buzzed the door of Peter Deal's apartment long and hard. He wasn't in the mood to be kept waiting. Davina Brooks had given them a new insight. The photographs of the baby in Jake Drummond's pocket matched the baby on the image of the mother with the two children and Grayson's ring proved he knew the children. They were almost certainly his. Poor kids. But even if their father had lived, Hogarth doubted life would have been easy for them. Now it was going to be even harder.

"Yes?" said Deal over the intercom. Hogarth eyed Palmer as they listened to the man yawn. It wasn't yet late, but Deal sounded ready for bed.

Hogarth nudged Palmer so she would do the speaking.

"Hello, Mr Deal. It's me, DS Sue Palmer. I just wanted a little word with you. If you don't mind…"

"What? Oh, DS Palmer, no I don't mind. No, I really don't mind at all. Come right up."

"Thank you, Peter. "

She waited for the buzz and the door clicked open.

"I just wanted a little word with you…" said Hogarth, as he imitated Palmer.

"Worked though, didn't it?" said Palmer, as Hogarth followed her up the stairs.

Deal looked decidedly nonplussed as he dropped his backside into the middle of his sofa. He picked a stray baked bean off his supper plate and popped it into his mouth. He chewed angrily. The smell of a beef and onion pie was thick on the air. Hogarth hadn't eaten, and his stomach gurgled.

"I suppose I should have mentioned DI Hogarth was with me," said Palmer, sitting down.
"Yes, you really should have," Deal said coldly. Hogarth leaned over his knees and caught the man in his stare.
"Don't worry, Mr Deal. You could always arrange another visit, I'm sure," said Hogarth, feeling Palmer's eyes on him. "But we're here on business."
"Yes. Now it's Grayson," said Peter Deal.
"So, you know he's been murdered."
"Around the back of that cheapy shop on the high street. The paper said the man was caught with his trousers round his ankles."
"That's The Record newspaper, taking a very serious crime and turning it into a sordid news story. Mr Grayson's body *was* found with his jeans pulled down. But it appears the body was probably staged that way by whoever killed him. The killer wanted to make a statement."
"A very apt statement, is what I'd say. That man was always at it. I told you people before."
Palmer nodded.
"You didn't like Mr Grayson one bit, did you?" said Hogarth. "The night when Jake Drummond was killed, Grayson was overheard mocking you for your business deal with Mr Drummond."
"Come on. We've been through that, haven't we?" said Deal, addressing DS Palmer.
Hogarth ignored the comment.
"Gary Grayson was rude to you. He patronised you frequently, didn't he? I'll bet he made you feel a fool. But tell me, why would Grayson go out of his way to do that, Mr Deal?"
"Because he was a prat. An arrogant no-mark. A no-account waste of space. The truth is that he was a drunkard with no

future, anyone could see that. Me? I've always tried to make the best of myself. People like him are jealous of people like me. I'm a trier. What was he?"

"He was killed, Mr Deal," said Hogarth. "Is that the point you were trying to make?"

Deal shook his head. "Uh. No. Not quite."

"So, what were you saying?"

"That I didn't like him. But I wasn't the only one, was I? The drink gave him a blabbermouth, but he did a lot more than drink."

"Oh?" said Hogarth. "Like what exactly?"

Peter Deal scowled and folded his arms.

Hogarth changed tack.

"You're a bit of an entrepreneur, aren't you, Mr Deal? I had you down as a standard grease-monkey who'd gotten fed up of hard work. But now I have you down more as a Dragon's Den type. Or maybe just a Southend Del Boy. I'm not sure which."

"What are you getting at?"

"Sticking ten grand with Drummond was a gamble, but it wasn't your first, was it? You've been quite understanding about the fact Drummond cost you so much money."

Deal shrugged.

"What other businesses were there, Mr Deal?"

"Other businesses? What do you mean?" said Deal.

"Gary Grayson told his girlfriend that you were always starting new ventures. Always looking for an angle. She'd seen you arguing with Gary Grayson at Club Smart on the one time she visited. When she asked him about your little row, Grayson gave her the impression that you were arguing about a business project you'd both been working on. From the sound of that argument, I'd say the project went badly wrong. Public recriminations mean bad blood."

"Lies!" said Deal. "That's a downright lie! What kind of business dealing would I have with a man like that?! I remember that woman. The double-glazing woman. I wondered what the blazes she saw in a man like that. I wanted to warn her off, but it wasn't my place."

"What were you arguing with Grayson about if it wasn't about a business interest? We'd love to hear your version of events."

Peter Deal clammed up and looked away.

"Are you telling us that Mr Grayson's partner lied about your argument with Gary Grayson?"

The man shook his head.

"Then what are you telling us?"

"I didn't kill Gary Grayson and I didn't kill Jake Drummond. End of story. You're barking up the wrong tree."

"That wasn't my question. But since you're changing the subject, so will I. Think about it this way. Someone comes to you with a proposition. Here it is. You provide them with space, you turn a blind eye, and you let them run a little import/export business for you. Who the hell cares what they sell, as long as you make the money." Hogarth leaned forward. "Dan Picton and Andy Cruddas will go down for possession with intent to supply the drugs haul we found at your old garage. Now what I want to know is whether you should go down with them. They say possession is nine tenths of the law, Mr Deal. And I'm afraid they're right. Those drugs were in your garage. The letter of the law means that ignorance is no excuse. You're virtually bang to rights, Mr Deal. I could make your life very difficult if I wanted to, whether you were complicit or not."

"No! That wasn't me! That was Picton, wasn't it? That's why he wanted access all the time. But I said no. I'm innocent."

"Of course, but the law might say otherwise. I think the CPS would go for it, don't you DS Palmer?"

Palmer gave a nod.

"I don't like your attitude," said Peter Deal.

"No, not many people do, Mr Deal," said Hogarth. "And it only gets worse. Maybe you should share some facts to get this moving in another direction."

"Facts. What facts?"

"You had a serious beef with Grayson and we need to know what it was. And we need to know now. There's a killer out there, Deal. Don't waste my time or I will make sure that I waste plenty of yours, are we clear?"

Deal stayed stiff for a moment. Then the man unfolded his arms and looked at his hands.

"I did have a beef with him. You know that."

"But we don't know why."

"You already know what he was like. He was an awful philanderer. The very worst kind of man…"

A buzzing sound started to come from Deal's armchair. He looked around, then shifted his backside and dug into the cushions beneath him. He lifted the phone and squinted at the screen. Deal's eyes flicked to Hogarth and Palmer.

"Take the call. Then answer the question."

Deal nodded. "Yes? What do you want?" he said. As he took the call, Hogarth's eyes narrowed. It sounded as if the man had almost lost his voice. "Y—yes?" he said, straining.

"But why?" said Deal. He looked away from them, his eyes staring down at his lap as if he wanted his own private space. "You can't do that. No. No. You don't need to… okay. Okay. Yes…"

The call was over. Hogarth studied Peter Deal as he lowered the phone to his lap. He watched Deal's string neck swallowing. He kept his eyes averted like he preferred to be alone in his own distant world.

"Mr Deal," said Hogarth. "We're still here, remember?"

The man nodded, but only looked up once the nodding was done. He looked weak and fragile.

"What's the matter with you?"

"Nothing. You should go."

"Mr Deal, you've still got questions to answer, and we still have a killer to catch."

"I can't answer anything else, I'm tired. I'm very, very tired."

Hogarth looked at Palmer and she raised an eyebrow.

"You're in trouble yourself, remember. I'll take you down to the station if I must, Mr Deal."

The man's voice stayed quiet.

"You'll arrest me?"

"If that's what it takes."

"But you know I didn't kill them."

"The drugs, remember. Mr Deal?"

The old man withered another degree and sank into his chair.

"Who called you just now" said Hogarth.

"What?"

"Just now. Who called you?"

"It was nothing. A business matter, that's all."

Hogarth stared at the man and Deal stared back.

Hogarth produced the two photographs from his blazer pocket. Deal watched him uneasily.

"Please take a look at these photographs, Mr Deal."

The man shifted in his chair and stretched out to reach them. Hogarth kept them close enough that Deal had to come near before he could collect them. So near Hogarth could read the man's eyes as he saw their subject matter. He watched the old man's eyes flare wide, his lips quiver. Then he looked at Hogarth, and drew back.

"Why are you showing those to me?"

"Because, Mr Deal. *Because*. You're holding out on us, Peter. And because of that, we're going to have to take you in."

The man grimaced. With lips tight sealed he stood up and put his plate aside. He pulled on a jacket and grabbed up a hat. Hogarth noticed that his trousers, jacket, and hat could all be described as dark. But by now, he wasn't at all convinced that Deal was his man.

Hogarth pressed Deal down into the back of his Vauxhall and shut the door. He leaned over the roof and spoke to Palmer as the busy traffic rushed by.

"We need to know who called him," said Palmer.

"Absolutely. That call shut him down. And did you see his eyes when he saw those photographs. He knows those children, Palmer. I swear it. And if he knows them, that gives us another clue. Look at Deal's family, Palmer. See what you can find."

Hogarth's phone began to buzz as he drove. Palmer offered a hand to take the call for him, but Hogarth shook his head. His mind was wired with the chase. He wanted every detail first-hand himself.

"Sir."

"Simmons," said Hogarth. "What now?"

"It's Marris, sir."

"Good. Has he got anything for us?"

"There's no rogue blood or DNA behind the SavaPenny, sir. Nothing conclusive like that. But they found a boot print. Like a Chelsea boot."

"Carry on."

"It doesn't fit the staff profile. It's a size eleven. The staff are women, sir, most of them have feet less than a size eight."
"Size eleven is close to a yeti, Simmons. Drummond? Do we know his shoe size?"
"I checked it, sir. He was a nine."
"And Grayson?"
"I spoke to pathology about that. He was a nine as well, sir."
Hogarth looked at Palmer with another fleeting grin. "Good work, Simmons. Did we get anything back on the shop's CCTV?"
"They got back to us. They've found the right footage, and are sending it across today. They said it doesn't show any faces, just the backs of a couple of guys. From the description they gave it could show Davina Brooks, but it's the same old story. They knew where the camera was and hid their faces. But at least someone left that boot print, eh?"
"That could be enough. Well done."
Hogarth's eyes flicked to the rear-view mirror. Peter Deal was watching him. He held back his smile as he ended the call.
"You know, Palmer, I think Simmons is beginning to earn his keep. Forensics found a rogue footprint by the wheelie bins. A large footprint by a man who wears Chelsea boots. Size elevens, too. I'd say a man who wears boots like those has to be tall, wouldn't you?"
"Then we're getting closer…" said Palmer.
"Much closer. But we're not there yet…"

Chapter Thirty-three

The phone he used to call Deal was the very same one he had used for his unpleasant dealings with Jake Drummond. A burner phone to keep identities hidden. But now he had used it to call Peter Deal, the phone was tainted once and for all. He could use it no more. He dropped it onto the tiles of his kitchen floor, raised a sturdy boot and slammed it through the middle of the device. The back of the phone came off easily, and out spilled the green circuit board and the sim card holder. He dropped his boot on it again, crushing the life out of the circuit board. If he was being thorough, he should have done more. But time was running out. The police chief on TV hadn't been lying after all. They *were* closing in. He'd been smart enough to keep an eye on the other suspects. He'd had to think one step ahead, like playing a game of chess. It was hard work and he had to spread himself thin, but his work had paid off just in time. He'd seen them haul Peter Deal out of his apartment block and watched DI Hogarth stuff the man into his Vauxhall. He was coming to hate that cop. But he had options, desperate options. There was always the knife. If he was going to lose everything he had worked so hard for, maybe he should take a cop with him. Even if he did, the worst he would get was life behind bars. And from the little he knew, most prisoners respected cop-killers more than any other. He supposed they would at least leave him alone. If he had to go to prison, then yes, he would have to kill a cop first. He grinned. Such thoughts would have been unthinkable a while back, but now they came easy. But they were still desperate thoughts. And for now, he still had options.

But none of them were perfect – because he had made a mistake.

He had made a slip of the tongue.

And now his lover had become a liability.

Even now he saw a way out, but if he was to do this, everything had to go his way. Because if it didn't, bloodshed was his only course of action. Bloodshed of the worst possible kind.

.

He picked up his knife and slid it into his jacket. He really wasn't ready to kill. He didn't have the rest of his equipment with him. But there was no time for that now. He had to put the rest of his plan into action, otherwise Peter Deal's fool mouth would tell that cop everything else he needed to know…

***

"Our finest interview room, Mr Deal. Tell me. What do you think?"

Peter Deal sat in the plastic chair across the table from Hogarth beside a solicitor who looked well past his use by date. Deal glowered faintly and kept his mouth firmly shut. Hogarth was all set to joust, but time wasn't something he could afford. Melford was on the prowl and had already peered through the glass once. Palmer was looking at Deal's family and friends and he'd entrusted Simmons with the job of looking at Peter Deal's phone. The last call Deal had received was of great importance. It was the call that had caused him to shut his mouth. Jake Drummond was dead, but someone out there was still pulling strings. Once he could discover who that was, Hogarth was sure the whole case could be closed.

"Comfortable? Cosy? No. I don't think so either," said Hogarth. "They fitted out this room a few months back and it already stinks of stale breath and pissed pants. The memories, eh? If you want to, you could spend a little time in here, or a long time. It's really up to you. The shame is I had you down as a nice man. Someone who'd been used, walked over. A bit silly, but generally a nice bloke. But now I'm not so sure. So, which are you? The nice guy or a villain?"

"My client's moral standing is not up for debate here," said the aging solicitor. Hogarth did the old man a favour and ignored him.

Deal shook his head, but Hogarth saw wild emotions flicker in his eyes. Something was troubling the man.

"You were very talkative back in your flat. You were about to tell us all kinds of things. I'm sure you were. Then that phone call came in, and you clammed up as tight as Fort Knox. Why is that, Mr Deal?"

The man looked up at him then looked away.

"You don't have to say anything, Peter," said the solicitor. Hogarth had the feeling the men were old friends.

"Who called you, Peter? What did they say?" said Hogarth. "They upset you. I saw it happen."

No response.

Hogarth shifted forward on the table.

"Okay then. Let's talk about those drugs. That's what we're here for, after all. Shall we talk about those legal highs you had stashed in your drug factory?"

"Drug factory?! My garage, you mean!" snapped Deal. "I knew nothing about them. It must have been Picton. How was I to know he was doing that rubbish?"

"Peter…" said the solicitor.

"Ah. Good to know you can still talk, Peter" said Hogarth. "But hardly convincing. Would you like to discuss the kind of stretch you might be facing for stashing all those drugs like that?"

"My client is not guilty. Those drugs were placed there by trespassers," said the old man.

"Trespassers? You're a solicitor, sir. Surely you know that's not an adequate defence."

The old solicitor looked troubled.

"Come on, Peter. You know Dan Picton. You were going to offer him a job in your import/export business. You told us that. Doesn't sound so clever though now, does it? Life can get complicated very quickly, can't it? I'm not sure a court would believe you knew nothing about it."

The solicitor squirmed and hid it with a cough.

"Or perhaps you'd prefer to help us find a killer, Mr Deal. I'd be grateful if you did. All you need to do is open your mouth and talk. Then maybe we can look favourably upon the misunderstanding about Picton's drugs. We need to stop this man, Mr Deal. He's a menace. *Do you understand what I'm saying?*"

Peter Deal looked Hogarth in the eye. Hogarth saw the man was struggling. It was all about the phone call. He needed to know who'd made the call…

***

Simmons jotted down the number of the last caller on Deal's mobile. It wasn't such a hard job as it sounded. Deal didn't

even use a pin code lock so everything was there for the taking. Which was handy. The trouble was the last caller's number had no name attached to it, so Simmons took the number and laid it aside. Out of curiosity he scrolled through Deal's recent phone calls. In the last week, there were three calls from someone called Sandra, and Deal had called her back once a ratio of three calls to one? Whoever she was, Sandra might have been a pest. Prior to that there were calls from Daniel P – it had to be Picton – and a week before there were calls from Peter Deal to Jake Drummond. Simmons was well up to date on the business between Deal and Drummond. The call list suggested Deal was doing all the chasing and Drummond was avoiding his calls. Which made sense. Hogarth and Palmer surmised there was some sort of poisoned relationship between Deal and Grayson. But the phone call records suggested otherwise. Grayson wasn't even listed as a contact and there were no calls to or from his number. Simmons grabbed the notes on Grayson from Palmer's desk. She didn't even look up. She was engrossed in something, squinting at a sheet of paper with a telephone pressed to her ear. He found Grayson's number and double-checked it in Deal's phone. He was right. Grayson's number drew a complete and total blank. The men may have known each other, but they had few dealings. Simmons shot Palmer a glance. She lifted her head.
"What?" she said.
"You thought Grayson and Deal conducted some business together, right?"
"Alison Craw told us that. She said Grayson offered her some line about them having a business arrangement which had gone wrong."
Simmons shook his head. "Someone lied. Either Grayson or Mrs Craw."

"Peter Deal said the same. Well, I know who I'd put my money on. Grayson was a habitual blagger. How did you know?"

"They never called each other. Not on Deal's mobile phone. I'd say that means they didn't have any such arrangement. Whereas with Drummond – Deal's phone shows he was forever calling the man. It underlines the fact there was no arrangement between Deal and Grayson."

Palmer nodded. "So, what was there between them? Something that Grayson wanted hidden?"

"Grayson was as dodgy as they come," said Simmons. "You got anything on the Deal family yet?"

Palmer shook her head. "Not yet. I've tried the easy stuff. Social media and all that, but he's got no web profile. A bit old school is our Mr Deal. I'll try council tax records or the electoral roll next… that might give us something."

"Hold fire on that. A name cropped up on his phone a few times in recent calls. Sandra. There's no surname, so she's either a close friend or family."

"Well, she's definitely not Deal's girlfriend. I can vouch for that."

"How come?"

"Both times I've been there I thought he was going to propose marriage."

Simmons grinned. "Maybe you should be flattered?"

"Please! His leery face almost makes me want to become a nun."

Simmons raised an eyebrow.

"Almost," said Palmer. "You were saying?"

"Sandra. I'll give you her number. If you call her and play it right, you could get what we're after…"

"Yeah, it would save on a lot of donkey work. But why don't you call her?"

"Come on, DS Palmer. You're a woman. It'd work better coming from you."

Palmer shook her head. "Okay. I'll give it a go. Keep digging through that phone. Let me know what else you can find…"

Simmons scrawled down the number for Sandra and handed it to Palmer.

As she dialled the number she wondered how to play it. But the phone was answered before she had decided. Palmer heard children at the other end before she heard anything else. Noisy, happy, and very loud. In stark contrast, the woman who came on the line sounded weary and depressed.

"H-hello?" she said. The word was drawn out longer than necessary.

"Hello. Is that Sandra?"

"Yeah. Who's this?"

Palmer racked her brain. In her position she couldn't lie, because there was a chance it would come back and haunt her. Instead, she sidestepped the question. "I'm just trying to track down Peter Deal, but I can't find his number…"

There was a half second pause at the other end, filled by the ear-splitting screech of a playful child.

"Peter? That's my dad. Why? What do you want with him?"

Palmer smiled. "Oh, your dad. How funny! Sorry to bother you… I must have got my wires crossed somehow."

"Who is this?" said the girl. "How did you get this number?"

As Palmer tried to extract herself from the call, she heard a jarring noise – a loud thudding at the other end. *Thud, thud, thud.* At the other end, the girl called Sandra sighed.

"Wait a minute will you," she said.

Palmer heard the girl groan with effort as she heaved herself out of her chair, and heard another subtle soft thud as the phone was dumped on the cushion. She listened to the girl's footsteps moving away from the phone. The kids continued to whoop, laugh, and play. There was some more thudding, and then Palmer heard a door creak open. Words were spoken rapidly, but all of them were hidden beneath the sound of the children. Oh well. The visitor had given Palmer an easy way out of that one. She ended the call.

"Bingo. Sandra is his daughter and it's odds on that she'll be the girl in the photograph. Nice one, Simmons. Come on. Hogarth should know about this right now."

"Yeah…" said Simmons, distractedly.

"What is it now?"

"I think I found something else. It could be nothing, mind. It's a small world and all that."

"What?"

"Deal has had regular phone calls with John Milford. It's here in his recent calls. Sometimes Deal will call him, occasionally Milford calls Deal…"

"But the last call Peter Deal took…?" said Palmer.

"Was from a pay-as-you-go phone. Totally anonymous."

Palmer walked to the whiteboard with the first important names they'd taken on the first night after Drummond's killing. Milford's name was there, halfway down the list. From the state of the first few letters it looked like his name had been almost wiped off and they hadn't even interviewed him yet.

"Milford, the man who owns Club Smart, remember. Then who knows. It could be nothing. Come on. I want to give Hogarth the news about this Sandra. I can't wait to see the look on Peter Deal's face."

As Palmer left the CID Room, Simmons frowned at the almost-wiped name of John Milford.

Palmer pushed into interview room one without knocking. Hogarth was staring at the men opposite, waiting for an

answer to one of his latest demands. He looked up grudgingly towards Palmer, as if she had stolen his thunder.
"Yes?"
"Thought you might want to hear this one, sir."
"Is it for public consumption?"
"I think so."
"Then fire away."
Palmer looked at Deal as she spoke.
"Mr Deal has a daughter and I've just spoken to her. And unless I'm very much mistaken, I believe she has a couple of young children."
Deal's eyes flashed with panic, and his mouth formed a circle exposing crooked teeth.
"You spoke to her?"
Palmer nodded.
"And she's okay?"
"Of course. Why wouldn't she be okay, Mr Deal," said Palmer.
"No reason," said Deal shifting in his seat.
"You've looked extremely uncomfortable ever since you took that phone call and now you're looking shifty again," said Hogarth. "Mr Deal. I am going to ask you a direct question and I want a proper answer."
Hogarth took out the photographs of the children and laid them on the table. He slid them across the desk. "Do you know these children?"
The man looked at his solicitor. They exchanged a brief but meaningful look. Hogarth saw that the solicitor certainly recognised them.
Deal looked back at Hogarth, then made a pleading look to DS Palmer. "You're very sure my Sandra is okay. She sounded totally fine?"

Palmer nodded. "She sounded tired maybe. At the end of the call, I heard she had a visitor."

The man's face changed. His skin pallor turned grey and his mouth became a straight line.

"A visitor…?" he said, shrinking in his chair.

"Mr Deal. Do you know these children or not?" said Hogarth.

"Yes," he said. "I know them."

"How?"

Deal shook his head even as he answered the question. His voice wavered in his throat.

"They're my grandchildren. They're my Sandra's children. Anthony and David…"

"Good. Very good, Mr Deal. And you knew Gary Grayson was their father, didn't you? That's the reason for your very public spats. Grayson had an affair with your daughter and left her uncared for like all the rest, except he left your Sandra pregnant with his own two children. To you it was a dereliction of his parental responsibility that irked you most, wasn't it? That's why you hated the man…"

Deal's eyes flashed darkly, but his skin stayed pale.

"I can't say a word."

"Why not? Gary Grayson's dead. So why can't you just say what you think?"

"Why does it matter what my client thinks? He's already answered your question."

"From the look on Mr Deal's face I'd say it matters an awful lot. One more question, Peter.

Perhaps the most important question of all. Do you know who killed Jake Drummond?"

"No. I told you that at the beginning." Deal's words finished abruptly as if there had been something more to say. And Hogarth knew there was.

"That's semantics, Mr Deal. Word play. You'd like to avoid this question, wouldn't you? But you can't. Do you know who killed Gary Grayson?"

"I didn't... not then..." he muttered. He looked at his solicitor friend. "I swear it..."

"But you know now, don't you?" said Hogarth.

"I mustn't say..."

Hogarth looked into Deal's eyes and saw the raw panic mounting. The trembling of his jaw. His eyes widened, and he turned in his chair.

"Palmer, this man's daughter is in grave danger... we need to find her address now."

"You can't! You mustn't!" said Peter Deal, hands beating down on the table as he shouted and floundered.

"Mr Deal. Someone is blackmailing you in the worst possible way, and it isn't Jake Drummond. Drummond is dead. So, who is it? Who called you? Who told you not to speak to us?"

"The man's got money. He's successful. I was pleased when they got together. I thought my prayers had been answered. I mean, I knew he could be moody, but I didn't ever think... never would I have thought..."

"Who?"

Deal looked at Hogarth and he almost read the name in the man's eyes. He saw the face of John Milford, inquisitive, friendly. The man who appeared as soon as he wanted access to the nightclub office. Milford, who enquired about the photograph of the children and why it gave him hope.

"If you want us to be able to save your family, Mr Deal, you won't dare waste another second, or I'll personally see to it that any and every charge we can bring against you will be brought and thoroughly pursued to prosecution. Do I make myself clear?"

Tears welled from under the man's eyelids and he broke like a dam.

"Yes, yes… okay. I'll tell you. Sandra lives at twelve Dalton Drive, North Leigh. Near the school off Manchester Drive… please don't let him hurt her. I'll have nothing without her. Nothing."

Hogarth nodded and grabbed his jacket. He stormed out of the door leaving Palmer in his wake. She followed him through the office. Hogarth slid his blazer on and hurried past the desks.

"Who is it, guv?"

"John Milford. Those killings were so close together we should have known. He's tall. He knows everyone involved. He knew where those cameras were because they were his cameras…"

The uniforms looked up from his desk as he passed by.

"Dawson, we could have a situation on our hands at twelve Dalton Drive," he said to PC Dawson as he passed.

"What kind of situation?" he said.

"An abduction, a siege, maybe even another murder. We need to be prepared for the worst," said Hogarth. "Come on, Palmer. This could turn nasty…"

"Sir?" said Simmons, across the office. "Do you need me?"

"Yes, Simmons. You've been coming through with the goods. I need you to get John Milford's address. It should be chock full of evidence. Call Marris and see what you can find. I think we're going to need forensics in there…"

***

Simmons knew witness contact details had been taken the night Drummond was killed. Dawson and Rawlins had done all that, and passed a list to Palmer. But scrabbling through the notes and files on Palmer's desk, he still couldn't find them. DC Simmons knew he had a bad rep on the team. Sometimes they made it so obvious. And it was out of that spirit he had complained about Hogarth to DCI Melford. It was a chance meeting. He'd seen DCI Melford at a local curry house, and the DI had asked him how he was getting on. Simmons should have kept his mouth shut, but he didn't. The DI had been berating him for so long and Palmer sometimes joined in. The bad feelings were there, so close to the surface, that it all came out. And so, Simmons had given the DCI his real feeling about Hogarth's policing methods and had regretted it ever since. But here Simmons had seen an opportunity to turn things around. There were glimmers of hope. And yet here he was again, with luck turning against him at the worst possible time. *Trust me to fail at the first hurdle,* he thought. If he couldn't even manage the basics, he would certainly deserve the next roasting which came his way. But Simmons was determined not to let anyone down. He stopped searching through Palmer's desk and started thinking. He knew Milford ran the nightclub under a well-known company name, Milford Enterprises. The firm which owned Club Smart had to be listed at Companies House. He checked with a quick web search and found the right company along with a whole list of other firms under the Milford name. An online search showed various addresses listed with each company, but only one address was repeated consistently. It was the address of an accountancy firm in Benfleet, six miles out of town. Why was nothing ever easy? Simmons took a moment, and tried to assume the air of a professional detective as he made the call to the accountant. The truth was his confidence had taken a knock and he needed to nurse his way back. Hogarth was a cop who enjoyed the hard knocks that went with the job. The gallows humour, the sarcasm, and all the banter. But as time went on, the jokes at his expense had started to weigh on Simmons. Yes, he was sometimes clumsy with his words, sometimes a little slow on the uptake. But he had always been a trier, until now. But Hogarth had caught a glimpse of what he could do, and he intended to show there was even more beneath the surface.

"Gulshari Accounts. Good afternoon?"

"Good afternoon. My name is Detective Constable David Simmons. I need to speak to someone about one of your clients. John Milford of Milford Enterprises. Can anyone help me at all?"

"I'm sorry," came the reply. We're not at liberty to discuss our client's accounts, I am afraid,"

"But you've heard about the murders in Southend?" said Simmons, borrowing a stern tone of voice he'd heard Hogarth use many times.

"Yes… it's awful. I've heard about it."

"I'm calling you as part of that investigation."

"Mr Milford? Is he involved in any way?"

"I'm not at liberty to say, madam. But in helping us, you may help to prevent another murder…"

Simmons waited.

"Wait one moment. I'll see what I can do."

Simmons smiled. He had used the woman's professional confidentiality shtick back against her and won. Now all he needed was the address. The woman soon came back on the line.

"Seeing as this is a serious police matter, you can have the details."

Simmons punched the air but kept his tone serious.

"Thank you. You've been a great help. Maybe you could help us with one more thing?"

"Yes?"

"Is there any chance we could look at his accounts?"

"His accounts? For which period?" said the woman. He could hear she was already typing.

"As recent as possible."

"May I ask why?"

"It's confidential, but I can tell you it's related to a possible fraud."

"I thought this was a murder investigation?" said the woman.

"Murder is rarely a simple matter, madam," said Simmons.

"I see," said the woman. "Management accounts will cover the period since the last tax return. But I'll need an email address to send it to. *A police email address*," she added with emphasis.

As soon as he put the phone down Simmons stood up from his desk, grabbed his coat, and made off. With any luck, he would be able to get into Milford's home, find some evidence, and make it to Dalton Drive with news for the DI about his finds. Hogarth would certainly think better of him then…

***

Less than ten minutes later, Simmons was climbing the stairs of the apartment block at the back of the high street. The block was situated above the shops and nightclubs – not those belonging to John Milford, but the few tucked around the corner beside the Quality Lodge. Simmons had known of the flats for years, but had never been inside them. He avoided the claustrophobic looking lift and took the stairs. He smelled family dinners and heard TV canned laughter as he climbed. At the top floor he found three doors. Number twenty-five belonged to Milford. A penthouse flat overlooking the top of the town, and out across the Thames Estuary. Nice if you could get it, but still not Simmons' cup of tea. He preferred houses to flats, but a single man on his salary couldn't afford one. Maybe if he could find a nice young WPC to settle down with or a pretty PCSO like Bec Rawlins, then he would be able to buy one. He knocked on the door and heard the echo in the flat beyond. He rang the bell and knocked again, hard. Still no answer. Simmons considered his options. Do nothing? Walk away and wait for a warrant? Or wait for explicit instructions to break down the door? But what would Hogarth have done? Yep. He would have kicked the bloody door down and sod the consequences. Simmons gulped and imagined Palmer warning against doing anything stupid. Then he backed away from the door, swore under his breath, and rammed his shoulder hard against it. The door didn't budge. His shoulder burned with pain, but the door held. He rubbed his shoulder and looked at the sturdy door.

As an angry afterthought, Simmons lifted one of his long legs and kicked it beside the lock. The door jamb instantly cracked, the lock gave way and the door opened into a wall of darkness. He'd done it now. His heart pounded at the prospect of reprimands and suspension. But it was done. And now he confronted a penthouse apartment which was nothing like he'd ever imagined. It was dark. It was musty. And there was a faint glow from the room at the end of the hall.

"You've got no choice now, Simmons," he muttered to himself. "In you go."

He took a deep breath and edged into the corridor. Slowly, he moved past dark doorways, his eyes on the faint glow in the room beyond. He heard the hum of a fridge in the kitchen. The clunk of a central heating pipe. He told himself to calm down. Simmons edged into a cavernous room at the end. He couldn't see much, but the room felt oddly cluttered. He rubbed his hands across the smooth walls until he flicked a light switch and suddenly the room was bathed in pale yellow light. He blinked until his eyes were accustomed to the light, and then he looked around. The curtains were drawn in a messy haphazard fashion. They fell in creases and folds over the back of sofas and windowsills with newspapers stacked over the curtain hems, along with pizza boxes and old yogurt pots. He stepped over the newspapers. Most of them were copies of The Record. A couple of them were printouts of the same edition, with headlines about the Drummond murder. The man was obsessed. Some of the papers were open on inside pages with the salacious reports by Alice Perry. He stepped over the papers and looked again. The faint glow he'd seen had come from the small white LCD light on top of a laptop left on a coffee table. Simmons used his fingernails to prize it open, to avoid leaving prints. He hit the on button with a knuckle and the computer flicked into life. The screen woke up. A moment later, the screen opened on the internet web pages left by the last user. Simmons saw several open tabs. One belonged to UKNews. Another to The Record. Another for the Basildon Recorder. All of them news media. Simmons didn't need to check what news the man had been looking at. But he decided to scroll the first page out of interest. And there he found the article from two days after the Drummond killing, with Alice Perry decrying the police's ineptitude. Front and centre was an image of Hogarth walking out of the doors of Club Smart, looking shabby and black-eyed as if he was the root of all evil. That Alice Perry didn't know what she was talking about. And maybe she

didn't understand that others paid the price for her lies. Blame Hogarth – that was her article. This useless cop is the reason you are afraid – nothing to do with the killer.
Simmons shook his head. He minimised the web browser and found the Weblook email icon on the desktop. Clicking it was a risk worth taking. He opened the mailbox and found a stack of emails. They were a mix of business and junk mail and he saw most of them had been read. Simmons drilled down quickly looking for any kind of meat relating to the case against Milford. His impatience got the better of him, so he opened the search box. He typed in 'Deal' and ran a search, but got nothing. Next he tried Grayson. He found a couple of emails about deejaying dates and payments, but nothing juicy. He typed in Drummond. Nothing. On a final whim he typed in Jake. *There. Twelve emails were pinged back.* All of them pre-read. Simmons opened one at random.

"**U need to pay now.**" Nothing more than that. It was pure teenage text speak. Basic. Blunt. No words spared.

He'd found gold – something not just to impress Hogarth, but something to sink Milford for good. Even DCI Melford would love this kind of initiative.

Simmons went to the first, bottom email in the stack.

Milford,

Nothing in my account again this morning. Let me remind you what's at stake. I know about the planning application for the nightclub and I know how you intend to get permission. I saw you with Cllr Brownlow. If you've got enough money for him, you've got enough for me. My fee just went up by another two hundred. Next time best not be late.

Your friend,

Jake

Brownlow? Hogarth would know about the councillor. But Simmons could already read between the lines. Planning applications went to the council wherever the high street was concerned, and impact on the community was considered, those permissions could be slow as hell and they were often rejected. It looked like Milford didn't want to take that risk. He'd met with a councillor and had been seen by Drummond, who had a nose for blackmail like no villain he'd ever met. And because of it, he'd eventually paid the price. Milford was on CCTV camera around the time when Jake Drummond died. He knew the club like no other. He knew where the cameras were. He knew how to hide and where to keep his knife. How had he done it? Maybe he had attacked from within the crowd. Maybe across the bar itself. The camera didn't show enough detail. All it showed was the result. But looking around Milford's dirty penthouse, the evidence was damning. Simmons grinned to himself. It was too late to go over to Dalton Drive and there was plenty to keep him occupied here. Simmons decided to stay and call in forensics along with some back up, just in case Milford decided to come back. He called Marris first. He dialled the number and paced the room. Outside the flat he heard the little elevator ping and the doors slide open. The neighbours would get antsy when they saw the broken door. Once his call was made he would knock on their doors to reassure them.
"Hello. Is Marris there please?"
"I'll just put you through."
Simmons heard the front door gently creak. He turned his head to see a tall man with a shaven head walking into the apartment. The man was looking directly at him. In one

hand he held a young child who was fast asleep. His other hand held tight to a young woman's wrist. He pulled her into the apartment behind him. Simmons saw the woman was holding another smaller child. Her face was a mess of tears. John Milford leaned back against the door.
"Put that phone down," said Milford.
Simmons face turned black with shock.
"Hello, Marris here," said the voice in his ear. "Hello…? Hello, who is this?"
Simmons lowered the phone from his ear.
"End the call."
"Simmons hit the end call button and the voice died.
"You look scared, Mr Policeman," said Milford, smiling. "Scared is exactly what you should be. You see, Sandra. Now we've got another human shield, you really don't have to be scared at all…"
Simmons shook his head in terror and disbelief.
Milford grinned and drew the knife from his pocket and raised it in the air. It glinted with the light from the living room bulb.Hogarth and Palmer had been at Dalton Drive for less than one minute when they knew something was wrong. Palmer drilled the doorbell with her finger for the fourth time, while Hogarth paced the garden path, stepping into the overgrown garden to peer through the front window. He saw the overturned plastic ride-on toys inside the front room, the Mega Bloks scattered over the rug, the baby bottle and the discarded nappies. The TV was still on, showing a happy little blue man holding a red blanket as he waved at the screen.
Hogarth hissed and walked back to the front door.
"They're not here. Milford's got them."
"We don't know that, sir. That's worst-case scenario. They could have gone out."

"In so much of a hurry that the TV is on? They had a visitor, what — twenty-five minutes ago? She's with him. He's taken her somewhere."

Hogarth's gaze turned inward. If Sandra Deal and her kids were killed, his career would be over. Melford would scapegoat him. The Record had already laid the groundwork for it. But that really wasn't so important in the grand scheme of things. Milford was a sick man who had seemed sane and friendly to speak to. Which meant he was one of the worst types. He knew Milford had done it out of choice not compulsion. Hogarth wanted to save Sandra Deal and her kids. Everyone else in this case had born some kind of guilt, but Sandra had been tricked and used not once, but twice. And now those children were in the worst danger of their brief lives. Hogarth burned at the thought of the children being hurt.

"Think, Sue. Come on. Where would Milford take them?"

"The club maybe?"

Hogarth shook his head. "No. Not there. There are fire exits and all sorts. It gives us lots of ways in and him lots of risks…"

"We don't know him. We don't know him well enough to make that call…" said Palmer. She was right. Hogarth racked his brains for insight. He was on the verge of shouting in frustration when his phone rang.

"Yes! What is it now!" he shouted down the line, venting at the unknown caller. He had expected Simmons. But it wasn't him.

"DI Hogarth. This is Ivan Marris. I received a call just now. One of your team, I believe."

"Marris? What?"

"Did you need something from forensics?" said Marris.

"No. I didn't call you. Neither did Palmer…"

"Wait there. I can check the number if you like…" said Marris.

Hogarth waited while Marris produced the number. As Marris called out the digits, Hogarth repeated them allowed.

"That's Simmons's phone," said Palmer.

"It was DC Simmons," said Hogarth. "Didn't he tell you why he was calling?"

"No. In fact, he left me hanging from the very moment I picked up the call. I heard him breathing. I heard someone else talking, but that was it…"

Hogarth looked at Palmer. "Simmons called you, but he didn't speak?"

He looked at Palmer and saw a grim look come over her face.

"I'm sorry, but there's been a development, Marris. I'll have to call you back." He hung up the phone.

"Sue?" said Hogarth.

"Milford's got Simmons."

"How do you know?"

"Simmons wouldn't do that to Marris unless he had no choice."

"But he could have lost the signal," said Hogarth.

"You know he didn't."

Hogarth's eyes narrowed, and he nodded once. The situation was turning from a crisis to a total disaster.

"We'd better go," said Hogarth.

"But where do we go?" said Palmer.

"You've got a list of contact information for the case back at the station. Milford's address will be in there somewhere."

"Isn't that the trouble?" said Palmer. "He could be anywhere."

Chapter Thirty-four

"PC Dawson?" said Hogarth. He was driving at speed along the tree-lined boulevard of Prittlewell Chase. And he was breaking the law – his phone was pinned to his ear as he drove but Palmer didn't say a word.
"DI Hogarth. What's up?"
"Have you seen or heard from DC Simmons?"
"Not since he left the station."
"When was that?"
Hogarth's Vauxhall reached the red tail lights of the cars queuing for the hospital car park. He accelerated and pulled past into the adjoining lane, receiving a blare of car horns behind him.
"About twenty minutes ago, sir. Maybe a bit more. He was in a hurry. I've not seen Simmons like that before."
"Did he mention anything? Say where he was going?"
"Hold on, sir." He could hear Dawson speaking to the officers around his desk before he came back on the line.
"PC Orton says he saw him heading into town."
"Club Smart maybe?" said Hogarth.
"No. Orton said he was round the back, opposite Warrior Square park."
"Warrior Square? What the hell would be doing there?"
"What did you find at Dalton Drive?" said Dawson.
"Nothing, Dawson. The house was a ghost ship. A woman and two children live there, the daughter and grandchildren of one of our key witnesses from Club Smart. It looks to me like they've been abducted. And now DC Simmons has done a bloody flit too. If he's done something stupid…"

"Do you need assistance?" said Dawson.

Hogarth was about to refuse, but stopped himself.

"I need to know where John Milford lives. The man who owns Club Smart."

"That should be easy enough. It was me and Rawlins who took down the names and addresses that night…"

Hogarth listened with bated breath. He heard Dawson rummage through the mound of papers on top of his desk.

"Here we are. Milford lives at twenty-five Warrior Court."

"Warrior Court!" said Hogarth. He looked at Palmer. "Then that's where Simmons was going. To John Milford's place. Dawson, Simmons could be in trouble. We're heading to Warrior Court now. I think John Milford is our man."

"Milford? Why, sir?"

"Drummond was leaching off everyone at that club. We don't know the specifics yet. But the evidence against him was mounting and I think he knew it. If Milford is our man, he could have a woman and two young children trapped with him. If Simmons is there, it could get worse. Do me a favour, Dawson. We need a police presence at Warrior Square but keep a low profile. Bring a couple of others, but only people who have their heads screwed on. Make sure you leave PC Orton and Matthews out of it."

"What shall I tell the chief?" said Dawson.

"Leave all that to me," said Hogarth. He cut the call dead and dropped the phone into his lap. Simmons disappearance was on him. He had told DC Simmons to find Milford's address, to start looking at Milford as the last suspect. If anything happened to Simmons it would be his responsibility. There would be an inquiry. Someone would get carpeted. There would be a scapegoat because when the shit hit the fan there always was. And Hogarth was under no illusions. He would be the man to go. Reaching the red traffic lights by Prittlewell Park, Hogarth flicked on the blue police lights hidden in his headlamps and the siren too. As the siren wailed he swung his car out into the oncoming lane and cut a diagonal across the junction, almost scything into an oncoming car.

"Simmons is at Milford's place?" said Palmer.

"I asked him to track down his address," said Hogarth. "Simmons was probably there when he called Marris, so he must have found something. Which means Milford is definitely our man. Then the call went dead. He was interrupted. Probably by Milford."

"But how did Simmons work out it was Milford?"

"Simmons has more of a brain than I gave him credit for. And who knows what he found there, Palmer. The long-lost knife, maybe? We just have to get there before something bad happens…"

Racing the wrong way across a busy town-centre junction Hogarth flicked off the sirens and police lights, then dabbed the brake. He parked the Vauxhall on a side street beside Warrior Square and looked up at the grey concrete block. High above shop level Warrior Court looked a little like a multi-storey car park with added windows.

"Where's the way in?" said Hogarth.

"Round here," said Palmer. "There's an entrance door by the bus stops."

Palmer led the way. She looked as tense as he felt. Palmer was pale, and her eyes were deadly serious. They jogged past the people at the nearby bus stops and opened the glass door which led into Warrior Court.

"What if he's armed?" said Palmer.

"But we have to do something. Besides Simmons, there's Sandra Deal and the children."

They came face to face with the option of the small steel lift or a very narrow staircase. Beside the lift was a plastic sign with list of apartment numbers. Flat numbers 23, 24 and 25 were shown as being on the top floor.

"We'll take the lift to the floor underneath. I'll try and deal with Milford. But I want you safe. Out of the way."

"Sir!" said Palmer, trying to resist.

"That's an order, DS Palmer. I need you to be a witness to everything that happens. This bastard has got to go down for a very long time."

The lift pinged and the door slid open. They got into a space barely bigger than a biscuit tin, only to face their reflections in the mirrored walls. Their fears were written all over their faces, inescapable.

The doors opened on the fourth floor. Hogarth got out and gave Palmer a nod.

"This is it," he whispered. "I lead the way."

"Sir, we should call this in. We should get armed back up."

"I don't want to ensure this turns into a siege, Palmer. Not if I can help it. Just do what I ask, and I'll carry the can, okay."

Palmer could see the fixed look in his eye. Brave was a word she had never associated with Hogarth. Dogged, determined, a bastard at times, but never brave. Yet here it was. They climbed the steps to the top floor carefully, quietly, then Hogarth paused at the top step. From their angled view, they could see the third door down the short corridor was ajar, showing a strip of darkness inside. The door jamb was cracked and splintered.

"Okay…" said Hogarth. He pointed at the top of the stairs and Palmer nodded in acceptance of the order to stay put. Hogarth started to creep forward. He moved past the first closed apartment door, then the second. With every step the tension in his body grew tighter, gripping at the sides of his head. He felt sweat dripping from his forehead. As he got closer, he could hear a mumble of words from within. A stink of cigarette smoke and rank stuffy air hit his nostrils as the voices started to make sense.

***

Simmons was on the sofa, hands on his knees to show he was following orders. Simmons wasn't armed. But his eyes were everywhere. He looked at the newspapers, the laptop, and the blade flashing in Milford's hand. Milford held the knife by his hip. He looked comfortable with it. Like it was an extension of his hand. As if it was a part of him. His hand covered the handle, and looking at the blade, Simmons reckoned it was six to eight centimetres long. It fit the bill of the weapon Ed Quentin had described almost exactly. There was no need to look any further. Simmons was nervous. In a quandary. Would talking help delay the violence? Would it help or harm them all? But as the aching dryness of his throat took hold he felt the need to speak. To lessen the tension. Besides, Simmons was a cop. He'd already been a cop for six years. He couldn't help being curious.
"No wonder we never found the knife…" said Simmons, with a shaky voice. "You kept it all the time, didn't you? You must have hidden it when you were body searched."
Milford looked at him like he was pathetic. He smiled and nodded.
"It's my club. I knew where to keep it. I wasn't going to let you lot have it, was I? Forensics and all that. I've watched those CSI shows before."
Simmons nodded and licked his lips. He looked right and scanned the young woman with the lank hair and the frightened eyes sitting at his side. There were deep, dark rings around those eyes. She held both children in her arms.

She was shaking while she held them and she never took her eyes off them. The kids had their eyes closed as if they were sleeping. They looked unconscious. But it was daytime. Their sleep wasn't natural. He wondered what the man had done.
"Those kids are very quiet," he said.
Milford leaned on the mantelpiece as he stared at him. Like a fox looking at a piece of chicken.
"Sandra knows I can't stand the noise – not at a time like this. I love Sandra, don't I sweet? And I can tolerate the kids, but not their incessant noise. A situation like this requires my full concentration."
"What did you do to them?" asked Simmons.
Milford grinned. "Don't worry. I'm not a monster. You can tell him, Sandra…"
The girl looked at him. Her smooth skin said she was in her twenties, but her eyes looked at least twenty years older. "He drugged them…" said the girl in a whisper. "A double dose of anti-histamine. It's too much for them, really… but what could I do?"
The girl was shaking now. Just about holding on.
Simmons nodded. Drugged. That made sense. So, Milford and the girl were together then. His cop brain chewed on it, while Milford stared at him. Milford seemed amused to watch his mind so busy.
"Sandra Deal, eh?"
The girl looked at Milford for permission to speak. Milford shrugged.
"Yes," she nodded. "That's right."
"You know then. But how do you know?" said Milford.
"Did you get that from her old man? Did he tell you Sandra was his?" His voice started to rise.
Simmons swallowed on his aching throat. He shook his head.

"No. Peter refused to tell us a thing. We had to work around him… we had to guess."

Milford grinned. "Good for him then…"

"So, you're together?" said Simmons.

"Perceptive little man, aren't we?" said Milford.

"I was just wondering, that's all…" said Simmons, his voice rasping.

"Wondering?"

"Drummond. I get that," said Simmons. "I know why you killed Drummond, near enough everyone wanted that man dead. He was an out and out villain… scum. But why Gary Grayson? Surely not just because of his past relationship with Sandra here…"

"Nosey little man, too. All these questions are a bit risky for someone in your position. But hey. I've never done last requests before. That is what this is, right? Your last request?"

Simmons refused to answer.

"Please don't…" said Sandra but her voice was like a whisper. Milford chuckled.

"Sandra used to be very upset with Gary, and for good reason, I'd say. He knocked her up once and she decided to keep away. But then he saw her again and made her promises as long as your arm. He even got engaged to her, just so he could get her into bed. Soon as he found out she was pregnant with number two, he cut her off. Ignored her. The full blank. He never returned her calls. He blanked her in the street. For a while she sent him letters and pictures to try and trigger something paternal in him, but the bastard never reacted. He could have organised maintenance payments, but that would have involved Gary admitting he was the father. *I knew he was the father.* I saw those photographs. He knew he was the father, but he wouldn't ever admit it. He left Sandra with nothing but stress. I felt sorry for the girl. But after I got talking to her, I liked her. She deserved better. She's a beautiful girl and the man ruined her life."

"But he worked for you…" said Simmons.

"I didn't know about her until later. Until I met her myself," said Milford. "Sandra denies it now, but she once told me she wanted to have him hurt for what he'd done to her. You know, to get a bit of revenge for all the horrible things he'd done to her. We only spoke about it once. But it got me thinking for a while after that. I watched his behaviour, and I soon started to dislike him too. Gary worked for me, yeah. He brought the customers in. But I hated him anyway."

"I still don't get it," said Simmons.

"You killed Drummond because of…"

"He was leaching off me. Roaming around *my club* like it was his own private kingdom. He tried to bleed me dry! As if I should have worked hard all my life to make him rich and me poor! Screw that. He pushed me too far. It was only a matter of time. Drummond always went to the same bar to drink. He gathered people around him like he was a film star or something. I watched him. I knew his whole bloody routine. All I needed to do was pick my moment…"

"But we saw the cameras. They never showed the moment he was killed. They never showed anything."

"Of course they didn't! I knew those cameras better than anyone. I knew what you people needed to see and what needed to stay hidden. You saw me behind the bar, right? So, it couldn't have been me, could it? Only I slipped out from the double doors, came back round and passed through the punters in the crowd. It was dark. It was busy. And all they want is a drink, and they're all fighting to make sure their drink is served before the man next to them. It's so easy to kill a man who's waiting at a busy bar. Everyone was looking the wrong way. The lights were flashing. I was out of there before Drummond dropped down dead."

"So, Drummond was blackmailing you. Killing Drummond made sense... but Grayson?"

"Grayson made sense to me. Once I'd started out, it was a lot clearer what needed to be done. You lot were so slack, I knew I could do what I liked. And dear old Gary finally got what he deserved."

Getting answers didn't make Simmons feel any better. He looked away, his eyes trailing to the floor.

"But I didn't want you to kill him!" snapped Sandra. "The kids might have wanted to know their father when they were older."

Milford shook his head. "That pillock didn't deserve them."

There was the faintest creak of the front door hinges. A very subtle noise, as if the door had been caught in a draught.

Milford looked back over his shoulder and he stared out into the darkness and the hallway beyond.

Then he looked at Simmons.

"For what we're going to do next, we'll need that door secured."

"Come on. You're not a killer. You don't need to do this. You're a businessman with a future, Mr Milford."

"But unless I deal with you, my future will be over..."

Milford turned away for the door. He walked towards the hallway. Simmons looked across at the girl on the chair beside him. He tried to get her attention, but her eyes stayed on her children. Simmons got it. They were the only things now which mattered. He was on his own. Simmons pushed himself up out of the chair, slowly and quietly. Now the girl's head flicked up and she looked at him. Simmons stared back for a split second. Her eyes were big and wide, and her pale lips fluttered. But she didn't speak. As Milford left the room, Simmons looked for something to defend himself with. He scanned the room for anything he could use, but the only thing he saw was an empty beer bottle left by the sofa. As he moved in the dark, his shin scuffed the coffee table and made a noise. Simmons froze, and Milford reappeared at the living room door. Their eyes met across the room. Milford's face turned dark. He ran across the room, the shining blade swinging at his side. Simmons was in trouble. He would have to fight for his life. As Milford came at him, the beer bottle was still well out of reach. Simmons stepped back, putting the coffee table between them. Milford grinned.

"You blew it. You knew everything there is to know. You found me. It's me. I did it. And even then, you know what? You still blew it. And now I'm going to kill you too…"

Simmons got ready to defend himself. Milford swung the blade at him in a wide arc and Sandra Deal whimpered in her seat. Simmons bobbed back out of range and Milford used the moment to dart around the table. Simmons moved to avoid the knife. He scrambled past the coffee table, but Sandra Deal's legs were in his way. He pushed himself over her, but ankles got tangled and he started to fall.

He was done for. He was dead. He knew it. He turned over, and found Milford breathing heavily as he leaned over him, the knife in his hand, a toothy smile on his face.

"I never knew killing could be this much fun," he said. As Milford leaned in, there was a noise in the hallway. But Milford was focused. He held the knife up high and took aim. In desperation, Simmons swiped the laptop down from the table and dragged the newspapers over him. The knife plunged down and struck the hard, plastic shell of the laptop. Milford growled and pulled his stabbing arm back again, ready to plunge a second time.

"No!" shouted Hogarth. He stood in the living room doorway, his hands raised, palms flat. Part appeal, part order. "Milford. That's enough," said Hogarth. "You've gone far enough."

Milford looked at Hogarth. "Really? Because I don't think I have. You know my only regret in all of this?"

Hogarth stepped forward, hands raised. "Tell me. Go on. Tell us all."

"That it couldn't be you instead."

Milford kicked the laptop aside and swiped at it with his free hand. He struck the laptop and sent it sliding down by Simmons side. Milford dropped down, and pinned Simmons down with a knee on his chest, then raised the blade. This time Milford had a clean aim at his chest. Simmons blinked and struggled as the blade began its final descent.

"No!" Hogarth dived at Milford and seized his blade arm with both hands. The knife slowly lowered, and Hogarth heard Simmons scream. He couldn't look. Milford was strong. Hogarth used every ounce of strength to pull the man away until he threw Milford back toppling against the coffee table. Hogarth looked down to see Simmons struggling on the floor. There was blood on his shirt and it glistened on the floor. Sandra Deal was whimpering with a low-level panic attack.

"I'll kill you as well!" said Milford.

He held out the blade as a warning and began to pull himself to his feet. In a few moments, Hogarth knew he would have lost any advantage. And Simmons was bleeding badly. Hogarth watched and waited, picking his moment. He waited until the man was on one knee, and then sent in a smashing fist. Hogarth knocked the blade hand out of his way and the knife spun down to the floor. The man looked shocked. Hogarth gritted his teeth and sent his all into a downward fist, smashing it through the side of Milford's head. His head lolled but he was still upright. Hogarth growled and sent another punch into him. Sandra Deal screamed as Hogarth drew blood. By the third punch, a voice called at Hogarth's back.

"Sir. You need to stop…" He aimed another fist and it crunched against the man's face. "Sir!"

Hogarth saw the blood and balled his fists again., "Sir," called Palmer. He was about to strike again. "Joe!" Hogarth stopped at the sound of his name. He looked back and saw Palmer. She looked pale faced and afraid.

Hogarth looked down at the bloodied face of John Milford. Dazed, yet still grinning with bloody teeth. Hogarth pushed back the coffee table and kicked the knife clear away from them. He looked back at Palmer and nodded, and she dropped down to Simmons side. As Palmer checked Simmons, Hogarth jabbed a finger close up into Milford's bloodied face.

"John Milford! I am arresting you on suspicion of the murders of Jake Drummond and Gary Grayson, and for the attempted murder of my colleague, Detective Constable Simmons…" Hogarth seized the man's wrists and cuffed him. Then he moved to Palmer's side. Simmons lay beneath her. He coughed and winced in pain as he raised his head up.

"I think he missed…" said Simmons, faintly.

"I think he did too," said Palmer, with a smile.

Hogarth steered Milford towards a corner, and pushed him down to his knees, facing the wall. Hogarth leaned over the cop and put on a stern face.

"Simmons, we haven't got enough decent coppers that we can afford to lose one to some knife wielding psycho, do you hear me? I need you fighting fit and back on the team as soon as possible, okay?"

"Yes, sir," said Simmons.

"And, Simmons… you're a better copper than I gave you credit for," said Hogarth. He gripped the man's arm once and let him go. Simmons smiled, and Hogarth took it as a good sign.

Epilogue

It was the middle of the day. Lunchtime, in fact. Which was how Hogarth had been able to use a flimsy excuse about meeting an old cop friend for a bite to eat. When DCI Melford had asked who he was meeting Hogarth had used an unlikely bluff. "Oh, you wouldn't know him, sir."
And Hogarth knew the only reason Melford hadn't challenged the assertion was because the DCI was in a very good mood. Today, The Record's lead story was 'Cops Face Down Nightclub Killer'. The killer had been found, been given a catchy name, a face, and a history. Now the press would feed off the story for weeks to come. And no matter which angle the trouble-making journos took, or how much they tried to spin it, Hogarth knew it was only a good news story as far as the police were concerned.
And it wasn't just Melford who was pleased.
It was lunchtime and Joe Hogarth lay in a bed which wasn't his own. It was too fresh, too warm, and too comfortable for that.
Hogarth held a soft, warm, and naked Ali Hartigan at his side. The plush bed was in a hotel beside the airport. Being with Ali like this was a risky business, but after facing down a killer, risk had been put into perspective. Being with Ali was exquisite. But now that the moment was over, Hogarth felt an odd mixture of elation and guilt.
"You took too many risks to set this up, Ali," he said.
She leaned up on her elbow and draped her blonde hair over his chest. He couldn't help but look at her. Her eyes were bright, and her cheeks were pink with the heat of passion.

She traced a finger over his hairless chest and Hogarth felt a little self-conscious. *How could a woman that bloody gorgeous be in bed with him?* He tried to put the thought aside, while she looked into his eyes.

"But I could have lost you to that psychopath and it made me think… life's too short and too fragile to go on living without doing the things you want to do."

Hogarth smiled, and Ali rolled her eyes.

"It's not just about the sex, Joe. Though, admittedly, that was pretty damn good too…"

"Pretty damn good?! It was better than that. If I didn't have to get back to those nitwits at Southend I'd make sure you got your money's worth from this hotel room."

She kissed Hogarth's chest and looked up. "I already have. Believe me."

"But aren't you worried James will find out?"

"Of course, I am. But I was very careful about this. I used aPayPal account attached to one of my old bank accounts. He won't know."

"But you're sure he's not, you know, suspicious…?"

Ali Hartigan sighed and rolled away from Hogarth. He knew he'd spoiled the moment, but he couldn't help it.

"Suspicious? Of me? From all the odd hotel charges I've seen on his credit card bill I'd say he's too busy bouncing around with that awful secretary of his to notice what I'm doing. These days I'm surprised he's got time to attend the House of Commons…"

Ali sat on the bed and slowly pulled on her underwear.

"Sorry," she said. "After your ordeal, here I am moaning about my awful husband."

"No, I should be sorry," said Hogarth. "But your husband is still a disgrace. You're in danger and he still does nothing about it…"

"No. But at least I've got you to protect me."

"But I have my job. I do my best, but I can't be there all the time. The man should assign someone to protect you. A proper security guard."

"But then… we couldn't have done this."

Hogarth sighed. "But I want you to be safe."

"And I want you to be safe," she replied. "But you can't do that either, can you?"

Checkmate. Hogarth got up and reluctantly grabbed his trousers and underwear.

"Why did that man turn into a killer?"

Hogarth shrugged. "He was a bad apple."

"Do you think everyone can become so evil, deep down?"

"John Milford was pushed to kill the first man. If he hadn't killed Jake Drummond, someone else would have done it eventually. It wasn't right, but it was going to happen. Milford planned it meticulously. He knew how to strike so as not to be seen and how to avoid CCTV. He'd been planning it for months. But the second kill, that was emotional. He said it was because of a promise he'd made to his girlfriend, but I think that was a lie."

"Then why do it?"

"He got a thirst for it, Ali. He crossed a line which should never be crossed, and he enjoyed himself. He found a reason because he wanted to kill again."

"Do you think all people are so bad?"

"No, Ali. There are a lot of dark souls out there. We both know that. But I also know a few very good ones," he said, smiling. Ali nodded at the compliment.

"What about the policeman who was hurt?"

"DC Simmons will live. If he still wants to be a cop after that? Well, only time will tell. Like you said, Ali. It was a happy ending."

If only they could have had their own happy ending, he thought.
"I wanted to be with you, Joe, but this is a one-off."
"I know," he sighed. "But I'll wait for you," he said. He watched her for a moment, studying her beauty. She leaned in and kissed him. The kiss lasted a few seconds, and then she pulled away and grabbed her bag.
"Give me ten minutes before you leave. We can't risk being seen leaving together."
"I know the drill, Ali. I'll watch you from the window."
"No. Don't. Someone could see you."
Hogarth sighed. "I need to be sure you're safe."
"It's broad daylight. I'll be fine. I'll get a cab."
"Okay. Fine" said Hogarth. Ali opened the hotel door and gave him a wave. Hogarth nodded and watched her go. Two minutes later he stood at the window, watching her walk out into the cold grey day. He lifted the net curtain so he could enjoy the full view of her until she was gone
"You've got it bad, Joe. You've got it bad…" he said, turning away. It was time to get back to the cop shop. Ali Hartigan was his oasis. But part of him wondered how long it could last.

***

Ali Hartigan climbed out of the taxi in North Shoebury. "And tell Mr Hartigan he needs to do something about the cyclists too," said the taxi driver. "They're always getting in my way. They think they own the bloody roads these days!"
"Yes, yes. I'll be sure to mention it…" said Ali, as she gave the man a ten pound note. She told him to keep the change just to shut him up. Ali Hartigan was happy. Joe Hogarth was a good man, a real man, and a hero. He was tough and austere on the outside, but soft and warm when it really

mattered. He was the kind of man she had always needed. Ignoring all her many problems, it was good to be alive. Ali smiled up at the gloomy clouds. A short way behind her, a second taxi slowed to a halt. A door opened and a man in a long grey raincoat handed over his money to the driver. He was in a hurry. The driver thanked him, but the man didn't say a word. He was focused on the slim, well-dressed blonde walking up the hill further ahead. The man pretended to look at his watch until the taxi drove away up the hill. Once it was out of sight, the man in the long grey coat started walking. His mouth was narrowed. His temples rippled with intent. He walked quickly and quietly, gaining on Ali Hartigan with every silent step.

Continued in book 2, The Darkest Grave…

The
Darkest
Grave
A Gripping Crime Mystery

The DI Hogarth Darkest Series Book 2

Solomon Carter

Great Leap

The Darkest Grave

Prologue

MP's Wife Attacked Outside Family Home
Exclusive by Alice Perry

The wife of Southend East MP James Hartigan, was rushed to hospital after sustaining unspecified injuries yesterday in a frenzied attack outside the MP's North Shoebury home. The violent attack took place at the house on North Lane around 1.25pm Tuesday afternoon as Mrs Hartigan returned home from a shopping trip at the Airport Retail Park, in Rochford yesterday. Police say that the attacker approached Mrs Hartigan undetected until she reached the driveway of the MP's home. Alison Hartigan is believed to have noticed her assailant in the moments before she opened the door to enter her house. Police say the attack would likely have had far worse consequences if the attacker had been able to follow Mrs Hartigan into her home. Police have yet to confirm whether a weapon was used in the attack and whether the attack is politically motivated, although police have already stated they do not believe the attack to be connected to terrorism. MP James

Hartigan was in Westminster at the time of the attack on his wife, taking part in a debate on the mandatory parliamentary vote on the European Withdrawal Bill. Mr Hartigan was not available for interview last night, although Mr Hartigan's parliamentary secretary, Honor Fulman last night issued this brief statement on his behalf:

"James would like to thank his constituents, colleagues and all those well-wishers who have sent him kind messages of support. He wishes to assure everybody that his wife Alison is in a stable condition and will soon make a full recovery. James does not intend to let violence win. James does not intend to let this threat affect his responsibility to the people of Southend or the freedom he and his wife have enjoyed up to now. Although it is not known if this attack was politically motivated, James wants to assure everyone he will not be cowed or swayed by violence. He and his wife will continue to bravely stand up for the residents of Southend undaunted and unbowed. Bullies and extremists of all kinds must never win and James Hartigan is sure that if we stand together we will ensure they never will."

This morning the Prime Minister said she wished Mrs Hartigan "a swift recovery" and hoped that "the culprit of this reprehensible and heinous crime" would be "found and brought to justice very soon."

Neighbours of the Hartigan household said they had noticed some unusual visitors in recent weeks. Mrs Hartigan had also recently voiced concerns to friends prior to the attack, yet it is believed no police presence had been assigned to protect the Hartigan house right up to the time of the attack.

Mr Hartigan's parliamentary secretary declined to comment on the issue of police procedure.

"James trusts the police will have done their level best. Any discussion about any police failure to respond to perceived threats is an internal matter for Essex police – and James is certain it will be dealt with in an appropriate manner."

Southend police chiefs and senior detectives have been unavailable for comment.

Chapter One

Nigel Grave's tall, withering body had become stoop-shouldered with age. The tired old farmer trudged down the track towards the blue barn, wearing one of his usual checked baggy shirts and corduroy trousers tucked into his muddy wellington boots. The long blue metal barn wasn't far from the back of the farmhouse.
The summer fruit and vegetable pickers usually thought the man was gruff and unapproachable when they first started work on Grave Farm, but those first impressions of old Mr Grave were always short lived. His gruff exterior had been carved by decades of outdoor life and toil, but inside the brittle shell was a warmth which burnt brightly. It was hard to see from the outside, but once seen it was hard to ignore. The summer was long gone, and so were ninety-five per cent of the seasonal work force. All that was left now was bare earth and plenty of cold. Nigel walked into the large blue shed where the potato sorting machine was being cleaned by some of his longest serving men. The foreign ones he liked to keep around for their old-fashioned ways and good humour. They loved work, as he once had. He watched them cleaning the machine with care, not knowing their boss was watching them. He admired them, and he feared for them now that this whole European immigration nonsense was going crazy. One of the men looked up and stopped. The man had soft eyes, his face wrapped in a hood and a scarf because of the January weather. He stopped work and his friend looked up to see why.

"Mr Grave," said Igor, the first man.

"Good to see you chaps working so hard even in this cold snap."

"Work is better than staying at home, Mr Grave."

The old man smiled. "I wish they made more like you. Is anyone else about? On the fields maybe?"

"No. The others have gone now. It is just us."

"Fine then. You might as well hear it too. Come up to the house this afternoon, will you?"

"Which house?" said the other man.

"Why, my house, silly. Grave House."

"What for?" said Igor.

"I've got something I'd like to say. It's about the future."

"But we're only the farm labour, Mr Grave," said Igor, looking confused.

"The kind of people which make the farm tick. You're as important as any other. Come up to the house. Susan is going to make a spot of lunch, if she remembers, that is."

The men looked at each other and shrugged.

"What time?"

"Call it one o'clock. And don't forget will you? You two haven't got age as an excuse for that."

They watched the old man look around the shed with an almost nostalgic air. He breathed out slowly and a wisp of vapour wafted from his lips.

He walked away from the men along the long shed, with his big gnarled hands swinging slowly at his sides. He stopped at the vast pile of logs laid at the back of the shed which stood beside the oversize chipper he'd bought on the recommendation of his son, Neville. He grabbed a few logs and traced a hand over the smooth cold surface of the industrial woodchipper. He'd forgotten how many thousands his son had spent on that contraption. It was one of young

Neville's brainwaves to create new income for the old farm. Old Nigel hadn't bothered to question if the idea would ever become profitable. He shook his head at the beast and strode back out into the cold. The morning clouds above were the palest grey. Behind him the two migrant workers exchanged glances as the tall, thin old man strode back up the gravel lane towards his huge red-brick country house. Halfway along, unwilling to face the trouble of home so soon, the old man stopped and cast his eyes across the flat fields towards town in the distance. Four miles away were the rectangular black shadows of the town centre office blocks, flats, and shopping centre. Some of those buildings had been there when he took over, but most of them were younger than him. The town had changed beyond description, life had changed, and farming too. Nigel Grave had a feeling that he had outlived all of it. He sighed.

On the other side of the farmhouse, a small shiny red Fiat 500 stopped at the edge of the country lane. The young man in the passenger seat looked towards the red brick house with its vast gated driveway. The gates were always open and the red brick pillars which framed them were spectacular. There was nothing else like it, especially around here. Neville's heart started to race, and he swallowed as he thought of what was to come.
"Nev, honey…" the woman in the driving seat beside him grabbed his big hand to bring him back to the present. The softness of her touch prompted sensual memories of recent afternoons and evenings. The memories were good enough to distract him for a moment or two. He looked across at the woman with the expensively cut hair, and well made up face. Nancy was about his age, maybe just a year or two older, but seemed so much more sophisticated. Looking at her glossy

eyes, her beauty almost stunned him. She held his chin to make sure he looked even closer. It was as if she knew the power she had over him.

"Nev, remember. It's all going to be okay. You and me. The farm. Everything that must be done. It'll be okay."

"But he won't approve, Nancy, I know he won't."

"Don't talk like that. You have to be confident about this from the very start or it won't work."

"Okay, then," he said, controlling his smile. "It'll be okay." The young man opened the door and got out of the car and straightened out his big torso. "You're sure you don't want me to come with you, Nev? This has to be done right. I could help you."

The young man leaned back down into the car and tried to look confident.

"I know you want to, Nancy. But you can't. If you come along now, it'll look all wrong. He'll think bad of me. Besides… you said you had something else to do first."

"Yes," said Nancy. Something flashed across her eyes. Neville didn't know what it was. "You're sure you don't need me?" she said.

He nodded but at that moment Neville wasn't sure about anything. But he knew what needed to be done. For the future. *For everyone's future.*

"I'll be along later, then," said Nancy, and blew him a kiss with her lustrous red lips. As soon as she closed the car door, Nancy picked up her leather business portfolio and dumped it in the warm leather seat where Neville had been sitting. She turned on the radio, and waved goodbye as she pulled away into the road. She started whistling to a tune on the radio. Behind her, Neville Grave lingered on the edge of the grassy lane. His feet were leaden, and his chest was tight. But he had made a commitment, and it had to be fulfilled.

Flames licked over the charred remains of the three black logs the old man had picked for the morning fire. His wife sat behind him in the oak chair beside the dining table which already bore six plates and two bottles of wine, one white, one red. There were two large bowls of French bread cut into pieces, most buttered, but some not, and a bowl of country salad. The old man looked round to see his wife sawing another baguette as she hunched over the edge of the table, her long silver hair draped over her shoulders. He thought he could smell aniseed on the air, but refrained from passing comment. Instead, the old man opened his mouth to say she'd cut enough for two gatherings already, but stopped himself. The old floorboards creaked, and he looked up to see Marjorie, his younger sister walking into the room. She still had some of the old blonde colour in her hair and life in her eyes. Whether the hair colour was bottled or not, the colour suited her. He saw Marjorie take in the bowlfuls of bread and the third loaf cutting underway, and Nigel gave his sister a weary nod. They shared a knowing glance but kept silent. Who cared if there was too much bread? There was no point upsetting his wife now.

"Hello, Nigel," said his sister, as if seeing him for the first time. She was wearing her big coat and wrapped his stick-like body in a soft embrace. The man was surprised by her warmth. He patted her on the back and drew away. Wherever Marjorie went, Trevor wouldn't be far behind.

"How can you walk around wearing just that thin shirt and trousers in harsh weather like this?" she said, giving him a sisterly look he knew of old.

"Because the weather isn't harsh, Marjorie. It's merely cold. It's called winter. I think you've forgotten what harsh weather is like. That's too much soft living with that husband of yours." He looked to the doorway and on cue, came Trevor. Trevor was aging now, but even so, he had the kind of looks which women used to describe as 'dashing'. And he worked hard to keep in shape. The man was about the sixty mark but looked ten years younger. Nigel reckoned his own face showed every single one of his seventy-one years. If anything, Nigel knew he looked far older than his age. Too much weather, too much living. And the Reaper was creeping in. Yes, it was time for change before changes were forced upon them all

"Nigel, how the devil are you?" Trevor seized his arm and pumped his hand, then slapped him on the back. It was his businesslike way of dealing with people. Trevor hadn't shaken off the boardroom since retiring from his career in the city. Nigel offered a half smile in response. It was the best he could. Especially seeing the way Trevor looked at Nigel's wife. Nigel saw the doubt and the pity in the man's big eyes.

"We're very well, thank you," he said firmly. Trevor nodded.

"Well, what's all this in aid of, eh?" said Trevor.

"What's wrong with a family gathering and a spot of lunch, Trevor?"

"But Christmas wasn't long ago…"

"Christmas is for Christmas, Trevor. The new year is for new things."

"New things? Hmmmm. How very mysterious. Finally taking my advice about the farm?"

"Oh, not necessarily…" said Nigel. He allowed himself a hint of smile as he turned away.

Through a side door, another tall man appeared. His face was big and ruddy, and he wore the agricultural uniform of checked shirts and wellingtons. He had steel grey hair and spectacles. "Pete!" said Nigel. "Glad you could make it."

"Well, you said to be here, Nigel. And who I am to argue with a free lunch…?"

For the first time his wife, Sue, looked up from her bread cutting with a laugh that soon turned into a cough.

"Hello, Sue," he said, and leaned in for a kiss.

Trevor leaned past his wife's ear, keeping his voice low and his mouth small and tight. "Isn't he the farm vet?"

"Yes," his wife muttered. "Peter Venky."

"What's he doing here?" said Trevor.

Marjorie shrugged. "He's Nigel's friend."

"What has your brother got in mind here?" he whispered.

"I told you, I don't know," she whispered, playing with her necklace. The vet, Peter Venky, seemed to know he was being talked about. He glanced at Trevor and Marjorie and nodded at them. "Hi," he said. It was all he said.

Nigel used a metal poker to prod the fire. He watched the last flames take hold of the logs he'd brought in earlier. He shook his head. "We're going to need more firewood to keep this going."

"Firewood? Nigel, I'm surprised you haven't used the woodchipper to turn all those cut logs into gold," said Trevor.

The old man rose up from his haunches and threw the iron poker down on the hearth with a clank.

"The chippings are selling. And what won't sell we can use for compost. I've saved some logs back for winter. As for Neville's woodchipper, it was worth trying, Trevor."

"Worth trying. Yes, I'm sure," said Trevor. Marjorie gently nudged him in the ribs.

Old Nigel grimaced. "I'll fetch some more wood now. Neville should be here soon with his girlfriend. Then after lunch I'll put you all out of your misery…"

Trevor and Marjorie wore thin smiles as the old man ambled past them. They watched him leave through the back door and walk away towards the distant barn.

A deep clunk echoed through the hallway. Everyone looked at the kitchen doorway as the footsteps approached.
"So, he's finally turned up," said Sue, looking up from the dining table. Neville appeared at the door and looked around with a pinch-faced smile. "If all the guests have arrived, we can get on with this farce." said the old woman. The young man walked in and embraced his mother with his big arms. The woman didn't resist the embrace but neither did she respond. Neville barely greeted the others but offered a warmer smile to Venky the vet. Venky raised his small glass of wine. "Hello, Neville."
"Hi Peter, where's Dad?"
"Gone to fetch some wood. You know how restless he gets when there's company."
"He's restless full stop," he said.
"So, does anyone actually know what this grand lunch meeting is all about?" said Trevor.
"Not a clue," said Venky.
Neville shook his head.
"I'll tell you what it's about…" said his elderly mother. She looked around with glee in her bright hazy eyes. "It's about the future. And it's a surprise… he's got something up his sleeve.
Trevor stiffened and raised his eyebrows at his sister-in-law's comments. Peter Venky smirked into his wineglass.
"Now, Neville, make yourself useful. Why don't you help me butter some bread? We must make sure there's enough to go round."

"You can use it so soak up all the sauce," muttered Trevor, under his breath. Marjorie gave him a sideways look.

Neville eyed the bowlfuls of buttered bread and picked up a spare butter knife.

"Oh dear…" said Susan. "I think we're going to run out of butter."

"That's okay, Mum. Look," said Neville. "There's plenty enough already."

"No, Neville," she said firmly. "You're wrong. There isn't enough at all. We need more."

The guests looked at one another before Trevor tutted.

"Okay. I could go down to the shop if you like, Susan?"

"Oh, that's very good of you, Trevor," said the old woman. "Shame everyone isn't so helpful." Trevor and his wife exchanged a glance, then Trevor sighed and left the room. Moments later they heard the great front door clunk shut and a beefy car engine fired into life.

The old woman looked round with a serene smile, pretending to be oblivious to the tension in the room, and the clock ticked.

"Well, isn't this nice?" she said. Everyone smiled. But every smile in the room was no more than skin deep.

***

The old man reached the long blue shed and walked inside.

"More wood boys," said Grave, expecting Igor and Borev to be where he had seen them last.

"In this cold, I think we're going to need a whole tree…" The old man's voice echoed under the high roof, passing between the black-plastic-wrapped hay bales and around the back of the dormant machinery.

Grave listened to the echo of his voice and looked around. The long potato sorting machine was shiny and clean. But there was no sight of the men who had been cleaning it. The old man blinked and looked around. "Damn strange," he said. "Igor?" he called along the length of the shed, wondering if they'd moved on to another machine or gone for a crafty smoke outside. Officially, no one was supposed to smoke around the farm – it was the law – but ever since he'd started employing Eastern Europeans back in the eighties, he'd learned the Eastern bloc boys loved cigarettes like no other people. They simply could not be parted from them. Over time he had turned a blind eye. Grave walked slowly past the potato sorter towards the bales of hay and just before them, the woodpile and the massive red woodchipper. The logs at the top of the pile looked more substantial, certainly big enough to keep the fire burning until he had made his announcement. He wondered how long any of them would stay after that. He grinned bitterly. Yes, there would probably be fireworks as well as a fire. He pulled four logs from the pile, and then reached up to grab one more for luck. The weight of the logs hurt his arms and brought on a touch of back pain. If he wasn't careful he'd do himself a mischief. But what did he care? He trudged towards the open front of the barn and peered out across the acres of land – those acres which were his and those that used to be part of Grave Farm before the family started to sell up. He wouldn't be a seller, no way. Not in his lifetime. But he was worried for the future though. If some in his family got hold of the farm, it wouldn't be long until the whole disappeared for good. The thought near brought him to tears. Farming was changing so fast he could barely keep up. Dairy would send them broke. Livestock was just about okay, but only just. Unless he changed things up, the business would die even before he did. But finally, he had a plan. To save the farm, to make it vital again. To produce enough profit to make it last another generation, maybe more. Then it would be their turn to save it. Nigel Grave's thoughts were interrupted by a whisper of movement. Then a sudden rolling noise, then a thud-thud-thud behind him. *Cripes!* He'd managed to knock the whole bloody log pile down! Grave turned back and saw a few logs rolling towards his ankles and he tutted and stumbled out of the way. He'd get Igor and Borev to fix that after lunch. It'd give them something to do. He bent over and set down the logs which were in his arms. Just as he laid them he heard the mechanical cough and grunt of a loud engine kick into life. Nigel Grave jerked upward in shock.

The chipper machine had come to life. It was as if there was a bloody ghost in the barn. No. The barn was too new for that. He looked at the chipper and saw the petrol engine was working full tilt and he could see the machine vibrating from the works inside. Nigel Grave stretched out his spine and looked around the barn.

"Igor!" he called. He looked left and right. No sign. "Borev?" Still nothing. Then how come the bloody machine came on? He was no expert, but surely being struck by a log couldn't start it. The machine was a Chinese effort. Who knew how these modern imported gizmos worked? Probably at the behest of a bloody smartphone knowing the way of the world these days. The old man sighed and started trudging towards the chipper, his eyes already darting over the controls at the side, looking for the off switch. A shadow moved between the tall black hay bales. It stretched down across the hay-strewn floor, but Nigel Grave was oblivious. "How do you work this damn thing?" muttered the old man. The shadow by the hay bales disappeared. Somewhere amidst the growl and shudder of the machinery, the old man caught a hint of sound. A sliding sound. Smooth. He stood up and looked at the black bales. Maybe a sheep on the loose? They were bloody cheeky animals when they wanted to be. There was a scuffing sound on the floor nearby and the old man wheeled around in fright. For a split second he was terrified, then his face settled and he gasped for breath. He was relieved. Clutching his chest, the old man almost smiled "What's this? A joke?" he said. But Nigel Grave's relief was short lived. He was shoved back hard against the metal lip of the chipper funnel and he grunted in pain as the metal hit his spine. His heart started to race and his smile disappeared.

"What are you doing? Come on? Eh? *What the hell are you doing?*"

Grave raised a hand to defend himself, but his arms were frail. The old man hadn't realised just how slight and fragile he'd become as he was seized in two hands and lifted clean off the ground. Finally understanding his fate, the old man cried out in terror, but the noise of the machine was louder still. As he screamed, the old man was turned and flung face down, headlong, into the wide mouth of the woodchipper. His scream was killed by the sound of the machine working at disintegrating what it had been fed. A spatter of unspeakable matter sloughed out of the waste bin and turned into a spray which coated the machine, the walls, the barn floor as it fell to earth. And those industrial blades could only cope with so much. Long before the shredding was done, the machine blades stopped spinning, caught on matter which had no business in a woodchipper. Two frail legs, and arms lolled either side of the feeder. The shadow turned, ran away from the barn and disappeared.

In the kitchen, the fire embers were flickering faintly.
"Here's your butter," said Trevor, dumping two foil-wrapped packets down on the table. He smiled at the old woman, but his smile waned as his gaze met Neville's eyes.
"I wasn't sure if that was enough," said Trevor.
"It looks so cold out there," said his wife.
Trevor nodded his head. "That's because it is," he said.
A deep doorbell chimed and reverberated through the hall.
"I'll get it," said Neville, eagerly.
Venky and Trevor watched him go.
"What's keeping old Nigel?" said Venky. "I thought he was fetching wood from the shed, not the forest."
"You know what he's like. He loses himself out there. I think he prefers it," said his old wife as she opened another pack of butter. Venky looked at the old woman and nodded.
Neville appeared back at the kitchen door, this time smiling. The door opened wider and they saw the glamorous young woman with the blusher, lipstick, and expensive hair-do appear at his side. She was smartly dressed in a stylish outfit. The smile on her face was warm enough to melt ice.
"Peter, Mother... you know Nancy Decorville, don't you?"
"Yes," said the vet. His mother gave a mixed-up smile.
"What is *she* doing here?" said Trevor.
The smile on Nancy Decorville's face stayed bright and faultless, but her eyes showed some frost.
"Neville invited me. You asked your mother if I could come along, didn't you Neville?"
"Yes, I did."
"You asked Susan?" said Trevor. "Of course, you did. Well, we all know why you did that."
"Trevor!" said Marjorie.
"I'm not going to pretend, Marjorie. The woman works for Crispin and Co. The property firm. I've seen her at the

auctions, gobbling up land for development, cheap as chips. It's bloody obvious why she's here. Insultingly obvious, in fact."

"You're wrong, Trevor," said Neville. "She's here because I asked her to be."

"Yes. Yes. *And the rest*," said Trevor, quietly. Neville surged forward like a dog straining at the leash, but the young woman laid a hand on his forearm to quieten him.

"It's okay, Neville," said Nancy. "Everyone's entitled to their opinion. Even when they're patently wrong."

Venky the vet stared into the bottom of his glass before necking what was left. If this lunch meeting got any worse, he would invent an appointment so he could leave. A breech birth at Belfairs stables perhaps?

"I'll go and check on Nigel," said Venky. "He's been long enough by now."

The tall vet walked out of the back door and left them to it. Shaking his head, he walked down the gravel track, past the overgrown garden and abandoned home allotment, towards the long blue shed, and he took his time. As he got nearer, Venky squinted. He thought he could hear an engine. A tractor maybe? Cheeky sod! It'd be just like Nigel to arrange an event then to bugger off and escape into some farm work. Venky smiled at the thought. Who could blame him? They were like vultures, the bloody lot of them.

Two men appeared from the end of the shed. He recognised them. The foreign migrant workers Old Nige had kept on, because he had a soft spot for them. Both wore puffer jackets with their hoods up in the cold. One blue, one green. They talked to each other as they turned into the darkness of the long shed. A moment later there was an awful shout. The shout quickly became a scream. A wild, blood-curdling scream. Peter Venky stopped walking. A few horrific possibilities skittered through his mind. He dismissed them all as ridiculous. This was just another day like any other. Yes, he knew worse were coming, but not today. Not today. He repeated the words like a mantra in his head, but something in him didn't believe it. The tall elderly man broke into a loping run. The foreigner in the blue coat emerged from the shed and fell to his knees. His face was ashen. There were tears in his eyes.

"What is it?" cried Venky. "What's the matter with you, man?"

The worker couldn't respond. Venky walked inside. Now he didn't need an explanation. The horror was evident enough. "Oh no. Oh please, no…" he said, walking forwards through the hay towards the mechanical feeder. He recognised his friend's shoes, his trousers, even his bloodied checked shirt. But the top of his torso was invisible, all held by the feeder. The engine chuntered, but the blades whined in complaint. Venky risked a glance to his left towards the end of the contraption which produced the wood chips and instantly regretted it. His stomach heaved. He felt faint.

The other migrant worker was pacing the hay strewn floor, muttering in his own language as if he had lost his mind. Then he said "Who? Who?"

The vet shook his head. And then he turned away, shouting for help. He ran outside shouting before he fell down in the cold rutted field and vomited onto the soil. Peter Venky couldn't breathe, couldn't think. His friend was dead too soon. From now on, the rest of Venky's life could never be the same.

Chapter Two

Detective Sergeant Palmer slowed as she drove along the end of Prittlewell Chase. She'd taken a call from Hogarth, and the DI had asked her for a lift. It was a strange request, and not just because Hogarth had a car of his own. The end of Prittlewell Chase was home to the driving test centre and a community garden for disadvantaged and disabled people. It was an odd place for someone like Hogarth to be out walking on a weekday afternoon. Hogarth hadn't been at the station during the morning and Palmer had heard the rumour he was off sick. After their recent case, Palmer wondered if it was a delayed stress reaction or an old-fashioned hangover. After all, Prittlewell Chase wasn't far from the nick. Hogarth could have easily walked the rest of the way. She had even thought about telling Hogarth to walk. Just as a bit of banter. But the strange, distant tone of his voice had changed her mind.

It was one-thirty-five pm when she saw him. Her dented Vauxhall Corsa turned onto the side parking bays of Prittlewell Chase and there he was, standing right outside the community garden staring over the hedge towards the well-tended allotments and greenhouses. Palmer parked her car and waited for Hogarth to walk over, but he didn't. In the end, Palmer looked at herself in the rear-view mirror and sighed. She checked the fringe of her blonde bob and blinked, making sure her eyes didn't look too tired. It was far too late to be bothered with any make-up. Hogarth had seen her in all kinds of states. He'd be able to see past the slap

and lippy in a heartbeat. Besides, it would only make her too bloody obvious. She didn't know what was bothering Hogarth, but at least it was an opportunity to get to know him better. Or something better than that. Palmer stopped and stared at herself. Her breath stilled. Did she *really* want to sleep with her boss? *Her direct superior officer?* No, not really. But if she'd met Hogarth in any other situation, she knew she wouldn't have turned him down. He was a bit of a bastard, but only when you first got to know him. After that, he was actually quite funny. And he didn't look too bad either, for a man of his age. And what with working sixty-hour weeks where else was she going to meet a man? It could only be in the force. And as her mother kept reminding her, she was still alone, and her body clock was ticking. *As if she needed reminding.* If she didn't meet a man soon and get on with it, any chance of a family and kids was going to go right out of the window – for good. So, if Hogarth was the least bit interested, she would have to go for it. Not because he was her ideal man. *Was Hogarth anybody's ideal man?* But because he was there, because he was real, and because she was unlikely to meet anybody else. If they got together she would have to transfer to the other CID team. Or maybe to another station, such as Basildon. But that was for the future. Right now, she was here for him and that had to count for something. Palmer got out of the car. Seeing how tired he looked, she wondered if he was about to quit. Even in profile, as he leaned over the fence, she could see he looked fragile. Burned out, maybe? "Guv?" she called, feeling butterflies in her tummy. Stupid, stupid girl. *Just bloody grow up.* She told herself.
"Palmer..." he said. Hogarth looked around at her sheepishly and scratched his chin. He looked emotional and tired... and something else. Palmer tried to read his eyes.

Then she saw it. He was angry. Hogarth was very angry, and she didn't know why.

"Sir, are you okay?"

"Why do you ask, Palmer? Oh, I suppose I might not look at my wholesome best right now."

"Something's wrong, guv. I can see that."

"You'll make a fine detective one day," said Hogarth, with a heap of irony. Palmer shrugged.

"Joke, Palmer. You're a pretty good detective already."

"Thank you, sir. You're not a bad one yourself," she said. The butterflies intensified. But Hogarth looked in a state.

"No, Palmer. Not true. I get by, Palmer, that's all. I got by for twenty years in the force, but right now I couldn't give a single solitary shit about it."

"But why, guv? DC Simmons is on the mend. And Melford's been singing your praises at the station, even the Super mentioned your exploits in the newsletter."

"They can both shove the newsletter where the sun doesn't shine."

"Would you like me to pass that on, sir?" said Palmer with a grin.

"No, Palmer. When I tell the Super to shove it, I'll do it in person. You can be there to watch."

Palmer smiled. "So, what is it?"

"It's bullshit, Palmer. That's what. We've got drug dealing scumbags coming out of our ear 'oles, so they assign a surveillance team to them to '*collate information*' like we're working on a stamp collection. We've got gangs carving up the districts like departments in Debenhams, and let's face it – if you close your eyes and point at anyone you like in this town my bet is you'd be pointing at a criminal."

"At least it keeps us in work," said Palmer. She mirrored Hogarth's body language, leaning over the fence and edged just a little closer. Hogarth seemed oblivious.
"Is it family? Did something happen over the weekend?
Hogarth grunted and shook his head. Palmer bit her lip and took a risk.
"Is it your partner?"
"Partner, Palmer? Me? Come on! A partner. Darts partner, maybe. Didn't you know I'm far too much of a sad sack bastard to keep a spouse. I'm all about the job, me. It's just a shame the job doesn't love me back."
"What do you mean?"
"I've given this job the best years of my life. I've been shot at, stabbed, and more for being with the police. I had my car burned out in Tower Hamlets. I had a cigar stubbed out on me in Holloway. I had my little finger bent back by a man in a frock at Aldgate bus station. And I've had every police chief I've ever worked for undervalue and underappreciate the work I've done. I know we don't do it for the thanks. We do it because it's what we do, but still."
Palmer nodded and made eye contact. Hogarth sighed.
"But even when we're dealing with all this crap, doing the very best we can, we still miss the bad ones."
"Like who?"
Hogarth shook his head. He stayed silent for a moment, then met her eye.
"Look at Alison Hartigan."
"Who?"
"Exactly, Palmer. Exactly. The MP's wife. The woman should have been high profile. High priority. Considered to be at risk from all kinds of threats, but no one even bothered to look at the Hartigans. She'd reported a stalker, apparently.

But nothing was done about it. And now the poor woman has been beaten up like a street scumbag."

Hogarth's jaw tensed as he spoke. Palmer was taken aback by the anger in his eyes. It shone out from deep inside.

"The Record newspaper insinuated we were to blame," said Palmer. "But that cheap hack Alice Perry was out to knock us again."

"Alice Perry was right, Palmer. I know. There's always a first time." The DI leaned up from the fence.

"What do you mean? We should have seen into the future and known she was in danger?"

"No, Palmer. The signs were there. We should have seen the risks. And that bloody MP should have told us he needed some protection."

"Sir? I don't get why you're so upset about this."

"It's the blind spots, Palmer. That's what it is. You know, I think I've got more blind spots than I ever realised. And in this job, that's not good."

"Sir," said Palmer, becoming a mite irritated at Hogarth's self-pity. "With respect, we all have blind spots. But last week you ensured a killer was stopped in his tracks, you saved DC Simmons from being stabbed to death, and you got four other collars along the way. You're doing all you can, sir."

"You reckon, do you?" said Hogarth.

"As a matter of fact, yes, I do."

Hogarth made a thoughtful face, pursing his lips.

"I didn't know you did pep talks, Palmer. You're pretty good at them, as it happens."

"I have been known to offer a little peer-to-peer support in my time."

"Bollocks to the work jargon. You're good at listening. Hope I didn't offload on you too much, did I?"

"Not any more than necessary, sir."
Hogarth straightened out his blazer and shirt collar.
"Where's your car?" she asked.
"I didn't feel good. I decided to take a walk this morning."
"From Westcliff?" said Palmer, with a quizzical frown. "Why?"
Hogarth shrugged. Palmer looked down the length of the boulevard to the distant brown and grey hulks of Southend Hospital on the horizon.
"Why did the MP's wife thing get to you so much?"
Hogarth met Palmer's eyes before he looked away.
"I don't know. I guess it's symbolic of something. The state of the police, maybe. The state of the town. I don't know."
"I didn't have you down as that much of a deep thinker, sir."
"Oh, DS Palmer? Contrary to popular belief I'm about as deep as they come. Now where've you parked your charming little motor."
"Charming?" she said.
"Yes, dents give it a certain rustic chic."
"I'll take that as a compliment," said Palmer, smiling.
"I would if I were you," said Hogarth with a gruff chuckle.
Palmer unlocked the Corsa and they both got inside.
"Sir. If you ever need to let off steam again…" said Palmer. She finished there, fearful of saying too much.
"Thank you for hearing me out, Sue. But I'll try not to dump on you like that again. I promise."
Palmer blinked, turned her eyes to the road and started the engine. As she drove, Hogarth's mobile phone started ringing.
"Here we go," said Hogarth. "Melford must be calling again to pretend he cares…" Hogarth put his phone to his ears.
"DCI Melford. I'll be along in… sir? You what?!" Hogarth turned to Palmer. The look in his eyes had gone from tired

resignation to wide-eyed shock. "Yes, sir. I'm on my way." He ended the call and dropped the phone aside.

"Where to?" said Palmer.

"Sutland. Just out of town. You know it?" said Hogarth.

"Yes," said Palmer. "The farmland in the sticks," said Palmer. She hit the accelerator and the Corsa took off.

"What is it?" said Palmer.

"It's another murder," said Hogarth. "And this one sounds grisly."

Chapter Three

Hogarth's tan brogues crunched on the pea-shingle which filled the long drive outside Grave Farm all the way to the house. He slammed the car door hard enough to make Palmer wince. The Corsa wasn't much, but it was hers. Looking at Hogarth, she saw he was oblivious. Hogarth stared up at the great old, red brick farmhouse before him. "This place must have been built long before the town," he said.

"Yeah. It looks Victorian," said Palmer. "Or thereabout…"

"You're a local, Sue," said Hogarth. "Do you know anything about the Grave family?"

"I'm not *that* local," said Palmer. "But I've heard a little. The family has been here for generations, and they used to own swathes of land out here – I mean almost the whole thing from the town boundary all the way to Rochford. They sold off most of it across the years. The only thing I know is they keep running these little odd events. Christmas things. Barn dances, that kind of thing. And look at the house, guv. It needs a fair bit of work."

Hogarth eyed the timbers supporting the roof. Where the great black beam protruded over the gable ends, he saw signs of rot. Rot wasn't something to be neglected if an old property was to hold together.

"I'd say they'd fallen on hard times, then," said Hogarth. "Which could prove instructive in itself… come on, we'd better get started."

They walked along the driveway as it curled past the big oak front door, which sat beneath a grand stone arch. Hogarth was about to press the doorbell when he heard loud voices from the side of the property. He cast an eye around the front and counted off the cars parked there as he walked. A top of the range Porsche estate – its fine shell was spoiled by a black roof rack and a cycle rack on the back window. Next was a ropey old Land Rover with muddy wheels and a battered body. An old fashioned mini, probably thirty years old, and a white mini-van with muddy tyres, not too old. The Land Rover had to belong to the farmer, probably the Mini too. Hard times and all that. But as for the estate and the white van? He'd soon find out. Reaching the side of the farmhouse he saw PCs Orton and Jordan squabbling beside their squad car. Hogarth gave Palmer a look.

"I've had enough of their crap already and we haven't even started yet."

"Yeah, I know what you mean," said Palmer. She took the lead and made a beeline for the uniforms.

"Hey. What's up with you two?"

Hogarth watched with satisfaction when the two men stiffened up at the sight of Palmer walking towards them. He was glad to have Palmer on board. She didn't take any crap, just like him. Hogarth strode on by, barely acknowledging them. He tried to put thoughts of Ali behind him. It was difficult. He'd tried to visit her – he'd had to. After seeing the article in The Record he had been shocked to the core. He'd been with her mere hours before it happened. He'd made love to her at the hotel near the airport. He'd watched her leave in that taxi. And less than twenty minutes later the bastard stalker had tried to cave her head in.

He couldn't help but feel it had been his fault. Being involved in a secret affair wasn't good for the soul. He felt like he was stealing from another man, even though the man in question was a total bastard. But stealing was never good. And seeing as Ali had been attacked so soon after the hotel tryst, he was sure they had been watched. How had he not seen the stalker? He'd tried to ensure they were clear by scouting the airport hotel twice after they arrived. But clearly his mind had been on other things at the time. Hogarth seethed, ashamed of himself. And in a way, he could not escape the feeling that *he* had been punished. Yes, dear Ali had been punished the most. But he was supposed to be a cop. A man of justice. *And he was doing wrong.*

Hogarth shook his head to clear it. He neared the long dark grey barn at the end of a rough garden track. The house was behind him now. He looked at the long shed and swallowed, knowing that the dead body was inside. A white van was parked at an angle across the track – Dickens and his crime scene assistant were already at work. Hogarth hoped it meant most of the horror had already been cleared away as he doubted he had the stomach for it, not today. He looked out to the low cold mist which clung to the fields ahead. Not far off he could see the red dotted lights of the airport. Somewhere out there was the hotel which had given him such pleasure and led to such pain. Hogarth started trudging towards the white van.

The barn was busy. John Dickens, the crime scene manager and his assistant were on their knees, covered head to toe in their white plastic overalls, gloves and masks. The suits were to protect the evidence from contamination. But as Hogarth surveyed the crime scene, he saw the suits were protecting them from the body matter too. The vast woodchipper used to kill the man was still firmly in place. Hogarth was pleased to see the body was gone. Well, most of it. Beneath the large metal feeding bucket was plenty of dark blood and other matter which had pooled on the hay-strewn floor, probably left behind when the coroner removed the body. Hogarth swallowed on a sicky feeling in his throat and strode towards the men in the white suits. Dickens was on his hands and knees aiming a powerful torch around the floor. Sensing Hogarth's presence, he stopped and looked up. His movements were abrupt. He raised a gloved hand towards the DI. "Stop there and don't come any nearer."

"Good to see you too, Dickens," said Hogarth. "With a bedside manner like that, it's easy to see you've been hanging around with Marris too long. Dr Ivan Marris was the police forensic expert. Marris was often brusque, yet managed to stay just on the friendly side of coldly offensive.

"So, what have we got, Dickens? It doesn't look like suicide, that's for sure. I wouldn't want to end it all by diving into a woodchipper."

"Normally, I'd appreciate the sense of humour, DI Hogarth, but as I need to concentrate at gathering flecks of flesh and bone, I'd prefer if we could postpone it. This hay all over the floor isn't exactly making my life any easier."

Hogarth swallowed again.

"Can't you move it out of the way?"

"Some of the hay grasses might contain evidence. Marris wouldn't thank me if I binned it. We have to be thorough and extremely careful."

"I can see all the evidence I need already. Mr Grave got tossed into the woodchipper. It must have been the worst possible way to go. The poor bastard got minced."

Hogarth's eyes traced to the production end of the chipper, where the long metal tray was spattered with gore. It seemed the more solid remains had been removed.

"The coroner's team must have had their work cut out. No pun intended."

"Yes. Took them a good long time to remove the bulk of the body. The pathologist better be good at jigsaw puzzles."

Dickens returned his eyes to the ground and started scanning the floor while his colleague continued similar probing behind him.

"Any idea what you're looking for?"

Not yet. We're doing our ABCs, Inspector. Assume nothing. Believe nobody. Check everything," said Dickens "I'm only looking for what's there. Assumptions are dangerous."

"I couldn't agree more," he said. "And I'm right with you on 'Believe nobody.'"

Hogarth kept his distance, but edged a little further across the hay-strewn floor. He sensed someone edging towards him. PCs Orton and Jordan had been shut up, so he guessed it was Palmer catching up with him.

"You see that?" muttered Hogarth, without looking up. He hoped his voice was audible to Palmer but not to Dickens. If Dickens was going to get possessive about the crime scene Hogarth knew it was best he kept quiet. But Palmer didn't reply. Hogarth glanced back over his shoulder and saw two men in puffer jackets and beanie hats standing behind him. They looked dark skinned, but ashen. From the look of their eyes – red, small, watery – at least one of them had been weeping.

"Who are you and what are you doing here?" said Hogarth. One of the men shrugged. The man in blue looked Hogarth in the eye. "He was our boss. More than that. He was our friend."

"You work here?" said Hogarth.

"Yes. For two years now."

"Name?"

"Igor Krescek." He pronounced his name *Kres-chek*.
"I'll need a word with you later. But please move away now. This is a crime scene. We need to keep it clear. Understand?"
The men nodded. Staying close to one another they made off.
"But don't go too far. I'll need to interview you," said Hogarth. Palmer passed the men by, nodding at them as she went. She joined Hogarth's side.
"What was Orton and baby Jordan's problem."
"Orton was taking the piss out of Jordan for losing his lunch all over the field."
"Jordan threw up?"
Palmer nodded.
"Who can blame him?" said Hogarth. "Orton's a prat. What happened in here is beyond wicked."
"Hardly says accident, does it?" said Palmer.
"Not in a million years." Hogarth edged forwards a couple of feet.
"Keep clear!" called Dickens. Dickens didn't look at Hogarth. He just raised his hand. But something caught Hogarth's eye. He ducked down to the floor. On some pale hay he saw a few pieces of black. Like small black dots. They could have been blood, flesh, or animal dung. He saw a few more of them dotted around. Hogarth took a risk. There was enough to share, surely? Dickens and Marris wouldn't miss out if he took a few. Hogarth needed to satisfy his curiosity. He reached down and pinched at a few.
"What are you doing?" said Palmer, tense but quiet.
"Nothing, of course," said Hogarth. He picked up a few of the specks and dropped them into the tiny watch pocket on the front of his chinos.

"Keep up the good work, Dickens," said Hogarth. Hogarth lifted a hand in farewell and left it hanging in the air as he turned away back down the track towards the farmhouse.

"What was all that about?" said Palmer.

"Dickens is one of those territorial types. Very procedural, methodical."

"That's because he's crime scene. Marris is just the same, isn't he?"

"Ed Quentin too," said Hogarth. Dr Ed Quentin was the pathologist. "And all these professionals have their place, Palmer, but sometimes I like to dance in the moment."

"Dance in the moment, sir?"

"I mean have a bit of a nose around. That black stuff didn't look right to me."

When he reached the other side of the crime scene van Hogarth stopped walking. He stuck his fingers into the tight watch pocket – tight enough to make him wonder if he needed to get back in the gym – and pinched hold of the black specks he'd taken from the crime scene.

He held them out in his palm and prodded at them with a bitten-down finger nail.

"There. What do you make of that?"

The small black pieces were bigger than sand grains, but much smaller than beads of polystyrene. One or two of them contained a strand of similarly black fibre.

"I haven't got a clue, guv. That's for Marris to decide, isn't it?"

"Yes, but there's nothing wrong with getting ahead of the curve. Come on, Palmer. Just risk an observation. Use those fine detective skills of yours."

Palmer pinched up a black grain with a strand from Hogarth's palm and lifted it to her eye. The texture was malleable, and the strand felt like cotton.

"I think it feels like… *nylon,* sir. Or… well, it's almost like rubber but not quite."

"Nylon. That would explain the strand, maybe, but not the other part."

"Actually, it could explain that too."

"How?" said Hogarth.

"Once upon a time I used to go swimming in the great outdoors."

"Skinny dipping? You're not going to confess you were a nudist or something are you? I don't think I could work with a nudist."

"A nudist?! What? I said I liked swimming. How did you ever…?"

"Never mind," said Hogarth, with a mischievous grin. "My mind works in mysterious ways, Palmer. Carry on."

Palmer shook her head. "It was a long time ago. The wet suits we used were made of neoprene which is basically synthetic rubber."

"That doesn't sound much better if I'm honest, Palmer. But go on. Tell me more."

This time Palmer ignored him.

"Divers wear it. Surfers. All water sports, basically."

Hogarth scratched his chin and frowned.

"So… you think this could be wet suit material? Hmmm. That doesn't help us much now does it?"

"It was a guess. You're asking me to do Marris's job in ten seconds with no analysis."

"Yes, I suppose so. Never mind. It was worth a go. Maybe it's from the farmer's wellies, then."

"I don't think so…" said Palmer. She dropped the crumbs back into Hogarth's hand. "But whatever they originated from can't be in the best condition."

Hogarth replaced the crumbs back into his pocket started the trudge towards the house. He eyed the silhouettes watching them both from the country-style windows. "Okay. Here we go. Grieving family and friends… awkward and uncomfortable, but then you know the drill by now."

"Yes. Keep an eye on all of them," said Palmer.

Do our ABCs, thought Hogarth. As he recalled Dickens words, his mind drifted to Ali Hartigan's stalker. He wondered if he applied Dicken's maxim to that matter, whether it would help him find the culprit? Woe betide the scumbag if he did. Justice came in many forms and Hogarth could issue more than one.

When they were near the back door of the farmhouse, Hogarth paused. Palmer stopped at his side.

"John Dickens says assume nothing, believe nothing, check everything."

"I've heard him say that before," said Palmer.

"I like it. I think it applies to most kinds of police work, except interviewing witnesses and suspects" said Hogarth.

"Why not?" said Palmer.

"Because we need to consider the context too, Palmer. The old man was turfed into that machine. But why kill him at all? That's context."

Palmer shrugged. "A grudge, perhaps? Murder as vicious as this demonstrates anger, don't you think?"

"Possibly. Or frustration. He was an old man. Maybe someone feels he should have got out of the way and given them their inheritance by now."

"Money then?" said Palmer.

"One of the oldest motives there is. But there are a few others. It could be a crime of passion, even." An image of Ali flicked through his mind.

"What kind of passion could cause that?"

"A sick one, Palmer. But besides money and lust what else is there?"

"Hate."

"Good. Yes. Hate, passion, or greed. And then there's this old farm to think about too. Keep it all in mind, Palmer. One of those will likely be our motive."

Hogarth narrowed his eyes then flipped into business mode. He struck the brass knocker on the stable door and rapped it three times. The door was opened before he had even let go of the thing.

"Good afternoon. I'm Detective Inspector Hogarth and this is Detective Sergeant Palmer. May we come in?"

By the time he had finished talking, Hogarth's eyes had performed their first fly-by of every face in the room. And he was intrigued by what he found…

Chapter Four

"Mr Venky. In what capacity were you here?" said Hogarth.
"I'm the farm vet. But more than that, I'm also a family friend. I've been coming to help treat the livestock on this farm since Nigel and Susan first took over. There's not much left in the way of livestock now, of course. But it's been a privilege to know them."
Hogarth saw the emotion in the man's eyes and nodded.
"Yes. You were close, then? And you were the one who first found Mr Grave's body?"
Venky took off his spectacles and rubbed his eyes. The rest of the family members watched as Hogarth started off. This was the time for soft questioning, not nitty-gritty detail. That nitty-gritty would soon come. This was a time for assessing and exploring the dynamics between these people. It was entirely possible the killer was among them. Any telltale reactions, slips of the tongue, or other signs would be seized upon and gratefully received.
Venky nodded idly, but then seemed to hear the question again. "Actually, no, Inspector," he said.
"Yes? No? What do you mean?" said Neville. "Did you find the body first or not?"
The young man sat pressed close to his mother. The woman looked bewildered, her eyes glassy and expressionless. There were tear tracks left drying in her pale wrinkled skin. Her long silver-white hair had been just about tamed but showed signs of dishevelment. Hogarth pondered if he could smell drink on the air. He was something of an expert on the matter, after all. It wasn't unusual for bereaved family

members to reach for Dutch courage in such times. But the old dear looked like she might have had one too many. Hogarth's eyes fixed briefly on the young man in the red and black checked shirt, a style more about fashion than farming. He was broad shouldered and fit looking. His clean face suggested he was in his mid to late twenties. The good looking young woman standing behind him had her hands on his shoulders. Her fingernails were painted bright red, the same shade as her lipstick. Hogarth looked at those neat feminine hands. The girl wore a smart work dress, the type worn to office jobs by girls who still wanted attention. She didn't look impoverished, either. And the way her hands were set on the young man's shoulders suggested a proprietary air. Like she was laying claim to him. Why? Was it insecurity in a family crisis? She was an outsider after all. Or was it something more? Hogarth logged the details as the woman blinked at his suspicious eyes. Interesting. Meanwhile the middle-aged couple at the other side of the room offered a mixture of scowls and blank looks. The woman's lips were pursed shut.

"I meant I wasn't the first one to find him. The two migrant workers were there first."

"Igor and Borev," said the old woman. "Nigel loved those two. Especially Igor. A very hard worker, and a very good man. That was his opinion, not mine."

"I think you should let the police be the judge of their characters," said the young man.

The old woman's face showed a hint of a scowl at her son's remark.

"Mr Venky – how do you know they were first?" said Hogarth.

"I watched them enter the shed just before me. Then the screaming started right after that. I knew something terrible had happened, so I ran into the shed as one of them came out. Then I saw him. I saw dear old Nigel stuck in that…" His eyes glanced over at Neville and the old woman. Venky cut his sentence short.

"It must have been an ordeal for you. For all of you," said Hogarth. "But with your help I believe we can identify and catch the killer."

"Who would even conceive of doing such a thing?" said the old woman. Hogarth's eyes drifted from the woman to her son. But Hogarth found another set of eyes ready to meet his. The man with the steely-grey hair and tanned skin.

"Susan – Mrs Grave… she isn't… isn't, um…" said the man. "How shall I say?"

"Trevor! How is it any business of yours, anyway?" spat her son. Hogarth's eyes flicked between them and then angled his head towards Palmer. None of the others seemed to notice, but Palmer did. Hogarth was noting the tension between the men, as if it needed underlining. The atmosphere was tangible and almost explosive.

"Your name, sir?" said Hogarth. Palmer's notebook and pen appeared from her pocket, right on cue.

"Trevor Goodwell. And this is Marjorie, Nigel's sister… my wife."

Hogarth nodded. The brother-in-law and sister of the deceased. From the look of his Aquascutum shirt and the pricey winter dress Marjorie was dressed in, they were the ones who owned the Porsche estate. He laid his eyes on the son. "And your name?"

"Neville. Neville Grave." His eyes filled up. "Nigel was my father."

"And this is your mother…?" said Hogarth.

Neville nodded. "My mother's been a bit forgetful lately, that's all."

From the smell of her, that wasn't all she was.

Goodwell tutted and Hogarth took it in. The tall vet seemed like an interloper of sorts. He wasn't connected to the deceased in the same way as the others. Hogarth wondered what he made of it all. Still emotional and pink-eyed, he seemed like a ghost in the room.

Hogarth glanced at the endless bowls of cut buttered bread on the table and pots full of food. "You were going to dine together," said Hogarth. He saw the third and fourth baguette by the woman's hands. The third baguette was mostly cut, and part buttered. It was excessive to say the least. The meal seemed mostly bread and butter.

"A special occasion, from the look of it. I'm sorry it's been ruined by such a tragedy," said Hogarth. He scanned their eyes for a reaction and found none. Time would tell.

"What was the occasion, if you don't mind?" said Hogarth. "An anniversary?"

Goodwell looked at him. "That's the problem. We don't know. It was to be a surprise. We think there was going to be an announcement. We hoped it was good news."

"Good news? About what?" said Hogarth.

"About the future of the farm," said Goodwell.

Hogarth's brow dipped low over his eyes. "The future of the farm?" he said.

"Yes," said Goodwell's well-dressed wife. Hogarth noticed the fancy bead necklace around her stringy neck. "My brother Nigel had been trying to keep the old family farm going for so long, but as you will have noticed, Inspector, it's become very run-down. Nigel was always a traditionalist when it came to farming, and never wanted to adopt new ways. I'm afraid it was one of the things that was slowly killing the farm."

"He was already beginning to turn it round," said Neville, in a forceful voice.

"What? With your wood chipping idea? What nonsense," said Trevor Goodwell, with a grin which was much more a grimace. "There were barely enough trees on the farm to make that project last a month. That machine was never going to pay for itself, let alone create an income for the farm. It was lunacy!"

"Diversify, Trevor. That's what farms have to do these days and Dad knew it. He was ready to try anything."

"Diversify? With that monstrosity? It was madness. How was he ever going to make his money back?"

"By hiring it out for use. They could come and chip their garden waste here. By offering to turn wood waste into saleable material. Face it, Trevor. You don't know anything about how farms work."

"And you don't know anything about business. The chipper was a total folly! Neville, you're not a businessman. If you took over, it'd be the end of the farm."

"And so would you."

Hogarth grimaced. Neville burst up from his chair and took another big step towards the man with the steely hair. The men were a generation apart, but physically looked an equal match. It would have made for an interesting fight. But the mother scowled, grunted and burst into tears. The good-looker with the red lips and nails pulled Neville back.

"Don't upset your mother… not now," she said.

"And she shouldn't be here at all," said Marjorie.

"She's my guest," said Neville. "Nancy's work is nothing to do with why she's here."

Hogarth glanced at Palmer and arched an eyebrow.

Hogarth coughed. "Does anyone here have any clue what this announcement might have been? Any idea at all? Mrs Grave?"

The old woman looked up. "He was going to make changes, that's all. He didn't tell me what. He never did. But the farm was his business…"

"I think he was going to take up some of my recommendations," said Neville.

"Rubbish. As if they would ever work," said Goodwell.

Hogarth kept his eyes on Neville.

"Diversification and changes in the structure of the farm to make it sustainable."

"Poppycock," said Goodwell.

"Well, Mr Goodwell?" said Hogarth. "What do you think he was going to say?"

"We'd been talking to him about the farm too. I'm certain he was considering what we'd said."

"Which was?"

"The farm needed to take on a partner to streamline the operation and run it like a modern farming business."

"Would you be that partner, by any chance?" said Hogarth with a glint in his eye.

"Oh, good Lord, no. This isn't our business. What do we know about farming. Our only care was that the farm survived. Not just saving it from decline, but saving it from the predators too."

Goodwell's eyes flicked to the pretty young woman in the suit. He was making an accusation with his eyes. Hogarth pretended not to pick up on it. Occasionally, it was best to play dumb.

"Then you suggested a partner to him?" said Hogarth.

"Not as such. Just that one of the larger farm businesses should take a stake in it. He would have been wealthy again in his later years. Of course, none of that matters now, does it?"

The young man bristled with unspoken anger.

"Calm down, Mr Grave," said Hogarth. "I think we should break here, let you have a little time to come to terms with what's happened. But we're going to need to speak to you again. I've got all the names I think. Except for yours…" said Hogarth as he passed the woman with the red lips. The more Hogarth saw her, the more he felt the confidence pouring off her. He could already tell she was the type people described as 'spirited'.

"And what's your name, miss?"

"Nancy Decorville."

"Decorville? Fancy name."

"Ancestral French, a long time back."

"I know it might be nothing, miss, but there's already been a reference to your work. Would you mind if I asked what your profession is?"

There was a titter from the other side of the room.

"I work in property. I am involved in sourcing commercial property for redevelopment."

Hogarth nodded. "I see."

Miss Decorville's face turned a shade of pink, but her pretty eyes stayed defiant.

"My career has nothing to do with my being here. I'm here as Nev's partner."

"Of course, you are," said Trevor Goodwell.

"I'd mind that mouth of yours, if I were you," she snapped.

"Or what, exactly?" said Goodwell.

Neville Grave chewed on his lip and kept quiet, as the young woman in the snazzy dress kneaded his arm to comfort him.

"I'm sorry for your loss," said Hogarth in parting. "But I'm afraid you'll be seeing a lot more of me until this is done.

Please keep your phones on and your diaries free. Come on DS Palmer. Thank you for your time."

He nodded at each of them, taking one last survey of their eyes and behaviour before he walked out into the bright cold day.

No sooner was the door closed than Hogarth let out a long sigh.

"My, my. I don't think I've ever encountered such acrimony in a family home right after a family member's death. And a murder too. The atmosphere in that old house was almost toxic," said Hogarth. "What did you make of it?"

"I felt sorry for that old woman. She was barely holding on."

"Hmmmmm," said Hogarth.

"What?" said Palmer.

"I'm not entirely sure Mrs Susan Grave is entirely with us. I think she might have let go of whatever she was holding on to a long time back. She'll need looking at too."

"But what for? She can't have done it, can she?" said Palmer.

"Context, remember. She's not going to be a suspect, but if the old girl's gone doolally there's a question about where the money, house, and business go now her husband's dead."

Palmer nodded. "Yes… I'd like to know what was in that old man's will.

"The vibe in that kitchen wasn't that the vultures were circling," said Hogarth. "I think they were already swooping to take their first bite."

Palmer nodded. "Fine. I'll look at the will and the solicitor."

Hogarth's eyes narrowed and glazed over with thought. As he walked he jangled the change and keys in his chinos pockets, thinking about the frightened pale faces of the migrant workers and the black crumbs they'd found at the scene.

"But what would drive someone to kill like that, Palmer? Such a hideous, brutal way to kill a man. Not much could drive someone to that. We need to know more about old Farmer Grave, more about this farm, and much more about that family of vultures. I think we've got our work cut out."

"Yes. Haven't we just," said Palmer. Palmer's eyes framed the faintest of smiles. Hogarth seemed to have forgotten his melancholy. The cut and thrust of the job suited him better than he knew. And Palmer was happy to have peeled one layer beneath his rough exterior to have found something new. Something vulnerable. But even so, Palmer was a realist. She knew there would likely be another thousand impenetrable layers to go before she ever really got to know the man at all.

Chapter Five

"DI Hogarth. You're calling me already?" said Ivan Marris. "If I didn't know better," said Hogarth "I'd say you didn't look forward to my calls."

Marris snorted a little laugh before he cut to the chase. Marris was an austere type, but then he was a scientist by trade. Even so, his tone was less brusque than Dickens, the crime scene manager's, had been. At least with Marris there was a hint of sophistication and wit to make the conversations a tad less dry.

"You're calling about the poor old farmer, I take it?"

"Who else? I haven't spoken with Quentin yet," said Hogarth.

Ed Quentin was the pathologist they consulted in every case involving a suspicious death.

"He'll have his work cut out with this one," said Marris. "From what I've heard the crime scene was hideous."

"I think so," said Hogarth. "I saw the aftermath. It was a bloody horror show. Whoever did this one was twisted, Ivan. Deeply twisted. So, have you got anything for us yet?"

"As a matter of fact, yes. There were shreds of paper rescued from the old man's trouser pockets. They came to me, so I could analyse them for traces of fingerprints. But the paper was so torn it was more like jigsaw work. Quite a chunk of the note had been torn away and looks to be missing. I think the paper had been torn up to be thrown away. I'm no expert in handwriting either, Hogarth, but I think it was written by the old man. The writing is very spidery, reminds me of my grandfather's actually."

"What does it say?"
"Something about a '*better idea*', whatever that means. There's not much of the note left and it ends on those two words – 'better idea'. Does that mean anything to you?"
"Not yet. But it might become clear as we go." Hogarth frowned in thought. *A better idea? Who's idea? And better than what idea?* New questions. He hoped they would lead to revealing answers.
"What else have you got?" said Hogarth.
"Brain, blood, and bone matter on the hay, and some on the blades of the woodchipper. It all belongs to the victim. We've got a mish-mash of boot prints and fragments of trainer prints in the barn too. But the freshest ones are well mixed up. There seems to be at least four or five different sets of footprints in there."
"What about the newest ones? The kill happened today, after all."
"It all needs work, DI Hogarth. Which takes time. We're talking about fragments of footprints here, just like that note. The grass and hay all over the show mean that the concrete floor didn't receive every full footprint, and they criss-cross over one another."
"But you might have an idea…" said Hogarth.
"A basic idea, yes. There were three or four sets of fresh prints. Two look like wellington boots from the shape of the print. But the others definitely weren't."
"One of them belonged to the victim, of course."
"And one of the other three could be the killer," said Marris.
"When will you have more on the footprints?"
"Hard to say. I won't be able to isolate or analyse them without a bit of legwork. And if you're after me presenting you with killer's actual shoe print, I warn you now, I might not be able to do that."

Hogarth grunted. "Okay. DNA. Fingerprints. Anything on that note which shouldn't be there?"

"Given time, I might be able to get something. Hopefully pathology can provide you more."

Hogarth gritted his teeth but kept his tone light. "Okay, Ivan. Thanks for the news on the note. Scan a copy to me if you would. Oh. And before you go, did you see any of those random black fibres on the floor?"

"Random?"

"Little black dots…?" said Hogarth.

"Oh, yes, I've picked up a few of those."

"What do you make of them?"

"That's easy enough. Those are neoprene fibres shed from a garment which has had too much wear and tear."

"Oh?"

"I've not run any chemical analysis on them," said Marris. "That's on the to do list. But it's definitely neoprene. And to be this broken down – broken down enough to shed particles – suggests a very old garment which has seen a lot of impact and pressure."

"Impact and pressure?"

"I'd guess whichever garment they came from really needs throwing away. Probably some kind of old PPE gear for the farm. Or sports equipment, even"

"Interesting."

"It *might* be interesting, Hogarth but it could be nothing. It's hard to say right now. 'll update you when I've checked it out."

"Thanks, Ivan."

Hogarth ended the call and tapped the edge of the phone on his lips. The neoprene mattered – he was almost sure of it. He just didn't yet know how.

Palmer breezed into the small CID room. With DC Simmons still in recovery from his injuries from the Club Smart case, the room seemed far less cluttered than before. Empty in fact, and it was quieter too. Hogarth didn't like the quiet. It made him brood, and inevitably, his thoughts turned to Ali Hartigan and the stalker. He still needed to see Ali. He hadn't even gotten close to her at the hospital. Instead he had only seen her bandaged face through the ward window at Southend Hospital. If he'd visited her bedside, it would have been taking a risk. It wasn't fair to Ali. But he *needed* to see her, to let her know he cared, that he was sorry for putting her at risk. But most of all, he wanted to see that she was okay. The yearning gnawed at him whenever he was alone.

He was all too glad for Palmer's return to the office. Hogarth looked up from his desk.

"Anything from the solicitor about the will?" he said.

"Not yet," said Palmer.

"Not yet! Now you sound like Marris."

"Nothing back from forensics yet then?" said Palmer.

"No. So what was the solicitor's excuse?"

Palmer shrugged. "The solicitor was busy. It's Gardner's & Co. They said they'll call us back."

"When it suits them, and they're solicitors, means we'll have to chase. I don't like sitting here waiting, Palmer. We already know it's got to be one of those scavengers back there in that farmhouse."

"Or maybe the migrant workers?" said Palmer.

"Hmmmm. They *were* the first to find the body," said Hogarth.

"According to Peter Venky, that is," said Palmer.

"But we've got no reason to doubt him, yet. The vet had the least to gain out of his friend dying. There's a chance he'll lose whatever business he had from them if the farm is sold up."

"But he was still present when it happened," said Palmer. "We can't discount him,"

"I won't discount any of them," said Hogarth. "Maybe it's the stench of all that greed which has me so suspicious. I'd like to put them under a bit more pressure. Just a bit, to see if any of them squirms louder than the others."

"That might look insensitive under the circumstances."

"Now you sound like the DCI. I think the Super's finally getting to him. All he cares about now are appearances and what the press might say. But he still wants results, of course. How about we swing past Grave Farm one more time, just to see what we else we can get?"

"But we only left them an hour ago. What for?"

"Who knows? I might need another look at the crime scene. We can always concoct a reason for another visit, Palmer."

"What's the real reason?"

"Thumbscrews, that's what. Marris was handed shreds of a handwritten note from the old man's pockets. The only bit he could read mentioned something about a better idea. I'd like to know what that idea was, wouldn't you?"

"The note was incomplete?"

"Yes, torn to shreds. Maybe partly thrown away. It had me thinking, when I'm tearing up a credit card bill, sometimes I put one part in one big bag and one in another."

"That's a little extreme," said Palmer. "I mean, you've already torn it up."

"Yes. Maybe a little paranoid even, but you can never be too careful, can you? Nigel Grave might have been the paranoid type too. If there's a chance the rest of that note is somewhere on that farm, I want it."

Hogarth stood up and grabbed his navy blazer.

"Come on. Let's go and see who's left among the vipers…"

***

The door chimed throughout the great house. When the door opened, it was the son, Neville Grave, who greeted them. Now that the young man stood framed in the doorway, Hogarth got a better sense of the man's physique. His trendy red and black checked shirt was snug around his muscles and broad shoulders.

"You're back," said the young man, with a hint of surprise.

"Yes, yes, we are," said Hogarth. "I did warn you. There's a couple of things we needed to check on. Can we come in?" Hogarth's eyes probed for more with his eyes, but the young man nodded and backed away from the door, breaking away from his gaze. Hogarth looked down at the brown walking boots on the man's feet. They were the kind with deep, thick-grooved soles. The kind worn by ramblers and people who watched Springwatch. Hogarth noted an edging of mud and gravel around the soles, but it was hardly incriminating.

"So, Mr Grave," said Hogarth. "Still very early days, of course. But how's everyone bearing up?" They stepped into the brown hallway and shut the door behind them.

"As well as can be hoped," he said.

"Is your fair lady still here, Mr Grave?" said Hogarth.

The young man looked Hogarth in the eye.

"Why do you ask?"

"Because I'll have to interview her soon."

"But Nancy was hardly here, and she wasn't even here when it happened."

"So, you know precisely, do you, the time when your father was attacked?"

"No… of course not – not precisely… how would I? But it stands to reason. Ask the others… my father went out to get firewood at around ten to twelve. He was outside for about twenty minutes when Peter Venky went to look for him, and found him… found him… found him like that…"

The young man's face fell, and he blinked to hide his tears.

"I'm sorry to press you on this, Mr Grave. I know it's a very hard time for you."

The young man sighed.

"My point is Nancy wasn't here, Inspector, so you needn't interview her."

"Thanks for pointing that out, but I will have to speak to her all the same. What time did Miss Decorville arrive then?"

"Oh… maybe around twelve fifteen, I think."

"Hmmmm," said Hogarth. "I've been wondering… there's no gate blocking public access to the side of the house, to the back garden, or those fields there, is there?"

The young man looked at both of them and shook his head.

"No… only the main gate and that's generally open. That's something we need to look at changing, maybe…"

"To be looked at when you come into ownership of the farm, perhaps?"

A hint of pink appeared on the sturdy young man's cheeks and neck. "I wasn't thinking along those lines at all."

"Maybe not. But people do," said Hogarth. "Even in times like this, Mr Grave. It's human."

The man nodded. "Well someone will need to look at it."

"Do you stand to inherit the farm – as things stand?"

"I wouldn't know about that, Inspector. I doubt it. My mother is still alive…"

"Yes… but I see there might be certain *extenuating* circumstances when an inheritance can be passed along…"

"My mother *is alive*, Inspector…" said the man, with firm emphasis.

"Yes, she is, Mr Grave." Hogarth decided not to push any further. Not yet. He gave Palmer a sideward glance. "Can we see who else is here?"

"Of course," said Neville Grave. "Come through."

As the man walked them through the hallway towards the country kitchen, Hogarth's eyes fell on the man's broad back.

"I'd say you must be a bit of a sportsman, Mr Grave, looking at that upper body of yours. What is it? Rugby? Or swimming possibly? Or some other water sport, maybe."

The man turned back with a quizzical look in his eye as they reached the kitchen door. Soft golden light poured out from the kitchen along with the sound of hushed voices.

"Water sport?" said the man. "Whatever gave you that idea?"

"You've got a swimmer's shoulders, Mr Grave."

"No. I'm not into swimming or any other water sport, Inspector. Most of the heavy lifting I've ever done was right here on the farm while I was growing up. But I do get down to the gym when I can."

"Good. It's good to keep in shape. In my job, we barely get the time to eat, sleep, or anything else. Not lately, anyway."

Neville gave an uncertain smile and led them into the kitchen.

"The inspector's back," said Neville. "And he's been flattering me about my swimmer's shoulders…" said the man, back on firmer ground among his family. Hogarth scoped them out. Every one of them was still around, even the uncomfortable looking Mr Venky. A shocking death had made their work routines redundant. It was a common result in a crisis. Who could return to their tawdry work routine after a tragedy? If the dead person mattered at all, it simply wasn't possible. They had stayed encamped in the kitchen, either unwilling to leave or unwilling to be the first to make a move. Poor old Venky looked as pale as the old man's wife. Trevor Goodwell sat by his wife near the warmth of the range cooker in the fireplace. The thin blonde woman held a mug of tea, while Trevor Goodwell cradled a glass of something resembling whisky. Neville returned to seats by the kitchen table. Nancy Decorville was still present too, looking young, pretty, and completely out of place. She looked like she'd been beamed in from a London recruitment consultancy and yet she seemed content to stay put. Her eyes flashed when Hogarth looked at her, but with what he couldn't tell. Nerves, maybe? Hogarth knew he was far too old and weather-beaten to be of any other interest. Besides, she seemed very content with her current beau. As Neville sat down at the table Miss Decorville draped an arm across his shoulders.

"Swimmer's shoulders?" she said. "Strong shoulders, more like. Shoulders which can bear anything."

Trevor Goodwell sneered from across the room. "Oh, please…" He whispered to his wife, but Marjorie remained implacable.

"Would either of you like a cup of tea?" said the old woman, with a lopsided smile. Her eyes were full of dark mirth. Hogarth wondered if she'd forgotten what had happened just a couple of ours beforehand.

Hogarth waved the offer away.

"We don't want to impose."

"And yet, here you are," said Trevor Goodwell.

Trevor Goodwell was clearly a total arse, but the situation made it impossible for Hogarth to respond in kind. At least for now. But he was able to offer a good mean smile.

"Seeing as I'm imposing," said Hogarth, "I'll do it quickly. I want to ask more about the purpose of today's event. About Mr Grave's announcement."

"We already told you. It was going to be a surprise," said Neville Grave.

"Yes, you did say that, didn't you?" said Hogarth. "But I'm keen to know what you think was about to happen. You must have been excited. I mean, your girlfriend, Nancy here, must have abandoned her workday routine to be here."

There was another sneer from across the room. "I doubt that one is ever off duty," said Goodwell.

Hogarth turned and glared at the man.

"I don't think we need your opinion for a moment, Mr Goodwell."

Goodwell responded with a glare of his own, but Hogarth kept his gaze firm until Goodwell looked away.

Nancy Decorville scowled and shook her head, but when Hogarth looked at her, she soon lost the scowl. Her face became sunshine and light once again. *I've got your number, sweetheart*, thought Hogarth. Maybe Goodwell had it too. But Neville Grave looked done for, the soppy fool. The girl had him hook, line, and sinker..

"Well? Come on. One of you, please. What do you *think* Mr Grave was going to tell you all? You must have had an inkling. Some of you drove a fair way to get here. Where did you come in from, Mr Goodwell?"

"We live in Upminster, Inspector. I'm retired. It's really very little effort for us to come here."

"And you came down here all the time? Or just today?"

"Trevor and Marjorie come too often," said Neville.

Hogarth watched Goodwell seethe for a moment before he regained composure.

"We only ever came here to help – that's all we ever came here for."

Details. Tones of voice. Nuances. It was all grist for the mill, useful to help draw conclusions about dynamics and motive, but Hogarth had heard enough of the bickering.

"Hold on, folks. I asked you a question. What did you think you were here for?"

The old woman was the first to speak. She coughed into her fist and looked up.

"Nigel told me he had a plan. He was going to tell us about it today. He'd made his decision. He was going to make the farm a success, just like the old days."

"He told you that, did he?" said Hogarth.

"He told me he had a plan…" said the old woman, in a harder voice.

"But that was all he said," said Hogarth. "I see. So, you don't know what his plan was?"

"No," said the old woman. "He wanted to tell everybody at the same time."

"Mum, with the greatest respect…" said Neville, hesitantly. "Dad wasn't going to make the farm great again. He was watching it slowly sink into the ground. Unless he was going to announce that he liked my proposal…"

"Stop it, stop it," said the old woman. "Your ideas came from him! Your father provided for you every day of his life…"

"But now is the time for the truth, isn't it?" said Neville. "Dad's been killed. There's a policeman in the room. We need to face the facts."

"You're being selfish and horrid. Horrid, I say. I expected better from you… but I don't know why I did." The woman turned away to face the table.

"Face the facts?" said Goodwell. "The facts are you're trying to manipulate people, Neville. And why? I think it's patently obvious, don't you? It's been obvious since *she* first started sniffing around here," said Goodwell, nodding at Nancy Decorville.

"Don't you dare insult us – her or me," said Neville, his face turning as dark red as his shirt.

"I wouldn't dream of insulting you, Neville. You're family. But she's a different story. You said it. Face the facts, didn't you just say that? I'm calling a spade a spade. That woman has been trying to manipulate you and your father for her own advantage."

"How dare you!" said Neville, launching out of his chair. Venky tutted loudly and hung his head. He leaned across the table and laid a hand on Susan Grave's shoulder.

"Come on, then Neville," said Goodwell. "Tell us all about your proposal for the farm! Tell me that it didn't have anything to do with her. Can you do that?"

"This has nothing to do with Nancy or her job…" he said, muttering. Trevor Goodwell's eyes sought Hogarth's. Hogarth met the man's gaze but didn't respond in kind. He didn't have to. Neville's mumbled reply proved his point. It seemed the girl had a stake in the farm's future after all.

"And you, Mr Goodwell," said Hogarth. "What did you think this announcement was about?"

"I don't know, of course. But it should have been about Nigel taking on a partner to run the business."

"That's a fast track to losing the whole farm," said Neville.

"No, son. You know nothing about it," said Goodwell. "By taking a partner Grave Farm would still be here in a hundred years' time. If you have your way, Neville – and if she has hers – it'll be closed, sold up for tuppence, and gone before summertime."

Neville shook his head and bit his tongue.

"Did you speak to Mr Grave about your idea too?" said Hogarth.

"Many times," said Goodwell.

"It was the only reason he ever came here," said Neville. "Uncle Trevor's got more pitch than Old Trafford, haven't you, Trevor?"

Goodwell shook his head and tutted like the accusation was beneath him.

"Be honest with yourself," said Goodwell. "Do you think you're the reason she's here, Neville?"

The girl in the bright dress leaned towards Goodwell.

"Yes, I am here for Neville," she said. "He's the only reason I'm here."

Venky's head snapped up. "Now listen you lot," said the vet, in a loud voice which seemed to surprise him as much as the others. "I think you'd all better shut up or leave. Think of poor Susan here, instead of yourselves."

Hogarth looked around and took in the silence. At last someone had finally said it. Hogarth waited until the silence and shame seeped into the atmosphere, then he spoke again. "Just a couple more questions."

One by one they looked at him. Hogarth made sure to meet their gaze.

"Is any one of you involved in a sport or activity requiring that you wear a neoprene wetsuit, or that you wear any protective equipment?"

He watched heads shake around the room.

"Not even you, Mr Venky? You're a vet, after all.

The tall man shook his head. "I wear plastic disposable gloves, much like the ones your crime scene people had on before. I don't wear anything made of neoprene. To be honest, I don't even know what it is."

"It's man-made rubber, essentially," said Hogarth.

"Why do you ask?" said Neville.

Hogarth looked at Neville Grave with careful eyes.

"It's just a question, that's all."

Hogarth watched his reactions for a moment longer before the young man's eyes fell away.

"What? None of you?" said Hogarth. "None of you wear anything like that? Not in the course of work or leisure? You don't use it." There was no response.

"Fine," said Hogarth. "That's been noted. And Mrs Grave… if you don't mind, may I ask you a question?"

Venky looked at Hogarth, with a protective air.

"What is it about?"

"A simple question, that's all."

The woman looked up at him with pink eyes.

"If your husband ever wrote anything down… where did he leave it? Did he have a work desk? An office, maybe? Something like that?"

The woman shook her head. "No. Not in the house, he didn't. He didn't like indoor work of that kind. He used to write letters at this table. Other than that, he used to do his business work, thinking and number crunching, in the tool shed."

Hogarth looked around for a reaction from the others but didn't see one.

"And where's the tool shed?" he said.

"Just out the back there. To the right of the garden."

Hogarth nodded. "May I take a look?"

"I'll show you the way," said Neville Grave, standing up from his seat.

"If you think that's necessary, Mr Grave," said Hogarth.

Neville Grave paused.

"It's locked. I meant I would get the key and open it for you."

"Who was the last person to go in there?"

Neville shrugged. "It was Dad's place. Come on, you can see for yourself."

Neville opened a plain wooden drawer in the kitchen cupboard and took out a long old-fashioned key. Hogarth nodded to the others as they left. Palmer followed suit. "Thanks again."

Neville led the way into the garden. Hogarth followed with Palmer behind. They crossed through the overgrown, strangled allotments to a battered grey shed which looked almost as ancient as the house. The lock crunched and complained as the key was turned in the door. Neville opened the door, bouncing it across the cold dry mud. Inside Hogarth saw old-fashioned tools and new hand tools hanging side-by-side from hooks on the wall. On one side, beneath a cracked glass window was a rickety table which looked as if it was made from an old door. On the floorboards below it was a plastic milk carton – a four-pinter, cut in half for a makeshift waste bin. There was a pencil on the table top. It had been cut the old-fashioned way – the wood and lead chopped away by a blade. Hogarth scanned the dim space, eyes reaching into every corner.

"Give me a moment, will you?" he said to Neville.

"Of course," he said. But Neville hesitated before backing out of the shed.

Hogarth ignored his presence and closed the door behind them, then dipped down and picked up the plastic milk bottle. He poked a finger inside, flicking a dried brown apple core and a dusty teabag out of the way to reach some screwed-up paper. He teased a couple of pieces free and laid them on the desk.

"A receipt for motor oil..." said Hogarth. "A shopping list... and...what's this? Hang on."

Hogarth pulled open a strip of paper as long and thin as a bookmark. It had rough torn edges on either side, and it contained a faint black spidery scrawl.

Hogarth tried to read it, holding the strip of paper to the light from the window. He moved the strip closer and further away from his eyes until the note began to make sense.

"I can't be the generation to lose the farm to the bailiffs. None of the alternatives were very good, but I've spent a long time considering them - much longer than some of you would have liked. Even so, I have made up my mind..." The note ended there. Hogarth looked at Palmer.

"You're a bloody tease, Nigel," said Hogarth.

"What is it?" said Palmer. "A page from a diary?"

"No. I don't think so," said Hogarth. "It reads more like a letter than a diary."

"He wrote a letter and then tore it up before he posted it? That doesn't make sense," said Palmer.

"He could have changed his mind and re-written it," said Hogarth. "But no, I don't think it's a letter."

"Then what is it?"

"I think this could be notes for his little speech. These notes could have been the basis for Mr Grave's announcement here today. But either Mr Grave changed his mind... or someone else decided to change it for him."

As he finished speaking, the door was knocked and shuddered outwards, opening into the daylight.

"Did you find anything?" said Neville Grave. Hogarth slid the note under his palm and into his shirt sleeve.

"A couple of scraps of paper, nothing much really."
"Oh. Sorry to hear that. Look…" said Neville, looking over his shoulder towards the farmhouse. "I just wanted to have a word with you before you left.
"Oh? What about?" said Hogarth folding his arms
"My father…"
They left the shed and Neville spoke to them as he locked the door behind them.
"My father was a great farmer. When he was a young man the farm flourished. But in the last ten or fifteen years he lost his way. He neglected it. He didn't keep changing the farm the way you have to these days. Look around, detective. You can see the place has gone to pot."
"But you were here the whole time, weren't you? If things were so bad, Neville, why weren't you doing anything to help?"
"Help? Of course I helped them in every way I could. But my voice used to be too young to be heard."
Hogarth eyed Palmer.
"What is it that you wanted to speak about, Mr Grave?"
"It's Trevor and Marjorie… they're trying to paint my Nancy in a very bad light. On top of that they're trying to make me look like a fool."
"Are they?" said Hogarth.
"Yes, Inspector," said Neville, frowning. "You must have noticed it."
"I notice a lot of things, Mr Grave. And the things I miss my colleague here picks up on."
"They're saying Nancy is only here to manipulate us for the benefit of her employer. To try and get her hands on the property for them. I mean, that's ludicrous."
"Is it, Mr Grave?" said Hogarth.

"Of course it is. Trevor and Marjorie have an axe to grind with me because I was Nigel's son. They don't like my influence, because they're worried it'll affect the family's wealth. Please. I'm not asking anything of you. I just don't want them to have shaped your judgment about Nancy, or me for that matter."

"Oh no. Their opinions haven't come into my reckoning, Mr Grave. You can rest assured on that score. Beyond the evidence, we'll look at every person in this case on their own merits, and their misdemeanours."

Hogarth's words were neutral enough, but they still sounded like a threat. Hogarth didn't mind at all.

"We'll speak soon, Mr Grave," said Hogarth, walking away. As he passed the kitchen window, Hogarth looked in to see tall Peter Venky consoling Susan Grave with a hand on her shoulder. But it was the eyes of Nancy Decorville which stole Hogarth's attention. As she looked out from the window, her eyes seemed brighter than all the rest. Hogarth watched her as he walked away.

When Hogarth was gone, Neville Grave walked into the kitchen and closed the stable door.

"Well, what was all that about?" said Goodwell.

"What?" said Neville.

"You bending that policeman's ear like that. We all saw you, so don't deny it. What did you say to him then? Spit it out."

"Nothing."

"Nothing eh? That was a lot of talking for saying nothing. Just what are you up to, Neville? Sometimes I wonder if you even know yourself."

Goodwell's eyes traced over Nancy Decorville's back.

"What did you make of that?" said Palmer.

"It's like watching a nasty, vicious, scrappy game of rugby on a muddy pitch. Everyone's covered in the crap, they're busily gouging each other's eyes out, and no one knows where the ball is. The poor old man's remains aren't even cold, and this lot are busy tearing each other apart. You've got to feel sorry for the victim's wife. If it wasn't for her having bats in the belfry she'd probably be next."

"But what about Neville and the girlfriend," said Palmer. "They bother me the most."

"He comes across as a slimy manipulating type, but she could be even worse. Let's look at them when we get back to base. Start digging and let's see what we can get."

Chapter Six

Back at the station, Palmer got busy. She called Gardner's & Co and got through to Norman Gardner, the man in charge. Gardner spoke slowly and enunciated his words like a Church of England vicar. And when she told him about Nigel Grave's murder, the man seemed genuinely upset.
"That's terrible, truly, truly terrible," he said.
"Yes, Mr Gardner, it was," said Palmer.
"Have you got any suspects as yet?" he said.
"We're just starting our inquiries," she said, keeping her cards close to her chest.
"Which is why you want to know about Mr Grave's last will and testament? You're looking for the motive, obviously. But you can't really believe it was family, can you?"
"At this stage, Mr Gardner, we can rule nothing out. Not until the evidence tells us what we need to know. There is a will, I take it."
"Yes, a standard joint will. The estate passes to the partner left behind, although I had started some preliminary work on an LPA for the Graves in case one or both of them became unable to manage their affairs properly. Just some initial inquiries, you understand."
"An LPA? You mean a Lasting Power of Attorney?" said Palmer.
"Exactly. Mr Grave came to see me about it only last month. In fact, we talked about it extensively."
Palmer thought of the old lady by the dining table, with the childlike petulant look on her face and the glassy eyes. She

seemed to flit between adult behaviour and slipping into the childish airs of someone with signs of dementia.

"Did Mr Grave mention why he was thinking of an LPA?" said Palmer.

"Not entirely. He was rarely an open book. But his age and his health suggested it was a concern. I didn't want to probe too much. I'd known him for a very long time, but only in a professional capacity. LPAs are sensitive matters."

"Can I ask who he wanted to act as his attorney?"

"He seemed caught between two different people. I could tell it was a struggle for him. Being an attorney is an awful responsibility in a time of family crisis. The powers usually come into effect after the subject becomes mentally incapacitated. Which is a problem for those involved already. An emotional drain, a time drain, and the like. Which often means the attorney has a lot going on when they are landed with this new added responsibility of managing someone else's financial affairs."

"So, you think that's why he couldn't choose?" said Palmer. "Nigel Grave was worried about putting on people?"

"Probably. He was a very kindly man."

"Do you know who he might have been thinking of?"

"I've known him long enough to guess."

"Yes?" said Palmer.

"There were two alternatives, DS Palmer. Either, Neville, his adopted son or Trevor, his brother-in-law. They are natural candidates for the role."

Palmer's mind had tripped over one of Gardner's words. She rewound the conversation in her head.

"Excuse me, Mr Gardner. Did you say Neville was Mr Grave's *adopted* son?"

There was a moment's silence.

"Yes. Yes, I did," said Gardner. "*You didn't know?*"

"It hadn't come up yet, that's all," said Palmer.

"Yes. Neville was adopted in the sense that he wasn't Nigel's own flesh and blood."

Palmer processed what she'd heard so far.

"That's a funny way to put it, Mr Gardner. Adoption is adoption, is it not?" said Palmer.

"Yes and no. I'm afraid I've overstepped the mark already here, detective. I feel I must leave the matter there."

Palmer scribbled furiously on a notepad beside the phone. *Neville – Adopted – What?* She circled the note.

"Very well, Mr Gardner, had you heard anything lately about their health – either Mrs Grave or Mr Grave, to suggest a power of attorney needed to be triggered?"

"Mr Grave wasn't as strong as he used to be. It was clear he was aging faster than before. But I didn't pry."

"And he didn't mention his wife?"

"I asked about her – as one does. He said Susan was fine. I didn't see the need to pry any further."

Palmer chewed her lip. Then why did old Nigel ask about an LPA? *It had to be for his wife.* But if that were true, did the old man have a premonition that he wasn't going to be around? Did he have an inkling someone wanted him dead? Or was it simply the inquiry of a man who always acted carefully and responsibly about his assets.

"He gave you no clue as to why he asked about it, Mr Gardner? None at all?"

"If you knew Nigel Grave, you would have known that he wanted to ensure the farm carried on. That was always at the forefront of his mind. The matter of the LPA would have been no different.

"How do you know?"

"Because it always was. He was afraid of being the one to kill off the family legacy. I knew the finances were precarious. That was easy to see."

"Tell me, Mr Gardner. What do you make of Neville Grave and Trevor Goodwell?"

"What? Their characters, you mean? Both seem fine from what I know. Trevor was a successful businessman in the city. I discussed that with Nigel. And Neville had shown immense loyalty and capability in running things for Nigel when he was busy."

"Busy?"

Silence again. When Gardner spoke again his voice was hesitant.

"Yes…" said Gardner. "There were periods of time when his mother had trouble."

"Trouble?"

Gardner sighed. "I suppose I shall have to tell you. Gambling and alcohol, detective. Never a good mix, I think you'll agree. There were times he had to take her away from the farm to get her fixed. Rehab and all that. Nigel used to go with her from time to time."

"I see… and when was the last bout of those problems."

"A few years back. The trouble is that those problems never really go away. They linger in the background. And alcohol causes plenty of other problems too, doesn't it?"

"You sound like a man of experience, Mr Gardner," said Palmer.

"I've had lots of clients with problems, detective. Booze is right up there at the top, along with cocaine. It makes people act out of character. They ruin their lives over it."

"So, did Mrs Grave ever act out of character?"

"Oh, a great many times, from what I hear. I think it was why Nigel hesitated about choosing who to have his power of attorney."

"Why?"

"Because she fell out with Neville, their son, a good few years back. She decided he was out to get them. Their money, the farm too."

Palmer took a long gulp of her lukewarm coffee, in lieu of something much stronger.

"Was there any basis for that – in reality, I mean?" she said.

"Who knows? But I very much doubt it. Listen, Detective Palmer… I've only told you all this because it'll come out sooner or later. But I had thought you would have known about the adoption business already."

"As you said, Mr Gardner, it would have come out soon enough. Did Mr Grave say if anyone else knew about that LPA?"

"I doubt it. Like I said, he was quite a private man."

"How far did things progress with the LPA?"

"Not far enough. We didn't even fill out the form. It was a discussion, that's all. He was going to book an appointment and fill it out with me at a later date. It'll never happen now, of course."

"No. No, it won't. You've been a great help, Mr Gardner."

"Yes. I hope you bring this villain to justice. Nigel was a kind man. He looked after the migrant workers, you know. No matter what had happened before, he always cared for them."

"Mr Gardner? What did you mean by that?"

This time the pause at the other end seemed final. Gardner clearly believed he had said enough already.

"Like I said, he was a very kindly man. I'm sorry. Duty calls. I must go now. Goodbye, detective."

The call was over. Palmer looked at the string of scruffy notes made on the pad beside her desk.

LPA not set up. Did Farmer Grave know he would be killed? The adoption. Mother believed him a threat.

To this Palmer added one more line. *Did Farmer Grave have a past problem with migrants?* It was worth checking.

Gardner had presented her with at least three possible gold nuggets. The LPA could have been a motive of a kind – either in believing it had already been set up, or in preventing it.

Then there was the son having a grievance with his mother. And now the possible migrant issue.

Gardner had given them a treasure trove of questions, but what they needed were answers. Palmer stared at her notes and chewed the end of her biro as the office door creaked open. Hogarth walked in with a few neat sheets of paper his hand. He laid them down on the desk in front of her.

"You see that?" said Hogarth. "The notes from the shed match the shred of paper copied from Marris. It's part of the same piece," said Hogarth, "but there's a ton missing. But wait for it," he said. "I only saw this part when I photocopied it. There was another line on the back. Can you see it?"

Palmer squinted to make it out.

"Even Peter had an idea of what to do, but there was no way I could do it without…"

"Peter," said Palmer, looking at Hogarth., her mind still swimming with her own discoveries.

"Yes. Peter Venky. The vet. Now why would the vet have given input on the future of the farm?"

"Maybe he didn't, guv. Maybe you're reading too much into it."

"No. It's about the farm. It has to be in order to make sense. But if Peter Venky stuck his oar in as well, then he's not the independent arbitrator I had him down for. And think; he was first on the scene after those migrant workers… I'd say this puts him back firmly in the list of suspects, wouldn't you?"

"About those migrant workers, guv…?"

Hogarth put his hands on his hips and nodded.

"I think your suspect list is going to get a bit longer."

"Longer?" said Hogarth with a frown.

"Something else has come up. I had a chat with the solicitor, and I think Nigel Grave had some kind of past with migrants, and not all of it good."

"Skeletons in the closet, eh?" said Hogarth.

"Where does it end?" said Palmer.

"That's the trouble, Palmer, it doesn't, does it? People just get murkier the deeper you go."

Chapter Seven

"Mr Venky!" said Hogarth, rubbing his hands in the winter cold.
"Inspector Hogarth," said the tall man, standing inside the front door of his vet practice. He pushed his glasses further up on his nose.
"Do come in."
"Busy with pets and livestock?" said Hogarth.
"Not quite. I was forced to cancel my appointments today. It's lucky there were no emergencies. But when a man loses a friend what can one do?"
"Nothing, Mr Venky. Take the blow and roll with it, I'm afraid."
"But what a wicked blow to take."
Peter Venky was his last call of a long day. Hogarth had the gist of Palmer's new information and had chewed on it during the four-mile drive to Rochford where Venky's vet practice was based. It didn't seem likely that Venky was their man. He seemed the least likely money-grabber of them all. Venky didn't stand to gain from his friend's death, not unless he planned on getting hitched to Susan Grave. As the power of attorney had not yet been set up, that was certainly one way to get the farm. But from what Hogarth had seen the woman was in no fit state to marry anyone. If it had been set up, the LPA could have prevented anyone getting the family money through the old woman, but the husband's love for his wife had prevented him from doing what needed to be

done. It was a theory which couldn't be proved, but it made sense to Hogarth.

The tall Mr Venky led them through a white clinical treatment room, beyond a holding area full of empty cages, and past a small reception desk. Beyond this last door the vet's practice turned into a dated but cosy living space with upholstered armchairs, shelves full of books and newspapers, a coffee table, and a rug. Work and home were clearly closely entwined for Peter Venky. "Take a seat," said Venky. "I didn't expect to see you for a third time today."
"Neither did I, Mr Venky, but when new information comes up, I need to consider it as soon as possible. Whoever killed Mr Grave needs to be put away quickly."
Venky's face turned ashen.
"Agreed. Can I get you anything? Tea? Maybe something stronger, detective?"
"You don't know how tempting that sounds, but I'd better not."
The tall man nodded, took off his white coat and hung it over a tea trolley in the corner of the living room.
Venky sat down and Hogarth followed suit. The room was musty, but not unpleasant. Add a real log fire and it was the kind of room Hogarth could have easily fallen asleep in.
"New information, you say?" said Mr Venky.
"Yes. Today's family lunch was set up, so Mr Grave could announce the farm's future, yes?"
"I believe so."
"You were Mr Grave's friend, is that correct?"
Venky nodded.
"You must have been or you wouldn't have been invited to the lunch."
"Yes, we were good friends for well over twenty years."

Hogarth nodded. "Then maybe you know what his actual intentions were for the farm?"

"I'm afraid not. Nigel was a secretive man, Inspector. Not in a bad way. But he was very traditional and careful. He liked to think about things a great deal before he committed to them, which is one of the reasons I think the farm was held back like it was. It declined because of his belief in the old ways. And not only that. He *liked* the old ways. It gave him a link to his father, and to the generations before him who'd looked after that farm. He felt a great sense of responsibility."

"But he didn't tell you his plan."

Venky shrugged. "He mooted a few things. I know he had finally relented. He wanted to modernise it."

"Modernise in which way?"

"I simply can't tell you, Inspector."

"I've already seen quite clear evidence of two divergent plans coming from Trevor Goodwell and Neville Grave. Do you know about those?"

"I have more than an inkling. I've been around and seen it when either Trevor or Neville was badgering him."

Hogarth waited.

"In short, Neville wants him to adopt new ways. He talks about a diverse range of incomes, a modern farm with varied crops, farm stay holiday accommodation, farm tours, workshops, a business centre. That kind of thing. He speaks of the farm as a brand and as a piece of land for multiple uses. He said the farm should be modern like that, but I think it reeked of far too much change for Nigel to handle. A farm was for growing crops and rearing livestock. Not a mere piece of land."

"Not like the way Neville's girlfriend, Nancy Decorville, might see it?" said Hogarth.

"That girl is quite a charmer, but I think Trevor might have a point about her. She appeared on the scene when Neville organised an event to promote the farm as a business centre. I don't think he actually asked Nigel for permission for that event, but he ran it anyway and I went along to support it, and there she was. It was the first time I laid eyes on her. It was only a matter of a few weeks and then they were an item. I don't want to cast aspersions, Inspector. It could be very innocent. But it seemed like a hasty affair given the timing.

"You think she's an opportunist, then?"

"I think her career is as important to her as her romantic interests, let's put it that way."

Hogarth nodded. He knew exactly what the man was saying. "And do you think she could have had anything to do with Mr Grave's death?"

"What? Are you serious?!"

"I have to ask," said Hogarth.

"I don't see how. And I think she arrived at the house after Nigel was killed. Besides… Nigel had become quite a slight old man in his final years, granted, but a girl like her couldn't lift him, surely. Whoever lifted poor Nigel had to be strong enough to turn him over and dump him into that bloody awful machine…"

Hogarth had already reached the same conclusion, but it was still possible that the girl was stronger than she looked.

"The machine, Mr Venky. It was purchased for another of the son's diversification ideas."

"It was. And it was a tragic mistake as we can see."

"Mr Goodwell questioned the purchase as a dead loss," said Hogarth.

"Trevor is Neville's second worst critic, Inspector."

"Only second worst? I can't imagine having a worse critic," said Hogarth. "So, who is the first?"

"His mother," said Venky.

"His mother?"

"Yes. There's a long-term love/hate relationship there, Inspector. It's always been like that."

"But why? They seemed close enough before."

"Did they? I suppose at times they're close. At other times, she's suspicious of him and resentful. As you may have noticed, she has wild mood swings, but Neville bears the brunt of it, mostly."

"Do you know why, Mr Venky?"

Venky sighed and leaned back in his chair. "I don't like talking about things which are not my domain, Inspector."

"You mean her medical condition? We already know that Nigel Grave made inquiries about setting up a Lasting Power of Attorney. It's possible the inquiry was made to put financial controls in place in event of Mr Grave dying and his wife being unfit to manage the estate."

"Susan would never have agreed to that."

"But if she was mentally unfit…?"

Venky shifted in his seat and folded his arms.

"What do you think is wrong with her, Inspector?"

Hogarth's brow dipped low over his eyes. "She seems a little confused. I'd guessed she was suffering from early dementia, maybe even Alzheimer's. I'll be able to look at the medical reports soon enough…"

Venky shook his head. "I'm afraid her variety of madness is the self-induced kind. Dear Susan is a drunk. Any brain damage she has suffered would have been caused by all her boozing. She's been that way as long as I can remember."

"What? She's a chronic alcoholic?" Hogarth remembered the aniseed smell on the air. His early suspicions hadn't been wrong then.

"And it's never been treated properly. Oh, Nigel would take her away from time to time to get her fixed up, get a little rehab and what have you. But it was always private. And she always went back to the bottle in the end. I am telling you because I know her too well, Susan would never have accepted the LPA."

Hogarth took it all in. The Grave family were a kaleidoscope of problems. Hogarth wondered what he would discover next. He needed progress, not more mess to contain.

"Mr Venky, we found some notes written in Mr Grave's hand. Nigel Grave. The notes look recently written, but they were torn up. Some were found on the body... a few were found elsewhere."

"Writing, eh? Nigel used writing as way of gathering his thoughts. He didn't talk much, so he wrote when he had bigger things to work through."

"We know he'd come to a decision on the future of the farm and I think he'd written it down," said Hogarth. "Maybe he'd even written these notes as the basis of the announcement he was to give at the lunch. I think he was going to tell you all his decision and how he'd arrived at it. Unfortunately, those notes are incomplete. But we've got enough to see that you had also advised him on the future of the farm. But it seems he wasn't convinced of your ideas, either, Mr Venky. What did you want to convince him of?"

Venky shrugged.

"I didn't want to convince him of anything. I wanted to help him."

That's what they all say, thought Hogarth.

Venky must have seen the suspicion in his eyes.

"Look. I recommended trying a rare breeds farm. They're all the rage these days and there's much more money to be earned that way. Yes, the animals need a little more care, but I could have provided that…"

Hogarth's eyes narrowed.

"At a discount, Inspector! This was never a money-making scheme. I wanted Nigel to prosper, not me."

"And you know he wasn't receptive to your ideas?"

"Broadly. I knew he wasn't receptive to anyone's ideas, much. Slow to think and even slower to act. That was our Nigel."

"Did that frustrate you at all?"

The vet's eyebrows tilted up into an arc. "Not enough to kill him! Nothing could frustrate me enough to kill anyone. Not even enough to have a spat. He was my friend, Inspector. Do you think I'm somehow implicated in this? How could I be? I only saw the body after the migrant workers did. Igor and the other one, Borev."

"So you say."

"They *were* there before me. Igor is an honourable man. He will vouch for me."

"Let's hope so."

"I don't have to hope so, Inspector. In all good conscience, I didn't do anything to harm my friend. I've helped Nigel out during the hard times with his wife. And I helped him out during the bad times with his son and on the farm."

Hogarth's eyes lit up, his mind brimming with questions. Hogarth's look continued to put Venky into defensive mode.

"Look…" said Venky. "Is it truly necessary for me to tell you exactly why I had no reason to kill him? No reason at all."

"Tell me whatever you think will help, Mr Venky."

The man pushed himself up from his chair with a pale, downcast face. He walked to a set of shelves by the fireplace and teased out some paperwork from between some books on animal husbandry. He handed the folded sheets to Hogarth and sat back down again, blinking at Hogarth from behind his spectacles.

"Well go on then. You might as well see," said Venky.

Hogarth teased open the pieces of paper. One had the blue NHS logo at the top. The other had the bright green insignia of MacMillan Cancer Support. Hogarth frowned and scan-read the documents. The NHS letter was an appointment for a meeting to discuss how palliative care worked, and the other was a first appointment letter with MacMillan.

"Do you see?" said Venky. "I'm dying, Inspector. I've got an advanced cancer. It's in my system and it's far too late to treat – not that I would bother anyway. I want to live before I die, not drown myself in radiation and chemotherapy."

Hogarth looked at the man who seemed as well as any other, but the evidence in his hand was undeniable.

"I'm very sorry, Mr Venky."

"At least you see. That's one very good reason why I would never harm another person for financial gain… but in case you wanted another, I've got another very good one."

Venky made him wait for it. Hogarth nodded for him to go on.

"Nigel was dying too," said Venky.

"What?"

Venky nodded. "It's true, Inspector. It brought us closer, of course. I suggested the rare breed animals not just for money, but to give him a passion for doing what he used to love, with the time he had left. I have months at most, Inspector, maybe a year. But Nigel had maybe a year left. He still had time to enjoy it."

"Cancer?"

"They say it gets one in three of us, don't they? Well for me and Nigel it was two out of two. Mine is pancreatic. His was prostate. He had a little time, but someone robbed him of it. That's the worst thing of all. I should have gone before him, Inspector. It's so bitterly sad."

Hogarth ran a hand through his hair and sighed.

"I'm sorry, Mr Venky."

"Yes, so you've said."

"But who else knew? His wife? His son?"

"In time, yes. But he was holding all of them off for now. I think that was one of the reasons he couldn't commit to changing the farm. He'd been in shock about his health. But now he had come to terms with it, he was ready to hand it on ready for the modern era."

"Was he going to announce his medical condition?"

"Oh no. Nigel really wasn't ready for that. This was all about the farm. He told me he'd only tell them about his health when it was about to become obvious and it wasn't going to be obvious for a while yet. Besides, he was worried it would send Susan on a killer bender when he needed them thinking straight."

"And they didn't know? You're sure? Not any of them?"

"No. I'm sure. But he *was* dying, Inspector. You'll be able to prove it too, won't you?"

Hogarth nodded. "Soon enough, yes… Mr Venky. I don't want to trouble you any further, but I must ask just a couple more questions."

"Very well."

"What was the issue with the migrant workers, Mr Venky?"

"Igor and the other one? There were no issue as far as I'm aware. They were well liked."

"I don't mean the recent batch. I mean the past issues. We've picked up information that there was a past issue surrounding migrant workers at Grave Farm."

Venky frowned and shook his head.

"Do you really need to go digging there, Inspector, at this unsavoury time?"

"I have to go wherever this case takes me, Mr Venky. The past always has some bearing on the present."

"Who told you then?"

"No one told us outright. A rumour slipped someone's lips."

Venky frowned.

"Now is not the time for this. But if you're demanding I tell you…"

"I'm asking for your full cooperation, Mr Venky."

The man sank back in his chair and folded his arms.

"It was a long time ago. It was 1991 when it happened. Nigel and I were mere acquaintances at the time. He told me about it afterwards. Nigel had always taken on migrant workers at the farm. Before then it had been the Irish ones and the students, but after '91 it was Greeks, Portuguese and people from all over. They were good hard-working folk. But he did have trouble with one of them. Susan complained. She said this one man kept making eyes at her. Said he kept on appearing near the house. Then one day she got in a dreadful state and said he attacked her. Nigel went wild and chased the man off, but in the end, they fought. Nigel eventually told me that he lost the plot and stabbed him with a pitchfork. Thankfully the man lived and didn't press charges. Nigel paid him up for his work the rest of the year without the poor man lifting a hand. Not long after, the truth came out. Susan had been the one making the advances. One of the older workers had seen it all. He told Nigel everything and it stacked up and made sense. Nine months later, Susan gave birth at the ripe old age of forty-two. Nigel had been childless. He didn't have an heir apparent, and even though he knew it wasn't his, he brought up that child as his own."

"Neville?"

"Yes. Neville."

"But I was told he was adopted."

Venky shook his head. "No. Not adopted. But certainly not favoured by his mother. She loved him and resented him in equal measure. She's the one who bandied that word about, bad as it is. She's treated him so badly through the years. I always supposed it was because Neville was the permanent evidence of what she'd done. She lied to Nigel and had a son by another man and kept the pretence going for years. Think – she almost had another man killed because of her drunken lies. And yet she somehow blamed her son for it all."

"Where did the adoption idea come from?"

"Oh, I heard a little about it. When he was a child she tried to have him adopted by someone else. It was another family secret. I doubt Neville ever knew."

"I wouldn't be so sure about that," said Hogarth. "Then in the eyes of the law, he is their son, and would stand to inherit the farm."

"But his mother is still alive, Inspector. And she will inherit everything before he ever would. You think Neville is the killer?"

"We'll all know who the killer is soon enough, Mr Venky. Thanks for your help."

Hogarth stood and gave the man an earnest nod, then slowly made for the door. Venky let him out.

"The family is a mess. It always was, Inspector. But I can't see how they could have killed a man like Nigel. It must be someone else. Just please make sure you get them."

"Oh, I intend to, Mr Venky. You can count on it."

The door closed, and Hogarth turned away to face his thoughts.

The family was a mess? The entire case looked like a quagmire. It was only day one, but everyone bar Venky was a suspect. And the dirty cover-up of the lies, the violence, and the migrant's child were a strong potential motive. Digging another level down, the case had just gotten even murkier. Climbing into his Vauxhall Insignia beneath a cold dark sky, Hogarth thought about the lies Susan Grave had told. He imagined how Nigel Grave must have felt as his wife recounted the tales of being followed and watched by a strange man on their own family farm. Of being attacked, of being raped at home. The farmer would have been beside himself. Rightly so. Hogarth understood all too well what the man had been through. Those lies had come with a cost for everyone at Grave Farm. Was it possible, that almost thirty years on, Nigel Grave had paid the highest price of all? Igor and Borev needed looking at, but so did Susan Grave. From a muddled old woman with a slipping mind, to a lying, cheating drunken harridan in one day. No wonder the job was taking its toll on him. Hogarth drove a mile before his thoughts of the case took him straight back to Ali Hartigan He thought about the stalker. He thought about embracing her in that hotel bed. Then he imagined the stalker bearing down on her, striking her on the doorstep of her home. Hogarth gritted his teeth and slapped the steering wheel.

"Screw it!" said Hogarth.

He doubled back around the Rochford roundabout and took the turning for Westcliff and Southend Hospital. By hook or by crook, he had to see her.

Chapter Eight

Hogarth marched right up to the Rigby Ward, and snuck in after a woman who held the door open for him. He breezed past the reception with a fixed smile, his tie flying back over his shoulder like a scarf in a high wind. There was a gallery window overlooking the wide ward where Ali's bed had been stationed. He looked in, his heart thudding as he considered that he was breaking the rules of their 'arrangement'. But right now, he didn't care. The curtains were drawn around the end bed where he had seen her before. Maybe they were giving her a bed bath or seeing to her wounds. Surely it didn't mean anything bad – because he didn't know if he could cope if it did. His heart rate thudded faster at the thought. Before he stopped to consider whether it was wise, he pushed the door into the orange-walled ward and stamped along the tiled floor. He waited outside the edge of the blue curtain and listened.

"I'll just do this, and we'll be done, okay?" said the nurse, hidden behind the curtain.

"Hello?" said Hogarth. He waited for a response, but none came. He shook his head, looked around and decided he couldn't wait anymore.

"Ali?" he called. He hung his head and looked at the tiles. "Ali? It's me."

A few of the people in the other beds looked around at him. He ignored them.

"Ali?!" he said.

The curtain was jerked aside, and a bespectacled nurse stuck her head out. Hogarth tried to steal a look past her, but she pulled the curtain and blocked him.

"Visiting hours don't start for another hour."

"I'm a policeman. I'm working on a serious case, and I took time off to come and see if she was okay."

"I don't care if you're the prime minister. The rules are the rules for the police as well as anybody else."

Hogarth shook his head. "Ali? Are you okay in there?"

There was no response from behind the curtains.

"Do you mind?!" said the nurse.

"I just want to see Ali Hartigan."

"Ali Hartigan? The MP's wife?" said one of the other patients.

Hogarth nodded.

"She's gone," said another.

Hogarth blinked at the nurse, his face aflame. The nurse disappeared back behind her curtain.

"You're sure about that?" said Hogarth, looking at the other patients.

"Yes. I heard an ambulance took her home this afternoon."

Hogarth bit his lip, then in one quick move tugged an edge of the blue curtain and peered inside. A large woman sat up in the bed while the nurse attended to some stitches on the side of her head. The nurse turned her head and glared at him. "Oi! I've warned you!" said the nurse. Hogarth had seen all he needed. He dropped the curtain back into place. As the nurse called out after him, Hogarth strode out of the reception and into the main hospital corridor.

Ali being sent home should have been good news, but somehow it made him feel worse. The stalker had been proved violent, and now Ali had been sent home he wondered if her husband had made any provision for her safety. This time he couldn't risk it. He had to know.

***

North Lane, Shoebury

The lights were on inside the big plush house. Classical music and warmth poured through the double glazing and net curtains, but it gave Hogarth no comfort. He walked past the big house, hoping Ali would see him and come to the door. But nothing happened. On a second whim, he chose to walk down the lane, hoping to catch the stalker hanging around. He felt wired with tension from the new case and with unspent rage after what had happened to Ali. But there was no one around. Hogarth looked back at the house and noted that the driveway was empty – the MP's jag was nowhere in sight, which meant the blighter was in London again, pretending to earn his inflated wages as an upstanding citizen. Self-righteous lying hypocrites, the bloody lot of them. Hogarth took a breath and crossed the street, making a beeline right for the front door.

He rang the doorbell and waited as the chime echoed deep inside.

"Come on, Ali, come on!" he muttered, as he bounced on his feet.

He tensed as a shadow came towards the front door. It lingered behind the glass for a moment and then the door opened. A tall man with a receding hairline opened the door. He had a neatly trimmed fashionable beard. His hair and his beard were dark brown. He wore a white shirt with an open collar and had a smallish paunch belly. Hogarth recognised the man from his posed smiling shots from the front of The Record. It was none other than James Hartigan MP. *Damn.*

"Yes? Who are you?"

"I'm… I'm Inspector Hogarth, Southend Police."

The MP looked confused. Hogarth tried to hide his awkwardness behind a stiff, professional air. His work face.

"I'm sorry. Are we supposed to be expecting you? I don't think…"

"No, I just came to ensure that Mrs Hartigan is okay?"

"Mrs Hartigan?" said the man. He looked at Hogarth and stiffened. "My wife is doing very well considering what she's been through."

"Then she's okay? She's not hurt?"

"She was hurt, but she'll be okay in a few days. Shouldn't you already know about that? She's stoic. Always has been. But I'm afraid I can't let anyone in to see her. She's resting."

The two men regarded one another for the first time. They exchanged a brief look, questioning one another in silence.

"What did you say your name was, Inspector?"

Hogarth didn't answer. As the man spoke, Hogarth caught sight of someone else moving into view in the hallway behind him. Hogarth made out a female silhouette and a warm but guarded smile briefly flickered across Hogarth's face. But it wasn't Ali. The woman drifted into view until she was close by the MP's side. She was in the forty-to-fifty bracket with tied-back blonde hair. She was pretty, but had hard eyes. She wore a white blouse and a dark work skirt.

"James, who is this?" As Hogarth looked at the woman, he couldn't help shaking his head.

"It's a policeman. He's come to check that Alison is okay…"

"Oh," said the woman, assessing him.

"Okay, Mr Hartigan, no problem" said Hogarth, trying to adopt a breezy tone. "I'll keep a look out for you. And if I catch this stalker scumbag hanging around, you can be assured that I'll handle it. But if anything else happens in the meantime, please call it in as soon as possible, okay? I'll make sure someone comes as soon as the call comes in."

"I'm afraid I'm rarely here, Inspector. Duty calls and all that. But I've already had a chat with your Chief Superintendent and he assures me we are a priority."

"The Super? That's all well and good. But If I were you, Mr Hartigan, I'd add in an extra layer of protection. You're an MP. Considering the situation, you must warrant some kind of extra support."

"My support and protection is the police, just like everyone else."

Hogarth bristled. "And after what's happened you think that's enough, do you?

"Now, look here…" said Hartigan. "What's your name? What's is your interest here exactly?"

"My interest is protecting people, Mr Hartigan. But I think I already know what your interest is." Hogarth's eyes flicked to the blonde in the suit. Her hand self-consciously traced to her throat under Hogarth's gaze.

"Excuse me?" said the MP, in a shocked tone.

"Forget it, Mr Hartigan. I think you're far too busy for the likes of me."

Hogarth turned away and stormed off towards the street. The MP and the blonde lingered in the doorway watching him, muttering to each other as he got into the car. Hogarth doubted he'd heard the last of the matter, but he was past caring. The scumbag's wife was upstairs in her sickbed, while his mistress was downstairs taking dictation… and the rest. Unbelievable. Hogarth still needed to see her, but tonight was a write-off. Instead, the only thing that beckoned was half a bottle of single malt to drown a head full of questions. Drink was going to be essential this evening. Which meant a workday hangover was on the cards. Hogarth started the engine, and sighed. His visit to the Hartigan household had become a messy mistake and he was going to pay for it one way or another. But he'd still enjoyed having a pop at the man. Hogarth had to hope it was worth the price he would soon have to pay.

Chapter Nine

"DI Hogarth, I'd like a word with you please."
Hogarth was about to cross the threshold of the CID room to start his day at work when DCI Melford called to him from across the open plan office. PC Orton raised his eyebrows and offered PC Jordan a sneery little grin to go with it, but PC Stephens was older and wiser and looked away as Hogarth passed their desks. Even young Jordan knew better. As soon as Melford had turned away to walk back to his office, Hogarth passed Orton and elbowed him in the back. Orton dropped a slosh of coffee over the forms waiting for completion on his desk.

"Messy paperwork, Orton," said Hogarth. "Tut-tut. You're setting Jordan here a very bad example."

Orton's face turned beetroot red as Hogarth marched on, but Jordan snorted with laughter.

Hogarth adjusted his shirt collar and tie. It was just a shame he couldn't adjust his head. He did indeed have the hangover he'd predicted, and now he had a feeling he was going to get the carpeting he had predicted too.

He walked into the oppressive room and felt Melford's eyes rake over his face. Melford wrinkled his nose as if he could smell the alcohol on him.

"Close the door please, Hogarth."

"Sir." He shut the door and met Melford's dark eyes.

"What is it with you, DI Hogarth? I gave you an upbraiding during the Club Smart case, and it paid dividends. You got the man before he hurt Simmons or anyone else. But here we are again, and look at you. You were late in yesterday, so now what?"

"I was in late, but I was working., sir."

"On what? I know DS Palmer went out to get you. I observe a lot more than people give me credit for around here, Hogarth. Don't let the fools out there convince you I'm just some old dolt you can do over at will. I paid my dues and worked through the ranks. I know how it goes and I know what the job does to people. Don't let yourself down. And don't blow your career for… for… whatever it is…"

"Sir?"

"I don't know what's up, but I know you have an issue. We can leave it there, if you like." Melford shifted in his chair and prodded a long bony finger at the corner of his desk. "This is off the record because you handled the Club Smart case very well. But, going from zero to hero and back again is not my idea of a useful copper. With DS Simmons out, you'll be under more pressure than ever – for a time. Listen. If you need someone to help get you through a tough spot, you can borrow someone from the other team, as a temporary support, that is."

Hogarth shook his head in thinly veiled disgust. Taking a member from another team was like waving the white flag. The tiredness was closing in on him. Hogarth needed to yawn but didn't dare. Something as trivial as a yawn could have him in deeper trouble if Melford was in the mood. Instead Hogarth's eyes tracked to the old tick-tock clock above Melford's head. It was hard to avoid. The presence of the ancient clock, as well as the DCI's height meant half the team called him Long Melford, after the Norfolk town well-known for its antiques.

"No…" said Melford. "I didn't think you'd want that. But if you're going to continue working on this farm murder – as just you and DS Palmer – then you need to pull your head out of your backside sharpish."

"With due respect," said Hogarth. "I am getting on with it, sir. I worked late last night to make up my hours. But yesterday morning couldn't be helped."

"But you were out all morning, Hogarth…"

"And the Club Smart case has only just finished, sir. I worked day and night on that."

"You're CID, man! You knew what you signed up for."

"I'm still here, sir."

"But it doesn't look like it…" Melford sat up in his seat. "This farm murder, are you on top of it or not? Who do you have in the frame?"

So, it was a test, was it? And Hogarth hadn't even drunk his first coffee of the day. Melford was on a stitch-up this morning. Hogarth wondered if Mrs Long Melford had denied the man his oats.

"Sir," said Hogarth. "I'm waiting on news from Marris regarding footprints from the barn where the old man was killed and on some unusual fibres we found on the floor there. They could be significant depending what we get back. I've spoken to all the witnesses and suspects yesterday bar two migrant workers who were the first on the murder scene."

"First? And you left them till last? Was that wise? By now they could have run off back to wherever they came from with blood on their hands."

"These men were very well known to the victim. They won't run. They'll be interviewed today."

But Hogarth's heart sank. Melford was right. He'd prioritised the family because of sensing they were a brood of vipers, but learning about the family's dark history with the migrants

had changed all that. The migrants could have been involved. But no matter. He'd grill them soon enough.
"That family are like sharks circling around dead meat, sir. Nigel Grave had summoned them together to make an announcement about the future of the farm, but it turns out that the family had been onto him for weeks, if not months about their own plans for it. The son wants to diversify into new areas of the business. The brother in-law wants to bring in partners and has some sort of agenda. Meanwhile even the family vet wanted to put his two-penny's worth in."
"They're after the farm then? You think that's the motive?"
"It stacks up for me. I'll need to look at those foreigners too, but I hope it isn't them. The last thing Southend's immigrant population need is a to be turned into worse bogeymen. You never know how that rag The Record will play it."
"Come on. You always know how The Record will play it. The lowest common denominator every time. Expect the worst and you're never wrong. But why might these foreigners have done it?"
"There could be many reasons. But one is history. Turns out the farmer's wife had got around a bit in her time. I thought she had bats in the belfry at first. I had her down as suffering dementia. But it seems she might have just been a randy drunk. Years back she had an affair with another of the farm's migrant workers – back in the early nineties. To cut a long story short, it seems that the only son, Neville Grave, was a product of the affair."
"Messy, eh? And she's still a drunk?"
"From the look of her, I don't think she's ever been sober."
"Hmmm. But the son of an affair… now there's motive alright. A son who finds out his father lies to him and loses the plot."
"I'm with you sir, but it's hard to make it stack up."

"Why?"

"Looking at the approximate time of death, the son was in clear view of the family the whole time. He never left the room when the old man was killed."

"So, who does that leave us?"

"Everything happened at lunchtime, from eleven-fifty onwards. The family were all together in the kitchen for most of it, with the exception of young Mr Grave's girlfriend, the vet, and the migrants who were always outside. We could be missing something there though. I'll run through the timings again today with Palmer. We'll nail it down before we progress things."

"It's the foreigners, isn't it?" said Melford, with a groan. Hogarth had a nagging fear his superior was right – and without knowing a damn thing about the case. After working so hard, Hogarth felt he was getting lost in the details. Ali Hartigan was getting to him, and the indulgence in the single malt surely hadn't helped.

"Anything on the body?"

"Nothing from Quentin yet, sir."

Melford sighed and leaned back in his chair. "Well you at least *sound* like you're on the ball. The migrant thing was a slip-up, but you can handle that. But sounding like you're on the ball and being on the ball are two different things. This is friendly advice. Get your house in order and shut this case down quickly. Do that, and you won't be doing your reputation any harm at all. It might even get rid of the other questions marks I'm beginning to see around."

Hogarth frowned.

"Question marks?"

"Let's not speak of it now, Hogarth. Speaking of it now makes it real and I don't really want to go there unless it becomes a problem. Which it won't, will it?"

"Sir?" said Hogarth, feigning confusion.

"You know exactly what I'm talking about. Whether it's politics, fanaticism of some kind, or some other special interest, make sure I don't hear of you around North Lane, Shoebury again. Don't you think that MP has enough on his plate?"

"I only wanted to help, that's all."

Melford looked at him doubtfully.

"Even if that were true, it's misguided. Leave it alone. You've got a full plate too. Don't pile it any higher."

"Yes, sir."

Hogarth left the office. Outside in the corridor he closed his eyes to compose himself.

"He's not on your case already, is he?" Hogarth's eyes blinked open and found Palmer standing in front of him.

"What?" said Hogarth. She'd caught him off guard – this time not just by her interruption but by something in her eyes. Hogarth knew Palmer was pretty, underneath her hard, weather-beaten cop exterior. The job did that to everyone. But he was surprised at himself for noticing. Like Melford said, he didn't need any more problems, and in his present plight even a hint of attraction to Palmer was unwelcome. Hogarth humphed and looked away.

"Guv?" said Palmer.

"Don't worry. Melford's got a beef with me but it won't affect the case."

"What was it about then?"

"He just likes to keep me on my toes, that's all. Have you heard from Ed Quentin yet?"

"No," said Palmer. "He said he'll call us back. Did you want me to go to the post-mortem, sir?"

"Not this one. We're shorthanded as it is. Come with me."

"Where?"

"We're going back to Grave Farm. If results will keep Melford off my back, then that's what he's going to get."
"But I don't understand why he's on your back in the first place, guv. You delivered on the Club Smart case. You'll deliver on this one. We only got landed with the case yesterday,"
Hogarth looked sideways at Palmer and nodded. At least someone still thought he could deliver. But it was a good thing she didn't know about his visit to the Hartigan house, or Palmer's faith might have been short-lived.
"Let's hope so," he said, as he walked. "Listen. I spent some time with Venky, the vet, on my way home last night and I learned more than I bargained for, I can tell you."
"Oh?"
"I'll tell you on the way. But what about you? Any news on our friends, Neville and Nancy?"
"Neville's pretty much off the radar as far as I'm concerned," said Palmer. "There's no criminal record or anything like that. Nancy Decorville doesn't have a record either, at least not in the way you'd think."
"Now, I am intrigued," said Hogarth. "And we're going to need to look at those migrant workers, too."
"Why? Anything specific?" said Palmer.
"Apparently the family had a lot of problems involving migrant workers back in the early nineties. Or depending on your point of view you could say the migrant workers had a lot of problems with the family," said Hogarth. "I'll let you be the judge of that."

As they drove out towards the flat green land of the Sutland area beyond the north edge of town, Hogarth use the hands-free to call Marris. Hogarth didn't like the hands-free. When he was on his own he preferred to flout the law and make his calls the old-fashioned way, pressing a phone between his ear and shoulder, but he couldn't set a bad example all the time. His conscience was playing up enough as it was. There was a beep as his call was picked up.

"Morning, Ivan."

"Morning, Hogarth. I must say, you sound a little rough round the edges this morning."

"Thanks for that. I suppose I probably do. Hard work and hard living, you know me."

"Yes…" said Marris. Marris wasn't going to deny it then.

"Ivan, I've got DS Palmer with me here."

The two greeted one another over the loud speaker.

"News, Ivan, what news?"

"Not much I'm afraid. The DNA which I've found so far only relates to the victim. There was DNA everywhere, remember. The woodchipper blades got stuck on the skull and muscle tissue in Nigel Grave's head. Looks like the soft matter clogged up the blades. It churned the poor man's head up like an aerosol spray. It's hard to find anything else down there apart from this poor old man. Crime Scene had the same problem."

"I can imagine."

"But," said Marris, "…the boot prints Dickens found are all fresh. There's a few trainer prints in there too, and plenty of prints which match the old man's shoes. The boot prints suggest wellington boots – the cheap no-frills kind. Size eleven or twelve for both. The trainer shoe is a bit harder, but it's a fancy one, and likely a size 10. I'll have to try and match it to a profile chart, but it could take some time."

"Size tens, elevens and twelves, eh?" said Hogarth. "Which rule out a female killer."

"Unless the woman planned it to look that way," said Palmer.

"Yes, I suppose it's possible."
"What about the neoprene fragments?" said Hogarth.
"Yes, they do belong to an old garment. I'd say the structure of the garment must be badly worn. The fragments I looked at seemed to be fractured and broken down from over-use. And there's no sign of water on them – by which I mean there's no sign of regular use in water. So, I doubt they were from a wetsuit."
"Which leaves us with… what exactly?"
"Protective workwear, boots or perhaps some other sport. There were some sweat salt particles on the neoprene, but no obvious DNA evidence yet. I'll keep checking though."
"Good work, Ivan. At least now we can rule out a marauding scuba-diving assassin then."
"Yes. I'd feel fairly confident about that," said Marris. Hogarth was glad the man had taken the comment in jest.
"Oh, and if I were you, Inspector, I'd check in with Ed Quentin. I take it that you're not going to the PM on this one?"
"I've seen the photographs, Ivan. I haven't even put them up on the incident board yet. They'd be enough to put DS Palmer off her bacon sandwiches. Besides, I don't think there's much contention about cause of death."
Palmer frowned at Hogarth and shook her head. She was hardier than most.
"You lot are getting soft," said Marris. "Anyway, Quentin mentioned some preliminary findings you might be interested in. Best call him after the PM to be sure."
"Care to drop any hints, Ivan?"
"No. I'd rather not. I don't want to steal the good doctor's thunder. I'll speak to you later on."
Ivan Marris cut the call before he could be pressed further. Hogarth looked at Palmer.

"Well?"

"The migrant workers are ruled back in. They have to be," said Palmer.

"Yes, agreed. But I'd have bet good money it was one of the sharks in that kitchen It still might be. But the trainers? Peter Venky wasn't wearing trainer shoes. I'd have noticed. He doesn't look the type either. Did you see any trainers around at the house?"

"No, but I can't say I was looking," said Palmer. "And Trevor Goodwell and the son weren't exactly wearing the sort of clothes which go with trainers. Goodwell is the smart type, all fifty quid shirts and forty-pound slacks, that kind of thing. But I'd put Neville down as a high street shopper. But more Topshop than Armani – he wasn't wearing trainers though."

"Maybe they did it and changed their shoes."

"Or it's someone else entirely," said Palmer.

"Now that is the idea I like least of all. Because that would mean starting from scratch." On their way out of town they drove past the stately red brick building of the crematorium. Hogarth noted Grave Farm and the crem looked similar. Both were remote. Built well away from the road. Both were tall and made of red brick, too. Only, the crem looked in better order, because at the crematorium business was always booming.

"One more thing to consider, Palmer."

"Yes, guv?"

"The time-window for the murder. In this case it's critical. If our killer is from that house of sharks – then which one is it? They provide each other's alibi. Neville Grave was there the whole time. He was seen by all the others from beginning to the very end. Physically, there's no way it could have been him. It's just not possible. Then we've got Goodwell and his

missus. Those two remind me of the snooty couple next door on the Good Life. Wasn't she called Marjorie, too?"
"I'm afraid I wouldn't know, guv," said Palmer with a grin. "The Good Life was well before my time."
Hogarth gave Palmer a hard look, softened by a thin smile. "You're no spring chicken any more, Sue."
Palmer chuckled.
"The old woman isn't what she seems, but she couldn't have done it either."
"Not what she seems, guv?"
"Definitely not. I think old Nigel should be made a posthumous saint for being so long-suffering. It sounds like Mrs Susan Grave had been a nightmare of a woman for decades. But either way, she didn't do it. Mr and Mrs Good Life were there the whole time, so it can't be them. Venky went out to see why old Nigel was taking so long to fetch the wood, which does give him opportunity to make the kill, but he didn't do it."
"You say that as if you're certain. How do you know?"
"Because I know the man is dying, Palmer. Cancer. He has months, maybe only weeks, to live, so he can have no real motive."
"Really?" said Palmer. "But what about revenge? Revenge is a motive that never fades away," said Palmer.
Hogarth toyed with the idea. He tilted his head left and right.
"Maybe. But I don't see it. These old boys had more in common than they had differences. Which leaves…"
"Nancy Decorville."
"The one and only naughty Nancy. Did you get anything on her?"
Palmer shook her head.
"Not much, guv. I found out she's the top earner and go-getter for Crispin and Co, the commercial property firm

based in Rochford. She's been Crispin and Co's golden girl for the last two years, finding them gold-card development opportunities in Thurrock, Leigh, and Chelmsford. The press reports on all those land buys suggest Crispins are set to make a killing on those land buys whether they develop them or not. That woman has a nose for an opportunity alright."

"Crispins – are they a big concern? I can't say I've ever heard of them."

"Not really. Looks like a big money outfit with a low profile. It's run by the Crispin brothers and a staff of five including sales negotiators, land finders and buyers like Miss Decorville, and has links to an Essex building firm, GMA."

"Our Nancy is as shrewd as she is pretty. I'd say she uses those looks to her advantage," said Hogarth.

Palmer gave Hogarth a look. "From what I've seen, I couldn't disagree."

"So, is there any clear sign that she's using our man Neville? My gut agrees with Trevor Good Life. She's a parasite waiting for the right time to strike... but the woman would have to be pretty desperate for success if she was prepared to kill for it."

"I got all the info from Social Media," said Palmer. "Crispin & Co's Twitter feed is pretty full on. George Crispin seems to spend more time on Twitter than the US President. And I checked out Nancy Decorville's Facebook, Twitter and IG."

"IG? You what?"

"It's Instagram, sir. Keep up," she said.

Hogarth humphed.

"Her Facebook profile says she's in a relationship with Neville Grave, but I've got to say it all looks pretty recent. I saw lots of luvvy pics after a short barren spell. Not long before that there was another man on the scene, and he was a very different guy. The older, suited and booted variety. Quite probably minted too, from the look of him."

"Maybe naughty Nancy sees our Neville as being minted too. And she didn't show up at the house until later. If I've got my facts straight, she showed up after Venky the vet went out to check on the old man. Which means she could be a possible killer…"

"Her social media certainly shows that she's a very fit and capable girl," said Palmer. "There are lots of images taken while running or at the gym… but I still doubt she'd be strong enough to lift the old man and dump him in that chipper."

Hogarth nodded, like he wasn't committed to deciding either way just yet.

"But you did get one detail wrong, sir. I asked some questions too, and according to my notes, Mr Goodwell did leave Grave Farm during the critical time window."

"*Did he now?*" said Hogarth, with a wicked grin.

"Did you notice all the buttered French bread?"

"You couldn't fail to notice them. It looked like the woman was about to feed the five thousand."

"She sent Goodwell out to grab some more butter. My notes say he was gone for between ten and fifteen minutes, depending on who you listen to."

"Goodwell went out? When the old man was attacked?"

"Yes, it does seem that he did."

"Oh dear, oh dear, Trevor," said Hogarth. "Maybe Life isn't so Good after all. We need to know where he went. We'll need to verify it and look at the timings."

"Yes, sir. I'll start as soon as we get back to the nick."

"Good work, Palmer."

Palmer ventured a look at Hogarth and waited. Soon enough he met her eye.

"Marris was right, sir. You do sound below par today."
"Well thank you for that little confidence booster. I was beginning to forget about Marris's little jibe until then."
"You had trouble with the DCI this morning, too."
"Long Melford. But you know what he's like. Everyone does. He wants blood from stones and he wants them to feel terrible if they don't bleed freely enough."
"But I don't remember him being on your case like this before," said Palmer.
"Then maybe he's found a new hobby – besides collecting antique clocks."
"Are you sure everything's okay, guv?"
"Yes, Palmer," said Hogarth with an exaggerated grin. "Everything's just peachy and tickety-boo. And don't worry. I'm not about to shed my clothes and run into the sea. I wouldn't leave you in the lurch, no matter who would like that to happen."
"That wasn't what I meant, sir. I was concerned – about you."
"Well then, thanks for your concern, but do yourself a favour and save it for the case. Don't waste your time worrying about me, sergeant. I'm honestly not worth the trouble."
Palmer felt put in her place. She looked out on the flat green fields to the airport for half a minute before she spoke again. They were almost at the farm.
"Those case photographs, guv. Of the victim. You shouldn't hide them on my account."
"What?"
"The murder pics."
"Oh, I was only joking Palmer. I was more worried about spoiling my breakfast than yours. I'll put them up alright. I

just didn't see the point until we have a proper meeting at the station. It's only the two of us after all."

"Putting those pictures up might show the DCI you're on top of things. He's always sticking his head through the office door."

"I never just want to do things just for appearances sake, Palmer. Not for Melford, or anyone else. Thanks all the same."

Palmer sighed. Hogarth started to speak, slowly at first.

"I know you meant well, Sue. Sorry if I snapped. This will come good. I promise."

Palmer couldn't tell if he meant the case, or his own situation, whatever that was.

Hogarth turned his car between the tall red pillars of the Grave Farm entrance and slowly crunched along the gravel drive until he pulled to a halt.

"Ooooh, I can't wait for this little chat," said Hogarth, with plenty of irony in his tone.

Chapter Ten

"Good morning Neville," said Hogarth.
Neville Grave was again the one to open the large front door of the farmhouse. The man's face grew stiff and awkward the moment he saw DI Hogarth and DS Palmer standing on his doorstep. Hogarth watched his reactions unfold, but then he had come to expect nothing less. Cops had that effect on people, and as far as Hogarth could tell, his own hard-bitten face had the effect more than most. Today the young man was wearing another fashion ensemble. A blue checked shirt with his sleeves rolled up to expose strong forearms. He wore skinny jeans shaped like carrots, the kind which made plenty of men look ridiculous, but such was fashion. Hogarth could still remember his trendy sunglasses from the eighties. The ones which looked like Jackson Pollock had attacked them with correction fluid. As far as Hogarth was concerned fashion was for the birds. He was getting old.
Neville Grave was holding a tea towel in his hands.
"Hard at work, I see," said Hogarth.
Neville glanced at the towel and dropped it to his waist.
"I'm here for my mother. It's far too early to leave her yet."
Hogarth looked at the man's eyes a little too deeply, probing for the truth. He quickly looked away.
"I'm sure you're doing the very best you can," said Hogarth. "Can we see your mother?"
"She's not feeling her best this morning."
"I'm sure. That's why we're here early. Before her *particular condition* gets any worse…"

Hogarth gave a nod to signal that he knew the woman's problem.

"I'm not sure that's a good idea, Inspector."

"All the same, I have to speak to her. And my guess is that mornings are best."

Neville didn't argue. "Very well. If you insist."

"That I do, Mr Grave."

Neville led them back towards the kitchen. Hogarth wondered if they were all still in situ, like some moving exhibit on the horrors of country life. Hogarth listened to Neville announcing their arrival. A moment later, Neville appeared at the kitchen door, beckoning them in.

"Come through. Actually, she's not too bad today."

Hogarth walked through, and Palmer shut the sturdy wooden door behind her.

They found the kitchen much as they had left it. The range was hot and there was the smell of bread baking in the oven. Odd, thought Hogarth, that the woman had found the inclination to bake after the death of her husband. But nothing about these people was run of the mill. Underlying the scent of bread he smelt that same old sickly aniseed wafting on the air. Pernod perhaps? Or a breath freshener to hide the booze of choice. Hogarth knew he would soon work it out.

"The police again" said the old woman. Her eyes were guarded and glazed as ever, and her mouth looked pinched. Somehow, there was a wicked look about her. In the eyes, maybe. If it was a hangover then Hogarth knew the feeling. Neville Grave lingered by the door behind them.

"We need to speak to your mother alone, Mr Grave."

Neville frowned.

"Is that okay with you, Mum?"

"It's better than you hawking around here interfering, wouldn't you say?"

Neville blushed. "You'll soon see what she's like, Inspector."

Hogarth waited until the man was gone, then he grabbed the back of one of the old wooden chairs from the dining table and pulled it to the centre of the room.

"Don't mind, do you?" he said.

"Help yourself. And the lady. You too," she said, pointing to Palmer. "Sit down. It isn't often I get to meet new people round here."

"You do remember we were here yesterday, Mrs Grave?"

"Course I do. I'm not senile, yet. Though, I know some of them like to pretend I am. Nigel liked to play that game. It made him feel better about everything else."

Hogarth shot a glance at Palmer. He sensed ripe pickings from this conversation.

"Everything else?" said Hogarth. His eyes roamed across the leaded-light windows towards the police vans and the white tent towards the end of the track. The tent had been set up as an awning over the open side of the big metal barn, and Hogarth could see John Dickens was still on his knees in the shadows. Days like this, frosty and bitterly cold, Hogarth was glad he had never become a SOCO.

"You want tittle tattle? Is that what you're after?"

"No, madam," said Hogarth. He glanced down at the distinctive Pernod bottle on the floor, hiding behind a table leg. "I'm here to try and find out who killed your husband. If you answer a few questions it would certainly help."

The woman nodded.

"Okay... if I must. We loved each other, of course, the way folks of a certain age do. It was comfortable, like an old pair of shoes. Easy. Safe, you might say. But boring as hell. But we were growing old together and well on the way to popping our clogs. I mean, look at me. You wouldn't believe I used to be a looker back in my day. Better than that girl Neville has taken up with. And Nigel was older than me, you know."

"So I heard," said Hogarth.

"We were friends, after a fashion, me and Nigel. I never wanted no harm to come to him. Damn it, all I wanted was him to snap out of his silly daze and do a bit better for us all. With a bit more brains, we could have earned much more from this place. We could have modernised before, decades back, when it mattered. But he was so obsessed with the past that he couldn't move on."

"The past?"

"His family history, and all. Grave Farm used to be huge when his grandfather and great grandfather ran it. It was his father who started to squander it. Nigel, poor Nigel, was content simply to limit the decay. But you can't stop time, can you? You either move on, or time moves you instead."

"You wanted Mr Grave to modernise, then? Did you know about the different ideas your family had to make things better?"

"Too little, too late. All I heard was a lot of hot air. Trevor wants to turn Grave Farm into a factory, letting in an industrial firm to run the place. Trevor might know about business, it might work, I suppose, but I'm yet to be convinced…"

"Would you have blocked the idea if Nigel had gone with it?"

"No. But I would certainly have held him to account if it went wrong."

The way the old woman's eyes shone as she said it left Hogarth in no doubt what an ordeal that would have been. No wonder Nigel Grave had trouble making a decision.

"And what about your son's idea?"
"Neville, you mean."
"Yes, your son."
The woman's lips shaped up to release some pinched words, but she held back and shifted on her seat. Hogarth felt he might have missed out on a revealing tirade.
"But your son had some ideas, didn't he?"
The old woman nodded. "Yes. He had ideas of his own before that lipstick hussy showed up."
"And?" said Hogarth. "Do you know about them?"
"He was responsible for ordering that woodchipper, wasn't he? To make wood chips for sale. Can you credit it? He wanted to turn fire logs into waste material for selling to the public. I could never understand it."
"People use them on the gardens," said Hogarth. "I don't, but people do."
"It was a fool idea. And that was the machine that ended up killing Nigel… I do wonder if that fool machine was what they were arguing about."
"Arguing? Who? Neville and Nigel" said Hogarth.
"Yes," said the old woman. She caught Hogarth's eyes and stared. "It didn't happen often, but they argued the day before Nigel died… I saw them out there on the field, having a proper set-to. Neville was the one doing the ranting and raving. And Nigel was shaking his head. Nigel probably refused to listen to the boy's ideas for the farm. And with good reason, I'd say," the old woman finished, with a bitter laugh.
"I'm no expert on the farming business, Mrs Grave," said Hogarth, "but unless you know something I don't, I think it would be hard to blame your son for…"
"Throwing him in?" said the woman. She raised an eyebrow and dipped her hand down for the Pernod bottle. She tipped

a good measure into an empty mug. The time for hiding her addiction was over.

"You're a man of the world, Inspector. I don't need to hide this from you, do I?"

"No," said Hogarth, though he hated the smell of it.

"Neville couldn't have done it, could he?" said the woman. "And do I think Neville did it? Why, those two doted on each other. Two peas in a pod, they were, both as daft as each other. I can't see it happening. The boy Neville is a nuisance and a fool, he always was. Uncanny really, how much they were alike. Considering…"

"Considering what?" said Hogarth, quick off the mark.

The woman sipped her drink and shook her head.

"It doesn't matter. He was here the whole time, anyways. Neville was here, trying to pacify me. Silly bloody sod. He's trying to butter me up now that his father's gone, I reckon. But I won't fall for it."

"Fall for what, exactly, Mrs Grave?"

"Nigel offered him safety and ease here. A simple life and an easy future. I can't offer him that. I wouldn't even want to. Life isn't to be hidden from, or to run away from. You've got to get out there and embrace it, no matter what."

Hogarth eyed the Pernod on the table.

"And you've done no running then, Mrs Grave? You're not one for burying your head in the sand or blaming others for their troubles, I take it."

The woman put her mug down and met Hogarth's eyes. Colour came to her pale cheeks. She looked angry. For an old woman, she looked menacing.

"You suspect Neville is only here for what he can get, am I right, Mrs Grave? Strangely, for a mother, you seem to resent that. But I thought that was part of the deal in parenthood."

Beside Hogarth, Palmer shifted in her chair. She looked at Hogarth as the room became tense, but then she recalled Hogarth's word of the case. Context. Maybe Hogarth knew something she didn't.

"Most parents are only too glad to let their children have what is theirs, aren't they?"

"I'm not most parents, Inspector."

"No. I suppose not," said Hogarth.

"What did you really come here for, Inspector? You're pussyfooting around. What is it?"

"To see if the past has affected the present, Mrs Grave. To see if it pertains to the murder. If it does, it might help us learn the identity of the killer."

"The past?"

"Yes. The past. People don't much like talking about the past," he said.

"I think you'd better ask what's on your mind, then get on your way."

"Very well, Mrs Grave. But I'll have to keep coming back until we find that killer."

The woman said nothing.

"Check the door, Palmer," said Hogarth, nodding towards the door to the hall. "We don't want to be responsible for any more family trouble, do we?"

DS Palmer opened the kitchen door and looked out into the grand old hallway. It was dim and empty. She looked up the wooden staircase and saw no sign of a lurking eavesdropper.

"Nobody there, sir," said Palmer.

"Good."

The old woman looked tense. She reached for her mug of Pernod, but Hogarth shook his head. "Not for a moment, please, Mrs Grave. I need your head as clear as it can be. Let

me take you back for a moment. Back to 1991 when your husband took on some seasonal staff. Migrant workers."
The woman coughed. "Nigel was always taking on seasonal workers. There must have been thousands through here."
"But these were different, Mrs Grave. You had people here who came from different parts of Europe. The first of the migrant workers from the EU. It must have been interesting though, all these new people, so new and different to the others before. But fascinating as it was, you had a problem with one of them, didn't you?"
The woman's mouth dropped open. Her eyes fixed on Hogarth's. He saw she now hung on his every word.
"This one kept hassling you. Coming to the kitchen window here, maybe. Ogling you. I mean, you must have been back in your prime still back then, a looker, like you said. You were a handsome woman of means. A catch. But you were a married woman, and off limits, and you knew it. So did he. But this man was a foreigner. He harassed you. He upset you. It got out of control and something bad happened. Something awful."
The woman nodded slowly. "That's right."
Hogarth looked into the woman's eyes.
"No, Mrs Grave. That's not right at all. I just described the version of events you told your husband. There was even an account of the alleged attack in the local press of the day. A short article about the foreign bogeyman in The Record. But no charges were ever made because that poor foreigner had already suffered enough because of you. Your husband became furious with him – enraged that a man he had trusted on his own farm had abused that trust and taken advantage of his wife. In a fit of rage, Nigel attacked the man, who denied everything, even when Nigel threatened him. And ultimately, blood was shed. Your husband attacked

him with a pitch fork. That's the truth, isn't it? But even that is only part of it. Your husband didn't want to go to prison, and he didn't want the shame of the true story in the press. He cared about his reputation because he wanted to live up to the Graves of the past. His old family heroes. So, he paid off that poor farm worker, gave him a whole season's wages in one go, and kept it all quiet to make it go away. Maybe Nigel also did it because deep down he knew *the truth*. That you'd led that man on – the foreign worker – that you led him on and flirted with him and eventually even slept with him, but when the deed was done you turned and blamed him for a sexual assault. Why did you do it? Was it the drink? Because you've been drinking a long time, haven't you, Mrs Grave? And gambling too. But even after all you'd done, Nigel tried to help you. He took you away to those rehabs. He stayed with you. He helped you… even though he probably suspected the child you gave birth to in 1992 wasn't his."

"Lies. Vicious lies. Nigel always believed Neville was his!"

"Even though Nigel was *smart enough* to see through your drunken lies, he accepted that child as his and brought him up as your son. But you didn't like it. You never liked Neville, did you? Because you were ashamed of where he came from. He was living evidence of your indiscretion and drunkenness." Hogarth lowered his voice. "Even though you hated yourself for it, you took it out on Neville. All these years on, I'd say you're still doing it."

"What is the purpose of all this poison?" said the old woman.

The look Palmer gave Hogarth suggested she was wondering the same thing.

"The past leads us right here, Mrs Grave. A bitter family vying to control this farm just hours after the owner was brutally killed. That could even have provided the motive for your husband's murder."

"I really don't know what you intend by dredging up the past like this…"

The old woman's hand was shaking.

"Mrs Grave. Am I right about what happened?"

The old woman regarded him with new eyes. Hogarth saw fear there. She bit her trembling lip. Hogarth recognised the look in her eyes because he'd seen it before. It was the fear of justice catching up with her. Hogarth shook his head.

"The past is not my concern, Mrs Grave. There'll be no charges for what happened. I only bring it up because it could bear relation to the present."

"No. You bring it up for the same reason as the person who told you. They all see me as a drunken harlot. They always did. Only Nigel didn't see me like that. But I punished him every day of his life all the same. Yes, I gave the man hell, when it was what I deserved. Let me have that drink now, will you?"

Hogarth relented with a nod. The old woman poured another generous measure into the mug and tipped it down her neck. In a drinking competition, Susan Grave could have given an old sailor a run for his money.

"I know what I've done," she said. "But I don't see how it bears any relation to what happened. That was nearly thirty years ago."

"What do you think might have happened if your son found out about it?"

"Neville?"

"Your *son,* yes," said Hogarth. He fixed the woman with his eyes, unwilling to let her off the hook.

"I think he would have hated me, but he would never have harmed his father. But yes, he would have been right to hate me."

"Is it possible that he could have blamed his father in some way? Think about it."

"No… the only thing Neville held against his father was his damn-fool stubbornness about the business. But I'm glad he was so stubborn when it came to Neville. The only ideas he had to save the farm were bad ones. Until that woman came into the frame. I'm civil enough, mind. But I know a troublemaker when I see one – no matter how pretty she may be. It takes one to know one, after all."

Hogarth nodded and watched as the old woman looked out through the window. Her eyes fell upon the men in the green and blue puffer jackets far out in the fields – the migrant workers who had found the body. Hogarth saw them and was relieved they were still around, but he wondered what the old woman was thinking.

"Do you think there's any chance those two men are related to the man who you took up with back then?"

The woman looked at Hogarth with angry eyes.

"Took up with?! You have a way with words, Inspector."

Hogarth didn't apologise.

"You mean do I think they are the man's sons? Is that it? Did they kill Nigel? That's your thinking, right? You're wrong. They aren't his. I remember that man's face very well, because I still see it every day. Igor and the other one are from Eastern Europe, he was Greek, no, they're not his sons. Neither of them."

"Then why was Nigel murdered, Mrs Grave? You must have an inkling. A suspicion."

"Because he was a stubbornly good man. Stubborn to the end. He *was* a good man, wasn't he?"

"Yes, so it seems," said Hogarth.

"This world can't stand good people, Inspector. At least I know I never could."

"Come on, Mrs Grave. You must have a feeling for who did it…"

"I drink for a reason. I drink so I don't have to look at my life too closely, any more. I don't know who did it. But I know I want you to get them. Whoever it is."

"Especially if it's Neville, eh?"

"No. It isn't him. Even if I can't stand him, this wasn't his fault. It wasn't him."

Hogarth sighed in frustration and changed tack.

"Peter Venky went down to the barn to find him – it seems to have been around twelve-ten or twelve-fifteen. So, your husband must have been killed shortly before then. Tell me, were any of the people in this room acting odd at the time? Did any of them make excuses to leave or vanish from the room. Think hard, please."

The woman looked away in thought and swished her cup.

"I wanted people full. I wanted people comfortable and we were running low on butter, so I sent Trevor down to the shop. It was good for him to go because he and Neville had been bitching at each other and it relieved the tension. Him and Neville are always scrapping."

"About the farm?" said Palmer.

"At present, yes."

"But no one else apart from Trevor came or went around the time of the murder?"

"No one. But that harlot Decorlay…"

"Decorville," said Palmer.

"Whatever, she came in a little late, didn't she? She turned up after Peter went to fetch Nigel. Now that was uncanny timing, don't you think?"

Hogarth studied the woman's glassy eyes. He could almost see them gradually filling with the drink. He ignored the remark, putting it down to jealousy.
"Do you know which shop Mr Goodwell used to buy the butter?" said Hogarth.
"Same one we all use. To go out and be back that quick, Trevor must have used the corner shop just past Furdon's Industrial Estate…"
Palmer jotted it down.
"We can time it, Palmer," said Hogarth. Palmer nodded.
"Would you know of any reason why Trevor might have wanted Mr Grave out of the picture?"
"None at all. He didn't stand to gain a thing from it, did he?"
"Then why did he care so much about the farm?"
"Like most hangers on, they think a farm is money. He's retired. If the farm thrived because of his ideas, he'd be hanging on for a dividend, wouldn't he? A few scraps from the table to make his pension go further."
"In spite of all that drink, you're not as addled as you seem, Mrs Grave." Hogarth put his hands on his knees and got ready to stand up and leave. He saw the foreigners were still working in the distant field, well past the police cordon around the barn.
"Just one thing… do you know anything about a power of attorney?"
"I've heard of the phrase. To do with your will, or something, isn't it?"
"Almost. It's more about taking responsibility for someone's assets while they are still alive, often because that persons knows they will no longer be in a fit state to handle them. Have you had any dealings like that?"
"The LPA? Nigel brought it up with me twice. Just twice. And I shot him down in flames. Nigel was worried I was lost

to the drink. He let other people think I was merely going senile, because he preferred that. Less to be ashamed of, I suppose. But I wasn't going to allow it. I like having my say."
"Did Nigel ever tell anyone else about the idea?"
"Not that I know of. He always kept things like that to himself. He was a very private man."
"And did Nigel ever discuss his health with you?"
"Not much. He was getting old, yes, but Nigel was one of those kind that go on forever."
Hogarth nodded. "So, you really don't know why he would have wanted that power of attorney?"
"I didn't care why he wanted it. All I knew, it wasn't going to happen. Not over my dead body."
"Well, thank you. It's been enlightening, Mrs Grave. Very enlightening." Hogarth stood up and looked out to the garden, as a swirl of new questions percolated through his head. He had to process them. He slowly walked to the hallway door and opened it. In the hallway, moving away as if he just happened to have walked past the door was Neville Grave.
Hogarth watched the man as he started to climb the stairs. The young man was a good actor, but Hogarth still wasn't buying it.
"I suppose you'll want to update Nancy on everything you've just heard, Mr Grave," said Hogarth.
Neville froze on the stairs and looked down at Hogarth. His face was strained, his eyes hard. "I don't know what you're talking about, Inspector. But you can leave Nancy out of it."
"But I'm not sure I can, Mr Grave. I'm going to need to speak to you, soon. Both of you…"
"When?"
"This afternoon."
"At the police station?"

"I don't think that's necessary. Not yet," said Hogarth.
"Then meet me here then."
Did none of them ever leave this damn farm?
"Two pm."
"Very well, Inspector. I'll make sure Nancy will be here."
Neville looked away and climbed the stairs. But as he turned, Hogarth saw bitter emotion overtake his face.
"What's the matter with him?" said Palmer, joining him at the door.
Hogarth waved at the old woman and pulled the kitchen door shut behind them.
"Sometimes it really doesn't pay to eavesdrop, you know. I think our Neville may have heard more than he bargained for."
Palmer made a face. "Oh crap. Then that could be on us."
"Well, he was going to find out soon enough."
"But if he was involved in the murder, finding out like that could prove to be dangerous."
"I don't have him down as a psycho, but I could be wrong, Palmer. If he was involved, we'll know soon enough…"

Palmer shut the once grand old wooden front door behind them and marched around to the front of the house.
"You heard my question about the Lasting Power of Attorney?"
"Yes," said Palmer. "The solicitor was going to set one up for Nigel."
"That's right. But Nigel only made an initial inquiry about it, didn't he? I couldn't understand it. But he wanted her to sign over her power to someone else. Initially the solicitor must have thought the power of attorney was to be given to Nigel. That he would have full control over the assets. But Nigel

didn't need any more control than he had already. He was the husband. He had full legal control of the estate anyway."

"So why then?" said Palmer.

"Because Nigel Grave knew he was dying and he was afraid what would become of the farm after he was gone. He knew he had no more than two or three years tops, and he knew how his wife had squandered money on booze and gambling so many times before. It's all interesting, but it doesn't help us find a culprit."

"Doesn't it?" said Palmer.

"Old Nigel never told anyone who he was going to sign those powers over to. Someone was in the frame to get those powers, that is until the old woman point-blank refused to agree to it. But Nigel took his secrets with him."

"Do you think his announcement was going to be about his illness? Or about the power of attorney?"

"Neither," said Hogarth. "Both were absolute secrets. I think old Nigel wanted to look like he was still in control – he wanted to give direction to the new methods he was about to adopt for the farm. Confessing a terminal illness would have got them all jockeying for position instead. The announcement was about leading the farm to security – securing his legacy before he popped his clogs. Yes, he was going to modernise, but we still don't know which way he would have gone. Taking on a partner, like Goodwell suggested, or diversifying like Neville wanted. If we could find that out, we'd have a huge clue as to who wanted to kill him."

"And the power of attorney thing?"

"Now, it'll be a footnote. A wrinkle of history. The old woman put the kibosh on it, so it was a non-event. This is either about greed, or revenge. And it's the revenge angle we need to look at now…"

"Revenge?" said Palmer.

"The old man put a pitchfork into the man who slept with his missus. That's a big deal. That's the migrant worker history we spoke about. Susan Grave diddled one of the migrants in '91, and nine months later bouncing baby Neville turned up. It seems old Nigel must have turned a blind eye to the timing and made Neville his. When it first happened, Nigel believed the old woman's line about being stalked and assaulted and went wild. But when he came to his senses, he saw things as they were and hushed it up with a pay off."

"The tangled webs we weave, and all that," said Palmer. Hogarth thought for a moment about his own sorely tangled web. "Yes, indeed."

"Let's interview those two migrant boys up there. We have to pin them down on exactly how they found the body… and their footwear is important too."

Palmer and Hogarth walked past the crime scene van and saw Dickens' team still poring over the woodchipper machine with torches, swabs and brushes. It was a painstaking business, and Hogarth didn't want to go into the barn unless absolutely necessary. Dickens was bound to be tetchy and Hogarth didn't need the aggravation.

But instead, as they passed Dickens looked up and peeled back his face mask.

"DI Hogarth. Just the man!"

Hogarth kept his eyes on the distant migrants and put on a weary smile as he turned to face Dickens.

"And DS Palmer, too," said Dickens.

Palmer nodded.

"I just thought you'd want to know," said Dickens. "We found some more of those fibres you were fussing about yesterday."

"Fibres?" said Hogarth, playing dumb.
"The black stuff. Marris told you that it's neoprene, right?"
"That stuff. Yes, I believe he did."
"Well, we've found some more. And we've found some other little pieces which could tell us more."
"What?" said Hogarth.
"The wide feeder of the woodchipper machine – the curved metal opening at the back. See it?"
"The part where they stuck the old man."
"Yes. It has a tin lip to it on all sides – right at the top. The lip curls around to the back but has a hidden sharp edge. It couldn't hurt anyone, but it's enough to catch a loose garment or thread. I found something on there that looks like Velcro. Just a few strands on the machine feeder. The Velcro is old too, it looks like it's gone loose and fluffy. I think there's a good chance they relate to your other find. But you'll have to wait for Marris before we can be sure. Is that any good to you?"

Velcro? What kind of garment used neoprene and Velcro? Hogarth chewed it over for a moment.

"Thanks for the tip, John. That might narrow it down a little."
"If there's anything else hidden in those fibres, it could narrow it down a lot," said Dickens, giving Hogarth a nod.
"The crime scene work must be coming to an end," muttered Hogarth. "Dickens is demob-happy. You don't see him being helpful very often."
"Must have been a pretty grim task, this one."

Hogarth's eyes moved to the far field and found that the men in the puffer jackets were gone. In the time of Dickens' update they had disappeared.

"The migrants have gone, Palmer. Come on. We need to find them, or Melford will have my guts for garters. Especially if it turns out to be them…"
Hogarth took in a deep breath and started to advance towards the field, with Palmer at his side.

Reaching the misty back field, Hogarth could see the red lights of the airport landing strip in the distance He turned his head left and right, but still couldn't see any sign of the migrants until he caught a fleck of bright green turning through a distant corner of the field into some hedgerows.
"There!" he said.
"I see them," said Palmer.
"But I wonder if they saw us first. Let's see if there's a short cut."
"I'll go this way, in case they come back," said Palmer.
"Okay," said Hogarth. He doubled back along the track towards the house, but stopped short of the barn. Instead he turned right across a wasteland strewn with ancient farming tools and a jungle of weeds. Hogarth picked though it until he reached the back of the hedgerow. He walked along gingerly, acutely aware of being a townie afraid of getting a little mud on his shoes. But by the time he stepped onto firmer land he saw his brogues were caked in mud as were the calves of his trousers.
"Bloody mess," he hissed. As he spoke, he saw the back of the man in the green puffer just ahead of him. Hearing Hogarth behind him, the man in the green coat turned. He saw Hogarth and nodded at him and gave him a flick of a wave. He seemed friendly and polite enough. But then the man kept walking. The other man in the blue coat joined him and gave Hogarth a friendly smile.
"Hey! Excuse me, boys. I need a word with you…"

The men kept moving. Slowly.

"Stop. I have to talk to you."

Hogarth heard the men exchange words in their native tongue, soft calm words. Five seconds later, with Hogarth still walking after them, the men broke into a hard run.

"Oi!" said Hogarth. "Stop!"

He ran after them, leaning so far and fast over his shoes that he almost fell head first onto the mud. He stumbled but kept running, his heels thudding and slopping on the cold ground. He felt mud spattering all over his trousers as he ran, and his breathing started to become laboured.

"Hey! Igor! Stop," he called, but the men were fit and strong. Hogarth hadn't seen the inside of a gym or gone for a recreational jog for longer than he cared to remember. In his mind he was still a fit man. It seemed he wasn't nearly as fit as he remembered. Whisky and freezer food was not a diet of champions.

"Don't do this!" called Hogarth, as the men broke through the wide hedge, and made their way into a neighbouring field. The scratching branches tore at the men's thick coats as they broke away, then the hedge sealed up behind them. Hogarth shook his head and leaned over his knees, dragging in short sharp breaths until his lungs were almost useable again. He looked at the mud caked all over his trousers. Sweat dripped from his brow.

"Did you lose them, sir?" said Palmer, appearing beside him.

"Now that you mention it, Palmer, I think I did." He stood up and put his hands on his hips.

"I'm screwed," said Hogarth.

"But there's no need to tell Melford, yet, is there, guv?"

"You think?" said Hogarth.

"We still might find them…"

"I bloody hope so, Palmer. I can't face another lecture from that man. Not today."

But Hogarth knew he would be in for more than a lecture. If the migrants ran because of the murder, his neck would be on the line for not nabbing them when he'd had the chance. As Hogarth contemplated the humiliating jobs he would face after discharge from the force – *Barman at the Old Naval? A private investigator snapping liars and perverts for cash? No way*, his mobile phone started to buzz in his pocket. Hogarth winced and put the phone to his ear.

"Yes?" he said.

"Oh, DI Hogarth. You sound just about ready for the slab yourself."

It was the pathologist, Ed Quentin.

"Everyone's out to cheer me up today, Ed. Okay. What have you got?"

"Are you ready?"

"You know me, Ed. Ready as ever."

"Okay then. It turns out that the old man liked a drink or two. His liver showed plenty of use. It looks like a large dead sea sponge. But much more interesting was his prostate. There were signs of a well-developed cancer. And when I opened him up I found tumours developing on the bowel and liver. The tumours had spread from the prostate, I think. Checking his records, I've found the man did have a cancer diagnosis. He was terminal. Still, I think I know which way I would rather have gone."

"I got a tip off about the cancer, thanks Ed. But it's good to know it wasn't just a red herring. Anything else?"

"Yes. There are a few grip marks, bands of bruising around the old man's upper arms and ribs. It certainly looks like there was a struggle to get him in that machine."

"Did the bruises give you any indication of the size or strength of the culprit?"
"Not really. There's not enough to go on I'm afraid. But there are some signs of friction and scratch marks around the bruised areas. No prints of course. Not on skin."
"Friction and scratching?"
"Yes. Caused by the struggle. When Nigel Grave was being handled, he incurred some very minor injuries."
"Hmmmm. Any idea on how they were caused?"
"Well, they don't appear to be made by fingernails, if that's what you were hoping for. From what I'm seeing, I think the killer was wearing gloves, but definitely not the surgical kind, or there'd only be bruising. These must have been made of rough material. Strange really. I can't get much insight into the size of their hands from the bruises either. The gloves seem to have distorted the pressure marks. But gloves that leave scratches? That's very curious."
"Any insight on those gloves?"
"Yes, a little maybe. I think you'll like this one, DI Hogarth."
"Go on."
"There are traces of neoprene material left on the skin. It's beginning to seem like this rogue neoprene came from the killer's gloves."
"Gloves! Of course!" said Hogarth. "And I've just had a heads up from Dickens at the crime ccene. They've found some loose Velcro fibres caught in the machine, too. I think it could be from the gloves."
"Could well be, but that's a matter for forensics, I'm afraid. The body came to me with almost all of the head missing apart from the lower jaw. Cause of death was simple enough. As you know, death was caused by the machine blades impacting the skull, and then penetrating the skull, before it made a total mash of the poor man's head. It's a small

mercy, I suppose, but from the lack of hand injuries and from attempting to escape, I believe Nigel Grave died within seconds of being pushed into that machine."

"Just his head? The pictures looked worse."

"There's a lot of substantial matter in the human head, Inspector. I'm told that machine sprayed it around the barn like confetti at a wedding. That's all for now. See you for the next one, eh?" said Quentin.

"Hopefully not for a while, Ed."

Hogarth ended the call. "It was true, then. The old man had been dying of cancer. Old Nigel should have told his family about the condition. It could have saved his life."

"But not if the motive was revenge, eh, guv? If it was revenge I think the killer might have hit him all the same," said Palmer.

"Hmmmm." Hogarth looked around for a sign of the migrants. Palmer was beginning to feel sorry for him, "Come on," said Palmer. "Let's try the corner shop at Furdon's. Who knows? We might even see our runaway foreigners on the way."

"Good idea." Hogarth started to fuss with his phone. "I'll get the stopwatch ready…"

Hogarth hit pause on his smartphone stopwatch the moment they went inside the corner shop. A tall bald Asian man stood behind the counter. There was old-fashioned Asian music on in the background, a female singer wailing with lots of clashing cymbals and drums. The shop smelt of warm food, Bombay mix, and curry spices. It was a smell that Hogarth had always liked. It reminded him of the sweetshops of his youth.

"Hello, sir. Detective Inspector Hogarth, Southend CID. I'm here in connection with…"

"Let me guess…" said the man in an accent more Dagenham than Delhi. "The murder of Nigel Grave?"

"You knew him, did you?"

"Yes. Old Mr Grave came in for his papers, chocolate, and drink for his wife. Such a shame. He was a very nice man."

"Yes. That's what they say. Yesterday – the day Mr Grave was murdered – a man came in here around lunchtime. Not a local man, not someone you'd know. He came in and bought some butter. Do you remember him at all?"

"Lunch time? Yes, I think so. Midday or something like that. A man with silver hair. Stocky."

"That's him. Can you tell us what happened?"

The man shrugged. "Why? There's nothing much to describe. The man walked in, he looked around the shelves and I asked him what he wanted to buy. He said he needed butter. I pointed to the fridge cabinet there and he picked up two packets of the Pyke's butter. The purple brand. It's cheaper than the rest. No one buys the other brand. I should really stop stocking it."

"How did the man seem to you?"

"Good enough. A little stiff, maybe. If you know what I mean. Why? Who was he?"

"Nigel Grave's brother-in-law."

"Really? He wasn't overly friendly, and not like Nigel at all."

"No, I don't think he is."

"What I mean is, the man picked the cheapest brand of butter, brought it to the counter and then complained about the price."

"What?"

"He said my butter was too expensive."

A long wrinkle appeared in Hogarth's brow. "Did he say anything else?"

"No. He said two pounds a pack was too much. I said he didn't know my overheads. It was nothing, really. Lots of people moan about prices these days."

Hogarth looked at Palmer. Was the price issue significant? "Do you remember what the man was wearing?

"Smart clothes. A shirt and trousers. That's all I can remember."

"What about his shoes?"

"I'm sorry. I look at their faces and their hands, not their feet."

Hogarth nodded. "Thank you, Mr errrm?"

"Pradesh. My name is on the sign. Pradesh Convenience Stores."

"Mr Pradesh, yes. Thank you. We may see you again."

"You think he did it then?" called Pradesh, as they headed for the door.

"After what you've told us… probably not."

"Oh dear. I hope you catch the killer. Good luck."

Hogarth waved and pressed the start button on his smartphone screen as they walked outside. They got into the car and sped off back to Grave Farm.

***

Hogarth was about to turn his Vauxhall onto the driveway when he saw them. Two men with olive coloured skin walking along the edge of the road. Hogarth hit the stopwatch pause button and tossed the phone into the backseat. He pulled the car over high up on the verge. As soon as the doors opened, the migrants recognised him. Hogarth watched as panic filled their eyes. One pointed across the street where a field climbed away from the road up a steep grassy bank.

"No, you don't!" shouted Hogarth. "You know English. You've been here long enough. If you do this, it only gets worse for you. So don't run. Stop here and talk to me. That's all. You run now, and I could presume you're guilty for the murder."

The men shuffled on the verge while the traffic passed by. The cars had kept them from crossing. "Well?" said Hogarth. He advanced towards them slowly, with his arms out, much like a farmer steering sheep towards a gate.

The man in the blue jacket seemed to nod in acceptance but the man in green looked wary. Hogarth moved in.

"Good. Very good. Just a word, that's all we want, isn't it, Palmer?"

Hogarth gave them a smile and nod of encouragement. He was almost in front of them now, almost blocking their way. But as soon as he got there, the man in the blue jacket barged right through him. The man's shoulder struck Hogarth in centre of his chest. Hogarth grunted in shock and was tipped back towards the road. He kept his balance long enough to avoid a car as it hurtled past, its horn blaring loud in his ears, before he fell on his backside. The men darted across the road, just as a lorry took the corner towards them. Brakes screeched. The lorry shuddered and shook, swerving across the centre of the narrow road and Hogarth blinked at the panicking driver.

Palmer took her chance and gave chase.

"Be careful, Palmer!" called Hogarth. As the truck drew to a shuddering halt, Hogarth pushed himself up and followed, his chest still aching form the strike to his sternum. Now he was angry. Melford had been on his case because of Hartigan. Now these two foreigners wanted to make a jerk of him too. He'd had enough. Hogarth scrambled up the grassy bank and growled as he pushed himself into a run. They were getting away. But he saw their trajectory. Up here the fields were flat again. Not far away was an allotment, and a long metal shed with some smaller buildings clustered around it. Hogarth couldn't keep up with them. But looking at those buildings, Hogarth now he believed he could take his time.

"Slow down, Palmer. We'll do this together." He called. Palmer reluctantly waited and watched as the migrants got away.

"I know this plot," said Hogarth when he reached her side.

"Do you?"

"Yes. They have a miniature railway at the back there. I've been past at Christmas time and seen kiddies hurtling around the edges of the farm on the back of a miniature steam train. I guess it must have been one of the first of Neville's diversification ideas."

"This land belongs to Grave Farm too then?"

"Yes. Which explains why they're running on it." Hogarth sighed and let himself enjoy a bitter smile. "Whether they like it or not, we've got 'em."

"They could be armed," said Palmer.

"I very much doubt it. First off, we'll search them. But we're looking for those gloves as much as weapons. And wherever they go, we'll need to check it out. And if they've got somewhere to hide, maybe they've stashed the evidence in there too."

Reaching the allotment and the secondary farm, they started to edge towards the buildings. The allotment shed was padlocked.

"Not in here then," said Palmer.

Hogarth pointed down the side of the shed and led the way. He moved carefully between the shed and a tall hedgerow, aiming for the large corrugated barn behind it – it was almost a duplicate of the barn Nigel Grave had been killed in by the farmhouse. As they walked, Hogarth caught the sound of a whisper and some noise through the hedge. He stopped and peered through towards the huddle of buildings half hidden by the conifer wind-break on the other side. Then he caught a flash of blue between the buildings.

"They're through there," whispered Hogarth.

He moved along the trees until he found a gap which had been almost entirely closed by rampant tree growth. By now, Hogarth's clothes were only fit for the dry cleaners, anyway. There was no use worrying about the conifer branches. He slid through the gap, bending the branches back. One bent branch thwacked Palmer in the face as she followed Hogarth through, but she didn't complain. Breaking out into the open, Hogarth saw a small single-storey house – a ramshackle tiny bungalow which had fallen into disrepair, right beside another allotment. This plot was well tended. The earth looked rich and dark. Beside the allotment was a greenhouse, every pane of glass had been blotted out with swabs of white paint. *There were in the greenhouse. Hogarth could feel it.* He moved across the sandy, soft brown earth and reached the door with a final surge of movement to prevent any escape. He snatched the door handle and yanked it open. There they were. Two sizeable gents in beanie hats and puffer jackets. Hogarth grinned at them.

"Hello again, chaps," he said.

The man in blue looked sensible enough but the man in green had a moody look to his eyes and the angle of his mouth. Hogarth addressed him first. He raised a finger and pointed at him.

"You! Don't cause any more trouble, sunshine. You're in my bad books already."

The fight left the man's eyes, and he looked to his neighbour, for a lead.

"Which one of you is Igor?" said Hogarth.

The man in blue nodded. "Yes. It's me," he said, with furtive eyes. His accent was strong, but his English was good.

"Igor. Yours is the name I keep hearing. This is a murder investigation. You must know that. I know you found Nigel Grave. So why the heck did you run? Go on. Give me one good reason why I shouldn't have you arrested for assaulting a police officer, as well as suspicion of murder."

The man raised his hands in frustration and threw them to his sides.

"Murder?"

"Yes, murder."

"But we didn't kill him!"

"But you were the first to see him. The vet told us so. He saw you with the body and your boot prints were all over the murder scene… do you understand?" Hogarth pointed at their big cheap wellington boots.

Igor nodded, but the other man looked confused.

"You're strong capable men. And you can run fast enough. You could have easily picked up that old man and thrown him into that machine, couldn't you?"

Palmer drifted into view behind Hogarth, closing off the rest of the gap in the greenhouse doorway.

"But why? Why would we do that?"

"That's what I want to know, Igor. Because there couldn't have been anyone else in there before you two. And we have no evidence of anyone in that barn after you until Mr Venky saw you. You were there. You had the opportunity to do it and you had the means. You know the farm and the equipment very well… so tell me why did you do it?"

Igor and the other man looked at each other. Hogarth folded his arms.

"Come on. Out with it. Was it the past?"

The men spoke rapidly in their foreign tongue.

The moody looking one barked a response and shook his head.

"What did he say?" said Hogarth.

"He says you're one of those English who doesn't like foreigners. A racist."

"Bullshit. You can tell him I say foreigners are welcome. It's just the killers we don't want."

Igor translated Hogarth's words and the man shook his head.

"We didn't do it."

"Convince me," said Hogarth.

"Nigel looked after us. He was our means of safety here. Now he's dead, what are we to do? There is no guarantee of work here now. There is nothing at all. The farm will probably close, yes? We'll be in bad trouble."

"What kind of trouble?" said Hogarth.

"Trouble is why we run from you…"

Palmer cottoned on first. "Oh…sir" she muttered. Hogarth wasn't far behind.

"Damn it. You're not from the European Union, are you?" said Hogarth.

Igor shook his head.

"We're not from Europe at all. We're from Syria. But the people who helped us get here, they said to use European names. They said it would be easier for us."

"Well you could have chosen a better bloody name than Igor, couldn't you?" Hogarth sighed. "Where'd you get that one? An old horror film?"
The man didn't answer him. "So… you ran because you were afraid of being deported?" said Hogarth.
The men nodded.
"Syria…" he said. Igor nodded again. "Then you people have nothing to do with Grave Farm's past history."
"We know nothing of the farm. All we know is that Mr Grave helped us. He didn't care that we were Syrian. He didn't write us off as terrorists as everyone does."
"Yes, old farmer Grave was a good old stick. Shame someone had to go and kill him. But your nationality doesn't exclude you for the crime. You *were* first on the scene."
Igor explained shook his head.
"No, that's not true. We weren't," he said.
Hogarth stiffened. "What? What do you mean?"
"We saw footprints on the barn floor before ours. We even talked about it afterwards. They were wet shoe prints which led all the way to the chipper machine. Wet prints from the path and they were nothing like Mr Grave's shoes…"
"You saw that, and you didn't tell us?"
"We were scared, you understand," said Igor.
"And then you messed those prints up with your own boot prints."
"Mr Grave was stuck inside the machine. We had to try and help him. We ran to help him."
Hogarth rubbed his chin and looked at Palmer.
"This is a right bloody mess."
Palmer frowned. "We'll need to verify what they're saying is true."

"Yeah. And we'll need prints and everything on these two just in case." *And we'll need them secure too*, thought Hogarth, knowing that it was the thing they feared most.

"Call the nick," muttered Hogarth to his sergeant. "Get some uniforms down here. Tell them to send Dawson for backup, in case these two get frisky."

Hogarth faced them again while Palmer made the call. He saw the men now wore an air of despair and defeat.

"Boys, I'm afraid you're going to have to come in with us."

"But you'll send us back…" said Igor.

"To Syria? It's a bloody war zone. I doubt it. Worst case is you'll end up with refugee status."

"You don't know that, Mister Policeman."

Hogarth met the man's eye and said no more. It was true. He didn't know for sure. But he still had no choice. The men had to be prevented from running until the case had been cracked. And it wasn't about pleasing Melford, not at all. The only thing that mattered was catching the killer.

"Did you see anyone in that shed, Igor? *Did you see the killer?*"

The man shook his head. "That, I would have told you."

"Tell me, who do you think did it?"

A bitter laugh slid from his lips and the man shook his head. "Truth?"

Hogarth nodded.

"The truth is it could have been any one of them. The old woman hated him. His son wanted him gone so he could have the farm now, and the other man is a shark."

"What about Venky the vet?"

The man shook his head. "No problem. All he cares about is animals. Venky is a nice man. Like Mr Grave."

"You've forgotten one of them. What about Neville Grave's girlfriend."

"I didn't forget. Just did not include her. If she was strong enough, I would say she did it."

"Why?"

"That girl looks like an angel. But I know a dangerous woman when I see her. That one could be worse than them all."

"But you say she didn't do it?"

"It is not possible for her," said Igor.

"Not without help…" said Hogarth. He looked at Igor's friend. Both seemed to understand the implication of his glare.

"I told you. It wasn't us, Mister Policeman. If you want to catch the killer, you need to find the person who wears those shoes."

And those gloves, thought Hogarth.

Hogarth looked around the area and aimed a thumb over his shoulder to the ramshackle bungalow. "You live in there, right?"

The men nodded. "Does anyone else use this area at all? Neville? Venky? Anyone else?"

They shook their heads. "This is ours alone."

"Then make yourselves useful. Help me search it. Then we can rule you out. Understand?"

"We didn't do it," they said.

"Then help me find who did. They could have stashed evidence here when you weren't looking. Come on. We'll start right here in the greenhouse."

When Palmer returned, she found Hogarth and the two men rifling through sacks and stacks beneath the potting shelves.

"Dawson is on the way, guv."

"Look here – I've found myself two new deputies, Palmer. Who said there was a manpower problem on the team?"

"Melford would just love that."

"Don't I know it? And that only adds to the fun."

***

Hogarth watched as PC Dawson and PC Jordan put Igor and Borev in the back of a police car. He waved them off before crossing the fields back towards Grave Farm. By now, Hogarth's clothes looked as if he'd worn them on a ten-mile cross country run. Somehow, Palmer's clothes still looked crisp and neat. Palmer smirked as she noticed Hogarth's self-conscious glances.

"We'll have to talk to Marris about those trainer prints," said Hogarth, changing the subject. "If he can split those prints apart somehow, or separate the timings of the prints, that would be a start."

"Maybe he can," said Palmer. "If one set of prints obliterates another, even that must tell us something,"

Hogarth marched through the field with his hands in his pockets, brooding. They found his car where he'd left it, parked at an odd angle on the verge just before the blind bend. All sign of the earlier chaos was gone. Hogarth opened the car door and saw his phone lying face down on the back seat. He remembered the stopwatch timer and picked it up quickly and looked at the screen.

"Eleven minutes, twelve seconds."

"So, does that leave any spare time at all for Goodwell to kill Nigel Grave?" said Palmer.

Hogarth frowned. "No. It leaves hardly any bloody time at all. And look, we're not even at the door of the farmhouse yet. That butter run puts our friend Trevor Good Life in the clear as well. Come on, Palmer. Who the hell did do this thing?"

"The only set of people we haven't questioned properly yet are Neville and Nancy."

"Yes, we need a result there," said Hogarth. "I think we'd better get some coffee and food down our necks before that. We need to be on our A-game with those two."

"But is it really possible that she could have done it?" said Palmer.

"Who knows? Marris. We need Marris to come up with the goods on those trainers – and we need more on those neoprene fibres. It's the trainers and gloves, Palmer. They're our way in."

Hogarth ran a hand over the streaks of dark brown mud on his chinos and the spatters to his navy blazer.

"Do you mind if I do a fly-by to my place before lunch?" he said. "I could do with getting changed before DCI Melford accuses me of staging a dirty protest."

"If it helps."

"It'll help stop Melford and all the wise-arses at the nick. I've had about as much piss-taking as I can stomach."

"At least it shows you can handle the dirty work. I wonder when DCI Melford last saw any action?"

"Action? What, Melford? I didn't have him down as your type, Palmer."

Palmer shook her head and tried not to blush. "Guv, you know exactly what I meant."

Hogarth grinned and started the engine of his Vauxhall. But the smiles didn't last long. His phone started to ring and vibrate on the dash. Hogarth grabbed it and saw the name on screen said 'A'. He felt Palmer looking and was glad he had chosen not to add Ali's full name on his contact list.

"Don't mind me if you need to answer it."

"No, it's okay. I'll deal with it later," said Hogarth, and he hit call reject, but his heart was thudding fast. He hoped Palmer didn't notice. Thankfully, she was busy staring out of the windscreen.

Palmer tried hard not to notice Hogarth's sudden tension, and the way he refused this call when he had answered the others. Maybe it was the mysterious fancy woman the uniforms had guessed about. Or maybe it was nothing at all. Deep down, Palmer couldn't help hoping it was the second option.

Chapter Eleven

Alone in his house, Hogarth pressed his mobile phone to his ear while he hopped around his living room with one leg still in his trousers. He dragged his chinos to the floor and shrugged off his jacket. When the phone call was answered he was down to his shirt, boxer shorts and socks

"You called me," said Hogarth, careful to say no more in case the call was a trap.

He peered out of the window towards his Vauxhall. Palmer was idle in the front seat, quiet and serious-faced, her head turning his way. She might have seen him at the glass, but thankfully the net curtains hid his modesty. By rights he should have invited Palmer in for a polite chat and a coffee, but he didn't want her to get the wrong idea. And he needed to make this very private call. Now Palmer would think he'd been rude. Life was a balancing act and it was always difficult to make the right call. Especially when one was having an affair with the wife of a local MP.

His heart thudded harder as he waited. Finally, a voice came on the line.

"Joe."

So, it was her. But Ali sounded odd. Hogarth forgot his chinos and dropped into an armchair with an open copy of The Record on it. He kicked last night's whisky tumbler over on the carpet but didn't care. The glass was empty.

"Ali, I wanted to see you. I tried to see you. I needed to know you were okay."

"Joe. You *really, really* shouldn't have come round last night."

"But your husband's car wasn't there. What with all this Brexit malarkey going on at Westminster, I was sure he'd be there voting or doing whatever else he can get away with."

"But you were wrong, Joe. Badly wrong."

"His car wasn't there, Ali! How was I to know? Look… I'm sorry."

"His car might not have been there because he could have gotten suspicious. He asked me why I was shopping at Rochford Airport when the attack happened. He knows I wouldn't shop there. That retail park is bloody awful. There's nothing there."

"How did he know about Rochford?"

"The Record reported it. I must have blabbed an excuse to someone when I was dizzy and hurt."

"I wanted to see you, Ali. I needed to know you were okay. You are okay, right? Tell me you're okay."

"I'm okay. I do look like a dummy from the Egyptian exhibit at the National Museum, but apart from that, I'm well enough."

"He hit your head?"

"He punched me, the bastard. He punched me as hard as if I was a man. Then I lost my footing on the doorstep, slipped, and my head hit the wall of the house. I honestly thought I was going to die, Joe. The man had a knife in his hand. I saw it. I was convinced he was going to kill me, but I was so dazed from the fall there was simply nothing I could do."

Hogarth's face darkened. A vicious light crept into his eyes. "Did you see his face… do you know what he looks like?"

"Oh, it was so quick. But I think I might remember if I concentrated hard enough. I should write it down. Or maybe draw him. But the thing is…" Her voice started to break with emotion. "I don't want to remember any of it, Joe. It's all so real. I'm scared, and I never get scared. That's just not who I am."

Swear words raced through Hogarth's mind in a long vitriolic chain. Thinking about Ali being hurt made him furious. He stood up, a fist clenched at his side. "If I saw that man, Ali… if I could spend ten seconds with him, alone, nothing bad would ever happen to you ever again. I'd make damn sure of it."

"I know you would…" she said. Her voice was quiet. He could hear she was still weeping.

"How injured are you, Ali?"

"He didn't stab me, thank God. But he kicked me a few times when I was down. He kicked me in the stomach, Joe. I thought this stalker was twisted before, but now I know he's a very, very evil man."

"Why? What do you mean?"

"Joe… he told me this was the least I deserved. He called me a whore. He called me all kinds of things, but he kicked me in the stomach and said if I had a whore's baby inside me, that his kicks would kill it dead. The sick bastard doesn't seem to have worked out why James and I never had any children."

Hogarth stayed silent. It was a topic they had never discussed but Ali carried on. She seemed to read his mind. "I can't have children, Joe. Even if I wanted them, I just can't do it. As if I needed that horrific man insulting me like that, reminding me, as he kicked me in the guts…"

Hogarth began to shake with anger and upset. He'd never asked about children. And although they'd never used a condom – and he hadn't complained about that either – he had always imagined that Ali had taken care of the contraception angle. The truth made him feel bad for her. And it made him feel a deep new hate for the stalker, and her husband too. The stalker had tried to kill a child they never had. The thought was like a fire in him. Hogarth felt like he could kill.

"When you're ready, you must tell me what this man looks like. I need a description, Ali. I need something to work with."

"Joe… you can't do that. You've done enough."

"Ali?"

"You came here – and you threatened James, didn't you?"

"I did no such thing. He was there, in your house, while you were in bed sick – he was there with his secretary, Ali. In your home."

"I know. But I have to play the long game, Joe. I have to be the smart one and wait for him to put a foot wrong or ask for the divorce. You coming here just gave him everything he needs to turn this thing against me. He's suspicious of you, Joe. Of us."

"How?"

"You made it plain you had a personal interest in my wellbeing. It doesn't take much to work out what that might be now, does it?"

"Ali…"

"No. Listen to me. You crossed a very serious line which I asked – *which I pleaded* – you not to cross. If there's any chance of me coming out of this marriage with a life at all, I have to put the brakes on this now. I can't give him any more ammunition to use against me. He can have his suspicions, but that's all."

"Ali… what are you saying?"

"From now on he'll be looking for signs of you in my life. But he mustn't find any. Do you understand?"

"So that's it? You're packing me in? You're punishing me for caring about you?"

"No. I'm saying we have to pause things. Put them on hold for a while. It could take time, and who knows how long… but. if we are meant to be – then you'll still be there for me when the time comes."

"That's a very fancy way of ending things without saying the actual words."

"No, it isn't. I mean what I say, Joe. What you did was very, very foolish, but I still care about you."

Hogarth gulped and shook his head.

"Has he put a guard on you, yet? Because you bloody need one."

"No. He said he's asked for police resources. He said paying for security would look too flash and show a lack of trust in the police."

"He's still thinking about the voters at a time like this! I'm a policeman, damn it, and I have a very justified lack of trust in the police! You need proper protection, Ali."

"Well, I'm not going to get anything more than what the police will provide."

"Don't finish with me like this, Ali. You need my help now."

"Maybe I do. But until the dust settles I'm going to have to manage without you. Wait for me, Joe. I hope that you will."

He heard Ali's movements at the other end – she was about to cut the call.

"Ali! Wait."

"What?" she said, quietly.

"What does he look like? This stalker – please?"

"I… I…"

"Ali?"

"He's a small man. Brown eyes. Dark hair with grey flecks. He's either in his late forties or early fifties. And one other thing, the only other thing I remember very clearly, was his grey raincoat. And he wore an aftershave that smelt like boiled sweets."

Hogarth blinked and fell silent.

"Joe? Isn't that enough?"

But Hogarth couldn't speak.

"Are you still there?" she said.

"Thanks for telling me, Ali. I'll keep well away from your house. And away from that waste of space you call a husband too. But I can't promise that I won't be watching you."

"Don't – his people could see you!"

"*His people?*"

"Now he knows about you, I wouldn't put it past him to hire someone…"

"What? You think he'd hire a PI, but no bodyguard to protect you? I *have* to keep an eye on you."

"Just don't ruin what's left of my life in the process, eh?"

"Ali…?" he said, slowly, before his voice dried up.

"I know…" she said. "We need to be strong. I have to go. I won't call you again for a while."

But her words sounded final.

"Ali…" he said.

"Don't say it. Not yet…" said Ali. The call ended abruptly, and Hogarth stared at the screen of his phone. A small movie played inside his head, over and over. The confrontation with the man in Southchurch. A smallish man with dark eyes, dark hair. *A man in a grey raincoat*. Hogarth growled and hurled his phone to the floor and watched it bounce once on the carpet. He ran a hand through his hair, stood up, and paced around his front room before he finally remembered that Palmer was waiting for him outside. He still needed to put some clothes on. Hogarth ran up the stairs and picked up last's week's chinos from the washing basket and dragged the cold dank things on over his legs. Then he snatched his old blue blazer from the wardrobe. Downstairs, he picked up his phone from the downstairs carpet, and found a fresh new crack running across the screen. He grimaced. It served him right. All this rubbish served him right. But he was still seething, and someone was going to pay. The killer in the Grave Farm case would pay handsomely. But when he found the stalker, that particular scumbag was going to pay most of all.

He opened the front door, stepped out into the cold and tried to set his face to a less abrasive look. His smile twitched at Palmer before it caved in. He let his shoulders sink and walked to the car.

"Guv? You okay?" said Palmer as he got in the car.

"No, sorry, Palmer. I could pretend I'm A-okay, spiffing and all that, but the truth is my life is rapidly sinking to deeper lows with each passing day. But hey. Now that's said, I hope you'll forgive me if I don't put on my jolliest smile. If I tried to do that all day, I'd end up in a loony bin by Friday night."

"What's the matter? If you don't mind me asking…"

"Life. That's what they call it, I believe. And apparently, it's incurable. Come on. Let's go and get a bite to eat. Scratch the coffee though, I think I need more than that. Then I am going to give Neville and Nancy a grilling like you wouldn't believe."

Palmer nodded, stony-faced and rebuffed. So, it was the secret lover then. But even having Hogarth shut the door on her stupid, illogical fantasy – a world where she and Joe Hogarth would become the most unlikely romantic couple since the Krankees, she still found a glimmer of hope. It seemed Hogarth's secret romance had hit the rocks. Yeah, it was mean, selfish, stupid, and nasty, but Palmer couldn't help it. Behind her glum face, she was just a little bit pleased. But Palmer didn't like herself for it.

"I'll get the sandwiches in, guv. My shout."

"Really? Maybe this once I'll let you buy me a beer too."

A dark glimmer of stupid hope grew just a little bit brighter. It was a phase. A moment. A brief crush. It would pass. Palmer told herself all these things. Don't make life awkward, and all that. And at the same time, her weird, foolish hope remained. Palmer hoped her serious cop side would outlast the silly crush. He was hardly a catch. But no matter what she told herself, the small awkward feeling still remained.

"A drink as well? Don't push it, guv," said Palmer.

"Sorry, Palmer. I can't change the habit of a lifetime."

Chapter Twelve

Hogarth refused every pub Palmer suggested, eventually taking her to a venue she'd never known existed. The Old Naval social club was tucked away on the Westcliff seafront, hidden from the estuary by a tall hedge and a row of parked cars. Palmer was hesitant as they walked in.

"Don't look so frightened, Palmer. This is lunch. It's not an initiation ceremony, if that's what you're worried about."

"I'm not worried," she said, looking around the white-walled interior as Hogarth led the way. The club was bright but old-fashioned inside. It smelt of carpet cleaner, cheap greasy food and strong beer. Hogarth walked in with the air of a man who felt right at home. He'd been grim and moody ever since they left his house on the other side of Westcliff, but the social club seemed to put him in a different air.

"You should be grateful," said Hogarth.

"Grateful? I wouldn't go that far," said Palmer, wrinkling her nose at the fading, yellowing prints on the walls. Seaside prints, naval prints, coastal maps, all in dated-looking wooden frames.

Hogarth reached the bar and clapped his hands in anticipation. A man who looked like a cross between a sergeant major and a cartoon fisherman appeared behind the bar. The man wore a bushy white beard, and wisps of white hair around a shining bald pink head.

"Joe Hogarth," said the man, wiping his hands on a towel. "With a woman too. About time, I'd say."

"You don't get many in here, do you, Henry?"

"They weren't allowed in until the eighties. Some of the older members haven't yet embraced the change in the rules," said the old barman, giving her a once over. "But you've got no worries with me," he said.

Palmer tried not to shake her head. So much for being grateful.

"What do you want? Scotch and water? Or is it just the scotch?"

"I'm working, Henry. I'd best stick to lager."

"Dear me, you must really be working."

Hogarth tapped the Aussie lager tap, and the old man poured him a glass. "And you, love?" he said.

"Vodka and lemonade," said Palmer.

"Right you are."

"We are having lunch, aren't we?" said Palmer.

"Oh, yes. Lunch for two please, Henry."

"No problem. Take a seat and I'll bring it out in two minutes."

He gave them their drinks and Palmer gave Hogarth a confused look as the old man disappeared into a room out back.

"What's he doing now?" said Palmer.

"Making lunch."

"But he didn't even ask what we wanted."

"Oh, Henry doesn't bother with all that. His menu consists of the sum total of pies and crisps. And he already knows what pie I like. Chicken and mushroom. You do like chicken and mushroom, don't you?"

Palmer thought it over and decided there was no point complaining or questioning things any further. In Hogarth's skewed view of the world, it was clear to see this club was close to Hogarth's version of nirvana. Palmer was grateful for the culture shock. Her view of Hogarth was becoming a little clearer – her rose-tinted glasses were beginning to slip.

"Do you know why I like it here, eh, Palmer?"

She looked around for clues, but didn't find any fast enough to respond.

"Because there's no scumbags in here," he said. "And guess what else – no coppers either. It's ideal."

"I've been working with you near on a year, and I don't think I understand you any better than I did at the start."

"Join the club. I understand less and less as I get older."

"You're not going to turn all philosophical on me as well, are you?"

"Don't fret. When the chicken pie turns up I'll stop talking altogether."

When the pies turned up, Hogarth did stop talking, and so did Palmer. While Hogarth rubbed his hands and looked at his steaming plate with delight, Palmer could barely hide her feelings. The old barman clunked their two plates down in front of them with a knife and fork each. The pies were still in their foil wrapping, and the pastry lids had the sunken look of a freshly microwaved affair. It looked less than appetizing.

"Voila," said Henry, and walked away rubbing his hands on his trousers. Hogarth picked up his knife and fork and looked at Palmer.

"What's the matter?" he said.

"I guess I'm just not that hungry," lied Palmer.

Hogarth raised an eyebrow. "You're soft, that's all. Henry's pies, once tried, never forgotten."

"I believe you on that score," said Palmer.

Hogarth cut himself a splodge of chicken and pastry goo when the phone started to ring in his pocket. He looked at the fork and stuffed it in his mouth in defiance.

Still chewing, he stuck the mobile to his ear.

"Yes?" he said.

"Hogarth, is that you?"

"Ivan. Yes, it's me, with a mouthful of chicken pie."

"Sounds disgusting," said Marris.

Hogarth refused to have his lunch talked down any further.

"What do you want, Ivan?"

"I've looked at those prints more closely."

"Prints?" said Hogarth.

"Don't get excited. I'm talking about footprints, not fingerprints. The ones in the barn at Grave Farm."

"Oh?"

"The boots look to be cheap and cheerful synthetic rubber soles. A common pattern. They have the same print, so they were probably ordered at the same time from the same firm."

"Yes. I've met the boys who were wearing them. Those boots were bought by the farmer, I'd say. Those two men are in custody because of their immigration status, but it's handy for us. It gives us time to look at them in connection with the evidence."

"Jolly good. I've looked at the other prints too…"

"The trainers?" said Hogarth.

"Yes. They're a cheaper sports brand. Nothing fancy. And they've been well worn-in too. The prints we found lacked a lot of the original definition to the sole pattern, but some of it was still there."

Hogarth stuffed his fork into the steaming heart of the pie and stirred it up.

"What about timings, Ivan? Any idea when those prints were laid? Which came first and all that?"

"That is about the degree of moisture left in the print, and which print is the last imposed."

Hogarth processed Marris's words. He wasn't much interested in the process. "Yes… and?"

"And the boot prints show up a lot. There are dry ones, ones half-hidden by the hay. Dickens found a ton of them. But the trainer prints are a mess. They show up along with the shoe prints belonging to the old man. From the mess of prints near the front of the woodchipper, we can assume the messy prints depict the struggle as the victim was physically overwhelmed. Then the trainer prints are much stronger, and the shoe prints disappear as they get closer to the chipper, just before the work-boot prints smear over them again."

"Have you got a hypothesis, Ivan? You usually do."

"As it happens, I do. The trainers are size nines and very well worn. The person who wore those used them a lot, over time. Maybe they are an everyday item."

"But nobody was wearing trainers at Grave Farm on the day of the killing."

"That's as maybe. The killer wears them a lot."

"Okay," said Hogarth.

"Secondly, we know from the moisture traces that the murderer tussled with Nigel Grave. The stronger footprints near the machine suggest a heavier load. This is where your man in trainers had picked up the farmer, and the extra weight impacted the prints. The other boot print smears were made when the migrants you mentioned probably attempted to rescue Nigel Grave when they found the body."

"How confident are you on that theory, Marris?"

"It's about the evidence. That's what I'm seeing."

Hogarth blinked at Palmer.

"Then the migrant boys are innocent?" said Hogarth.

"It's very likely."

"And our killer wears trainers?"

"Your killer is the one in trainers, yes."
"So, if we factor in the neoprene gloves…" said Hogarth.
"I'm sure you're beginning to come to some conclusions of your own."
"As a matter of fact, I am… and in a very timely way. Thanks for the update, Ivan."
Hogarth ended the call and stuffed another fork-load of pie into his mouth. He washed it down with a slurp of lager.
"You get any of that?" he said, still chewing.
"I think so," said Palmer. "The killer wears old size nine trainers."
"Indeed, he does. Which doesn't eliminate naughty Nancy from being involved – a woman can put on big trainers just as well as a man."
"But Marris said they were old and worn in, didn't he?"
"Yes. Maybe like a pair you could buy in a charity shop."
"You think it's her? Seriously. Do you think Nancy Decorville is strong enough to move someone like that?"
"If she had to. The old man was slight as a bird. He was withering away from cancer, preparing for the end with the LPA and his business announcement. I'm not sure how much fight he had left in him. And if that girl is as spirited as she looks, she could be capable of anything."
Hogarth finished his pie and drained his pint to the halfway mark. His eyes fell to Palmer's pie, still untouched in the foil.
"I do hate waste, Palmer."
"It's all yours, guv."
Hogarth swapped their plates around and stuck his fork into the pastry. Palmer looked away to spare herself. If she was worried about developing an unhealthy close-quarters crush on the DI, then this little chicken pie break had done a great deal to allay her fears.

When the pint was drained and the plates empty, Hogarth wiped his mouth with the napkin and stood up. "The lady is paying, Henry."

"How very modern of you," said Henry, at the bar.

"I'm a New Man, Henry. That's me all over."

"Eight pounds fifty, miss," said Henry.

Hogarth was right. It was the cheapest lunch for two Palmer had heard of in twenty years. Shame that it wasn't edible. Palmer took out the eight pounds fifty from her purse and left the money on the bar top, right beside old Henry's open hand.

Chapter Thirteen

Hogarth put on a calmer, friendlier air as he stepped back into Grave Farm house and wiped his brogues on the thick brown mat. The pies and beer had contributed something to his new demeanour, but for the most part it was an act. He was getting himself into the zone. The new main suspects were coming into view, and this afternoon, he intended to make a full study of them. To be thorough he needed them at ease. He wanted to catch them off-guard. It didn't take long to see the couple had been at ease long before Hogarth and Palmer had arrived.
"Mr Grave," said Hogarth, nodding at the man.
"Inspector," said the young man. His tone was confident, but his eyes betrayed just a hint of nerves. Neville greeted Palmer as she came in and closed the door.
"And where is your good lady, Mr Grave?" said Hogarth.
"Oh, don't worry, Inspector, I promised you she would be here, and she is. I think we'll leave my mother to it down here… we'll go upstairs to talk."
At the mention of his mother, Hogarth watched Neville's face hardening. Yes, the boy had heard too much.
"Okay, is she, your mother?" said Hogarth, picking at the sore.
"Okay? By now you have probably noticed that she's never okay. She's drunk. And she's worse today than most times, but she's always drunk. I don't know how to address it anymore."

"No," said Hogarth. As they climbed the creaky wooden steps, Hogarth peered through the gap in the door towards the kitchen. He caught a glimpse of the woman huddled at the table. It seemed she was fast asleep.

Neville Grave led them to a comfortable upstairs living room. The room had a window looking out over the allotment and the long blue barn where the old man had been killed, to the wide flat fields beyond.

The young man pointed to a couple of empty and worn red-upholstered armchairs.

"Please take a seat."

Hogarth did as he was asked. Palmer followed suit, her stomach growling loudly enough for all to hear.

For a second there was silence, and then the door opened behind Neville and out came Nancy Decorville. Her cheeks were flushed, and her hands were busy as she replaced an earring. As the door shut behind her, Hogarth and Palmer caught sight of an unmade double bed. Hogarth raised an eyebrow at Palmer. Neville and Nancy were well rested.

"Miss Decorville," said Hogarth.

"Inspector," she said, her eyes a strange guarded mix of flirtatious and aggressive.

Hogarth ignored the vibe.

"Thanks for agreeing to see us."

"No trouble at all. It's in everybody's interests that this matter is resolved as quickly as possible. *So the family can move on.*"

"It would be good for the farm too," said Neville. Hogarth watched Nancy give him a pointed look. A look like a rebuke. A warning.

"Neville wants what is best for his family, and for the farm."

"I'm sure he does. It must be difficult to think straight with so much grief weighing you down, eh, Neville?" said

Hogarth. But the lack of emotion on Neville's face made his words seem ridiculous.

"I am grieving, Inspector. In my own way. I loved my father deeply and I'm still in shock at the moment. But he was an old man and he was getting frail. My mind had been on the future for a long time."

"But this wasn't dying of old age, Neville. This was murder. This was sudden and brutal and horrific."

The man's face changed and flickered with emotion. "Do you think I don't know that? He was my father! I know how horrible it was. He must have been in agony when he died."

"I am sure he was," said Hogarth. "Which is why we must find the killer and bring him to justice. Killing a man like that, it's a despicable crime."

Nancy Decorville perched her backside on the edge of a chest of drawers and folded her arms.

"But you have arrested the migrant workers, haven't you?"

"News travels fast around here, miss. Yes, we have. But I have a few reasons to doubt their guilt."

"Oh," said Nancy.

Hogarth's eyes tracked across the floor of the room. He looked at their feet, sizing them up, trying to be discreet all the while. Decorville was barefoot except for her tights. Hogarth guessed she was a size six, or maybe a seven. Not small feet by any means, but not large either. She would have had plenty of spare room in a size nine – maybe too much to wear them easily. Neville's Grave's feet were bigger and wider, maybe a ten. But his feet could still fit into a nine. They'd pinch a bit, but otherwise be fine. Hogarth's eyes took in their body shape next. Both looked fit and strong. The woman's bare arms looked supple and toned.

Both Neville and Nancy waited and looked at Hogarth with awkward eyes.

"Why did you want to see me, Inspector?" said Decorville, playing with her necklace. "I've taken time away from work for this."

"Yes, you do seem very busy," he replied, with a hint of sarcasm. "Neville. You were in the kitchen the whole time when your father went out to collect the wood from the barn. You were still in the kitchen when Mr Venky went out to bring your father back. From the notes we've gathered so far, your father went out around eleven-fifty am, and Venky found him around twelve-ten. That's a window of no more than twenty minutes between approximately eleven-fifty and twelve-ten. But you were seen at home the whole time by your family. Which means, physically at least, you could not have been the killer. Trevor Goodwell left a few minutes after your father and went to get the butter, meaning he had virtually no spare time either…"

The young man shuffled on his feet and scratched his cheek. "I had never thought you'd think me guilty!"

"Murder, Mr Grave, is a messy business. Murders are often committed from mixed motivations, and it's even worse when family are involved. We need to look at everyone involved in this to be certain."

The man offered a weak nod and looked at Nancy.

"Now, Miss Decorville. Correct me if I am wrong, but you didn't arrive until just after Mr Venky went to fetch Mr Grave senior from the barn. That puts your entrance at Grave Farm at around the twelve-ten mark or just after."

"Yes, in time for lunch."

"And perhaps, maybe at the perfect time for having just committed a murder."

"What?!" said the woman. She looked incredulous and defiant, her eyes flashing at Neville and at Hogarth.

"You don't have an alibi for that time from eleven-fifty to twelve-ten, do you, Miss Decorville?"

"What do you mean? Isn't it obvious. I was driving, wasn't I? I had to drive to get here."

"Of course. But it's feasible that you could have set off earlier, waited for your moment, and sprung on the old man when you saw the chance."

"What? Surely you don't believe that? You make me sound like some kind of monster! As if I could ever do such a thing! I've never hurt a person in my entire life."

Hogarth looked at her blankly.

"Not even in pursuit of business, Miss Decorville? Because you strike me as a very driven individual."

"Driven? Yes, of course I'm driven. Driven to be successful in my career, but not at any cost."

"Really?" said Hogarth.

He let his words sink in.

"How dare you?!" she said.

"This is a murder investigation, madam. I have to look at everything in front of me."

Hogarth turned to Neville.

"Mr Grave. You were seen arguing with your father on the day before the murder. Can you tell us what you were arguing about?"

The man blinked at Hogarth in surprise.

"Arguing?"

"Yes. That's how it was described…"

"I didn't think we were arguing, but… I was trying to persuade him to see sense. To listen to my ideas before it was too late."

"Too late? For what?" said Hogarth.

"He still had a brief window of opportunity to diversify the business here at the farm. If he sold just a little of the land to a developer – just a sliver – it would have released enough capital to reinvest in the new tech and crops which could have brought life back to the farm."

"But your father wasn't too receptive to the idea, was he? From what I've heard, he never was very receptive to your ideas. As I understand it, you'd tried a few things already and none of them had worked out."

"And why was that? Because they were sticking-plaster solutions. Vain attempts to stick a finger in the wall of a cracking dam. I was working with the tools I was given. But to save the farm we needed to do much more."

"And let me guess, the sale of this sliver of land would have gone through Crispin and Co, meaning a healthy commission for Miss Decorville here."

"That had nothing to do with it," she said, all too quickly.

Hogarth's mouth formed a bitter grin. "Of course not."

"If you want to convince me you were elsewhere at the time of the murder, Miss Decorville, I'll need to know your whereabouts for the entire day but especially for the hour between eleven twenty and twelve fifteen."

The lovers exchanged a glance.

"What is it?" said Hogarth.

"I suppose it's probably best we tell you," said Nancy Decorville, finally.

"Tell me what."

"We had our own plan for the lunch. We were worried – Neville was worried – that his father had made the wrong choice and was about to announce something desperately foolish. Neville and I talked about how to give him a last minute talking to. As a way to turn his thinking around before he made a very serious mistake…"

"A last-minute talking-to, eh?" said Hogarth, looking at Palmer.

"No, no, no. Not like that. The plan was about showing him a better way. Persuading him."

"Why were you so desperate to persuade him, Neville? I think I can see Miss Decorville's angle here, but what about yours?"

"My father wanted the farm to go on and so did I. I didn't want him listening to Venky's absurd rare breed ideas, or the bloody industrial partnership thing Trevor was always on about."

"So?"

"So, I was about to confront him with a truly golden, once-in-a-life-time offer."

Hogarth frowned. The young man's words sounded like a sales-pitch. His eyes narrowed, ready to hear some bull. In suspicion, Hogarth glanced at Nancy Decorville.

"Nancy and I had talked it through after the argument which I assume my dear mother must have told you about."

"And?"

"We came up with a perfect plan – to keep three quarters of the farm, all the best land there was, while freeing up some of the disused wasteland on the fringes, the parts nearest Rochford and Sutland village. Those would be sold for new housing, and all the money would go back into the farm."

"Isn't that the same deal you've described already?" said Hogarth.

"No – this was a better deal. The clincher – was this. I would take over the running of the farm. And the ownership. My father would sign it over to me, with one extra, crucial proviso written into the agreement. I would never completely sell the farm. I would always ensure that Grave Farm went from my generation to the next. This would ensure my father had a peace-of-mind guarantee that the farm would go on. That was what he cared about. I was going to guarantee it."

"The way you say it, the phrases you choose… excuse me for saying, Mr Grave, but you make it sound like an advert from TV," said Hogarth.

Neville Grave's face dropped. "That was never my intention."

"You've got the wrong end of the stick, Inspector," said Nancy Decorville.

"I'm telling you what I hear. So, according to this plan, you were going to own the farm? Taking it over from him? Interesting. But I picked up on the word *completely*. You said you would never completely sell the whole farm."

"That's right," said Neville.

"That must have made Miss Decorville here very happy. Because that word would leave the farm open to lots more sell-offs over time. So long as you kept a small farm operation going while you sold off everything else, you would be honouring your promise."

"You're out of order," said Miss Decorville.

"That's a wilful misrepresentation of what I wanted to do. And our plans had no bearing on father's death."

"On the contrary, Mr Grave. The future of this farm seems of critical importance to everyone who was here the day your father was killed. So, you cooked up this agreement for the farm… when did you plan to pitch it to him?"

"Before he made his announcement. I was going to ask him for a word just before lunch. That was the intention. As a matter of fact, it was Nancy who dropped me off for the lunch. We talked it through, and knew what we were going to say… and that's why I know Nancy couldn't have killed him – because she was driving."

"Driving?" said Hogarth. "You had this plan to talk to Nigel before lunch. But you dropped Neville off and came back, what, twenty minutes later. Why? Where did you go, Miss Decorville?"

"To my office - to Crispin and Co. You can check it out if you like. I was there."

"But this was your last chance to persuade Nigel Grave to adopt your plan, yet instead you drive away to your office, and for such a short time… it doesn't make sense."

The woman blushed, just a shade, but Hogarth still saw it. "I went there to provide an update on proceedings for Mr Crispin."

"An update on your plan, eh?" said Hogarth.

"Our plan," said Decorville. The woman toyed with her necklace.

"All very dignified and above board then," said Hogarth. "You set out to take the farm out of his hands and sell some of it off – maybe just one piece or maybe lots of pieces over time. That sounds like Nigel's worst nightmare."

"That was *never* my plan!" said Neville.

"Trevor Goodwell's been in your ear," said the woman sharply.

"You're wrong there, Miss Decorville. Tell me. Do either of you wear trainers?"

"Trainers?" said Neville, like it was a trick question. "Sports shoes? Or fashion shoes?"

"Either," said Hogarth.

Neville shrugged. "Yes, I've got a pair."

"Can you get them for me please?"

Neville looked at Nancy Decorville and she shrugged.

Hogarth saw a marked bitterness on her pretty face. She had been called out and she knew it.

"And you, miss. What shoe size are you?"

"This is absolutely preposterous," she said.

"Miss, this is a murder investigation," said Palmer.

"Fine. Whatever you say. I'm a size six…" she said, shaking her head.

Neville Grave opened the bedroom door and walked inside. He left the door open and passed the unmade double bed. Palmer and Hogarth's eyes followed Neville into the room, and though the young farmer seemed oblivious, Hogarth and Palmer couldn't fail to notice the brassiere hanging over the bedstead, or the lingerie abandoned on the floor.

Neville Grave returned holding a pair of black sporty trainers with a red swish down the side. Hogarth was still looking at the skimpy underwear on the floor when Neville Grave handed him the trainers. Hogarth coughed and looked at the insides then turned them upside down and looked at the soles. The soles were neat and new the tread was deep and thick.

"And these are the only pair you have?"

"Yes."

"Then have you replaced them recently?"

"No," he said, looking confused. "Why?"

"Just a question. From your physique, it's clear that you must lift a few weights, Mr Grave. You said you were a gym goer?"

"When I get the chance. I used to go a lot more than I do now."

"Life gets in the way, eh? Gloves, Mr Grave. Do you wear weightlifting gloves?"

"To stop myself getting sore hands. Yes. Hold on. I'll fetch them. Why do you want all this stuff?"

Hogarth's eyes flicked to Nancy Decorville. "It's something we have to look into, that's all. And how do you keep fit, Miss Decorville?"

The woman's eyes flicked to the open door and the unmade bed. She shifted on her feet with awkwardness. "All the usual ways, Inspector."

"Gym goer, are we?"

"No. I prefer to run, and I run in my size sixes. What is all this about?"

"All will become clear in due course."

Neville Grave returned and handed the gloves to Hogarth and he inspected them. They were smooth black neoprene stitched with nylon – just what the doctor ordered. In this case, Dr Ivan Marris. Hogarth prodded the Velcro strap and passed the shoes and gloves to Palmer.

"Mind if we borrow these for a few days?"

"Not at all," he said.

"Very sensible, Neville. I think you should both know that Miss Decorville's lack of alibi, late arrival for the lunch and the nature of your business proposal leave me with serious questions to be answered."

"But I do have an alibi, Inspector," said Nancy.

"So you say. But Crispin and Co may not be watertight. Can any other Crispin staff vouch for you?"

"No. The office was empty. It's not like an estate agent's. We can come and go. I left a note for Mr Crispin."

"You see my problem, then," said Hogarth.

"No, Inspector. There's something else."

Miss Decorville looked increasingly awkward. Hogarth's eyes locked onto her discomfort, and Neville was watching too.

"What then?" he said.

"I did meet someone at Crispin's, albeit very briefly, and face to face. They are my alibi."

"Then who did you meet?" said Hogarth.

Nancy Decorville turned her eyes towards Neville. "I made a small investment for the both of us, Neville. Just a little of my own money. I hired someone to help us."

"Spell it out, Miss Decorville," said Neville.

"I met with a man called Fred Schapps. He's a private detective."

"Excuse me? You did what?" said Neville.

"Go on," said Hogarth.

"I had some suspicions that your uncle and aunt were up to something. That they were trying to out-manoeuvre us."

The young man kept quiet.

"Trevor and Marjorie Goodwell," said Hogarth. "In what way?"

"I didn't know exactly. But I knew they had their own plan for the farm's future."

"And?"

"I was going to tell you about this later on, Neville. But seeing as the inspector won't give us time alone to talk…"

The woman hurried back into the bedroom and returned with a large handbag. She made sure to close the bedroom door behind her, but it was far too late for all that. From her shiny red patent leather bag, she produced a paper wallet with two photographs in it.

She handed them to Hogarth. The first photograph showed Susan Grave looking animated as she spoke with Marjorie, her sister-in-law. Looking closer, Hogarth saw they were arguing.

"So? What is this supposed to prove?" said Hogarth.

"Not much. But the second one does."

He handed the first photo to Palmer while Neville Grave looked on, confused. Hogarth looked at the second photograph.

"That shows Marjorie in a restaurant in Brentwood. The man she is seated with there is Daniel Crump. Does that name mean anything to you, Inspector?"

"No," said Hogarth. "Should it?"

"Really? I am surprised," said Nancy Decorville. "Head anywhere into farming territory – East Anglia, Wales, the South West – and you'll see the Crump brand name everywhere. Milk tankers, farms, feed factories, farm gas supply and utilities, farm transport and engineering, Crump is simply everywhere you look. They are the biggest brand of the new industrial farms. Officially, Crump's way of business is to become a partner with the local farmer, moving in their industrial equipment to streamline the business. In reality, they buy a stake and take over stage by stage. If Crump got hold of Grave Farm it would remain Grave Farm in name only.

It would soon become another pin in the map of the Crump farming empire."

"My, my," said Hogarth. "That picture must have scared you witless, Miss Decorville. What with how much you care for the Grave farming legacy and all."

"I don't care what you think of me, Inspector. This photograph here shows I was perfectly right to hire my investigator. They're out to take the farm from right over your head, Neville. And while that hateful mother of yours is still alive, they can do it too."

The words stuck in Hogarth's mind. *That hateful mother.*

"Do you think Susan Grave is of a mind to accept such a deal?"

"It depends on how much alcohol they offer her, wouldn't you say, Inspector?" said Decorville.

Neville Grave was silent and looked upset. Nancy Decorville went to his side, but he didn't look at her. Instead he looked at Hogarth.

"It's true, Inspector. You see how my mother is with me. Even if I figured in my father's will, any mention of me will soon be removed. She owns the place now, and she can do what she damn well likes with no one to stop her."

"What are you going to do?" said Hogarth.

"I'm going to do my best to persuade her it's in her interests and the farm that I take over. If Trevor and Marjorie are making promises to look after her, then so I can."

"That's the spirit, Neville," said Nancy, taking hold of his arm.

Hogarth's eyes glinted as he watched them. He had heard enough to be getting on with.

"Thank you for your time, Mr Grave, Miss Decorville. It's been most enlightening – for all of us. I'll need to borrow these photographs too. Don't worry. You'll get it all back in due course. In the meantime, stay local. I'll need to speak to you again."

Hogarth shared his weighted glare between both of them, but only Neville Grave responded with a nod. Nancy Decorville was too busy attempting to clean up the mess she'd created. Her attention was devoted to Neville. Hogarth opened the door and waited for Palmer to walk out ahead of him. When they were halfway down the creaking steps, Hogarth muttered. "These bloody people…"

Palmer agreed. "And I think we've just found the supreme candidate for the worst one of all," she said.

"I don't think so, Palmer. Not yet. But we're certainly getting closer."

Chapter Fourteen

By late afternoon, the trainers and the gloves were with Ivan Marris. The photographs went up on the incident board, along with the graphic images depicting the old man's body stuck in the chipper. Hogarth left the goriest ones in the file where they belonged. When the day was done, Hogarth could think of nothing more than the whisky bottle waiting at home, or another of those chicken and mushroom pies at the Old Naval club. He didn't want to be at home alone with his thoughts and fears, or the words of Ali's brush-off echoing through his head. Even so, three chicken and mushroom pies in one day would be the world's slowest form of suicide. Instead, Hogarth made a cheese sandwich for dinner and chomped through the stale bread as he watched the news. The grim-faced newscaster spoke about the tragedy of another US shooting by a lone nut in a shopping mall. The local police chief said the killer wasn't a terrorist, but to Hogarth these nut jobs were all the same. By the time he was on his second half of the sandwich, the whisky bottle was out – just one small glass – just a nip – and the news had shifted to North Yorkshire. Police had failed to react to a warning that a teenage boy had a fixation on a female teacher. One month after the teacher asked police for help, she was killed in the classroom. Hogarth stopped chewing the dry bread and flavourless cheese. He clunked his plate down on the side table and poured the entire nip of whisky down his neck. Time to go out.

North Lane, Shoebury. After news like that, Hogarth had no choice. He sat in his car staring into space from behind the windscreen, tired and alone, feeling something like a stalker himself. The hilly road was empty of pedestrians. The evening was quiet and cold, and already dark. At least the days were lengthening again. He started the engine to take another drive by. He just wanted to see her, that was all. To make she sure she was alright, because he *had to know*. *Had to see*. Hogarth started the engine and pulled the car out onto the street. Just as he passed the Hartigan house, he dabbed the brake and turned his head to look towards the big gallery window. Inside, the lights were on, and the thick curtains had not yet been shut. There! He saw her. His Ali, her fine slender figure as she walked across the room, heading towards the window to close the curtains. He saw a square bandage taped to the side of her head, otherwise she looked fine. Or was that a black eye? Even at a distance, it was good to see her. But the bandage annoyed him. That bastard had almost killed her, and if he got another chance he'd probably succeed. And there were *still* no police around. None in sight, at least. James Hartigan had said he'd spoken to the Super. If so, then the tight bastard still hadn't agreed to post anyone on the MP's front door.

Hogarth waited, his eyes flicking between the blinking dots of his dashboard clock, and the cold dark street. He knew he should have gone home. The sicko had already taken what he could from the woman and it was late. Surely he wouldn't try anything now, not with Ali safely locked away at home. But Hogarth couldn't bring himself to start the engine, so he stewed in his driving seat and waited. After a while, a walker came into view. A man in a long dark coat., pacing down the road down from the top of the hill. His face was obscured in shadow, mostly from the hood pulled over his head. It

wasn't raining, but the night air was freezing cold. Hogarth sat up in his driving seat and squinted over the steering wheel. The coat was a long puffer-style coat, the kind football managers wore in the coldest months. It wasn't a raincoat, that was for sure. The man's head flicked across his right shoulder every so often as he checked the windows of houses where people were still awake – with the lights on. When it came to Ali Hartigan's house, he slowed down. Then he almost stopped. Hogarth didn't wait a beat. He opened his car door, stood up and slammed it behind him. The man in the puffer coat jerked around to see Hogarth striding towards him and he took a step back. Then another.
"Oi. Don't you move," said Hogarth.
"What? Why?" said the man, stepping back.
"You heard what I said,"
"Leave me alone."
Hogarth sped up, bounding along the kerbside as the man backed away.
"What? What do you want?" said the man in a panicked voice.
"The question is, pal…" said Hogarth, seizing the man by his hood. "What do *you* want?"
He dragged the hood away from the man's face and found a hollow-eyed, pasty-face man with a shaven head. The guy appeared to be in his thirties, and had a nasty, shifty look about him. He was vermin alright, but not the vermin he was looking for. But Hogarth was still caught off guard. He pulled the man upright and held him by the collar of his coat.
"What are you doing hanging around here?"
"I'm walking home, that's all."
Hogarth picked up the drink fumes from the man's breath.

"I saw you staring into that window. Someone put you up to it, did they? Did someone ask you to do their dirty work?"
"You're flipped, mate. Get your bloody hands off me!"
"Then why were you looking at that house?"
"Come on! You know why?! It's the MP's house, innit? That MP's missus got attacked there. It was in the news."
Hogarth stared into his eyes, looking for the lie.
"I was being nosy. So, there's a law against being nosy now as well, is there, *copper?*"
He spat the last word like a swear word. Yes, he was the kind of vermin who recognised a cop. Hogarth let go of the man and shoved him away. Then he raised a finger and pointed at him.
"If I ever see you round here again, I'll..."
"You'll what?"
Hogarth sighed. "Use your imagination, cretin. Now piss off."
"Pig..." muttered the man as he moved away, trying hard not to hurry. Hogarth sighed and looked at the Hartigan house. He wasn't exactly doing much to restore public faith in the police. In terms of outreach to the community, that momentary encounter was an epic fail. And Ali Hartigan had dumped him. For better or worse, he had pushed her too far, so she had ended it. "Bollocks," said Hogarth. He thought about the real stalker, the skulking rat who had struck hard when no one was looking. Hogarth looked around the street, sensing that the man was near. But there was no way of knowing and the thought made him want to hit out. Hogarth thought what a pleasure it would have been to own a gun. To find the man and simply remove him from the face of the earth. Hogarth knew the ways to get hold of a gun, but he shook his head and walked back to the car.
"You're not shooting anyone, you daft bastard," he muttered.

The dashboard clock told him it was too early to go home to bed and he was too burdened to be alone. And Henry the barman was no company at all. Talking to Henry was like having a conversation with a soggy beermat. Hogarth started the engine of his Vauxhall and drove away. But he didn't go home.

"Time to break some more rules, eh, Joe?" said Hogarth, talking to himself again. He passed the man in the puffer coat, tooted his horn and gave the man a big, friendly wave. The guy flipped him a finger and left it high in the air to ensure it could be seen in Hogarth's rear-view mirror.

Beyond the Hartigan house, a lone figure sat in a small dark car parked across the street. The man watched every detail of the encounter unfold until Hogarth's unmarked Insignia disappeared at the bottom of the slope. And when he was gone, the man in the dark picked up his phone and dialled. "Yes. It's me," he said, in a soft, well-spoken voice. "Listen, I've got something for you. And I thought you'd want to know…"

BZZZZZZZZZ. Hogarth hit the buzzer on the door for 121b Beedle Road, Westcliff. And just in case the buzzer wasn't loud enough, he waited two seconds more then hit it harder. A second later the upstairs window opened onto the street, and Sue Palmer leaned out. She was wearing a white towelling dressing gown and her hair was slick from the shower or bath.

"Who is it?!" she snapped. Then her tone changed. "Guv?"
"You got any whisky, Palmer?"
"No. But I've got some wine."
"They say never mix grape and grain. But who cares? It'll do."

Palmer studied Hogarth for a few seconds before she replied. "Okay."

She closed the window and a minute later she appeared at the foot of the stairs and opened the door.

"What's this about, sir?" she said.

"It's about me being a selfish idiot and needing a little company. I'm only after a drink and a chat, but you're free to tell me to piss off."

Palmer looked at his glum face and stepped back. "Come in, guv. But I hope you don't mind the smell of garlic."

Hogarth shrugged.

"I hope you don't mind the smell of whisky," said Hogarth. But when he reached the upstairs of Palmer's cluttered flat, he smelt the full force of the garlic butter scent.

"Bloody hell, Palmer. It smells like you've had a squadron of the French resistance in your kitchen. What've you been eating?"

"Garlic bread," said Palmer. He looked at her sofa in her living room and saw her laptop open while some music blared out from her TV. The TV had been switched onto radio mode, or something. Beside the dent in the sofa left by Palmer's backside was a plate with a third of a garlic baguette left on it. It looked like Palmer had polished off a loaf and a half by herself.

He thought of making a quip about her choice of food or about watching her waistline, but neither seemed appropriate. They weren't at the nick. This was Palmer's home. He cancelled the banter and sat down.

"Looks like you're working, Palmer," he said, looking at the laptop. Palmer was nowhere to be seen, but she returned with two brimful glasses of red wine.

"Here you go, guv. The rest of the bottle is in the kitchen if you need it."

"Sounds like a plan."
Hogarth noticed Palmer was self-conscious. She moved to the far end of the sofa, picked up her laptop and covered her legs with it. Hogarth smelt a new fragrance on the air. Mint. Palmer was sucking on a mint. Hogarth glanced at her laptop screen.
"I thought I'd look at the Grave family history," said Palmer. "Seeing as they have all that history behind them, I guessed there would have to be something about it online."
"You never stop, do you, Palmer?"
"And you do? Look at you. You're still wearing your work gear and you look like you haven't been home."
"Spoken like a true Hercule Poirot," said Hogarth, sipping his wine. "I'd rather focus on the case than stay at home."
"If you don't mind me asking," said Palmer, looking at him carefully. "What's the matter, guv?"
Hogarth took a big gulp of red wine and sucked his teeth.
"I don't mind you asking, Sue, but right now, I don't even want to think about it. Let's just talk about the case."
Palmer nodded. Hogarth felt close enough to her to drop round her house on a whim when he wanted, but still closed her out when it mattered. Nevertheless, Palmer decided that was progress of a kind. She watched Hogarth take three gulps of wine, leaving the glass half empty.
"Thirsty, are we?" she said.
"You're not wrong," said Hogarth, with a mirthless smile. "Now? What else have you learned…?"

When Hogarth eventually woke up, he was stretched out on the wide beige corduroy-coloured sofa, with a tartan blanket over his legs. The room still stank of garlic butter, though Hogarth was immune to the additional scent of copper stewed in wine. For a fraction of time he wondered where he was. A moment later, wide-eyed with panic, he wondered if he had made a pass at Palmer. The idea almost brought a cold sweat and the feeling wouldn't leave him.

"You're awake then," she said. Hogarth bolted upright on the sofa, like Frankenstein's monster shot full of lightning. Thank God. There was Palmer, standing before him, clean and fresh and in her standard work outfit – skirt, blouse, and jacket. Her hair looked neat and she was smiling, with a cup of coffee in her hand. There was something coy about her look, something girlish which made him double-check his memory banks. *He had been a good boy, hadn't he?* She saw the look on his face.
"It's okay, don't panic. You finished the wine and fell asleep on the sofa, guv."
"I've taken liberties, Palmer."
"Not really. At least, not any you need to confess. Actually, I saw another side to you."
"Oh no…" said Hogarth. "Should I be worried?"
Palmer grinned. "Not overly. I made a pot of coffee. The proper stuff. Want some?"
Hogarth nodded and rubbed his temples. "Please."
"And I left a towel by the shower for you."
Hogarth looked up at the clock on Palmer's front room wall. It was seven-fifty – high time he was at work. "No thanks. I'll skip the shower and nip out later. Unless Melford is watching my every move, which he might well be."
Palmer handed him a scalding hot black coffee and a slice of buttered toast.
"So, what did we find out?" he said, nodding at the laptop. He could barely remember a thing.
"Only what we knew before, sir. There was the migrant trouble in the nineties, and before that nothing."

"Nothing new then. We'd better hope Marris has come up with something on those trainers and gloves before Melford asks for his update."

"If I were you, guv, I'd take up the offer of a shower. Melford seems to have enough of a problem with you already. You don't need him turning up his nose at you as well."

Hogarth considered his options.

"I don't suppose an extra minute would hurt, would it? And you don't mind, Palmer?"

"That CID room is pretty cramped, sir. I think it might be for the best."

"Yes, good point," said Hogarth. He left the living room and headed for the bathroom in a hurry.

Arriving at Southend Police Station a well-coordinated five minutes after Hogarth, Palmer joined him in the CID room. By the time she walked in, she saw Melford was already standing in the middle of their little room taking up far more space than was necessary. His arms were folded. He reminded Palmer of a stern Soviet statue. Hogarth was trapped in his seat, in the full flow of giving his excuses.

"…but the lack of evidence says we were right. It couldn't have been the migrants, sir. Besides, the old man was keeping them safe. They're not Eastern European as we were led to believed. They're from Syria, no doubt on the run from IS."

"Even so, leaving them aside wasn't your gamble to make. They were the obvious candidates."

"Obvious, but it still wasn't them, sir."

"Which means what? Have you got anything at all?" said Melford. As Palmer slid past him into the room, Melford nodded at her then returned his gaze to Hogarth.

"Yes, sir," said Hogarth. "We've narrowed the field back to those in the family kitchen at Grave Farm at the time of the murder."

"But I thought they all had alibis. How is that supposed to work?"

"Because one or more of them is lying. We'll have to test every word of their alibis. And we've found underlying motives on all of them. I'm certain the motive for the murder was connected to ownership of the farm. The son wanted the old man to transfer ownership to him, so he could sell it. The brother-in-law and sister want the farm to be industrialised for short term gain. Then we've got this other chiseller by the name of Nancy Decorville. Dangerous little thing, she is. I think she's been playing her own game for a while. Her alibi is the weakest of them all. And she hired a PI to dredge up some dirt on the in-laws."

"*Dirt?* Did she find any?"

"Yes. They met with a man from Crump Agro Industries. Crump is the one who could buy up the farm."

"But they don't own the farm, do they? The old man did. What motive did anyone have in seeing him dead."

"The son, has less and less. I think Nancy Decorville's plans are shot to pieces too."

"Which leaves you with a bunch of suspects with watertight alibis, am I right?"

Hogarth blinked and looked away.

"It's not as bad as you're making it sound, sir."

"Is that right? Because to me, it sounds like a shit-show. Which is exactly how you've been looking the last few days. Palmer, if your team is losing its grip of the case, I need to know it now, so I can do something about it. You're clearly underhanded, but that isn't all that's going wrong here."

Palmer turned quiet and pensive. She looked at Hogarth. His eyes lingered on hers. He wasn't asking for a favour. He was waiting to hear her response.

"Sir," she said.

Melford nodded for her to speak.

"Go on," he said.

"I believe we're on track to solve the case," said Palmer, as calmly as she could. "We're well equipped to finish the job. If you hand this case on to the other team they'll be starting from scratch."

"And that's your honest opinion, is it?"

Palmer nodded. "Yes, sir, it is."

"Okay then. Get this case fixed. Then you can take a few days off or do whatever you need to, okay, DI Hogarth. But for God's sake, keep it together until then."

"Sir," said Hogarth, gritting his teeth. Melford stared down at him with stern eyes.

"Yes?"

Hogarth felt Palmer appealing to him at his side. It was just a feeling. She wanted him to hold his temper in check.

"I'll wrap this one up for you, no trouble, sir," said Hogarth.

"Glad to hear it, Hogarth. I'll want an update before the end of the day, okay?"

Melford turned out of the room and shut the door.

"Bastard!" hissed Hogarth.

"That was out of order," said Palmer. "He shouldn't have done that. He shouldn't have put me in that position."

"You didn't have to lie for me, Palmer."

"I didn't lie, guv. We're progressing the case. But the DCI had no right to put you and me on the spot like that."

"That's because someone's put a fire under his backside about me," said Hogarth.

"Why?"

"Because Melford thinks I'm a problem, so now he probably wants me to leave. But I've got nowhere to leave to, Palmer. I transferred in to this place for the long term. Who'd bloody have me after this? I'm staying put whether he likes it or not."

"That's not what I mean, guv. I meant what has he got on you?"

Hogarth looked at her, his throat full of words. For a moment it seemed he was about to speak. Then he shook his head and swallowed his words away.

"All you need to know is that I haven't broken any laws, and haven't done anything – or should I say, much, wrong. No corruption. No crime."

"Then I don't get it," said Palmer.

"Don't get involved in the psychodrama, Palmer. Just stick to the case and you'll come up smelling of roses."

Hogarth took a deep breath and wondered. The DCI was worse than ever. The MP must have been on to him again. Melford was under pressure and passing it on. The office phone rang and Hogarth snatched it up as a welcome distraction.

"Yes?"

"DI Hogarth?" said the police call-handler. "I've got Andrew Gardner of Gardner and Co solicitors on the line for you."

"Gardner and Co," said Hogarth aloud. Palmer nodded and turned her chair to listen. "Yes, put them through."

"Detective Inspector Hogarth speaking," he said.

"Hello there. I've had some dealings with you lately," said the well-spoken man at the other end.

"Yes. The Nigel Grave case. You advised us on the lasting power of attorney issue."

"Yes… I did. And I've had an interesting development in the light of that inquiry…"

"Oh really?" said Hogarth. "My colleague DS Palmer is here with me. Mind if I put you on loud speaker, Mr Gardner?"
"No. That's fine."
Hogarth hit the speakerphone button and the man's voice filled the room.
"I shouldn't be doing this, really," said Gardner. "If it wasn't for our recent conversation I certainly wouldn't, but, well…"
"What is the matter, Mr Gardner?"
And I think I now know why Mr Grave wanted to make that power or attorney. Susan Grave called to ask if she can make changes to her will. I put the brakes on that, of course, and advised it's a bit of a tricky time at the moment, what with Mr Grave's recent death. I said there was a process to slow her down. I exaggerated because there is no such process apart from obtaining an appointment."
"A shrewd move, Mr Gardner. And what was the change she wanted to make?"
"Neville Grave was to be the main beneficiary of the will once both mother and father were deceased…"
"Yes," Hogarth already knew where this was going. It was as the son had predicted. He was about to lose his inheritance.
"Susan Grave stated that she wished to bequeath Grave Farm and all her assets to Trevor and Marjorie Goodwell."
"Goodwell?" said Hogarth, sitting upright.
"Yes, indeed," said Gardener, his words charged with judgement. "It strikes me as such a cruel blow."
"Cruel, yes," said Hogarth. "But I think there could be more than cruelty at work here, Mr Gardner. I think we could be talking about a criminal level of greed."
"I had wondered that myself," said Gardner. "And the woman was drunk as a lord. Now I know she's grieving, and I knew about her issues before, but Nigel's LPA inquiry

makes an awful lot of sense to me now. He wanted to bypass exactly this kind of madness, didn't he?"
"I think he did, Mr Gardner, I think he did. Listen. I appreciate the risk you've taken in calling me, but I don't think you'll regret it. That call from Susan Grave could shape the rest of our investigation…"
"I'm in a tricky position here, Inspector. Mrs Grave remains my client."
"I'm aware of that. If I can keep you out of it, I certainly will."
"Thank you, Inspector."
Hogarth put the phone down.
"But what does that tell us?" said Palmer. "We already know the Goodwells had influenced her. And they've acted like sharks under the circumstances, but it hardly means they're our killers."
"You think their gambit is mere opportunism then?" said Hogarth. "A meeting in a restaurant with one of the agricultural-business's top names. That's planning. That would have taken time. Those two are on a mission."
"But Goodwell couldn't have done it, could he? And the rest of them were in the house the whole time, busily hating each other."
"The mood music is changing, Palmer, so let's not rush it. We're getting closer. If we keep closing in and don't reveal our hand, the killer might just out themselves. We need evidence. Let's get Marris on the phone, then maybe we'll book a meeting with our friends the Goodwells and see what they have to say for themselves." Hogarth picked up the phone and dialled.
"Morning, Ivan. Any news on those shoes and gloves?"
As Marris answered, Hogarth hit the speakerphone button. Marris' smooth voice filled the room.

"Yes, I've got news alright. The trainers and gloves you supplied have nothing in common with the shoe prints found in the barn. Furthermore, the gloves have even less in common with those rogue black fibres. Those gloves in are mint condition. There's no sign of any damage or loss of fabric."

"Damn," said Hogarth, running a hand through his hair. Palmer's hair conditioner made him smell of strawberries. He wasn't sure if the scent really suited him.

"Chin up. It's not all bad, Hogarth. Those fibres were good for a baseline comparison. Yes, they are neoprene, and yes, they have Velcro straps. But the Velcro on these gloves is new and tacky. The hook and loop weave is in perfect order. The gloves you're looking at have Velcro which has gone strandy and soft. The neoprene is deteriorating too. These gloves are like new.

"But how is that helpful, Ivan? The man might have ditched the murder equipment and replaced it yesterday."

"No. I considered that. These newer trainers and gloves have been in use for at least a few months. There is some sign of mild wear – enough to prove it. So, either your killer must be someone else, or the person who owns these gloves has been preparing for this murder for a very long time and has provided this equipment only to throw you off track."

It was possible, but the tone of Marris' voice implied he didn't believe it. Marris was good at his job. His advice couldn't be ignored lightly.

"Thank you, Ivan. You've come good again."

"As always, I hope."

"So do I," said Hogarth, then cut the call.

"Fancies himself a bit, our Marris, doesn't he?" said Palmer.

"Who cares? I think he helped us more than we expected."

"Help? He just ruled out your main suspect."

"He only ruled out Neville Grave, and to tell you the truth I'm glad. I think that young man has put up with enough crap, and with that girl he's probably in for more to come. And I expect between the PI meeting and the journey to Crispin's office we might have to rule her out too."
"Then that would mean everybody's been ruled out."
"Which means, Palmer, everybody has to be ruled back in," said Hogarth. "Do me a favour. Call Crispin's and then track down Nancy Decorville's investigator. We need to test her alibi before we go to the next phase."
"The next phase?" said Palmer. "What's the next phase?"
"Shit or bust."
For a moment, Palmer wondered if Melford had been right about the DI after all. Maybe he was cracking up. Hogarth smiled thinly, picked up the telephone and dialled a number from a scrap of paper on his desk.
"Mr Goodwell, Hello. It's DI Hogarth here. Listen. I was wondering if we could meet up again today? So, you're local, are you? Well, isn't that, handy…" said Hogarth. Palmer heard a hint of the shark in the DI's voice. Somewhere nearby he smelt blood in the water. And with the pressure coming from the top, there would soon be a feeding frenzy. Palmer hoped Hogarth could win out before Melford scented blood of his own.

Chapter Fifteen

Palmer drove out to Crispin and Co by herself, rather than conduct the matter by phone. She believed it was always easier to elicit the truth face to face. The pressure of a face-to-face interview reduced the temptation to minimise or dress up the truth. It was a brave person who lied as they looked a seasoned CID detective in the eye.

Crispin's was situated above the old town square in Rochford. The small town on the edge of Southend which still looked a lot like a village. Rochford had old streets, cobbled paths, and even a tea room, but it wasn't a place Palmer had spent much time. Work dominated everything. Rochford was a 'one day' place and that day had never come. She parked on the little square and noted the sedate air, feeling a hint of resentment at her busy existence. She saw the sign for Crispin's above the big TV shop. She went to the side door entrance and climbed the steps.

"Good morning," said Nancy Decorville, with a hint of the ice queen about her. It was all in the eyes.
"Hello, Miss Decorville."
Palmer's heart sank. She hadn't wanted to deal with her again so soon.
"So, you're here to check up on me, are you? Perhaps you want to damage my reputation at work?"
"Not at all, miss," said Palmer. "It's a matter of procedure. I have to check your alibi. I'll have to check on the others too."

Nancy Decorville readjusted her face at the news. "Oh. But I don't think Mr Crispin can help with that. You should try the private investigator instead."

"You never know, though, do you?" said Palmer. "Is Mr Crispin in, at all?"

Nancy Decorville sighed. "Yes, he's in. Very well. Come through."

Palmer looked around as Decorville led her into the spacious office. It was far plusher than the exterior had promised, Evidently, property was still a big paying business. And the way Decorville worked it, it was probably the best business in the world. Decorville knocked on a glass door at the back of the office, then opened it onto a fancy private office.

"Mr Crispin, this woman is one of the police officers I mentioned. She wants to ask you about my whereabouts for Monday. I told her I dropped in here for five minutes just around lunch time."

"Some time between eleven-fifty and twelve-ten to be precise," said Palmer.

The man at the big desk had short-cropped silver hair which was very thin on top. His red-framed half-moon spectacles suggested a liking for flamboyance.

The man peered at Palmer from behind a large white laptop. He sat back.

"Now, that could prove difficult," said the man.

"See I told, you," said Decorville.

"But you used the office as part of your alibi, Miss Decorville. If it can't be proven that you were here, then you're back on shaky ground."

Decorville shook her head in disgust.

The man at the desk raised his finger. "Ah. Now, I said difficult, but not impossible," said the man. "Please sit down." He gestured for Palmer to take the seat in front of his glass-topped desk. Palmer took the seat.

"Nancy, if you don't mind," said Crispin. He nodded her towards the door. Decorville didn't look happy, but she acquiesced and closed the door behind her.

The man typed and stared at the screen for a moment before he turned the laptop towards Palmer. "Here… we… are," he said.

"I think this might be useful to you. It certainly gives me peace of mind."

Palmer studied the screen, unsure of what she was looking at. There were three images framed by one white box. The images looked a lot like CCTV footage. They seemed to depict an area in Crispin's outer office, with its pale wood floors and the edges of the desks she'd passed outside. Next there was an area with a bank of filing cabinets and cupboards. Finally, the third image, was of the door to the very office she was standing in.

"I do have a standard CCTV system here, but I like technology, Inspector. This is another layer of surveillance, and I'm the only one that knows about it."

"Sergeant, Mr Crispin. Detective Sergeant Palmer."

"Of course," said the man, without caring. "I had these installed myself. Hidden cameras. You could stare at the locations of these lenses and still not see them. I had it done on a whim, I suppose. But it does give me a sense of peace. It's like an insurance policy, I can check on the office any time I like, just using an app on my phone."

Palmer nodded. The man clearly didn't trust anyone. But then again, she wasn't too far behind him. "And with these, we can look at the day in question? And the time in question?"

"We can scroll back to the exact times you mention very easily, yes. Like this."

The man rolled a mouse across the smooth glass surface of his desk, dragging the play-point across a line at the bottom of the white box on screen. The images jerked as the man played with the timings.

"Ah. Here we are, I think." Crispin let go of the mouse and the images started to move. The first high-angle-view image showed Nancy Decorville still wearing her jacket as she entered the office. Palmer eyed the time and date reading as the images showed Decorville hurrying about the office. She appeared in each of the three images, before she eventually walked back to the main entrance and reappeared with a man. The man was middle-aged with dark iron-grey hair. He looked small and solemn. They sat down at one of the outside desks and started to talk.

"Now, I haven't the faintest who this man is, but this the time slot you were after. See. The time is shown down here." Crispin pointed a well-manicured fingernail to the time clock. 11:58am.

"And this is Monday?"

"Yes, it is," said Crispin. "So, you see, she was here, and I can prove it. Nancy is not your killer, detective. She's one of the crown jewels of our business."

Palmer looked at the man over his half-moon spectacles.

"You didn't sanction her hiring of a private investigator, Mr Crispin…?"

"Excuse me?"

"It seems that Nancy Decorville hired a private investigator to look at some of Nigel Grave's relatives. Miss Decorville suspected they were going to try and obtain Grave Farm for themselves, which would have prevented any plans Miss

Decorville and Crispin's had for Grave Farm. You didn't instruct her to do that?"

The faintest smile appeared on the man's face. He leaned his chin on his soft hands.

"One of the reasons Nancy is so good at this business is because she thinks like a self-employed person. She's a strategist and she always wants to win. I can imagine she wanted to remove any unfair advantage the other party had in this situation."

"But Miss Decorville shouldn't have had any part in it, should she? She's a property buyer. She's in a relationship with Neville Grave. That's a conflict of interest."

"Isn't it odd the situations we sometimes find ourselves in? But I'm certain everything is above board. There was no conspiracy, detective. Nancy is going to be a stellar success, I know it. Why? Because opportunity always seems to come her way."

The man smiled at her but sealed his lips. The implication was clear. Decorville's play for Grave Farm wasn't his responsibility. Only her successes were his interest. And if Nancy Decorville wanted to play her own games in order to win, who was Crispin to stand in her way?

"She's innocent," said the man, as he took back his laptop.

"Innocent of murder, maybe," said Palmer. "But I wonder about the rest of it."

"Innocent of murder is all that matters, isn't it?" said the man.

"For now, yes. Could you forward those videos to me, Mr Crispin?"

Palmer took out one of her police business cards and pressed it to the desk in front of him.

Crispin gave it a cursory glance.

"Yes, fine, fine. I hope you find the real villain, detective."

"Yes, sir. We will. We get them all in the end."
Palmer didn't mind if her words sounded pointed. Crispin was protecting his assets and nothing more. Palmer walked out into the outer office and Nancy Decorville stood up from her desk.
"Well?" said Decorville.
"Seems like you're in the clear," said Palmer. The woman smiled back. "But I wouldn't get too excited just yet. Detective Inspector Hogarth wants us to look at everyone more closely. Just in case there's anything we've missed."
"What?" said the woman.
"Sorry, Miss Decorville. I've got to go. I've got an appointment with some friends of yours."
Decorville narrowed her eyes.
"Trevor and Marjorie Goodwell. I'm meeting them at Grave Farm."
"Does Neville know about this?" she snapped.
"That's not my concern, Miss Decorville. See you soon."
Palmer walked down the steps back towards the town square. When she was halfway down she glanced back up. As expected, she caught sight of Nancy Decorville on the phone. Palmer smiled, shrugged, and carried on her way.

Chapter Sixteen

Hogarth and Palmer regrouped at the end of the driveway at Grave Farm house. They parked their Vauxhalls side by side, Palmer's looking the poor relation to Hogarth's Insignia by a large margin, while Hogarth's car in turn looked inferior to the Porsche estate. As Hogarth locked his car he glanced at the Porsche. It had been cleaned recently and looked good, but those bloody racks needed to come off. They were an eyesore.
"Who wastes that much money on a bloody Porsche and sticks ruddy great utility bars all over it?" said Hogarth.
"People with more money than sense."
"Good answer. And with no taste. They're greedy bastards, Palmer. I've smelt greed here all along. There's been an attempted carve-up ever since that man died. I think he was the only good man near this bloody place." Hogarth blinked at the black metal roof and cycle racks on the back of the Porsche. His eyes softened as he got lost in thought.
"Sir?" said Palmer, reading his eyes. "What is it?"
"Nothing much, Palmer. Just more questions popping up in my head. That's all I get lately. Questions – and I can't find the answers for toffee."
He looked at those racks one last time before he made his way along the long gravel drive.

"So, did you check Naughty Nancy's alibi?"
"Yes, guv. It looked a bit leaky at first, but her boss showed me some CCTV footage. It shows her at the Rochford office

at the time of the murder. She was with her with her private investigator too. She didn't do it. Shame, eh?"

"People like that one never get their hands dirty. She's a manipulator, Palmer. If she had Nigel Grave killed, she would have got someone else to do it for her…"

Palmer nodded. "But Neville didn't do it either."

"Which leaves us with a lot of nothing. Let's hope we get something here."

By the time they reached the big wooden front doors at the end of the driveway, the noise inside alone suggested they had something. Loud raised voices, male and female – an argument at the higher end of the spectrum.

"Crikey. They're going at it hammer and tongs in there. They'll probably never even hear the doorbell," said Hogarth. But Palmer saw the mischief on his face. He stepped away from the front door and instead walked around the side of the big old house. The voices grew louder and more distinctive the closer they went.

"I'll do whatever I bloody well please!"

"You can't! You mustn't do that. Dad's only been dead, what, two days, and you want…"

"Stop! Stop your whining! This was never your farm in the first place. It was ours."

The dynamic was clear. Old Susan and the son were arguing with gusto.

"Sounds like Neville knows about her wanting to change the will. The drunk old biddy probably only told him to wind him up," said Hogarth.

"You have no right to try and intimidate Susan like this, she's your mother for heaven's sake." The new voice was deep, condescending, and male. It was Trevor Goodwell. Hogarth grinned and rubbed his hands.

"Oh, that bugger just can't resist sticking his oar in, can he? Come on, Palmer. Let's gatecrash the party."

Hogarth walked past the kitchen window while the argument was still in full flow. The raised voices became stifled as they passed, and a second or two later as Hogarth knocked on the kitchen door, the voices stopped altogether.

When the door opened, it was Trevor Goodwell who stood in the doorway, with a hard smile stretched across his face.

"Inspector Hogarth, good to see you."

"Yes. You being here has saved me a journey, but it doesn't sound like everyone is happy about it."

Hogarth watched the man bristle but Goodwell kept his smile in place. He stepped back and the others looked his way. The old woman was still in place at the dining table, and the unmistakable scent of booze was strong on the air. It smelt so strong Hogarth wondered what would have happened if he'd lit a match.

"Neville," said Hogarth, with a nod of greeting. "Mrs Grave."

The woman's eyes were distant and glassy but like a typical hardcore drunk, he saw the woman was able to veer between spit-flying rage and smiling innocence at the drop of a hat.

"You went to see Nancy at work," said Neville.

"Did you? Jolly good" said Goodwell, with a smile.

"All part of the process," said Hogarth. "And it seems Miss Decorville's alibi stacks up," Hogarth's eyes roved the room, but there were no clear give away responses – no signs of irritation or panic.

"I told you, Inspector," said Neville. "She's not the woman these people have painted her to be."

"Oh, I wouldn't go that far, Mr Grave," said Hogarth. "But it still doesn't look like she killed your father.

"Not on her own, anyway" said Marjorie Goodwell.

"You should mind your own business" said Neville. "We know all about what you were up to. It's out of the bag now. You can't deny it anymore."

"What's there to deny, dear boy?" said Goodwell, with a laugh.

The son turned his eyes to Hogarth.

"I bet you don't know yet, do you, Inspector? If you want to find the motive for killing my father, then here it is in spades."

"Poppycock! You're off your head, Neville," said Trevor Goodwell. But Hogarth wasn't listening. His eyes were trained on the son.

"They've come to some sordid arrangement with my mother. *An arrangement, can you believe it?* My mother who can't even arrange to be sober for a half day, can suddenly arrange the whole future of the farm."

"Neville! You're speaking out of turn," said the old woman.

Marjorie Goodwell, who had been quiet, moved into the centre of the room.

"Your mother is right. There's no need to discuss this with people outside of the family. And certainly not with the police. It's our business and has nothing to do with what happened to your father."

"If you don't mind, madam" said Hogarth. "I'd like to listen to what young Mr Grave has to say."

Marjorie Goodwell gave Hogarth a scornful look then withdrew. Neville's face was full of barely contained emotion.

"They've begun to arrange a deal with Crump Agricultural Industries. Can you believe it? Admit it!" Neville turned and jabbed a finger at Goodwell. "Admit it!! He cried.

It wasn't the news Hogarth had been expecting. Maybe the son didn't know a thing about the changes to the will, after all.

"Admit it? Like it's a sordid secret? This is for the good of the future of this farm, it's not a sell off. They are investing, not buying it out."

"That's how it starts. I know about them as well as you do. Before you bloody well know it, Grave Farm will be nothing but a franchise skimming the profit off the top of our earnings. It'll be their farm. It'll be gone."

"That's backward thinking, Neville. And if you can't see the virtue of the deal, then at least your mother can."

Goodwell looked at Hogarth. "He's not right, Inspector," said Goodwell. "It's not a sell off. Crump wouldn't even use half the farm. They'd come in and use the dormant or failing areas at first. It'd bring life and capital back in."

"They will turn the farm into a factory. A bloody factory!" Neville was shaking, his face was red. "How could you do this? We're not done grieving and you've already persuaded this poor, drunk old woman to give up the farm my father worked so hard to keep."

"Don't insult your mother," said Marjorie.

"As if you care! You're only here to scavenge and steal what you can. I was trying to safeguard my father's heritage. You're a bloody thief, Trevor."

"Heritage, you say?" said Goodwell. "And what *heritage* do you think that is, exactly? Because I think you'll find your *heritage here* is a lot flimsier than you think."

The words hung in the air like a guillotine blade ready for the fall. Goodwell had presumed Neville was ignorant of his origins. Hogarth's eyes flicked to the son, and his mouth dropped open, ready to speak. But it was too late. Neville Grave roared and leapt across the kitchen, his arms flailing at

Goodwell. He seized the man and punched him full in the face. Goodwell stumbled back, but quickly recovered. He flung his arms out and knocked Neville back on the floor. Hogarth intervened. He pulled Neville Grave away and pushed him toward the table. "Calm down, Mr Grave, for your own good."

Hogarth turned to Trevor Goodwell. "You want to watch your mouth, Mr Goodwell. Comments like that don't do anyone any favours.

Goodwell wiped his lips checking for blood.

"I think you've just seen all the evidence you'll ever need of who the violent one is in this family. I suppose he must get it from the other lot."

Hogarth jabbed his finger at Goodwell.

"I told you, that's enough!" he snapped.

Goodwell stiffened and closed his mouth and rubbed a hand on the back of his neck. For a man of his age, he was in good nick. In better nick than Hogarth, he had to admit, who was between fifteen to twenty years his junior. Hogarth took a quick look at Goodwell's thickset torso. His tucked-in shirt showed little fat. And he had big, thick legs. And after the way he virtually threw Neville Grave across the room, Hogarth knew he had strength.

"I didn't kill my father, detective. No matter how much they try to discredit me, about this farm, about my work on it – or about my history, I was my father's son. This man is the robber, here."

"It's not robbery. It's an agreement, man. It's been arranged."

"But when?!" said the son. Hogarth kept quiet and looked at Palmer. It was a good question. Marjorie Goodwell stepped up once again. Right on cue.

"In recent days, of course. Your mother clearly is in no fit state to think about the future. And you know it can't be left like this. Grave Farm needs managing properly. Come on, Neville. Your recent business decisions hardly merit you as being the one left in charge."

"It was not your choice to make," he snapped.

"No," said Trevor. "But it was your mother's. Just reflect for a moment. You bought the instrument which led to your father's death. Think, about it, man. How could you be left in charge?"

Hogarth stared at Goodwell and shook his head. "Mrs Goodwell, let's be clear." said Hogarth. "Are you saying you arranged this deal since Mr Grave was murdered?"

The woman's eyes flicked to her husband then back to Hogarth.

"Of course."

Hogarth looked at Neville. For once, the young man looked defiant and confident at the same time. Hogarth nodded.

"What would you say if I could prove you had been dealing with Crump days, maybe even weeks before Mr Grave's death?" said Hogarth.

"I'd say you were mistaken," she said, but her voice trailed away quietly.

"He can prove it," said Neville. "Nancy knew you were both up to something. She had you put under surveillance. You were seen with Crump, Marjorie. *You were seen*. How long did you have to court them to arrange this? Now who's devious and lying?"

Marjorie Goodwell's face darkened and she looked away.

"Your girlfriend had us watched, did she? I think it's you who need to be careful, Neville. You think you've got a catch there, don't you, eh? But she's got you by the short and curlies. Soon as she realises she can't get her mitts on this place, you won't see her for dust. Mark my words."

"You were seen," said Neville. "You planned this before my father died and now he's gone you've stitched it up just the way you wanted it. Does that sound suspicious to you, DI Hogarth?" said Neville.

"Suspicious? There's no crime involved, is there, Inspector?" said Goodwell. "Just wisdom and good business sense. And you shouldn't worry about your future, either, Neville. I'm sure we'll find a place for you here, working on the farm."

"Scum!" said Neville.

"That's enough!" snapped Hogarth. "All of you – that's enough… Mr Goodwell, Mrs Goodwell, I think we need to talk."

Hogarth opened the stable door to the garden and held it open, waiting for the Goodwells to join him. The sound of the traffic from the country lane mingled with birdsong and the whisper of the breeze. Compared to the blazing row in the kitchen, the outdoor world sounded like a heavenly retreat. Shame Hogarth had to spoil it by taking the Goodwells with him.

It was cold and when they joined him and Palmer, he was glad to see the pinched, cold looks on their faces. Hogarth intended to put them through their paces.

"I'm going to ask you some questions – both of you."

"About the meeting with Crump, I suppose? That was just common sense. We had meetings with them to plan ahead. Who doesn't plan ahead?"

"But planning ahead for something that wasn't ever likely to happen? Can you explain that to me, Mrs Goodwell? Nigel Grave shouldn't have died like that. The farm was his and eventually his son would be the heir. So why would you plan for something which was, in all likelihood, never going to happen."

"But it has happened, hasn't it?" she said.

"Yes. It has. Because someone made it happen. So, it seems very fortunate that you had a plan ready for such an outcome."

"Of course, detective," said Goodwell.

"Did you know in advance about Mr Grave's announcement?"

"No. How could I?"

"So, you didn't find any of his torn-up notes?"

"No," said Goodwell, looking confused. "I didn't know they existed." Hogarth nodded. He led them along the track by the old back-garden allotment, leading them past the long blue corrugated barn. Dicken's white crime scene van had gone, and the tent was slowly being taken down. Only the blue and white police tape sealing off the open barn remained. But looking carefully, Hogarth could still see a faint spattering of gore left on the chipper machine. Eventually nature would see to those marks, and then all traces would be gone. The man. His legacy. And now his farm too.

Hogarth dismissed the torn notes. They were an aside. An old man's aide-memoire, signs of a note making habit. Hogarth's blazer pocket vibrated as he walked. He took out his phone and peered at the screen. Beside him, Palmer glanced at it too. He saw he'd missed a call and received a voicemail. The call was from Melford. Not good news. Hogarth's jaw tightened, and his temples rippled, and Palmer saw all of it. Hogarth took a deep breath and slid his phone away.

"We've looked at every person in connection with this family, and we've looked at them in depth," said Hogarth.

"We've looked at the family history, at Susan Grave's past. We've looked at Neville Grave in detail. And we've checked all the alibis given by family members for the time of Nigel Grave's death, and they stack up. Which should tell us that none of you committed the crime. That it had to be someone else."

"The migrants, maybe?"

Hogarth shook his head. He stopped walking when he reached a spot outside the open barn as the cold winter wind blew across the miles of flat fields, whipping at Marjorie Goodwell's grey-streaked hair, and making all their faces radiantly pink with cold.

"The current migrants Igor and Borev, had no relation to the past, if that's what you mean. We've looked at the stories circulating in the press from 1991, about Susan's allegations of being sexually assaulted by a migrant worker. Now I don't think there's any need for us to rake over that nasty past any more, do you? That incident caused a lot of damage to this family already. But let's just say I know the details…"

"Then you know Neville was fathered by one of them?" said Marjorie.

Hogarth nodded. "And in this particular situation, I don't believe it made a rat's arse worth of difference to anyone except those with an axe to grind against Neville and his father."

"And that's your objective point of view as a policeman, is it?" said Goodwell.

"It's more objective than anything I've heard at Grave Farm since I took this case on. The last two migrant workers who remained were here under Nigel Grave's care. Do you know why they stayed while everyone else had gone?"

"Because they needed the cash?" said Goodwell.

"No. Because they didn't have homes to go to. They were from Syria, Mr Goodwell. They'd fled their homeland. The old man knew it and decided to let them stay so they could hide from the authorities and try to build a new life here."

"Those men could have been bloody terrorists, the silly old fool."

"But Mr Grave had faith in them. Like he had faith in his son."

"Where are you going with all this officer? I don't need a lesson in how to be a pillock. You know we couldn't have done it."

"Yes. Your alibis all stack up. But now I'm seeing more than the alibis."

Goodwell stuck his hands on his hips. A faint sneer crossed his face. He glanced at his wife then turned to Hogarth.

"And in your world where watertight alibis don't mean a thing, what do you see, Inspector?"

"At the moment I'm seeing two sets of people who got worried that their window of opportunity to bag the farm was coming to an end. They were worried if they did nothing, they were going to lose it forever."

"Opportunity?"

"The land, Mr Goodwell. Farms are all well and good, but making food produce is hard work. And it's a cutthroat business. It's all over the news. Milk loses money. Supermarkets pay a pittance for vegetables. Livestock poses risks, gets TB, prices go up and down. And then there's the investment, and the costs. It's a bad racket. But one thing which doesn't cost is land you already own. And because the land is already here, it's just waiting to be turned into cash, isn't it?"

"Now, hold on a minute," said Goodwell. "We proposed to keep this as a farm. We said Crump would come in as partners, not buy the damn thing."

"That's what you say now. But when that old woman dies – and once she signs that will over to you, you'd be free to make up your mind all over again. All that dead land, Mr Goodwell. And all that money. It's prime real estate too. Someone smart like you could even play off Crump against Gillespie Homes. You could start a Dutch auction. You'd be free to do whatever the hell you liked to maximise the value of that land and screw the legacy that Nigel and his son cared about so much."

Trevor Goodwell's face turned stiff and serious.

"Why do you mention Susan's will?" Hogarth looked hard into the man's eyes and saw the lie.

"Do you need to ask, Mr Goodwell?" said Hogarth.

"The property isn't ours. Everything you've said just now is supposition, pure and simple."

"I can assure you it's not, Mr Goodwell. You've made all the running you think necessary to get the farm sewn up for you. So, come on. Tell me, Mr Goodwell. I'm keen to know… what prompted all this? What made you panic and kick-start your little takeover right now?"

"Takeover? What are you on about, man?" said Goodwell.

"You saw your window of opportunity and you got all your plans in place. Meeting Crump's top people takes time to arrange. That much is obvious. And you worked so hard to persuade Mr Grave to see your way of thinking. You've also worked very hard to discredit Neville Grave in all kinds of ways. It's a comprehensive business strategy and you are a businessman, aren't you, Mr Goodwell?"

"There's nothing wrong with business," said Marjorie. "Businesses make money. Neville doesn't get it. He would almost certainly cause this farm to fail."

Hogarth's eyes narrowed. "But what made you panic?"

"Nothing? We didn't panic about anything. That horrible thing happened to Nigel, and we were here…" said Trevor Goodwell.

Hogarth shook his head.

"Yes, you were, weren't you? The idea of the lunch announcement made you panic. It was a new uncontrollable factor. You didn't know what Mr Grave had decided because he always kept his cards so close to his chest. It was the habit of a lifetime. And you knew Neville had been on at him about the future…"

"On that little witch's behalf," said Marjorie. "If you think we'd sell the farm for profit, then why do you think she's here? You should be talking to Neville, not us."

"Neville doesn't have the motive. I've looked at it. I've searched high and low. To me, Neville Grave looks like the second victim in this tragedy."

"Then Neville's taken you in, Inspector."

"No one takes me in for long, Mr Goodwell. Then there was Venky, the vet. All these people had their own ideas about the farm and were trying to sell them to old Mr Grave for different reasons. Then came this big lunch with the grand announcement and you panicked. What if everything you had been working towards was done in vain. What if the old man had gone against you? It was unthinkable, wasn't it? You had to act. You had to win, Mr Goodwell. This land is gold, after all. Nancy Decorville knows it and so do you. And Neville would have squandered it, because you are a businessman and he is a wastrel. Am I right?"

"Of course, you're not right! How can you be right?! You can't fit us up – I have an alibi, Inspector. And no matter what fantasy world you live in, my alibi would certainly hold up in court. No matter how much you dislike me or how much you might be jealous of my hard-earned success, I worked for it. I deserve everything I have. That doesn't mean I killed Nigel, does it? Not even if you wanted it to. My alibi is real, and it will stick. Come on, Inspector. After all those forensics, have you even got any evidence telling you that I did it? Because, frankly, I don't think you have. If you did, you would have arrested me by now."

Hogarth smiled and nodded slowly.

"But you still think I did it, don't you?" said Trevor Goodwell.

"Maybe I don't, Mr Goodwell. Maybe I was just playing devil's advocate. I'm a police officer, after all. I do that kind of thing from time to time. And sometimes, when I'm having a bad day, I might even do it just to get a rise…"

Goodwell's face darkened.

"But I think it gave us all something to think about, don't you?"

"I think at the end of this case, you're going to offer me an apology, DI Hogarth."

Hogarth looked down at the man's neat tan shoes. They were brogues, not unlike his own. But they had a lustre to them which said they had probably cost five times what Hogarth had paid for his on the high street.

"Nice shoes, Mr Grave. Size nines, by any chance?"

"Are we done, Inspector?" said Goodwell.

"I think so, for now. And thanks for putting me in my place, Mr Goodwell."

Goodwell wrapped his arm around Marjorie's shoulders and led her away from the barn back towards the house.

Hogarth waited a minute before he turned to Palmer.
"What do you think?" said Hogarth.
"I think he's right, sir. At least about the alibi and the evidence."
"Yes, it is a bit of a problem that," said Hogarth, with a grimace. "But I'm working on it, Palmer. He outed himself in there. It's him. He's got it all. Motive. Means."
"Opportunity? He's got a cast iron alibi, guv…"
"One thing at a time. Now we need to focus all our efforts on the evidence. It must be there somewhere…"
Hogarth started walking away along the track, but Palmer stayed where she was. She looked at the dark empty barn for help. Palmer was beginning to believe the case – and DI Hogarth – were heading for serious trouble.

Chapter Seventeen

"DI Hogarth, I'd like a word with you please."
Hogarth had only just dropped his backside back into his chair in the CID room when Melford's lanky frame leaned around the door. Hogarth looked at the man and nodded. "Yes, sir." As Hogarth stood his eyes tracked towards Palmer, and he found a hint of sympathy in her eyes. He offered her the acknowledgement of a single raised eyebrow in response. With all these tellings-off, coming back to the police station was beginning to remind him of his school days, with Melford in the role of his vicious old headmaster. Hogarth hoped he'd seen the back of those days but as they trudged into Melford's office and he stood before the desk and the old-fashioned clock Hogarth felt a grim sense of déja vu. "Well? Any progress?" said Melford, as he arranged his long limbs behind the desk.

"There's little more to report than before." *So why don't you let me get on with the bloody job?*

"I think I have a good idea of who has done it, sir, but I need a bit more time to get the evidence together before we can make the arrest."

"Ah. And would I be correct in assuming your suspect would be Trevor Goodwell?"

Hogarth frowned. Not good.

"Not a friend of yours, is he, sir?"

"Of course not. But Goodwell called the station with allegations of police harassment. You know how the climate has changed in recent years. In the nineties the criminal justice act meant we could do what we damn well liked…"

"It was easier to do the job then, yes, sir." And easier to get all kinds of prosecutions, including the wrongful ones, thought Hogarth.

"But those days are over," said Melford, wistfully. "From the Lomax inquiry onwards, every other bloody conviction seems to have been called into question on account of weak evidence or bad policing…"

"Bad policing, sir?"

"Hold your horses, DI Hogarth. No one has accused you of anything…"

Hogarth nodded. But it was coming – whatever it was.

"The police are in the dock more than the bloody defendants. Which means?" said Melford.

"Which means someone made a complaint against me and the Super is panicking?"

"Enough of the attitude, Hogarth. It means the rules of our game have changed."

But the rules of Melford's game seemed to be changing by the hour. Hogarth held back a sneer and kept his face blank. Just like in the headmaster's office at school.

"Trevor Goodwell made the complaint," said Melford, telling him what he already knew.

"He did that bloody quickly. He must have someone's ear around here."

"You know how it goes," said Melford. "These days, if someone makes a complaint using the right keywords, it shoots to the top of the warning list. Harassment, Hogarth. Goodwell says you took him and his wife out by the murder scene to question them. *You questioned him by the bloody woodchipper, Hogarth.* If you were trying to induce their family to suffer a collective PTSD I'd say that was a pretty good way to start. What were you trying to do, encourage them to start a lawsuit against us?"

"Of everyone I've interviewed, it has to be those two, sir. It must be. They have the motive. They've manipulated the old woman to sign over the farm to them and write the son out of the will to their eventual gain, and with the amount she's boozing, it won't be too long before Mrs Grave carks it and follows her husband. They've done all that in just two days since the old man went into the mincer. I don't have them down as the kind who grieve too much. I took those two there by that barn because I wanted to see their reaction. I wanted them on the spot."

"You put them on the spot alright," said Melford. "But from what I hear you don't have a shred of evidence against them. You barracked them, and accused them of murder without having any real evidence to back it up. If it turns out you're wrong, I'd say you've just given them a cause of grievance. Enough to cause us all problems. When Trevor Goodwell made his complaint he mentioned solicitors, Hogarth. That's the last bloody thing we need."

"I didn't barrack them. I questioned them. And I didn't accuse the man of anything. I said I was playing devil's advocate."

"Devil's advocate? Bloody brilliant. You could use that line come the court case. *I was only playing devil's advocate, your honour.* How do you think that'll go down? Like a sack of the proverbial, and no mistake."

"With due respect, if I am not allowed any leeway to question suspects I don't rightly see how I can do my job at all."

"It's all about the right questions for the right people. Wouldn't you say, Hogarth?"

"Sir?"

"Goodwell complained that you haven't looked at those migrants thoroughly enough."

"Sir… respect, should one of our main suspects really be allowed to dictate the course of the investigation? I questioned those migrant workers, alright. It wasn't them. And Marris hasn't found anything to prove otherwise."
"But did you check their recent history?"
Hogarth's eyebrows dropped low over his eyes.
"*Recent history*?" said Hogarth. "How recent are we talking?"
"Exactly," said Melford. "Goodwell told me there was a massive row between the two migrant workers and old Nigel Grave shortly before Christmas. Now, any guesses as to where the argument might have taken place?"
Hogarth shook his head. He saw the question was another of Melford's rhetorical beating sticks. Offering a reply would only worsen the beating.
"In the barn where Grave was killed," said Melford. "And guess what… they argued about the woodchipper, no less. The whole row was about that bloody woodchipper, how it worked, how expensive it had been, how terrible it would be if they broke the damn thing. If the scale of that row was anything to go by, I'd say you should have looked at those foreign boys much more closely."
Hogarth's face darkened, but he kept his voice level.
"Goodwell reveals this now? But not to me? Not when he had the chance? This argument probably never even happened, sir."
"I believe it did. Goodwell reported it to us, but he wasn't the one who saw it. Peter Venky saw it happen."
"Venky the vet? Venky never mentioned it, either," said Hogarth, with annoyance
"The right questions at the right time, Inspector. It's called due diligence. Goodwell implied you're not checking your facts and that you're making wild accusations, giving him grounds to claim harassment, Hogarth. On the one hand he

implies incompetence, on the other he suggests you've got a grievance against him. *Harassment* was the word they used. And that's not good at all considering your recent activities."
Hogarth stiffened and swallowed before he replied. "Sir?"
"You were seen – *again* – outside the MP's house. Specifically, you were seen confronting a stranger in the street. The confrontation was abrupt and aggressive – and I'm told you were the aggressive one… is it true?"
Hogarth waited and narrowed his eyes.
"Sounds like a case of mistaken identity, to me, sir. In this town there are plenty of scallywags itching for a fight."
Melford's eyes stayed on Hogarth. They were unrelenting, like lorry headlights on full beam.
"So, it wasn't you stomping around near their family home last night? And it wasn't you threatening members of the public?"
Hogarth coughed into his fist and shook his head. "No, sir."
Melford shifted in his chair. Hogarth couldn't decide if it was DCI Melford's chair or his backside which creaked the most.
"No, sir," said Hogarth, his thoughts already elsewhere. So, someone *was* watching the property. A private security firm perhaps? Maybe James Hartigan was spending some of his hard-earned salary on protecting his wife after all. But protection may not have been what he had in mind. And what if the stalker had been the one watching the house? *What if the stalker called it in?*
"If I request CCTV footage for North Lane, Shoebury, what will it show me, DI Hogarth?"
"A lot of big posh houses. Apart from that I couldn't tell you, sir. I wasn't there." Hogarth's heart thudded along like a freight train. He felt his armpits begin to drip.
"Very well, Hogarth. I have no real cause to doubt you… the MP's people must be getting a bit paranoid. Understandable,

I suppose. And you did well to deliver on the Club Smart case. But now I'll need you to deliver again, and quickly, to prevent these allegations getting out of hand. That's two sets of people on your case, and no matter what I say to the top brass, they'll tell me that there's no smoke without fire. You playing fast and loose is not helping you at all. Please, play this one by the book for the rest of this case – and bring me that killer."

"Playing by the book, sir? Shame the criminals never want to play along."

"Very dry, Inspector. That's all, we're done here. You can go."

Hogarth loosened up. He'd won on his bluff, but he still couldn't be sure that the DCI believed him. Hogarth opened the door into the corridor and made to leave.

"Just a final thought," said Melford.

"Sir." Now Melford fancied himself as Jerry Bloody Springer.

"You have accused Trevor Goodwell of the crime, so you'd better be right. If you are, then these legal threats of his are nothing."

Hogarth waited for the next pearl of wisdom with bated breath.

"And whatever problem you've got with our local MP, DI Hogarth, *now* is the time to let it go. Is that understood?"

"Understood, sir."

"Good. I wouldn't want to see the word 'harassment' used as the epitaph on your policing career. I don't suppose you would, either."

Hogarth let Melford's final thought go unanswered. He closed the door and sighed. Hogarth hoped that now he'd be able to get on with the job, if there was enough time between bollockings from the DCI.

Hogarth hung his head as he walked through the open police office. The uniforms who'd watched him from their desks went about their business. Hogarth knew some of them smiled and nudged their companions at the sight of his downcast face. Some of the buggers loved it when he was having a bad day. But others, like PC Dawson, had a sense of the bigger picture.

"Problems, sir?" said Dawson, as he passed the big constable's desk.

"That obvious, is it?" said Hogarth.

"Melford," said Dawson.

"Saying a word against Long Melford is like committing hara-kiri round here, Dawson, so I'll keep schtum if you don't mind."

Dawson nodded. Hogarth saw he wasn't pushing.

"Let's put it this way, it's not just Melford. Hassle from the DCI is a symptom, not the cause."

Hogarth changed tone. He stretched out his spine and tried to shake off his hangdog air.

"The immigrant workers, Igor and Borev. Are they still here, Dawson?"

"No, sir. They've been transferred to IRC Harmondsworth this afternoon."

"Eh? That was bloody quick?"

"It's politics, sir. It turns out they're Syrian, not Eastern European, sir. So, the immigration boys were called over sharpish. Their nationality earmarks them as a terrorist risk, so they were fast-tracked to Harmondsworth."

"Terrorists? But I got the idea they were over here running from the terrorists."

"Shame, that. Harmondsworth will be their last port of call before deportation back to the war zone."

Hogarth nodded. "They call these detention sites Removal Centres now, don't they? Harmondsworth, hmmm. Sounds like I've got a long drive ahead of me."
"Why?"
"New evidence has come to light, Dawson. But before I go to Harmondsworth, I think I'd better have a chat with a certain vet."
Hogarth walked into the CID room, and found Palmer busily making notes for the files on her desk.
"Got a lot on, Palmer?" said Hogarth.
"When haven't we?" she said.
"Fair point. So then… fancy a day out of the office?"
Palmer closed the files and turned in her chair, curious.
"Sightseeing, Palmer. Sightseeing."
Hogarth could feel Palmer reading his eyes for news about the Melford meeting, reasons for the bitterness behind his humour.
"Sir?" she said. "How did it go?"
"If ever there was a cause to quit this profession, Palmer, it's being undermined by your superior officers and all the petty political bullshit which frightens them to death. There. I think that sums it up nicely. Now, are you ready?"
Palmer offered a lopsided smile and gathered her things. "I am now."
There was a handwritten sign on the door of his surgery recommending another vet for emergencies, with an apology to everybody else. Venky was ill, but Hogarth was undeterred. He knocked and rang the door until the tall man's shadow darkened the glass on the other side. When he opened the door to them, his eyes betrayed a great deal of pain and he walked slowly. Venky seemed much paler than the last time they'd seen him. Even so, the man made a good fist of smiling at them.

"Visitors," he said, as if pleased, which of course, he wasn't. "Do forgive me if I don't play the host very well today, I'm a little under the weather."

"Yes, Mr Venky. We're sorry to disturb you, so I'll make this as… quick as I can." Hogarth nearly used the word 'painless', but managed to avoid it at the last second.

They sat down in his cosy lounge. With Palmer present, the room seemed too small for the three of them.

"Mr Venky, it's come to light that there was a serious altercation between the two migrant workers and Nigel Grave last month."

"An altercation?" said the man. He shook his head, confused.

"So, I'm told," said Hogarth. "I'm told you saw it happen. It happened in and around the barn where Mr Grave was killed. Curiously enough the argument centred around the woodchipper machine. Does that ring any bells?"

Venky looked away, racking his memory. Slowly, he began to nod.

"Why, yes. There was a row. Igor and his chum can get quite lively, you know. They don't mean any harm, but they are still young men. The work on the farm dies off around Christmas time. The crops are done, and there isn't much in the way of livestock to manage at Grave Farm these days. I was there that day to run some health checks on the sheep. Those two men were mucking about around in the barn by the hay bales, chucking stuff around. There were plenty of logs to be chipped, and they were making a great bloody racket throwing them around. I think they threw a couple into the chipper for sport, like they were playing basketball. Neville warned them against it, but Neville's still a bit soft and those boys didn't take him seriously. Soon they were doing it again. When old Nigel cottoned on, I saw him march down that track like he was on a mission. He gave them what-for, I can tell you. Nigel was a quiet man, but when he lost it, he lost it alright."

"How do you recall the argument? Was it angry? Violent?"

"It wasn't an argument. It was a stern telling off."

Hogarth raised an eyebrow.

"The migrants didn't take offence or start gobbing back at him?"

"Not that I recall, no. They seemed quite meek and contrite as I recall. They took their medicine, and Nigel sent them back to the other field to do some digging."

"Let me get this absolutely crystal clear. There was no argument."

"Not unless there was something I didn't see. It could have had consequences later, I suppose."

Venky had a point. But Goodwell had said Venky was a witness…

"Considering this telling off, do you think it was likely that there would have been any consequences? I mean, was the old man out of order? Did he go over the top?"

"Not at all. That chipper machine was very expensive. He didn't need them breaking it. He told them off in strong terms, then he calmed down and sent them on their way."

"Did they seem upset, resentful, angry, anything like that…?"

"No. I've told you that already. Inspector, are you asking me if this ticking off – which was given more than one month ago – was grounds for these two men to *kill* Nigel?"

"I suppose I am, Mr Venky."

"Then I'll make it plain for you. Those two men would have to have been mentally unhinged to think of killing anyone for that. That telling off was no grounds for his murder, no grounds at all. It ended amicably."

Hogarth nodded.

"You've been very helpful, Mr Venky."

"Good. Now tell me, Inspector, where did you hear about this?"

"Trevor Goodwell passed the information to my superior earlier today."

"How odd. I remember laughing with Nigel, Neville, and Trevor about this over Christmas. That's the only time I ever mentioned it. I suppose Trevor must have got the wrong end of the stick. It was never an altercation. He's completely misunderstood the situation."

"Then I'd say Mr Goodwell seems to have grabbed the wrong end of this stick pretty forcefully," said Hogarth.

"Then he's just plain wrong."

Hogarth nodded and stood up.

"Is there anything we can get for you, Mr Venky. Fruit. Groceries… painkillers? I couldn't bring it back until tonight, mind."

"Painkillers, you say," said Venky, with a flicker of a smile. "You don't happen to have a stash of opiates, do you?"

"Not on me," replied Hogarth.

"Then I'll have to pass. Thanks all the same."

They let themselves out and Venky waved at them from his chair.

"Goodwell's a troublemaker," said Palmer.

"Have you ever watched that Blue Planet programme at all, Palmer?"

"Can't say that I have. I didn't have you down as a nature watcher, sir."

"Didn't you? Watching human nature is all we do. Goodwell strikes me as a squid. He's slimy. Totally unpalatable. Doesn't show many human characteristics. And the moment a predator starts to close in on him, he shoots a cloud of ink out of his backside to muddy the waters, while he jets off to safety."

"You think this stuff on the immigrants is his way of muddying the waters."

"Yes, I do. And I think it shows he's worried. He's worried we're getting close."

"And are we, sir?"

"Not yet, but we will. But first we need to clear the water. Next stop, Harmondsworth."

Hogarth got into his car and Palmer joined him.

"Harmondsworth?"

"The immigrant removal centre. The powers that be have decided to send Igor and Borev back home to whatever smoking crater they crawled out of. I'm sure the boys will be keen to thank me when they see me, aren't you?"

Chapter Eighteen

Harmondsworth IRC was a stone's throw from Heathrow Airport. The airplanes taxied above in vast wide circles as they waited for landing slots. The swooping metal underbellies of the passenger airlines were a constant sight as Hogarth manoeuvred around the IRC's visitor car park. Having never been a huge fan of air travel, Hogarth found the sight of the planes unnerving. How the hell did those metal monstrosities hang in the air like that, let alone take off? It was a miracle he preferred not to contemplate. Which made his infrequent holidays to the Costas a particular ordeal. Palmer watched Hogarth's flinty eyes turn skyward as he closed the car door. She misread the pensive look on his face.

"I'm sure they won't blame you, sir," said Palmer.

"Blame me?" said Hogarth, catching on. "The immigrants? Of course, they'll blame me. Who the hell else have they got to blame? But I didn't know they'd get fast-tracked like this. Those poor buggers will probably get shot as soon as they step off the plane. But at least the government immigration targets will be met, eh?"

They walked towards the entrance security checkpoint. The front of house area looked bland and unintimidating enough. The front of the building was a pale beige brick four-storey affair, much like a Quality Lodge motel – the kind you'd find tucked behind a petrol station on a semi-rural A-road. But the signage told a different story. There were lots of signs giving instructions with accompanying diagrams, as if pictures were necessary. But the biggest giveaway was the security checkpoint with its red and white barrier gate. The Quality Lodge motels hadn't installed those yet.

Hogarth's phone buzzed in his pocket as they walked towards the security guard window. It couldn't have been Melford. It was far too soon after his last rollicking. He took the phone out and glanced at the screen. The letter 'A' was on screen. Hogarth felt his eyes flare and his heart start pounding. He slid the phone away and hit call-reject in his pocket, hoping Palmer hadn't seen the screen. Even though the letter 'A' was innocuous enough, he also knew it would pose a mystery, and cops had an inquisitive mind. People like Palmer – and Hogarth too – couldn't help but try to solve any puzzles put before them. Hogarth reckoned he should have changed the name to 'Terry' or 'Dave A'. No one would have cared about that.

"Do you need to take the call, guv?"

"No," said Hogarth, all the while wishing he could. Ali had called off their… what? Their *romance?* He couldn't think of a suitable name for such a fleeting affair. It was an almost-thing. And yet she had called him again. What if she was in trouble? Hogarth winced at the thought and pushed it aside. It was too late to help now, he was miles away and busy. He'd be sure to call her as soon as he got the chance.

"Anyway," said Hogarth, changing the subject. "I won't have to worry about those two getting shot in Syria just yet."

"The situation is supposed to be getting better over there, or so they say," said Palmer.

"That's not what I mean," said Hogarth.

"Oh?"

"These Syrian boys have got to survive Harmondsworth, yet."

There was a glint of curiosity in Palmer's eye.

"You don't know, then?" said Hogarth. Evidently, Palmer didn't.

"There are suicides, Palmer. Who knows what these places are really like? We'll never know for sure. But I think we might just get a glimpse…"

A man in a peaked security cap looked up from his desk behind the glass window. He was an old duffer wearing a uniform with a corporate logo on it. MERTIE. Hogarth had never heard of them. Last time he'd been near the place, a different outfit was running it. G3P. Another bunch of corporate jokers fleecing it for all it was worth.

"Hello. We are Detective Inspector Joseph Hogarth and Detective Sergeant Sue Palmer, from Essex Police. We're here to see two of your recent inmates. Two Syrian gentleman."

"Righto. Names. Do you have their names?"

"Yes… I believe so…"

Hogarth looked at Palmer in hope. Palmer hurriedly fiddled with her phone and took half a minute to dredge up the names from her emails.

"Here they are. Khaled Al Maghout and Salim Saqqal…"

"Not much like Igor, then," said Hogarth.

"Pardon?" said the security man.

"Nothing," said Hogarth. "We need to see those two men urgently. It's in connection with a murder investigation."

The man wrote the names down on a pad, then picked up a phone. The look on his face suggested he was struggling with something.

"Did you phone ahead?" asked the man, carefully.

"Did you hear the words *'murder investigation'?*" said Hogarth. "We need to see those men now. If not, there will be repercussions, please ensure you pass that on to your bosses. Okay?"

The security guard nodded as his call was answered. The old boy stood up from his desk and turned away as he spoke down the line.
"Did you really need to be that harsh?" said Palmer.
"With these outfits, yes, every single time… incompetent bureaucracy comes as standard.
They waited for the guard to finish his call before sitting back in his seat.
He looked relieved.
"One of the senior managers, Mr Abberetz, will come and collect you shortly. He says he should be able to accommodate you, but any meetings must not be very long."
"Oh? Really now?" said Hogarth. "I can't wait to meet him. Can you, Palmer?"

After twenty minutes of waiting at the internal reception, watched by a big bald man in a black Mertie jumper, a set of double doors opened and a man in a steel-grey suit appeared. His hands were clasped together in front of him and he wore a paper-thin gameshow-host smile. His eyes were so small it was impossible to see how fake the smile really was. Hogarth guessed it was ninety-nine point five per cent. It had probably taken him twenty minutes to prepare.
"Mr Abberetz?" said Hogarth, standing up from a line of plastic seats.
"Yes. George Abberetz, People Services Director."
"People Services?"
"Yes. Serving people, in the centre and visitors too. Why? Is that a problem?" said Abberetz. His eyes opened a little wider.
"It shouldn't be, providing you can provide us a room with those two Syrian gentlemen."

"Murder, you say? Are these two a danger?" said Abberetz. "It would have been helpful to have known in advance."
"And you should have known in advance, Mr Abberetz. Your people picked them up from Southend, didn't they?"
The man grinned and nodded like a nodding dog, but he clearly didn't have a clue.
"Are you wearing lanyards?"
Hogarth flicked his tie out of the way and lifted his lanyard.
"In here they must be visible at all times."
"They're visible. Can we see the Syrians?"
"Yes, but you should know that the people in our care…"
"The inmates, you mean? Or do I say detainees?"
"We don't use either of those terms here. They are *people* to us. The same as you are."
"Of course. Just the same as us. Except you're holding them against their will before you ship them back to hell."
Abberetz fell silent but kept his smile in place. He kept his hands meshed together and walked them into a sterile corridor without windows.
"The people in our care are dependent on us providing positive structure and routine as part of their stay with us. Your visit could have been handled much more effectively if you'd called ahead…"
"Listen, Mr Abberetz. Your firm's business operation is not my concern here. I'm not a mystery shopper. You've kept us waiting twenty minutes already, so you could put all your skeletons back in the closet. Now stop asserting your non-existent authority over us and let me see those men before I think of raising a complaint."
Abberetz finally dropped his smile as fast as penny tossed into a well.

"Very well, Inspector. But these men really aren't too happy to see you. So, for your sake, we're going to put a security man in the interview room, to ensure your safety."

"For my safety? Or to listen in, Mr Abberetz?"

Abberetz didn't nod or smile. This time he said nothing until they reached a door on the first floor of a neighbouring building. This building smelt of disinfectant and unhappiness. The floors were shiny as if waxed. The walls were white, as if painted every week. Everything was functional and bland and safe. Just like any other modern prison Hogarth had ever been in.

Abberetz opened the door and led them into a room where two familiar faces sat in stony silence behind a big desk. It was much like a police interview room, but for the addition of a homely pot plant and some very faint classical music coming from the speakers. Without their hats and coats, Igor and the other man looked far more middle-eastern than Hogarth remembered. Their clothes had been changed entirely. Instead of winter wear, they wore plain unbranded sweatshirts. Both men had their arms crossed. And, as Abberetz had promised, neither man looked happy to see him.

"Are you well?" said Abberetz. The men ignored him. "Very good," said Abberetz. "Well then, I'll leave you gentlemen to it."

Abberetz nodded to all of them and made his exit.

Hogarth paused by the door, making his presence felt as he looked around the room. He took his time to feel the vibe from the migrants. They were in a sanitized prison doing its best to feel friendly - and every part of the friendliness felt like a great big lie.

"I'm sorry about all this," said Hogarth, gesturing to the room. He advanced to the table.

"This wasn't part of the plan. Just a few years back it wouldn't have been like this. You'd have been set up, given a home…" Seeing the look on their faces, Hogarth stopped apologising.

They men offered him nothing but a long brooding stare.

"Have they told you how long you'll be in here?" said Hogarth. He took a seat and Palmer sat down next to him. The one with no English hissed and sucked his teeth. The other man, Igor shrugged and sat back in his chair.

"They are creating a case for us," said Igor. "If we are lucky, our stay here could be indefinite. If we are lucky. Lucky! You know in this place they kill themselves just to be free."

Hogarth knew about the suicides. It wasn't everyone. It was a percentage, and that was bad enough. There was no response worth giving. He knew he could offer no comfort to anyone in the room.

"If I can add anything to your appeal, I certainly will."

"I think you've done enough already, don't you?" said Igor.

"You can blame me if you like, that's fine," said Hogarth. "But you should also blame the man who killed Nigel Grave. If old Nigel was still alive none of this would have happened. You know that as well as I do."

"Of course," said Igor. "The old man helped us. He protected us. He gave us work and money."

They were angry and defensive, and Hogarth couldn't blame them. But he needed to get past that as soon as possible. It was time to change tack. Time to stir the pot.

"Do you know Mr Venky? The vet?"

Igor shrugged. "Yes, of course. But not very well. He comes to the farm, treats the few animals. He talked to the old man. They were friends."

"Yes, I think they were," said Hogarth. "Before Christmas Mr Venky said you were told off by the old man for messing

around with the woodchipper machine. You were throwing logs around, chucking some of them into the machine."
The men looked at one another. It seemed the one with no English could understand more than he let on. The other man shook his head and frowned.
"Well? Did it happen or not?" said Hogarth.
"Yes, it happened."
"The son told you off."
"He's a young man," he said. "He can't tell us off very well."
"So, you didn't listen to him. Then the old man came out and saw you messing about with his new machine and gave you a reprimand. Then what? Did it make you angry? Did he offend you?"
"Stop, stop, stop…" said Igor. He shuffled in his seat and gave Hogarth a nervous smile. "You know we didn't kill him, already. The only reason we ran was because we imagined you would have us deported. And here we are. You see we were right to run."
Hogarth didn't deny it.
"You didn't kill him," said Hogarth. "But I need to know who did."
"The vet blames us?" he asked.
Hogarth sighed and shook his head.
"No. I think he believes you are innocent. But your row got discussed by the family. I had to come here and check it out. It's part of the process."
"That family! Come on, Mr Policeman. You know it has to be one of them. The Neville boy is weak but ambitious. His girlfriend is far, far worse. The old woman is spiteful and drunk. Then there are those other two fools…"
"Fools?" said Hogarth.
"Trevor and Marjorie. The snobs. They look at us but never say a word. They don't like foreigners."

The other man humphed and made a bitter face at the mention of their names.

"I'll agree, they're not exactly my cup of tea either," said Hogarth. "But neither one strikes me as a fool. Quite the reverse, I think they're as sharp as they come."

"They are vain fools. They show off their money, their car, his clothes, her dresses. And he is the most vain of all."

The foreign men looked at one another, spoke in their native tongue, and then laughed out loud.

"What are you laughing for?" said Hogarth.

"The first time we met the man we saw him with his bike. Dressed like an idiot. We saw him wearing his black Lycra and his sport sunglasses, helmet, and gloves. He was dressed like an athlete but looks no more than a fat old fool in women's clothing."

Hogarth's eyes narrowed. His mouth turned pinched.

"Trevor Goodwell?" he asked.

The men carried on laughing, sharing words in their own tongue.

"Yes, Trevor, the world champion of fat old fools," he added. "And then he always cleans that car. He cleans it so much I wonder if there is any car left under the wax."

Hogarth's eyes flicked to Palmer. He bit his cheek as he processed what he'd heard.

"Guv?" said Palmer.

"Gentlemen…" said Hogarth, sitting forward. "This is important. Have you seen him wearing that stuff often?"

"What?" said Igor.

"Trevor Goodwell's cycling outfit. Have you seen him wearing it often?"

Igor shrugged, "Many times, yes."

"Many? How many? More than five or ten?"

"Ten at least. He lives near the city. He comes to Essex to cycle near the coast."
"So, you must remember *what* he wears?"
"Yes. It has left a mark in my memory," said Igor, with a grim smile.
"And he wears gloves… what colour are they?"
"Black."
"The fingerless type or the ones with fingers? Can you remember?"
"He does everything with a flourish. I remember. They are not fingerless."
Hogarth nodded with enthusiasm.
"And what shoes does he wear for cycling?"
Igor shrugged. "I don't know. I never paid attention."
"Think, please think. This is an important question."
Igor spoke to his companion. The other man looked at Hogarth and pointed to his feet. His spoke with enthusiasm, but everything he said was in Syrian. Hogarth waited for the translation.
"Grey… my friend says he wore grey trainers. Not a famous brand. But he could be wrong about the colour, of course. The trainers could have been white and become dirty."
"But you say he was vain? Surely Goodwell would have cleaned his equipment if he is that vain?"
"Vain, but also, how you say? *Tight,* with his money. The only new part of his cycling clothes was that black cycling top. It said Sky on the front. But his bike was a much older road bike. The colour was bad. It was purple and the bars were thin. They don't make those types of bikes anymore."
"You know about cycling, do you?"
"Only because it's on TV. I know as much as anyone else."
"So, you think Trevor Goodwell's equipment was old. Well worn? Out of date?"

"Like the man, himself. Yes," said the Syrian, grinning. Hogarth decided one good last stir might be helpful. "Trevor Goodwell is the one who said I should interview you about the argument with Nigel Grave. The way he described it, he said it almost bordered on a fight."

"What?! What would he know?! The man wasn't there. If there is a killer in that house, it is him. The greed and vanity of those two stinks far beyond anything else at Grave Farm."

Hogarth stood up, a faint smile appearing on his face.

"Gentlemen, thank you for your time. It's been very, very enlightening."

"Good. And now you'll leave us to rot, yes?"

"No. I'll do what I can, I promise," said Hogarth.

Hogarth gave each man a nod. "You'll be hearing from me again."

"Make it before they send us back to Syria. Or before we hang ourselves like the others."

"Because of your help your deportation will be far less likely now," said Hogarth.

"Why?" said Igor.

"We'll need you here for the duration of the murder trial at the very least."

"What?" said Igor, with panic in his eyes.

"Don't panic. We'll need you *as witnesses*." Hogarth nodded a goodbye and left them in the cell. The security man who had been watching the interview leaned out of the door after them.

"Wait," he called. "You should wait for Mr Abberetz!"

"Tell him we're leaving," said Hogarth.

"The gloves, the trainers," said Palmer. "You think it really could be Trevor Goodwell?"

"I'd be overjoyed… I'd love it if we could nail the bastard for this one. He's too smug and smarmy. And it's beginning

to look like being thrifty could be the man's downfall. If we can find those old cycling gloves and trainers…"
"He must have got rid of them by now. Goodwell isn't stupid. You said so yourself."
"True. Trevor Goodwell is smart. But even getting rid of evidence is a clue in itself. And Goodwell hasn't got the secret weapon that we have."
"Secret weapon?"
"Ivan Marris, Palmer. Trevor Goodwell thinks he's got me in hot water, and side-tracked me with the Syrian boys. Hopefully that means we can catch him off guard…"
"What do you mean?"
"Trevor Goodwell lives in Upminster. That's about an hour's drive from here, maybe a little more. If we head over there now, who knows what we might find? Hopefully, the man is so tight he didn't throw anything at all."
The nervous, smiling face of Abberetz appeared through the porthole window of a security door dead ahead. Abberetz looked in a hurry. He opened the door and clasped his hands together.
Hogarth could barely look at the simpering little man.
"Everything went well, I take it?" said Abberetz.
"They're not the killers, if that's what you're worried about."
"Oh," said Abberetz. "That's good."
Hogarth walked on and Abberetz walked with him, using his lanyard to wave them through a set of electronic barrier doors.
"Were there any other problems?"
"No, Mr Abberetz. And there won't be…" They reached the reception and Hogarth turned around to face the man.
"Provided you keep those men well fed and happy."
"No problem at all. That's the Mertie way."

"Funny? I heard suicide and hunger strikes were the Mertie way. I need those two as witnesses. Keep them well and keep them happy."

Hogarth stuffed his lanyard into Abberetz' hand and walked out under a sky full of roaring planes hanging in the air like zeppelins. He turned to Palmer, and spoke as he started walking away.

"Call the station. Get Goodwell's home address. We'll go there and surprise him, see what we can find before the smarmy bugger can try hide anything."

"Guv? But where are you going now?"

Hogarth walked away with his phone in hand.

"I'll only be a minute, Palmer. I just need to check on something. Back in a sec."

Hogarth dialled Ali's number and put the phone to his ear. The phone rang on for a good long time before the call went to voicemail. He didn't leave a message. Instead he thumbed a quick text.

"Ali. You called me. R U ok? Please let me know."

He turned back towards the car park. When he reached Palmer, she was busy talking.

"Thanks, that's great." She hung up. "Okay. I've got the address."

Hogarth unlocked the car. "Then off we go." He looked up once more at the full skies, before dipping his head under the safety of his car roof. He couldn't wait to leave.

Chapter Nineteen

It took just over an hour to get to Upminster from Harmondsworth and the place surprised him. The only part of Upminster Hogarth knew at all was the A127 corridor as it cut its grey way though Essex in a hurry to reach the heart of London. But if Champion Lane was anything to go by the A127 view had failed to give a true impression of the place. Champion Lane was a road of well-set semi-detached houses, three and four bed places from the look of them, all doubled glazed and well cared for. It wasn't exactly a dream-home street. It wasn't even leafy. But it had the look of self-satisfied achievement about it. Which suited someone like Trevor Goodwell down to the ground, but if anything, Champion Lane made his pretensions seem even more ridiculous.

"Goodwell's house will be the one with the Porsche, then," said Hogarth, slowing to a crawl as he nosed his Vauxhall down the street.

"The Goodwells live at Number thirty-eight," said Palmer.

"Hmmmm." Hogarth didn't bother to look at the door numbers. He scanned the cars on the driveways. He saw the Nissan Qashqais, the BMW estates, the Mazdas.

"It doesn't strike me as a Porsche kind of road," said Hogarth.

"No. Goodwell and his wife do seem a little flashy. She has all the jewellery. He wears the Aquascutum shirts. Could be that it was all for show."

"It doesn't impress me," said Hogarth. "In fact, quite the opposite. And I get the feeling old Nigel would have felt the

same way… there!" said Hogarth. He dabbed the brake as he saw the back of the Porsche Cayenne overhanging the driveway. The bike rack was prominent past the hedge, but there was still no sign of the bike. Hogarth pulled over and parked at the side of the street, still a way off Goodwell's home.
"Okay, then," said Hogarth. He turned off the ignition and clapped his hands.
"How are you going to play this, guv?"
Hogarth showed Palmer his narrow, glinting eyes.
"There's only one way to play someone like Goodwell, wouldn't you say?"
Palmer looked uneasy but gave a nod.
"Sir, just remember what Melford might say if we push too hard."
"Melford? He's the last person I want to think of. I'm thinking about Nigel Grave, his son, and that drunken old biddy back at the farm. Come on. Let's see how this goes."
Palmer let Hogarth get out first, so she could take a moment to sigh alone in his car. Once finished, she got out and followed Hogarth as he marched across the street, dragging a hand through his unkempt hair.

The door-bell chimed, long, pompous and deep. It still resonated as Marjorie Goodwell opened the door. They saw her hands were clad in bright pink washing-up gloves. An upright vacuum cleaner stood in the hallway behind her. Her face moved from welcoming smile to cautiously blank, to full blown displeasure.
"Mrs Goodwell. I see the housemaid is ill."
"What?" said the woman, before she looked at her gloves. "We don't have a housemaid." She said, her cheeks blushing with confusion.

"I'm very glad you're here," said Hogarth. "And I'm glad your car is here too. What about Mr Goodwell? Is he in residence?"

"Who's asking?" came a voice from deep in the house. Hogarth watched the man's feet thud down the wooden staircase. Hogarth studied those feet and the old-fashioned diamond-patterned socks they came in. Size tens, maybe. But it was just as likely he wore size nines.

"It's the inspector," said Marjorie.

"Oh," said Goodwell, as he finally came into view. "Well, what's he doing here?"

"Mr Goodwell," said Hogarth, giving the man a grin. "Good to see you again. Thanks for putting that little word in for me at the station."

Goodwell stiffened, and anger flashed across his face.

"You're well out of your area, Inspector. Off your patch. This is exactly the kind of treatment I was talking about when I contacted your superiors. You're singling us out. The way you interrogated us beside that barn, the very place where Marjorie's own brother was butchered – it was unthinkable. It was a sick thing to do."

"Murder is sick, Mr Goodwell. I'll admit, I may have become a little desensitised to some aspects of the crime. Just a little. But what always gets me most is the depravity and the audacity of the murderer themselves. That, I'll never get over."

"Don't think I won't be recording every detail of this visit, Inspector."

"I'm counting on it, Mr Goodwell. And so will I."

There was a moment's silence between the men as they locked eyes. Palmer noticed the grappling and coughed to break the spell.

"May we come in, Mr Goodwell?" said Palmer.

"If you really must," said Marjorie, standing aside.
"Actually," said Hogarth. "I'm not sure that we need to ruin your clean carpets just yet, Mrs Goodwell," said Hogarth.
"Why not?" said Goodwell.
"I'm interested in your little hobby, Mr Goodwell. The one you don't mind showing off about."
"What?"
Hogarth stepped away from the door. His movement brought Goodwell down the rest of the staircase and out into the porch. Hogarth walked down the front path alongside the Porsche. He pointed at the bike racks on the back of the car.
"You're a cyclist, I see. And a keen one."
"Yes. What of it?"
"And what about the roof racks? What are they for?"
"Why? Because we like to travel. France and such. Very good cycling country, France. The roof rack carries all of our belongings, as well as the cycling gear."
"Good for you," said Hogarth. "It's good for a man to keep fit as he gets older."
Goodwell bristled. "I'll bet I'm a darn sight fitter than you are at any rate, no matter my age."
"That's a bet you'd easily win, Mr Goodwell, so I'll keep my money, if you don't mind. I admire people like you. The weekend warriors. The ones committed to the cause of fighting the middle-aged spread."
"I'm committed to living well whilst I'm alive, Inspector. That's all."
"*I'll bet*," said Hogarth.
"What's that supposed to mean?" said Goodwell, anger straining his voice.
"You've done well for yourself here, eh? Nice house. Paid off your mortgage too, I bet. Means you can get about and

use all your spare time travelling and enjoying the good life, am I right?"

"My affairs are no business of yours, are they?" said Goodwell.

"But I'm right though, aren't I, Mr Goodwell? You took early retirement because that city life isn't all it's cracked up to be once you get past forty-five odd, is it? I've seen people burn out long before then. I've seen people die because of it. And you didn't want that, did you?"

"Who the hell does? I'd earned enough money to call it a day, so I did. We paid off the mortgage and down sized, and here we are. We live very well. But I don't understand why you're here punishing us for it. I have you down as jealous, Inspector? Is that it? Well, there's no point in that. We all had the same life choices back at the start. You can't blame anyone else but yourself if you're unhappy with your lot."

"I'm not unhappy, Mr Goodwell. I'm just inquisitive," said Hogarth. "Nice street, eh?"

"It's nice enough," said Goodwell, frowning.

"Nice enough, but for someone of your standing, your status, if you will, would probably like something just that little bit better. Maybe a fully detached house with a big garden like a moat, all the way around the house. Tall privet hedges. Four bedrooms to host your friends for the night after a dinner party. You know what I mean?"

The man's face darkened. "What is this? You're insulting me now? Calling me a snob?"

"No, sir. You know I'd never dream of it. I was wondering, that's all, if maybe you might think you've settled for less than you deserve. I mean, your car certainly speaks of ambition and wealth… but this neighbourhood, well. It's nice enough, eh? Those were your words, not mine."

"My social status and economic standing is not on trial here."

"Quite right," said Hogarth.

"And neither am I."

"Definitely not," said Hogarth, supressing his smile.

Goodwell jabbed a finger at Hogarth. "I'll make a formal complaint about this. I'll speak to my solicitor as soon as you're gone. I could even call them now if you like."

"No, sir, that really won't be necessary. Call them in a little while, if you like. I haven't quite finished yet. Now, sir, can I take a look at your bike?"

"What?"

"You have a racing bike, don't you?"

"That's what they used to call them. But it's a road bike, Inspector. Now what the blazes do you want with my bike."

"Because you suggested that the migrant workers might have been the killers, I've been to visit them. I interviewed them earlier on, just like you wanted."

"Well? You should have done that the first-time round," said Goodwell. "Surely they must be suspects."

"Everyone is a suspect, Mr Goodwell. Can I see your bicycle? Those migrant workers mentioned it and I'd like to see it for myself."

"They mentioned it? How?"

"Put it this way. They said it showed another aspect to your multi-faceted personality, Mr Goodwell."

Goodwell gnashed his teeth as he turned away from the front door. A second later he returned with a handful of jangling keys. He stepped outside and opened the garage door, flipping it up into the ceiling space. Inside, the garage space was dim but perfectly neat, a place of tidy wall racks and empty space. In the back corner was the shiny black bullet-shaped capsule of the car's roof box. Against the side was the lilac coloured road bike Igor had described. The saddle was white, like it was making a statement. The old-fashioned question-mark handlebars were white. The rest of the bike was lilac with a streak of purple. By modern standards, Hogarth decided it was garish.

"Do you mind?" said Hogarth.

Goodwell's eyes were sharp and alert. He shook his head and they stepped inside the garage space together. Palmer followed, feeling almost as confused as Goodwell looked.

"Very colourful, Mr Goodwell, just like the boys said."

"Colourful?"

"Yes. Not quite as sleek and futuristic looking as the bikes the cyclists ride these days. This is more tubular shaped. A classic style, I suppose."

"That's because it is a classic, Inspector. It's twenty-five years old, and it's immaculate. I have it serviced each year and I do the basic repairs myself. I used this one at La Rochelle Triathlon in '05."

"Very nice. I see you must have adapted it too."

"Eh?" said Goodwell.

Hogarth pointed down at the pedals. "The pedals – don't the serious cyclists have shoes that clip into special pedals?"

"Some do. I don't go in for all that nowadays, but it doesn't mean I'm not a serious cyclist. I just prefer normal shoes."

"Normal shoes?" said Hogarth.

"Trainers. I don't compete much these days, so I wear trainers. I prefer them."

"What do you wear with this. One of those Lycra suits?"

"Everyone does. A helmet, shades… gloves, trainers…"

"And are they classics too? I mean, are your cycling clothes from the same vintage?"

"What? Twenty-five years old? Of course not, man. In fact, I just upgraded my shoes and gloves a few days back."

"Really now? How long ago, exactly?"

"Um. Well..." said Goodwell. "I'm not sure. A week. Maybe more, maybe less."

Hogarth's eyes pinned him to the spot. "Fine. But I'd be grateful if you would confirm that for me. I'll need you to be very precise on this."

"But why?" said the man. Hogarth scanned him for signs of panic. If there were any, they were very well disguised. Hogarth didn't answer his question.

"Your old cycling gear... did you happen to keep it? Because I know what I'm like. I hate to throw old stuff away. My old trainers are still kicking around at home somewhere and I don't think I've even worn them in two years."

"I threw out my old ones, Inspector. I'm not the sentimental type. I'm efficient. And as you can see, we like to keep the place clean."

"I can see that. Not sentimental and very efficient. Very good qualities for business, eh? But those qualities could prove quite contentious in a family setting."

"What? What are you saying now?"

"Nothing, sir. Just an observation. So, when exactly did you throw your trainers out?"

"The same time as I got my new ones, obviously."

"Obviously," said Hogarth. "Did you put your old ones out with the rubbish?"

"No. I'm not sure. I can't remember. I think I dumped them when I was on the move somewhere. A public waste bin, maybe. I'm not sure exactly."

"Where though?" said Hogarth. "Did you dump them in Southend?"

"I told you. I can't remember."

Hogarth nodded.

"And what about your gloves?"

"Eh?"
"Your cycling gloves. Are those new too."
"As a matter of fact, yes they are. Is it illegal for a cyclist to update his kit now and then?"
"No, Mr Goodwell. But let me get this straight. You updated your cycling kit in the last week, maybe less. And you *specifically* replaced your trainers and your gloves. Did you buy anything else to go with them? A new helmet? New top? Shorts, maybe?"
Goodwell's eyes narrowed to match Hogarth's.
"No. I only replaced what was needed."
"I see. And your trainers and your gloves happened to get tired at *exactly* the same time, and you dumped them at *exactly* the same time. Maybe at the same place?"
"I never said that. Did I ever say that?" said Goodwell.
"It's odd how they got so worn out at the same time."
"Not at all. People always tend to batch things when they replace them, don't they? When I need a new pair of trousers, sometimes I might buy a shirt as well. It's not remarkable in the least."
"But these were very, very tired items, were they not? They were almost falling apart. Particularly the gloves," said Hogarth.
"What? But you know nothing about my kit. Nothing at all."
Hogarth kept quiet.
"Where did you dump the gloves? The same place as the trainers?"
"I told you. I don't recall."
"I'd like you to try and remember."
"I said I don't recall. Look, this is ludicrous. Absolutely ludicrous…"
Hogarth stared at the man and scratched his cheek.

"Mr Goodwell, if it's alright with you, I'd like to have a look inside your car."
Hogarth felt like he was gambling again. He was out on a limb in a high stakes game. It wasn't that he thought Goodwell was innocent. Far from it. But he was playing a game where Goodwell might still come out a winner. If so, Hogarth knew he would become an extreme loser. His career was on the line again.
"My car? Why? Have you ever been inside a Porsche Cayenne before, Inspector? If you like I could take you out for a little spin," said Goodwell, with fake levity.
"I'll admit I'm curious," said Hogarth. Goodwell turned away to retrieve his car keys from the hallway. He watched husband and wife exchange a momentary glance and tried to read them. Was it fear he saw in Marjorie Goodwell's eyes? There was certainly none in her husbands and that bothered him. Hogarth glanced at Palmer. She was looking right at him, warning him of something. She looked unsettled. She doubted his approach and was worried for him – for his job. But he couldn't be swayed by her, not now. DS Palmer was good, but at times he could read her like a book. At other times she was a closed one, a mystery, but her unsettled look wasn't helping. Hogarth turned his head so he couldn't see her appeals. Goodwell returned waving the little black key fob with the Porsche badge on it.
"Let me show you, Inspector. It looks even better on the inside, believe me."
"I can't wait," said Hogarth.
Goodwell opened the doors and pulled them wide open, both front and back.
"As you can see, there's plenty of leg room and a luxurious interior."

Hogarth's eyes raked the floors, and the carpets. There was not a single trace of dirt in sight.

"And it's been very well looked after. You've must have had it cleaned. Recently?" said Hogarth.

"You already know we like to keep things shipshape, Inspector."

"Did you clean it yourself?"

"No. I had a mini-valet done. One of those Eastern European car washes you see around."

"Oh? Which one?"

"I don't remember."

"You don't remember," said Hogarth.

"Yes. There are so many of them around these days."

"And there I was thinking you had something against migrant workers. Good to see you supporting their businesses. Now let me guess. You had the car cleaned at some time in the last week?"

"How did you ever guess?" said Goodwell, folding his arms.

"I'm no genius," said Hogarth. "It fits the pattern, that's all.

"And what pattern is that exactly?" said Goodwell.

"I think you know what kind of pattern, Mr Goodwell. Don't you?"

There was a momentary silence. The man's face became inexpressive, refusing to be reveal any emotion.

"I haven't the faintest idea what you're talking about. I think my solicitor should bring this up with your chief superintendent.

Hogarth kept firm. "Palmer. Look in the footwells, will you?"

"Yes, guv. What am I looking for?"

"Anything at all," said Hogarth. "Tell me if you see anything at all."

"It was a very thorough clean," said Goodwell. "There's nothing for you to find here."
"There's always something, Mr Goodwell."
"Sorry, Inspector. This time there really isn't. You should stop wasting your time on me and look at those migrants, or at that gold-digging tart that Neville has got himself involved with, the poor fool."
"The trouble with that one, Mr Goodwell, is that Nancy Decorville has an alibi."
"As do I. You are you still ignoring alibis?"
"No, I never ignore alibis, Mr Goodwell," said Hogarth, blinking at him.
"You tell me, Mr Goodwell. Do you think it's plausible that Nancy Decorville picked up Nigel Grave and threw him into the woodchipper – a man who had worked in the outdoors all his life? Do you think she was strong enough?"
"Well," said Goodwell. "Nigel wasn't the force he was. He'd started to look weak…"
"But he was still a fighter, wasn't he? He refused your ideas to change the farm. He ignored Venky. He'd rejected his son's ideas too. He was stubborn. I'm sure he would have put up a fight if anyone tried to hurt him."
"So?"
"With due respect, I doubt Miss Decorville had the physical strength to subdue the man."
"Then maybe she had help."
"From who exactly?"
"From the migrants."
"And why would they help her?"
"Use your imagination, Inspector," said Goodwell. "I think it's plain for all to see what she is about. Marjorie saw through her from the very beginning."

Palmer stood up from the side of the car. She shook her head. "The footwell's been well cleaned and vacuumed sir. I can't see anything there at all."

"It was a very good valet for the price," said Goodwell, smiling. "But then again, you wouldn't have found anything in the first place, would you? Because I'm not guilty."

"They offer a very good valet, but you've forgotten where the car wash is…?"

"Yes. I picked the place at random."

"Of course, you did. Open the boot, Mr Goodwell."

Goodwell glared at Hogarth. "You're going to regret this visit, you do know that, don't you?"

"I've had far worse regrets, I can assure you. Now please, open the boot."

"Of course," said Goodwell. "I've got nothing to hide."

Goodwell popped the boot and lifted it high. The vast boot interior was spotless and immaculately clean.

"What were you hoping to find, Inspector? I told you. I disposed of all that junk last week… long before poor Nigel was killed."

Hogarth ignored him. He looked around the interior, his eyes tracing over the top of the wheel arches, the neat boot carpet, into every nook and cranny. The metal gleamed. The boot lining was spotless.

"Your valet seems to have been very thorough, Mr Goodwell. I hope you tipped them well."

Hogarth stood away from the boot and left it open. He walked past Goodwell back into the interior of the garage, heading once more for the lilac bike.

"The bike looks clean too… though I do wonder…"

Hogarth bent down and leaned his face low and close to the handles. The tops of the handles – coated in white binding –

were pristine. They had been well cleaned. Hogarth dropped to a lower crouch and studied the underside of the handles.
"Now what, Inspector?" said Goodwell.
The cleaning had been good, but the underside of the handlebar curls showed a grubbier colour. It was ingrained. And where the binding was wrapped over and over across the handlebars, the edges showed fine traces of black colouring.
"What is it, man?" said Goodwell.
"Not much, to be honest" said Hogarth. *He needed more.* Just a little something. More from despair than anything else, Hogarth walked back to the open car boot. Goodwell let out a faint titter of amusement. Without asking Hogarth reached in and peeled back the bottom layer of rubber-linin at the bottom of the boot.
"What are you doing, man. That's my car!"
Hogarth didn't listen. He looked at the bare metal of the boot cavity beneath. In the centre of the metal floor was a red-coloured metal spare wheel. Hogarth leaned close, inspecting the metal surface. There had been no cleaning under here, but whatever dirt had collected over time was minimal. Hogarth closed the compartment and pulled back the carpet. Just as he was about to give up, he saw something. On the very edges of the flimsy carpet were the merest fragments of black. The carpet was a tight weave grey and the loose black fibres didn't match. Hogarth suppressed his new faint hope. He needed to play it careful. He dropped the carpet lining down into place and followed its edge with his eye. *There.* He saw a few more black dots. Slowly, he leaned back out of the boot, raised his hand and closed the boot gently.
Goodwell studied Hogarth's face but Hogarth stayed blank.
"Well. What is it?"

"I don't know, Mr Goodwell. But I'll be delighted to let you know as soon as I do. Palmer?" said Hogarth.
"Guv?"
"Keep an eye on that bike and on the back of this car. Make sure no one touches them until Marris gets here."
"Marris?" said Palmer in surprise.
"Look here. Those are my belongings. You can't tell me what to touch and what not to touch."
"I really don't think you'd want to interfere with a murder investigation, would you, Mr Goodwell."
"Investigation? This isn't an investigation. This is harassment, pure and simple."
"You can plead harassment if you like. Yes, it might frighten the PC brigade, but it doesn't bother me in the least. And if forensics find anything here, you can pick any bloody word you like, or any solicitor you like, and the result will still be the same."
"The result? What do you mean."
No, thought Hogarth, it was too early yet to share his thinking.
"You'll know when I do," he said.
Hogarth walked to the roadside and took out his phone. He turned and watched Palmer guarding the bike, while ignoring the Goodwells altogether.
"Ivan, yes, yes, it's me. Listen. I'm going to need a favour. And this one is urgent. I have something for you on the Grave Farm case, but it's out of area, I'm afraid. It's in Upminster…"
"Upminster?" said Marris into his ear.
"Don't worry. I'm sure our hosts will make you a cup of tea when you arrive."
Hogarth gave him the rest of the address.

"Damn it. Okay, Hogarth. I'll be there in an hour. Just keep everyone away from that evidence," said Marris.
"Oh, with pleasure, Ivan," said Hogarth. Hogarth ended the call and gave the Goodwells a bright smile. The smile was much brighter than the truth. Hogarth had gambled on a hunch.

***

"You see those black dots?" said Hogarth, whispering. Ivan Marris moved his pen-torch along the boot lining, slowing every time he found a stray fibre.
"See? There."
Marris nodded. "Ahhhmmmmm. Yes. I see them," he said, keeping his voice low. Goodwell was still nearby, trying to eavesdrop. "These are really not the best circumstances for this kind of work. If you believe there is something here I think we should impound the car."
Hogarth frowned. "But do you believe there is something?"
"Hard to say," said Marris. "Without analysis those fibres could have come from anywhere. They could have even originated at the car factory."
"But they look like the black dots we saw in the barn," said Hogarth.
"But at the microscopic level – they could be entirely different. That's what counts. And then there's any traces of DNA. Those would be the clincher."
"You don't seem convinced," said Hogarth, rubbing his jaw.
"I'm not convinced about anything until it's been analysed. If you want me to do this, we should do it properly. I'd work as fast as I could."
Hogarth grimaced. "Come over here, Ivan."

The tall man walked past Goodwell, who looked pale and wary. He watched as Marris ducked under the garage door, and Hogarth led him directly to the bike.

"This is ludicrous!" said Goodwell.

"You keep away," said Hogarth. "This is police business. We need space."

"This is my home!"

"And you'll have it back shortly, Mr Goodwell, now back off."

Goodwell tutted and backed away, but only by a few feet. Ivan dropped into a crouching position beside Hogarth.

"What am I looking for here?"

"Black fibres again," said Hogarth. "The neoprene. The bike's been well cleaned, just like the car, but with a little less care. The murderer would likely think to clean stuff used directly after the kill… but the same care might not have been applied to the stuff used before, will it?"

Ivan Marris clicked his pen-torch into life and pointed it at the underside of the bike handles. The spotlight lingered on the grubby-patches and stayed still over the darkest spots by the rims of the wrapped white tape.

"Well?"

"Hmmmm," said Marris. He lowered his torch beam to the pedals and shone the light on the flecks of mud caught around the edges of the metal.

Hogarth watched the man's methodical movements with bated breath.

"I'll need access to the car and the bike away from here. I need more than a few samples to be sure of what I'm looking at."

"Fine. Let's do it."

"Are you sure?" said Marris.

Hogarth thought about the ton of shit he'd be under if he was wrong. But he had to make the call. He squinted at Palmer, then at Goodwell and then back to Marris.

"I'm sure. I'll call it in and have the vehicles impounded."

"I can arrange that, Inspector," said Marris. "Perhaps you'd better square it with those two over there."

Hogarth nodded to the Goodwells. The pensive couple were standing together by the edge of the garden path.

Hogarth walked towards them.

"Mr Goodwell. I'm afraid we're going to have to borrow your bike and your car for a short while."

"What? You can't do that!"

"In this instance, I assure you, we can."

The man's face quivered and his expression darkened.

"You'll lose your job over this."

"Life's a gamble, Mr Goodwell. But then I think you know that. You've had all your dice rolls already. Now it's my turn. We'll need your bike and your car for no more than a couple of days. Will you object, or will you let us take them?"

The Goodwells looked at one another.

"If you're as good at cleaning as you think you are, you won't have anything to worry about, will you?" said Hogarth.

"Take the car and the bike," said Goodwell, his eyes flashing with anger.

"That's the spirit," said Hogarth.

"But when this case has been solved – and we're proved innocent – I'm going to have you sacked, Inspector. Just so you know."

"I wouldn't doubt it for a second, Mr Goodwell."

Chapter Twenty

"Anything yet, Marris?" said Hogarth. Hogarth was sitting at his desk in the CID room he shared with Palmer. He leaned over his knees with the phone in his hand, brogues tapping on the floor, his eyes looking down at the grey office carpet. "Come on! I've only had the Porsche and bike here for the last hour. I need time."

"But we were there hours ago, Ivan."

"They weren't dropped off until two-thirty. I'm good but I can't work miracles, no matter how much you need them."

"It's that obvious, is it?"

"It is, yes. I'll do my best for you, Hogarth. But I'll need more time."

"Fine, Ivan. I'll leave you be for a while."

"Very good," said Marris and hung up.

Hogarth sighed and put the phone back in the cradle. He looked up to find Palmer's face a mirror of his own internal concerns. Her eyes looked large and worried. She looked almost mournful. And for a moment, he noticed that she was pretty. *Palmer. Pretty.* But she was a sad kind of pretty. It wasn't often he noticed Palmer's looks, but even so the worry on her face irked him. He decided to ignore it. He didn't need to be under any more pressure, but of course he asked anyway.

"What's the matter, Palmer? You look like you think my goose has been cooked already."

"No. Of course not. But I know the strain you must be under. And we're not exactly close to finding the culprit yet."

"We know who it is. And even if I am wrong about this, the murderer is someone we've already spoken to. They were around that bloody house on the day of the murder. It's smoke and mirrors, Palmer. That's all this killer has got to hide themselves with. Smoke and mirrors. We just need Marris to come through… but maybe there's something else. Something we haven't considered yet."

"Sir, I think you've looked at everything."

"No. There's always more."

"Like what?" said Palmer.

"Don't become a fatalist, Palmer. That's my job. This office needs an optimist. And Lord knows we haven't got much comedy without Simmons as the butt of my jokes."

"He'll be back soon," said Palmer with a smile. There was that look again. Pity, fretting, and those eyes. Hogarth shook his head and turned away.

"Yes. And no matter who wants me gone, I still intend to be here when Simmons gets back."

There was a knock at the office door. Hogarth stiffened and felt the buzz of his mobile in his jacket pocket. He knew who that would be. Unfortunately, he had also guessed who was at the door. Melford's moustachioed head leaned through the doorway and nodded at Hogarth. The single nod was a summons. If Hogarth had to endure one more meeting with DCI Melford, he was going to have to hurt someone.

"Yes, I'll be right with you, sir," said Hogarth.

Melford withdrew and Hogarth raised his eyebrows at Palmer.

"Told you I need an optimist on the team," said Hogarth.

"I'll do my best," said Palmer.

"Then that better be good enough," said Hogarth. Melford was out already long gone by the time Hogarth left the room, so he took his time. He took out his mobile, ignoring the uniforms who passed him by, and scanned the mobile screen, slowing to a halt in the half-light by the vending machines.

"Sorry for what I said, Joe. I was wrong. I mean it. I can't do without you. Will you forgive me?"

A smile flickered across Hogarth's grim face. Ali had dumped him, and now she wanted him back. It was barely more than a twice consummated affair. In the old days, he wouldn't have counted that as anything more than a roll in the hay, worth nothing more than an idle boast to the lads down the pub. But he was getting long in the tooth. The old Joe would have told her where to go then blanked her altogether. But, he knew he was caught with this one. There was no way he could abandon her, and he knew it

Of course. I'll be here as long as you want me.

He thumbed the text then pinged it on its way before he could change his mind. "You bloody sap," he chided himself. But the smile still crept around the corners of his lips looking for a way out. But Hogarth tamped it down. A smile would never do – not in Melford's office beneath his antique clock.

Hogarth knocked.
"Come in, Hogarth."
In he went. There he was, reclined and resplendent in his authority, ready to dish it out once again.

"You do recall our chat about the word *harassment*, don't you?"

"How could I forget, sir."

"And you didn't happen to forget about it, did you?"

"Sir, your words are indelibly imprinted on my mind."

"Cut the facetious bullshit, Hogarth. You know damn well why you're in here."

"The Goodwells have complained again, I take it."

"Right after what we discussed, you went straight round to their house and have given them even more grounds to claim that they've been victimised."

"But they are not being victimised, sir. They are suspects. Key suspects."

"How? The man has an alibi and you have no evidence."

"I think we may have found some evidence."

"You've taken his car and his bike off him…"

"To try and locate the evidence. Sir, if this man is the killer, I think he used his car to transport the clothes he wore during the murder. He would have had nowhere else to put them."

"But you didn't find the clothes."

"The gloves and trainers he wore have been disposed of. He told me so. And he's had the car valeted. He's cleaned the bike too."

"So, you've got nothing, then. Square one."

"Not quite. I saw some black fibres in the car, just like at the barn. It's him, sir. It's Trevor Goodwell. It stands to reason."

"Black fibres."

"Yes."

"You went back and insinuated the man was the killer and found some black fibres for your trouble."

"Most likely belonging to the gloves the killer wore when Nigel Grave was killed."

"And? What does Marris think?"

"He's running the tests now, sir."

"You'd better hope those tests come out in your favour, Hogarth."

"No matter whose buttons Goodwell is pushing, sir, I know this man is the killer."

"With an alibi and no evidence?"

Long Melford was turning into a stuck record.

"Sir, what's going on here?"

"What do you think is going on?"

Hogarth's eyes shimmered with a few thoughts, but he held his tongue. It was better to be quiet than sacked.

"Come on, speak your mind. I know you're sharper than most," said Melford.

"I think Goodwell knows someone in the force, someone on high. From the way he uses the Super's name like he's a get-out-of-jail-free card, I'd guess it's him."

Melford nodded. "Not that the Super would admit it. And I won't be the one pressuring him on that front, either," said Melford. "But no matter who this man knows, I can assure you no one has a get-out-of-jail-free card with me. I'm under pressure as well, remember. That's the job these days, as you know. But you're not helping matters. Every time you go out and undermine my orders, the pressure on me goes up another notch, and you make me look like a complete idiot before my superiors. I don't like these Goodwells any more than you do. They're troublemakers, and threatening the force with legal action won't endear them to anyone."

"So, where does that leave me, sir?"

Melford glanced up at his clock as if it would give him the answer. He looked at Hogarth and considered his response. "Well, DI Hogarth… after all the fuss you've caused, you'd bloody better go and prove this bastard did it, or we'll both be in deep trouble. Is that clear enough?"

"Crystal, sir."
"Be honest with me, Hogarth. Do I need to be worried?"
"No, sir."
"Good then," said Melford. "Now bloody well prove it."
A faint smile crept past the defences of Hogarth's stoic mouth. Melford noticed but didn't respond. It seemed Melford could play the bastard in a variety of ways and he did so with aplomb. But this variety – honest, understanding even, was one Hogarth had never seen before. Hogarth nodded. "Thank you, sir. I'll get right on it," he said. He shut the door and let out his grin. PC Orton passed by Hogarth and saw the strange spectre of a smile on the DI's lips. It was such a rare sight that Orton shook his head in confusion.

Hogarth leaned through the CID room door and watched Palmer snap up from her desk. "How did it go?" said Palmer.
"Let's call it a stay of execution. Or one last try. Whatever it was, Goodwell is connected in police circles and he's making it count against us."
"So, what can we do?"
"Do what we do best, Palmer. I think it's time we proved this scumbag is our killer, don't you?"
"Isn't that what we've been doing already?"
"Don't dampen my enthusiasm, Palmer. It's usually short-lived at the best of times."
"So, where to?" said Palmer, standing up.
"Where do you think, Palmer?"
"Grave Farm…" she said.
"Spot on," said Hogarth.
Palmer shook her head.
She was pleased to see the return of the gleam to Hogarth's eyes, but she couldn't help wonder at its source.

Chapter Twenty-one

Hogarth parked up by the farmhouse. He got out and dispensed with the customary front door greeting at the house, instead walking down the track along the side of the house towards the back garden. When Hogarth and Palmer reached the barn, he saw the blue and white police tape flapping in the breeze and the tyre ruts left by the crime scene vehicle. The police vans were gone. The case was in a make or break state. They needed to break the impasse or it would soon be taken out of their hands.

"What are we looking for?" said Palmer.

"Who knows? Something new. Something Dickens didn't see. We're still doing our ABCs, just like Dickens said. This is letter C. *Check everything.*"

With her hands on her hips, Palmer surveyed the barn. The evidence of murder had been cleared away, but she could still detect a faint smell of bodily decay. Or maybe it was her imagination.

"Where do we start?"

"The hay bales over there by the chipper. And behind the chipper too – who knows. We'll only know what we're looking for once we see it."

"Sounds like a long afternoon," said Palmer.

"*I want Goodwell.* He did this, Palmer. If he gets away scot-free it'll only be because of a lack of evidence. Then it'll be me in the dock instead of him."

Palmer glanced back at the house and saw a shadowy shape watching them from the kitchen window. It was hard to make out exactly who it was, but Palmer suspected that it was the old woman drinking at the dining table.

"Okay. Where shall I start?"

"By the chipper. I'll check the hay bales."

Palmer trudged towards her task. Hogarth walked briskly towards the pyramid of black shrink-wrapped hay bales, and the shadows at the back of the barn. He slid to the back and peered into the darkness behind the vast stack. Yes, the gap was big enough for a man to get inside. It was a dangerous hiding place, especially if the bales collapsed. But it would have been a great place to wait for the right moment to strike. Hogarth took out his phone, flicked to torch mode and shone the light deep behind the bales. He saw a layer of straw on the floor, deeper than everywhere else. He trailed the light across the back of the bales and saw a muddy smear on the lowest in the pile. The mud stain looked dry and it was faintly patterned. Hogarth nodded to himself. It looked like the print of a sports shoe, but with the original shoes disposed and lost, the shoe prints offered nothing which would stand up in court. Hogarth bent down and raked at the straw with his fingers. He teased the straw away and scanned the concrete. There were a few black dots on the floor, but he had more than enough of those. He needed something new. But if something new was to be found, its wasn't behind the hay bales.

Palmer decided to stop breathing through her nose. Imagined or not, the smell of death seemed thicker than ever. As a murder weapon, the woodchipper should by rights have been removed. But the size of the contraption must have prohibited it. The imported machine was nothing like its smaller, mobile counterparts, at least not in scale. Essex Police didn't have a facility for storing something like this.

But looking at the blade area, she saw that most of the blades had already been removed. The blades which had killed the man were gone. But the minute organic particles of body matter were still around. Palmer wasn't too bad with death, but the smell of it was always too much. She kicked at the straw around the floor by the machine and squinted at the dried mess of prints beneath. By now, all of them would have been photographed and catalogued. Double-checking like this made her feel useless. They were stuck, and she knew it. But it was no use telling the guv, because deep down she felt he knew it as well.

Palmer looked up from the floor and found him looking at her. The weary look in his eyes matched her thoughts. "Nothing new here, eh? I suppose we should try the shed… that's where the old man tore up his notes, after all…" said Hogarth.
Palmer offered him a nod and hoped it looked enthusiastic. They walked out beside the overgrown garden and picked a diagonal path towards the battered old shed.
"Look who's turned up," said Hogarth, nodding towards the house. Palmer glanced towards the kitchen window, but the old woman had barely moved. Then Palmer looked up and found Neville Grave was leaning on the windowsill. He looked impassive, unreadable. When her eyes met his, the young man lifted a hand in a half-attempt at a wave. Palmer nodded back. She saw Nancy Decorville appear at his side, nestling catlike against his shoulder. And if Neville Grave's eyes conveyed nothing at all, Decorville's couldn't have been more different. They sparkled and burned through the glass.

"That woman hates our guts," said Palmer.

"Because she thinks we're standing in the way of her ambitions," said Hogarth.
"Are we?" said Palmer, staring back.
"That depends on what we find. But a cutthroat like her, I couldn't care less what she thinks."

He saw the padlock was gone, tried the shed door handle and the door came ajar. Curious, thought Hogarth, but welcome too. From now on, he didn't fancy dealing with the Grave family any more than he had to. He opened the door and stepped into the damp-woody darkness. The shed was empty and cold except for the detritus Hogarth had seen on his last visit. As his eyes raked the bare wooden floor, he saw something had changed. It seemed as if a wind had blown through the ramshackle structure and blown the plastic plant pots, seed packets, and garden paraphernalia across the floor. Hogarth looked at the muddle and Palmer leaned into the doorway beside him. She could see the mess but saw no hope in it.
"You tried in here before, didn't you, sir?"
Hogarth's eyes picking at the mess on the floor. "What? Yes, I looked. It's where I found the shredded note from the farmer's planned announcement…"
"Then you probably already found all there was to find."
"Pretty much," said Hogarth, his voice trailing away.
Palmer saw the hope was fading from Hogarth's demeanour. He was turning dour and introspective again. Now it was Palmer's turn to panic. If Marris didn't come through, they had nothing at all.
"I'll look around the garden," she said. "Maybe bits of the other notes will be out here. There might be a bonfire site or something."

"The Graves would have mentioned if there was," said Hogarth.

"Not if the old man kept it a secret. It's worth a look."

"Sure. Okay. It's worth a look."

Hogarth nodded, and Palmer turned away. Hogarth closed the door when she'd gone. He could see the mess had been spread behind the door too and there was the little bin, emptied. Ransacked. Hogarth bent low and checked the shed floor with his eyes, prodding at the debris for new information.

"Who did this…?" he muttered. *"And what were you looking for…?"*

Hogarth dredged the floor with his fingers.

"Yow!" said Hogarth as he snagged his fingers on one of the floorboards. A splinter. He sucked on his finger and grunted in irritation. The way things were going, the splinter was all he was going to get out of this case. That and a badly sullied reputation. He wondered what Ali would think of him then. Everything seemed so fragile. But Melford had effectively given him another chance. He couldn't bear to squander it. Hogarth hurriedly delved into the corners of the shed and started rummaging again. For long moments he found nothing. And then his hand knocked against the edge of a very small slat which came loose and tilted up to expose a thin line of darkness beneath.

"DS Palmer?" said Marris.

The man's well-spoken voice betrayed his surprise as soon as he answered the call. Palmer paced around the edges of the garden, with her phone pressed to her ear. She was under watch from the windows of the house. But as she looked over her shoulder, Palmer only cared whether Hogarth could see what she was up to. But Hogarth was safely out of sight in the shed.

"So now DI Hogarth has got you to do his dirty work, has he?"

Palmer didn't answer that one. "I've taken the liberty of calling because we're under a bit of time pressure, Dr Marris."

"Well, aren't we all? I'm still the running tests, Palmer. I'm looking at fibres from the car boot, traces of dirt in the driver's-side footwell of the car and the black stains on the bike handles. If you want me to supply you with anything we could safely call evidence, I need the time to get this right."

"But are there any?"

"What?" said Marris.

"Clues?" said Palmer.

"Of course not. This is a binary matter. What we'll find is either evidence or the absence of evidence. There are no grey areas in forensics."

Palmer sighed. She should have expected Marris to give such an answer. "How long will it take?"

Marris tutted.

"Give me at least another hour. Maybe two. And next time, I'll call you, okay?"

"Thank you. DI Hogarth is under the cosh on this one."

"Then it's good to see he's so adept at passing it on. I'll call as soon as I can."

Marris hung up abruptly, and Palmer was all too glad to get her ear away from an upbraiding.

The possibilities had Hogarth blindly wedging his fat nail-bitten fingers into the slot beneath the floorboard. The loose floorboard was no more than a sliver of wood. A wooden patch to cover a gap where the floorboards barely joined by the wall. But he struggled with the thing, until he realised he didn't need to yank it at all but slide it back. Then the angle made it pop free. Hogarth looked down into the earthy blackness below the floorboards and guessed there was a good foot gap between the floor and the cold soil. A few desperate strands of grass had tried to break through the floorboards, but failed and yellowed to death. Hogarth wedged his hand down past them, scraping his wrist on the wood as he turned it left and right, searching for anything at all, fearing he'd be nibbled by vermin. The tips of his fingers grazed past something. The edge of a paper sheet? No. *Something.* His finger flicked past it again – something with a little spring in it. A bent blade of grass? The ear of a bloody rodent. Who knew? It was like one of those absurd segments on the old TV show *Game for a Laugh*, the guest trying hard to work out what disgusting thing they were touching, eating, or smelling. Hogarth didn't want to think about it. Then he found it again. This time he snagged it with his little finger and pulled the thing towards him. He lost it, found it again, then tugged. There. The top of a dirty old carrier bag came up out of the floorboard.

"Come on you bugger!" said Hogarth. He pulled the thing free and found the bag was brittle and old – bearing a Co-op logo he hadn't since his childhood. The bag had been knotted in the middle, leaving the bump of contents beneath. Carefully, he teased the knot open, thinking of the rebuke he'd get from Marris for handling it like this. But he didn't care. He needed a result, Melford had made that plain. The knot came open and inside he saw an untidy mismatched sheaf of different coloured papers, stained by age, folded, creased, and bent. It reminded him of the mess of receipts his dad used to toss to the accountant every year with his tax return.

Hogarth dropped to his backside and leaned against the rough shed wall. He peeled a note free from the bottom of the sheaf and scan-read the old spidery scrawl. Not much made sense. But some did.

"…Neville is still my son. I'll always love him no matter his biological parentage…"

Hogarth shifted gears and looked at another note.

"…the very worst kind of alcoholic there is. At this rate she'll be in an early grave and leave me a very lonely old man…"

"You wish," said Hogarth.

He raced through the notes, knowing he needed something else, but not knowing what it was.

"Come on, Nigel!" said Hogarth, shaking the papers, speaking to the dead.

Finally, he believed he had found something. But only perhaps. He found notepaper which looked familiar – it reminded Hogarth of the paper shreds he had found before. But this sheet was a hole piece. He couldn't help a burst of excitement as he started to read.

"I'm no longer sure if she is of sound mind. These days they say the drink diminishes the brain. Actually, the brain shrinks, so I hear. Which comes as a surprise to me. Half her time is spent on the bottle, a quarter of her time spent in a demented trance, the other quarter devoted to the kind of bitterness one associates with an angry old tramp. I know I used to love her once, but now I think I love the memory of her. These days she makes me worry for the future. Neville is the only future here, of course. The only question is which one of us will die first, me or her. I cannot believe I am able to write such a thing as this. It shows how bad things have become. But the alternatives need considering. I must speak to her, catch her in a moment when she's sensible – no more than three drinks in – to see if she'd be willing to pass it on to Neville."

Hogarth flipped the page. The writings turned once more into bland musings, then a shopping list for the hardware store, before they returned to matters of substance. There was a new paragraph.

"I'm coming to a new mind. The boy was right, but not in the way he thinks. Renewal at Grave Farm is about change. But change does not have to mean selling the land, or jumping into bed with a wolf in sheep's clothing. Perish the thought. And it doesn't mean wasting money on nonsensical ideas, whosoever they come from. The chipper will become a classic folly, but Neville must be given room to learn his way. But it is my responsibility to help him, and so, after all the deliberations, I have decided. The future of this farm lies in a new crop. It is a risk because any change is risky. But my forebears were not averse to taking risks, as history shows. So with trepidation but certainty of heart, we will tread a new path. We must aim for a modern cash crop. I've done the research, and I believe it should pay. Maybe for a generation, maybe for two, I don't know. But I think it will work…"

Hogarth scanned the sheet for the next words, but the sheet ended abruptly. He grabbed the sheaf of papers and flicked through for the page that followed.

"Don't do this to me now, Nigel…" he whispered. Frantically he picked the sheets apart and dumped the useless ones at his side. As he was in the middle of the chaos, the shed door opened, Palmer walked inside, and she froze as she saw her superior scrabbling about on the floor. Palmer looked down at him like he was a lunatic, but Hogarth didn't care. He carried on searching until he found another sheet of the same yellow hue.

"Yes!" he said.

"What is it?" said Palmer. But Hogarth held up a flat hand to shush her, and turned his eyes to the page.

"They say soya is the way to go. The weather is changing (global warming?) and the crop is hardier now, so you can grow it in England, and in this part of the country we have the warmest., driest climate available. It's a crop that pays well. It'll be hard work at the start, but it'll work, I'm sure of it. Soya will save my son's inheritance. And it will save Grave Farm too…"

Hogarth shook the sheet of paper like it was a hard-won trophy.

"You little beauty, Nigel…"

"Guv? What are you doing?" said Palmer. Hogarth near leapt to his feet.

"These are the old man's musings. Turns out the old man was very wise to keep his thoughts to himself – even after he was dead."

"Is that his speech?"

Hogarth shook his head.

"No. But someone's been in here. I think they were looking for that speech, which is worth considering… but these other notes are recent enough to mention the woodchipper, and they talk of a future for the farm. Which means they must be dated in the last six months. Maybe less. And it contains the very plan with which the old man intended to save his farm. He knew what to do, Palmer. He had all kinds of plans. Nigel Grave was the smartest of the lot of them."

"So, you've found his plan," said Palmer, without enthusiasm.

"Yes."

"But there's still no evidence, every alibi is sound. We don't have a killer."

"Tempting as it is to wave the white flag, if I do that, Goodwell and Melford will have me lynched. I won't give up until Marris tells me the scoundrel didn't do it. I have to believe the evidence is coming. Everything else about this is telling me Goodwell is the man. Marris. We need Marris. Maybe I should call him."

"No! No. I wouldn't bother with that," said Palmer. "I'm sure he'll come through when the time is right."

"Fair point," said Hogarth, checking Palmer's eyes, before he let it go. He waved the sheaf of papers at her.

"But I've got another idea."

"Please, not another search, guv?"

"Why not? This one paid off, didn't it?"

"I suppose."

"Then let's try one more. Not a search – a double-check."

"Double-check? Double-checking what?"

"Our man Goodwell likes his cycling. Racing bikes and all that."

"So?"

"You ever heard of a time trial, Palmer?"

Palmer shrugged. "It's a type of race, isn't it?"

"Yes. One cyclist goes at a time. It's about who is the fastest over a set distance. It's basically an all-out sprint, and the fastest person across the distance wins. I think we should do a time trial right now."

Hogarth grinned at Palmer. "Don't worry. I've not lost it quite yet. And I promise there won't be any Lycra involved. Come on. I'll show you what I mean."

Hogarth led the way back into the cold air, and Palmer followed. The look on Palmer's face said she wasn't sure whether her boss had lost it or not. But if the bookies took odds on it, Palmer guessed they would have been shortening.

Chapter Twenty-three

Hogarth doubled back and walked past the kitchen window, ensuring his walk was slow and unhurried. This time he wanted everyone at Grave Farm to be aware of his presence. He knocked on the stable door, and Palmer watched him try several versions of the same, mean smile before he settled on the one he liked best. When the stable door opened, it was Neville Grave who answered it, with Nancy Decorville appearing close behind at his shoulder.

"Mr Grave," said Hogarth.

"You've been busy, Inspector. Did you find anything out there?" Hogarth's eyes tracked past the pretty, feline face of Nancy Decorville to the others. The old woman looked as befuddled and vicious as the last time they'd met, and her perfume of Pernod still laced the air. Towards the back of the room, standing as stiff and pale as two mannequin dummies, were Trevor Goodwell and Marjorie. The woman scowled at him. Trevor Goodwell forced a look of imperious calm onto his face and folded his arms.

"You could say that," said Hogarth, finally answering the young man's question.

"Really? What could you have found out there after all this time? Poor old Nigel was murdered days ago, and you've done nothing so far. As far as I can see, the killer is still on the loose," said Goodwell.

"Loose?" said Hogarth. "Mr Goodwell. Your favourite suspects are the migrant workers. But they're hardly 'on the loose'. They're banged up in a deportation centre and they'll be there as and when we need them for this entire investigation. And the coming court case beyond."

Goodwell glanced towards his wife, but their eyes didn't seem to meet. "So then, Inspector, you think it's possible they did it?"

Hogarth fixed the man in his eyes. "The evidence suggests not."

"The evidence? What evidence? Come on. You've been floundering here, haven't you? Trying to pin the blame on any of us, or all of us, because the fact is you simply haven't got a clue who did it. Frankly, this whole thing has been a bloody shambles."

"That's certainly what you keep telling my superior officers, isn't it, Mr Goodwell?"

Neville and Nancy's attention turned towards Goodwell. He met their eyes unabashed.

"Well? What if I did complain? Your father is dead, and all this man can do is throw his weight around and threaten people. I complained because he interrogated me and Marjorie out in the cold – right beside the very place where dear old Nigel was killed. That shows a complete lack of sensitivity to anyone here."

"That was your first complaint, yes, Mr Goodwell. Your second was regarding the suspects. You wanted me to interrogate the migrant workers. You suggested I had ignored the fact that Igor and the other chap had been involved in a disagreement with Neville and Nigel Grave about misusing the woodchipper, just before Christmas. You gave me the impression that the incident left a very sour taste in those men's mouths. Indeed, that it could have even given them motive to want to kill Nigel Grave in an act of revenge."

"What?" said Neville. Nancy Decorville's red-painted lips flickered with a smile and she raised an eyebrow.

"He's exaggerating because he's got everything wrong," said Goodwell.

"What else did you want me to think, Mr Goodwell?" said Hogarth.

Goodwell pursed his lips and became silent.

"Makes you think, doesn't it?" said Decorville.

"You keep your bloody nose out of it. We all know your game here," said Trevor Goodwell.

"Don't speak to her like that!" said Neville.

"Neville, Neville, are you the only one who can't see what she's after," said Goodwell. "She's used her charms to get into your head. You're not thinking clearly, are you, dear boy? That's one of the problems we're here to solve."

The old woman at the dining table cackled then coughed. Hogarth wrinkled his nose as a spray of spittle flew through the room.

"Shut your vile bloody mouth, just for once, will you!" snapped Neville. Hogarth's eyes glinted in delight, as did Nancy Decorville's. "I'm thinking clearly enough, thank you, Trevor."

Goodwell shifted on his feet, face red, looking like he was about ready to explode. But Neville wasn't done.

"You put the blame onto Igor? Seriously? Because of that pathetic argument? Don't be so bloody absurd, Trevor! I didn't take it seriously. They were pissing around, that's all. There was nothing for them to do out there, so they were mucking about. I just didn't want them breaking the chipper…"

His words trailed away at mention of the instrument of his father's death.

As Neville diminished Goodwell seemed to gain a little succour. But Neville still wasn't done. This time he spoke to Hogarth.

"Dad told them to belt up and he gave them some work to do. That was it. It was hardly a life changing moment."

Goodwell jabbed a finger at Hogarth.

"But I only complained because that so-called detective hadn't even considered the option. The man's got his own agenda, and that has nothing to do with solving this case. He's been harassing Marjorie and me because we had the audacity to complain. Listen to him now. He's ranting about the complaint instead of the murder case. Where are your bloody priorities, man?" said Goodwell, fuming.

"I'm coming round to that, don't you worry, Mr Goodwell," said Hogarth.

He took his time. Palmer and Hogarth had been lingering on the threshold of the kitchen door, their backs still in the cold.

"May I?" he said to Neville, nodding towards the interior warmth.

"Of course," said Neville. Hogarth and Palmer stepped inside and shut the door behind them,

"You talk of agendas, Mr Goodwell. Let's be honest. There are more bloody agendas in this kitchen than there are at a town hall council meeting. It doesn't take too much imagination to see through it. Poor Mr Nigel Grave is dead. His assets, and the farm he has seen passed down from generation to generation is up for grabs. The farm is an asset, worth what? At least a couple of million in land alone. Then there is the business. It has a value too. I see that. And the farm has value to the family too because it's also part of their heritage. But then there's the question of legitimacy, isn't there? A point you raised and fixated on, Mr Goodwell. Just who should be the legitimate heir to this farm. That's a mess which has been stirred up by people in this room, probably for their own reasons, because in the eyes of the law the legitimate heir is the legal heir. The one mentioned in the will."

"Here you go again," said Goodwell. "Casting your aspersions…"

"Wrong, Mr Goodwell. This isn't harassment, Mr Goodwell. This is analysis. It'll all go into the court case, where everything I'm explaining now will be opened like a Pandora's box to the scrutiny of the media. Everything. Every skeleton in every closet will come out into the open, believe me. You can use that harassment buzzword all you like with my superiors, but it doesn't cut any ice with me – and it won't work a jot when this case reaches court."

"Aspersions. You've been the one casting aspersions, Trevor," said Nancy. "You've cast them on me, on those poor migrants… and you have knocked Neville time and again. You've made out he can't fill his father's shoes. That he's somehow unworthy because…"

"Because of my heritage," said Neville. His words were like a full stop. "I know it was you. You used my mother's fixation against me."

Eyes briefly turned to the old woman, but Susan Grave resolutely ignored them and instead picked up the Pernod bottle.

"I know about it," said Neville, nodding. "Whatever doubt there is about my heritage, I was my father's son. No matter what anyone says."

Hogarth nodded. "I believe you're right, Mr Grave," said Hogarth. "Heritage doesn't count for a thing, these days. Birthright means nothing. It is only the last will and testament that counts…"

"And the living will of the owner too, let's not forget" said Goodwell, smugly. "And as for a court case, Inspector. I've not seen any sign that you're anywhere near a court case. Not unless it's one for police negligence and worse."

Hogarth grinned. His time was coming. "Birthrights. Wills. Living wills. You've spent a long time thinking about this farm, haven't you, Mr Goodwell? And ever since you worked out there was a question over the birthright issue – ever since you saw that there was a chance to make a grab, you've pondered how you could get it. You saw a hint of opportunity, and so you studied it closely. You're retired. You had all the time in the world, after all. While Neville Grave spent his time working, trying to find a practical solution to the farm's woes in the here and now, you were busy concocting other ideas. Business arrangements, like the ones Miss Decorville exposed with her own investigation. You spoke to Crump Agro Industries with the future of this farm clearly in mind. It wasn't even your farm to discuss."

"Come on!" said Goodwell. "Someone has to take charge and use their brain. All Neville came up with was a bloody woodchipper! I was doing the decent thing before he sent the farm to ruin," said Goodwell.

"Oh, you always do the decent thing, Mr Goodwell. Don't you? You were the one with the business brain. You were the smart one. You were the one who knew how to turn this farm into multi-millions, and you sincerely believed Neville Goodwell would squander the opportunity and lose the whole farm. You believed in your abilities and denigrated your nephew's. Which gave you two reasons to hatch the plan you came up with. One, by obtaining control of the family farm you would be serving the old man's memory. You would be honouring him by ensuring the farm thrived for future generations, just as he wanted. But that story was a lie only you believed, because it justified your actions. Because you were prepared to go into partnership with a firm which has a history of asset stripping and taking farms from farmers hands. You weren't so stupid as to think that wouldn't happen here. But you didn't care. In the end all you wanted was the money. On that count alone, you stand guilty of every insult and accusation you have tossed at Miss Decorville."

"Lies! Terrible, horrible, lies!" said Goodwell, shaking. "You can't prove them, and I'll make sure you pay for them."

"You can try, Mr Goodwell. You can certainly try. But I'm really not worried."

"Well, you should be," said Goodwell.

"Your influence with the police is about to wane dramatically, Mr Goodwell."

"Why?"

"Because everything we've said so far underlines one thing not yet said."

"Which is?"

"Nigel Grave would have never given you this farm if he had lived. Grave Farm was his. There was a tradition of passing this farm down the family line, from father to son and grandson, and so on."

"But Neville is not Nigel Grave's son," said Goodwell.

"You bastard," said Neville, quietly.

"But we've already heard how Neville loved his father," said Hogarth.

"He would say that now, wouldn't he?!" said Goodwell.

"And now we have written proof of his father's intentions for the farm."

"What?" said Neville.

Goodwell blinked and shook his head.

"Someone – one of you, I believe – went into that shed very recently – looking for Nigel's missing notes. The ones which revealed what his announcement was to be in advance. I don't think they found what they were looking for. I think they knew about Nigel Grave's announcement, because they found some of his notes after they threw the poor man's body into the woodchipper. The killer was in a hurry. He didn't take all of the notes from the man's pockets or we wouldn't know about them. And so those notes are probably gone forever. But the killer panicked thinking there were other notes hidden elsewhere. They didn't find them, but they tried, alright."

Neville frowned. "But to open the shed they'd need the key and the key is…" Neville went to the cabinet where the key was kept and opened the door. His fingers traced over the empty hook. "It's not there."

"No. I think someone borrowed it. Who might that have been?" Hogarth's eyes traced Goodwell's face.

"Nigel Grave liked to hide his thoughts until he was sure of himself. With all your separate plans and agendas, I can well see why. But the man wrote down in these notes that he wanted his son to inherit the farm. That is no longer beyond doubt."

"What does that matter now? He's dead," said Goodwell

"Yes, Mr Goodwell. You said the words already. It's the living will of Mrs Grave that matters now. Because her husband is dead. Because the killer feared that Mr Grave's announcement would ruin all his plans, so the announcement had to be stopped. And seeing as we all know Mrs Grave's feelings towards her son, I think it's clear that she was open to consider offers from different parties about the future of this farm which excluded him. And it's got to be obvious to everyone here why Mrs Grave is open to manipulation."

"How dare you," said Goodwell. "Have you no respect?"

"Yes. And with all *due* respect, Mrs Grave has been at least three sheets to the wind every time I've been here. According to what I've seen, heard, and read, she's spent most of the last thirty years the same way. And she's been in and out of rehab for alcohol abuse."

The old woman shook her head and looked down. "I believe Mrs Grave's drink problem is probably rooted in an old and damaging lie, but that's not my business. My business is catching the killer. Do you see where this is going, Mr Goodwell?"

Nancy Decorville gave an emphatic nod and stepped into the middle of the room. "You did it, didn't you? You killed Nigel, so you could persuade Mrs Grave to hand over the farm into your hands."

"Rubbish. Pure evil rubbish," said Goodwell. His face was red, his eyes bright. But this time his face rippled with emotion. Hogarth saw nerves alternating with defiant rage. "You all of people, how dare you?! You harlot! Don't you ever accuse me of…"

"It doesn't matter what anyone says, Mr Goodwell," said Hogarth "You know that."

Goodwell stopped his raging and gathered himself.

"That's right. It doesn't matter what anyone says…" he said. "All that matters is that I didn't do it. I couldn't have done it. I went to the shop when poor Nigel was killed."

"Yes, you did. And it's very a strong alibi, sir. I tested it. The shopkeeper remembers you. You argued with him about the price of butter."

Goodwell blinked at Hogarth and maintained a brittle smile. "Good. There you are then."

"It's a good alibi. But when I remembered your keenness for cycling, I realised you might have seen creating an alibi as something of a sporting challenge. You had a near impossible mission, but you were up for it. Creating an alibi for the short timeframe of the kill would have made you safe as houses. But, I decided to see if I could follow your route and beat the time slot – to make it back to the house, butter argument and all, and still have time to kill."

Hogarth let the implication sink in.

"The butter argument was a stunt, Mr Goodwell. It was designed to show you were calm. Unhurried. To ensure you were remembered, you even argued about the price of butter. It was clever, I'll admit that. But if I was a sportsman like you, I could have done it. There was just enough time to buy the butter from Pradesh stores, to come back here and hurl that poor old man, that frail man, into the woodchipper, then to get rid of your bloodied clothes and come back into the house here as if nothing had happened. That takes a very cold, calculating brain. That takes the commitment of a man who will stop at nothing until he wins."

"Preposterous. And impossible," said Goodwell. "I could never have had the time to do that."

"Yes, you had enough time. Just enough. And then shortly after that, you disposed of your old cycling gloves – the gloves which you used to protect your hands and prevent leaving DNA and fingerprints. And you disposed of the trainers which you wore when you went into that barn and killed him."

"Lies. Fabrication. I swear I will…"

"Yes, yes. You'll have my job. I've heard it all before now and it's getting boring. The neoprene fibres of your deteriorating neoprene gloves were all over the barn. And they were still in your car. The ones in the barn and in the car, contained your sweat, your DNA. And you used to wear a pair of Fiafora Speed Lite trainers didn't you?" said Hogarth.

He saw the stunned look appear on Goodwell's face.

"Yes, Mr Goodwell. The news is, Mr Goodwell that if you hadn't have been such a bloody skinflint, you wouldn't have kept those running shoes going for so long. That made them much more identifiable. The forensics people said they are rare these days. They've not been in production for six years."

"I don't understand…" said Goodwell. Everyone in the kitchen watched the man as his voice weakened and his eyes turned glassy.

"Forensics are better these days than many give them credit for. The cheap mini-valet of your Porsche looked good enough to the naked eye. For a while there, I thought we were stuffed. I knew it was you, but I couldn't prove it. I thought you'd gotten away with it. But my colleagues in forensics located almost invisible dirt prints from your old Fiaforas – in the footwell and in the boot. There were microbes and particles of mud in those prints which match the material in the barn. And the prints match the areas where the struggle took place. It was you, Mr Goodwell. You had been making your plans for a long while, hoping the old man would die so you could talk Mrs Grave here into giving the farm away."

"No, no, no," said Goodwell.

"Yes. But when you heard about the coming announcement, you were terrified that you were about to lose your chance. Maybe the old man had decided to hand the farm over to Neville before he died. Maybe he'd had another idea which would have seen your hopes go up in smoke. Either way, you couldn't risk it or your long-held plans would have never come to fruition. You had to win. You had to get this farm. Even if it meant killing your brother-in-law to make it happen. You don't have to listen to accusations anymore, because we're well past that now. Your alibi has been broken, and the evidence says it was you. You went to the barn and you confronted him. I think you'd already made up your mind to kill Nigel, but you wanted to hear it from him. You needed to know, didn't you?"

"No."

"You confronted him, and he told you. And after the confrontation started, you were never going to get your way. By then you had to kill him. But you could have chosen a better way, a nice way to do it, Mr Goodwell. A quick knife wound. A simple farm accident. They would have been feasible."

"Horrible lies…" said Goodwell.

"But you were furious, weren't you? The old man wouldn't see sense, so you lost it. You became cruel, and vengeful. And that was why you decided to use the woodchipper. It was symbolic for you. You were punishing the man with his own mistakes…"

"How can you invent such hideous lies?" said Goodwell.

"Lies?" said Hogarth. "Nigel Grave's blood was found in the back of your car, from when you dumped those gloves and trainers out of the way just moments after his death."

"No!"

"Mr Goodwell, it's time for *you* to stop the lying. You're as guilty as sin."

Goodwell looked around the kitchen. Nancy Decorville's face was marked by a sneer. Neville's was a mask of wide-eyed shock. The old woman looked up from the table, her voice croaking and weak.

"I was afraid to ask…" she said.

Hogarth looked at her. "I saw you, Trevor," she said. "But I was afraid to ask why. I thought I'd imagined it. I saw you a moment before you came back with the butter, but you were coming the wrong way," said the old woman, in a croaky, lisping voice. The old woman looked at Hogarth. "You know why I was afraid? I was afraid if I asked why, that I'd be next."

Goodwell turned away and wrenched the door open into the hallway.

"Palmer! Guard the back door!" called Hogarth, before he broke into a run. He ran into the hallway to find Goodwell snatching at the latch of the great front doors. In his hurry his hand slipped and Hogarth caught up with him. Hogarth slapped a hand on his shoulder, and spun him around. Goodwell was wild eyed. He threw a punch, his knuckles lashing across Hogarth's jaw. Hogarth grunted in pain and fell back to the floor, but scrambled back up to his feet as fast as he could. Goodwell wrenched the doors, and flinging them open stepped out into the cold grey light. But as soon as he stepped outside Goodwell stopped. Two uniformed police officers in their hats and stab vests were walking purposefully towards him. They were close. And further away at the front gate, a second police car swung through the gate between the two vast brick pillars. Hogarth leaned forward and grabbed the man again, this time he held him hard. He yanked him close and stared into his eyes.

"You used that harassment word a bit too much for my liking, Mr Goodwell. Now I've got a few words for you. Premeditated murder. And not only that, but assault on a police officer. And don't think I won't bother with the assault charge, old bean, because I most certainly bloody will. Just so you know, that's fifteen to life for murder, and twenty-six weeks for my jaw. Trevor Goodwell, I am arresting you for the murder of Nigel Grave. You do not have to say anything. But, it may harm your defence if…" Hogarth grinned as he gave the man his rights, and looked deep into his eyes.

"One more thing…" said Hogarth, as he pushed the man into PC Jordan's grasp. "Did you know?"

Goodwell looked back, his face blank with shock.

"I don't think you did, did you?"

"What?" said Goodwell.

"Nigel Grave was going to die anyway…" said Hogarth, as he pushed the man into PC Jordan's grasp.

"What?"

"He was becoming frail. You said it yourself. Think about it, man."

"What are you saying?"

"Nigel Grave had cancer, Mr Goodwell. Greed made you hurry. You killed a man who would have been dead soon anyway. I've seen the evidence. Something else to ponder, eh, Trevor? You'll have a lot of time for pondering now." Hogarth saw the man's arrogance was gone. His defiance was gone. All Hogarth saw was an empty husk whose life was all but over. Justice was hard but fair. And it had finally been served. With a sigh, Hogarth walked back into the house, rubbed his jaw, and nodded at Marjorie Goodwell. The woman was pale and still, hands clasped, head turned towards the floor.

"The very least you are, is an accomplice. Do the honours, will you, Palmer." DS Palmer nodded and duly obliged in reading the woman her rights. Hogarth joined Neville Grave in the corner of the room. The shock had faded from his face. At Neville's side, Nancy Decorville wore a triumphant, preening smile as she threaded her arm through his. Hogarth ignored her and nodded at the man in respect. The case was closed. Neville nodded back in acceptance and thanks. Hogarth was set to turn away when he heard the young man call his name. He turned to see Neville pull his arm away from Nancy Decorville. The girl's smile faltered as Neville approached him.

Hogarth narrowed his eyes.

"Yes, Mr Grave?"

"A word if I may…"

There was a look in the young man's eye. His shock was more than understandable, but Hogarth saw something else too.

"Of course," said Hogarth. They walked to the stable door, leaving Nancy Decorville and the old woman looking at one another as Palmer dealt with Marjorie Goodwell.

"What?" said Decorville, as Neville shut the door.

The old woman didn't answer.

Nancy Decorville folded her arms and stood an isolated figure in the farmhouse kitchen. Her eyes trailed after Neville and Hogarth as they walked away talking. Inevitably, her eyes fell on the old woman once again. Susan Grave had been watching her the whole time, and when their eyes met, Mrs Grave offered her a deeply unpleasant smile. Her smile soon became a laugh.

"I'm sorry about that, Mr Grave. There can't be much worse than discovering that your own uncle killed your father. I can barely imagine what you're going through right now."

"But in the end, it always had to be one of us, didn't it?"

"There were other suspects," said Hogarth.

"Peter Venky?"

"Yes. Briefly."

"And then there were Igor and Borev."

"They were quickly ruled out. Maybe too quickly at first."

"It had to be one of us though…" said Neville.
Hogarth nodded. "The people waiting for the lunch announcement had the most to gain and the most to lose by whatever your father had planned to say. There was plenty of motive in that room. But it's still hard to believe that a family could do that to one another."

"As you know, Inspector, ours is not a normal family."

"The truth, Mr Grave, is that I believe there is no such thing. Every family has a past, has bitter regrets, and has skeletons in the closet. But thankfully, not every family has a Trevor Goodwell."

"Yes. And at least I now know for sure that I was the biological child of a man I will never meet. I know my mother too well. She'll never ever tell me who it was. She never speaks of it except to allude that she detests me for ever having been born."

"Maybe she does. But I've seen a few glimpses of affection from her too. I think her bitterness comes from the bottle. Either way, she has no one else to turn to now, apart from you. And now you have written proof your father wanted you to inherit the farm and no one else, that must count for something."

"It counts for a great deal, Inspector."

Hogarth held the slim sheaf of notes in his hand. "And it says a lot more in here than that. No matter the bloodline, you were his son, Mr Grave. There is no doubt about it. And your father's legacy to you is a plan to make this farm a success again. He discovered a crop which could bring in a good income for decades, so he said. A crop with global demand – soya."

"Soya! Yes. My father was a thinker. I should have known he'd come up with a solution. But he was getting weaker. I didn't think he had it in him any more to be even just the brains."

Neville and Hogarth stopped walking before they reached the edge of the barn where the old man had been murdered. They looked at one another, and Hogarth saw that look in Neville's eyes.

"You knew he was dying, didn't you?" Hogarth saw his words caused no shock.

Neville nodded mildly. "He was getting weaker and spending more and more time alone. He insisted on driving himself to his appointments without telling us what they were about. I got a little suspicious. In the end I found he'd run a couple of web searches on cancer symptoms, treatments and the like. But that was all. He never told us a thing."

Hogarth nodded. "It's not my place to say anything more, Mr Grave. But I don't think he had long. I think he was trying to get his house in order before he died."

Tears bloomed in the younger man's eyes.

"I wish I could have spent some of his last months close to him. Trevor's robbed us all of that."

Hogarth nodded and looked at the frozen earth beneath his feet. There was no comfort he could give for that. After a moment had passed, Neville sighed and wiped his eyes on the back of his sleeve.

"Still… I won't let him down. You can be my witness on that, Inspector. So long as my mother doesn't do anything to deny my father's wishes."

"I don't think she will. In my opinion, she doesn't have it in her anymore. Her malice comes from nowhere but the bottle, and has been encouraged by Trevor. She'll depend on you now."

Neville nodded and his eyes drifted away.

"You know, I was dreading that announcement," he said. "I couldn't have cared less about the farm in the end. I thought he was going to tell us he was dying."

Hogarth nodded. "That would have made sense. But I think his death was a secondary concern to him. He cared more about the farm, the legacy, and he wanted you to be a success. So, then," said Hogarth, changing tone. "I suppose you and Miss Decorville will start enacting your grand plans for the farm when everything calms down."

"Nancy? Oh no. She won't have any part of it. Not anymore."

Hogarth raised an eyebrow.

"Oh?"

"That stuff with the private investigator – she never told me about that. Like Trevor said, she had her own agenda all long. You said there were more agendas in the house than at a townhall council meeting. I don't think Nancy's agenda was much different to Trevor's…"

Hogarth's lips formed a wry grin. "And I thought you were head over heels for the girl," he said.

"So did I," said Neville. "But if she thinks I'm going to let her tear this farm apart on the back a few heated moments, she's got another think coming."

"Plenty more fish in the sea, as they say," said Hogarth.

"Except I don't think I'm going to have much time for fishing from now on."

"Hard work helps with grief of all kinds, Mr Grave. Hard work and whisky."

"Thank you, Inspector. I'll remember that recipe."

Hogarth looked up to the crisp cold sky and watched the steam of his breath curl away above him. He gave Neville a final curt but friendly nod. As he turned away the young man called him back.

"Inspector?" said Neville.
"Yes?"
"You did my father proud. Thank you.".
"Pleasure, Mr Grave."
Hogarth walked away, hands deep in his pockets. He avoided the back door, instead he passed the kitchen window and looked in on his way. The old woman didn't see him, but Nancy Decorville did. For all her good looks, there was no denying the bitter look in her eyes. The farm had moved beyond her grasp. The game had changed, and it was far too late for her to swap her cards.

Chapter Twenty-two

"How are we doing?" said Hogarth. He had his foot pressed to the floor, his sleek Vauxhall saloon swinging around the tight curves of the country lanes, Palmer shunting left and right in her seat with every turn.

"Two minutes twenty seconds, guv."

"Good. Good," he said. "It's not often I get to push this little car to the limit. Not often I can be bothered, to be honest."

"No," said Palmer, struggling to keep her decorum.

"But DC Simmons is a proper petrolhead. When I let him drive it he acts as if we've turned into Bodie and Doyle."

"Bodie and who?"

"Come on, you're not that green, are you?" said Hogarth. He shot Palmer a glance and saw she was blank-faced.

"Damn. Maybe you are. Bloody hell. You're in your late thirties and you're making me feel old. There really is no bloody hope, is there?"

"Two minutes forty, guv."

"Oh. I'd better speed up."

"You're well over the limit already!" said Palmer.

"Do you think the killer gave a shit about the speed limit? Neither do I."

As they headed for the painted roundabout of the Furdon's Way Industrial Estate, Hogarth judged the oncoming traffic, and made a quick call. He slammed his foot down and shot straight across the roundabout, preventing any other lane from pulling out unless they wanted to crash. A horn blared long and loud behind him.

"Police business!" said Hogarth with a shrug.

He pulled over on the verge opposite the Pradesh Convenience Store and got out quickly. Palmer followed, slamming the door behind her.

"You really think Goodwell would have got to the shop this fast?"

"Tell me. Have you seen any police cars out here apart from ours?"

"No," said Palmer.

"No. And we saw none on the last trip either. On a clear run, driving at fifty miles an hour in a thirty, yes, I think a man like Goodfellow would thrive on the challenge. He's the kind of bastard who likes to win at all costs. Come on, don't hang about," said Hogarth.

Hogarth jogged across the street. But as soon as he walked inside the shop, he slowed a little. Hogarth walked to the fridge and stared at the different packs of butter. He picked up a pack and put it down. Then he grabbed the other brand and put it down again. The shopkeeper gave Hogarth a strange, questioning look as Hogarth moved back towards the exit door.

"Just browsing," he explained.

"Browsing? At butter? Wait," said the shopkeeper. "You're the policeman…"

Hogarth stepped out of the shop without a reply. Palmer looked back in to answer the man.

"Nothing to worry about, sir, just testing a theory."

"There's nothing wrong with the butter in here, I can assure you…" said Mr Pradesh.

Palmer nodded as positively as she could, while withdrawing and closing the door. Hogarth was already halfway across the street.
"How we doing, Palmer?" he called.
"We're down to four-minutes and fifty-eight seconds to go," she said, glancing at the stopwatch on her smartphone.
"Get a move on then!" said Hogarth.
They jumped back into the Insignia, and Hogarth pulled out onto the country lane with a wide U-turn that made the tyres screech. He put his foot down and the car lurched away before Palmer had even clunked her seatbelt into place.
"Well, isn't this exciting?" said Hogarth.
"That's certainly one word for it," said Palmer.

Hogarth pulled between the tall red brick columns into Grave Farm with a drastic lurch and applied the brake.
"Time?!" he said looking at Palmer. His eyes were wide, his face tense.
"To be more accurate you would need to drive to the house," said Palmer.
Hogarth cursed under his breath, before pushing the car down the track towards the side of the house. He pulled up the handbrake and looked at Palmer again.
"Now?"
"Eight minutes forty-one seconds door to door. I didn't think it was possible…" said Palmer.
"No. Neither did I, but Goodwell must have fancied his chances. I bet he'd thought about it a few times during his cycling tours."
"But this might not be accurate. You hardly wasted time haggling about the butter."

"No. But I looked at it. Okay. Knock off another twenty seconds for the butter nonsense. That still gives us two minutes. Start the timer again…"

Hogarth and Palmer got out of the car and walked alongside the great old farmhouse at a clip. Hogarth stalked along like a man on a mission while Palmer kept her eyes on the time. Hogarth walked a tight angle, working to avoid the eyes behind the kitchen window as much as he could, then he changed angle at the last second, risked being seen, and dived into the barn.

"Now?"

"One minute fifteen left."

"Out of how much?"

"Twelve minutes, which is what we worked against last time."

"And the real window could have been longer – up to twenty minutes."

"No. He couldn't have used all that time on the butter run. There was leaving, stowing his equipment, getting into position in the barn…"

"Yes, yes, I get all that. And here we are. We've done it. We've cracked his alibi! Goodwell did it, as sure as eggs are eggs."

Hogarth clapped his hands in delight, but he saw his enthusiasm wasn't matched by the look in Palmer's eyes.

"What?" he said.

"But you could time it again and fail. You could do it again and fail five times in ten."

"But Goodwell wouldn't. That's the whole point. Goodwell would drive on the bloody pavements if he had to."

"It won't stand up in court, guv. The CPS might consider it, but only as throwing a degree of doubt on his alibi. But it won't absolutely disprove it."

"*Doubt* is the beginning, Palmer. A while back they all had cast iron alibis – but Goodwell's isn't cast iron any more. And we're not done with this yet. Let's take it a stage further. How long did we have left?"

"One minute, fifteen seconds."

"Okay. Go towards the chipper. Let's pretend you're the old man. Take your time, go over there, head towards the wood pile…"

Palmer shrugged. She started the timer and walked towards the woodpile. As she moved, Hogarth moved past her, and slid into the gap behind the hay bales. He looked at the dried trainer print. When Palmer was in position, Hogarth slid out again, and stalked towards her.

"The man moves in…" said Hogarth, narrating his moves so she would know what he was doing. "He seizes the old man… they struggle." As Hogarth lightly grabbed Palmer by her shoulders, they simulated a struggle. "Goodwell dominates him… picks him up…" Hogarth lifted Palmer clean off her feet. "And tosses him in." Hogarth looked Palmer in the eye, his grim smile faltered, and he dropped her back down to her feet. "Yes… sorry about that."

"Um. No problem," said Palmer, with awkward eyes. There was a momentary silence which Hogarth quickly quashed. "How long now?"

"Thirty-five seconds."

"Keep the timer going. Follow me outside."

Hogarth broke into a slow jog, running along the edge of the track until he reached the side of the house and then his car. He opened the door, counted a second slammed it shut. He opened the boot, counted a few seconds and closed it again. Then he ran back to the corner of the house near the kitchen door.

"Stop the clock!" said Hogarth. "Now what's the time?"

"You've got three seconds to spare."
"Three seconds? Then even being tight with the time, it fits. It really does fit."
"But no one saw him – surely someone would have seen him from the window."
"Goodwell was careful. He knew the lay of the land very well. And in the kitchen, they were busy, tense, distracted."
"And when he returned – no one reported that Goodwell was red-faced or out of breath."
Hogarth felt Palmer's eyes tracing over his face.
"That's because Goodwell is a darn sight fitter than me. He wasn't red–faced at all, that's why it wasn't mentioned. He did it."
Palmer met Hogarth's eyes and nodded once. But she gave it nothing more than that.
"It's still not enough."
"Maybe not. But you know it's him, don't you?"
Palmer shrugged. "Yes… I think so…"
"Where the hell is Marris when you need him?" said Hogarth. He took out his phone and kicked at the gravel with his brogues.
"Marris said he would call us, guv," said Palmer.
Hogarth's brow dipped over his eyes in confusion. "Did he now?"
Palmer bit her tongue.
"Well I've had enough of waiting." With drooping shoulders, Hogarth walked away. She heard him greet Marris before his voice faded out of earshot. Palmer's heart thudded in her chest. She recalled the strange moment where Hogarth forgot himself and lifted her off the ground. He was desperate, caught up in the moment, wanting to prove his theory. A good few other female officers she knew might have reported the incident, especially as it involved the

prickly, and occasionally sexist DI. But Palmer knew he'd meant nothing by it. And somewhere inside, she had been taken aback by her own response to his sudden manhandling. She'd felt vulnerable – not a feeling Palmer was comfortable with – but had she almost enjoyed it? Palmer shook her head and winced at the thought.

"You're turning into a bloody perv, Palmer…" she whispered to herself.

She straightened her back and looked at the ground with a sigh. Palmer hoped the new hints and hues of this juvenile attraction would simply fade away. They had to – before Hogarth noticed – before the rest of the nick did too.

In the distance, she saw Hogarth turn around.

"Okay… fine… thanks, Ivan," she heard him say. But Hogarth's face looked shadowy and downcast. Much less than fine. She watched him end the call and slide the phone into his jacket. In his customary style, Hogarth stuffed his hands into his chino pockets and paced towards her. His shoulders were hunched, his face serious. As she watched him she had the feeling of them both standing on a knife edge, though in truth, only Hogarth's fate hung in the balance.

When he was halfway towards her, Palmer could bear it no more.

"Guv?"

Hogarth looked up. His voice was low and quiet.

"You were right, Palmer. The alibi wasn't enough."

Palmer nodded and blew out a long, gutted breath.

Then Hogarth's grizzled face cracked a smile which grew wider with every passing moment. His eyes narrowed but let loose a glint of light.

"But now there's evidence too. Marris found a trace of blood – a minute amount of blood – in the boot lining of the

Porsche. The mini-valet vacuumed the carpets, but they didn't clean away the fibres. The blood is a match for Nigel Grave. I think we've just found a very good example of how Trevor Goodwell's penny-pinching might have just landed him in jail for murder."

"What?" said Palmer, smiling in shock.

Hogarth nodded. "Murder, Palmer. It was him. If he'd had a proper valet, those carpets would have been cleaned. There'd be no DNA to find."

"Are you sure? I mean, Goodwell could still argue the blood got there another way…"

"Hold your horses. The fibres in the boot space were neoprene. They contained sweat particles and skin particles which almost certainly belong to Trevor Goodwell. They are from neoprene cycling gloves. And they are the very same fibres as we found in the barn. And there's more. There is the ghost of a shoe print in the boot. We couldn't see it, but Marris has the tools to see what we can't. There's also a similar fractional trainer print in the footwell below the pedals. The stuff the vacuum left behind."

"But we don't have the shoes…" said Palmer.

"We don't need them, do we? Marris has a print out of every training shoe sole pattern ever made in the last thirty years. Can you believe it? It's true. He says those shoe prints belong to a pair of budget running shoes, Fiafora Speed Lites, which haven't been made for over six years. Whatever. And guess what? Those match the fractional prints Dickens found in the barn."

"Then we really have got him?"

"There's one more thing, Palmer."

"What?"

"Marris."

Palmer maintained a blank face, but her cheeks started to turn pink.

"Marris told *you* not to call him back. Not me. I just got my ears burnt for not following his strict instructions. Next time, Palmer, leave Marris to me. You know what he's like."

"Yes, guv. Sorry."

"No harm done. We've got him, Palmer and I can't wait to see his face…"

From the side of the house, they heard the modest chunter of a small car engine pootle through the tall gates onto the driveway of the house.

Hogarth walked to the front corner of the house and watched a red two-seater city car dawdle along the driveway. The vehicle had the name of a car rental firm emblazoned on the side. *Valu-Rents*.

"Who the devil is this…?" said Hogarth. Then he rose up on the balls of his feet. "Or should I say speak of the devil…?"

Palmer's eyes followed Hogarth's as the light of the cold grey day reflected off the glass and hid the identity of those inside. But as the car moved, the light faded, and Palmer saw Marjorie Goodwell's pinched face and stringy turkey neck, pressed awkwardly close to the ageing brawn of her husband.

"Okay. Let's get out of sight," said Hogarth.

"Why?" said Palmer.

"I don't want them to see us until the very last second. That scumbag has put me through the ringer. I want to enjoy this one to the full," said Hogarth. They stepped back into the shadows at the side of the house and watched as the Goodwells extracted themselves from the city car.

"Bit of a step-down from the Porsche Cayenne," whispered Palmer.

"But it's good practice. Trevor Goodwell's going to have to get used to cramped spaces and confinement. Looks like he's started early."

The Goodwells muttered to one another as they walked, hurrying along towards the big front door. The couple were bickering as they pressed the doorbell. A moment later, they were safely inside the house.

"They didn't see us," said Palmer.

"They were too busy arguing to notice. Maybe they've come to try some last-minute chiselling with the old woman. All to no avail, of course. Okay, Palmer. Call in some backup but tell them not to hurry. Goodwell's a killer, but he's not the dangerous type. I think five or ten minutes should wrap this up nicely…"

Palmer observed the glint in Hogarth's eyes and speculated as to what he had in mind. In the end she gave up trying and made the call. Hogarth enjoyed being inscrutable. With Palmer around, it wasn't too often that he succeeded.

Chapter Twenty-four

This time Hogarth closed the door of the DCI's office to face Long Melford with relish. This time his heart beat slower, and the angst was mostly gone.

Melford watched him quietly. Hogarth kept his poise.

"I just don't know how you do it," said Melford, eventually.

"Do it? Do what, sir?"

"You know what. You saved your own bacon. And mine too, I might add. The pressure from on high has gone ever so silent since you brought in Goodwell. And it stacks up well. The evidence is good. Forensics came through."

"And his alibi is broken."

"Yes, it's solid enough for a prosecution."

"And it's the right man, sir. He was using those complaints to steer us left, right and centre – anywhere away from him."

"Yes. You did seem convinced of his guilt. The CPS seem confident in the case too. Hopefully there's enough humble pie being eaten to keep them upstairs from opening their mouths for a while."

"Is there ever enough humble pie for that, sir?" said Hogarth.

"Maybe not, Hogarth," said Melford. "Besides, you know how it goes. You make your boss eat humble pie, he'll only want to make sure you're served a slice too."

There was a moment's silence while this sank in. Hogarth marshalled his face muscles to keep that smile in place a little longer.

"All that matters is that you're off the hook, Hogarth," said Melford, leaning back in his seat. "Well done."

"Thank you, sir."

"But you can't keep up this workload, can you? Any idea when Simmons will be back?" said Melford.

"Another week at least, sir. He's healing well. He wants to come back, but I'd rather he came in when he was fighting fit than lose him again if he freaks out on the job. He went through a lot in John Milford's apartment."

"Yes…" said Melford slowly. Hogarth sensed more coming. "But I'm also concerned about your welfare too, DI Hogarth."

"Welfare, sir?" said Hogarth.

"You know what I mean, Hogarth. I asked you to close that case on the double, and you did it. So now, for your sake, I'm asking you to leave that MP's house alone. I don't know what it is about. You don't strike me as the political type, so maybe it's just down to stress. I don't know. But whatever it is, make sure you keep away from James Hartigan. Because if you don't, I'll hear about it. Just listen to what I'm saying, okay?"

"I always do, sir. You know that," said Hogarth.

Melford regarded him with a steady, cynical eye.

"That will be all, Inspector."

"Yes, sir," said Hogarth.

The fresh clean air of relief blew through his mind as Hogarth stepped out into the corridor. With every step he felt better, but the sting of the Hartigan warning stayed uppermost in his mind. "*Screw you, sir,*" muttered Hogarth as he walked away.

"Cheer up, sir. You won," said PC Orton, as the thickset copper passed him in the corridor. Hogarth nodded with irritation. He walked out past the hotchpotch of desks towards the CID room which was his home. Young PCSO Rawlins gave him a grin. "Well done, sir," she said. Even

Dawson looked ready to deliver some sort of positive remark. It was all too much for Hogarth.

He stopped walking and gave Dawson and Rawlins a look. "Hold on. Trevor Goodwell is just one scumbag out of how many? Thousands, got to be. Tens of thousands, even. That town out there is full of them. So, thanks for the compliments. But let's not get carried away. I can't afford to get too big a head. I've got get out there on the lookout for the next one."

As Hogarth reached his office, PC Dawson shook his head "He can't afford to get a big head?" said Dawson. "If big heads cost money, he'd need a bloody second mortgage on that one."

CID always tended to work later and longer than everyone else, but with a nice big scalp in the bag, and the pressure lessened, Hogarth was looking forward to a few sips of whisky in front of the television. Tonight, maybe he would skip the news channels. He considered the soap operas for a moment. No bloody way. The comedy channels. The nature shows. A moment later he settled back on the news channel again.

Palmer looked up from her desk. The pensive eyes and tension seemed to have been wiped away. Melford's high-pressure antics had spread stress throughout the whole team. Or maybe that part was down to him. Hogarth realised he was still looking at Palmer's eyes. With the strain gone, the woman seemed brighter and happier than he'd seen her in a while. This was the pretty Palmer again. Funny. Hogarth doubted a woman like Palmer would ever think of herself as pretty. She had probably worked too long in CID to think of herself as anything other than a cop. For her sake Hogarth hoped she could find someone to tell her. Everyone needed an outlet, cops especially. They needed to feel like a human being outside of the job.

"Did Melford congratulate you?" said Palmer, mischief written on her face.

"Come off it," said Hogarth.

"Surely he had something positive to say. PC Orton is calling you DI Lastminute.com."

"Lastminute.com? Is that what he's saying?" said Hogarth.

"It's true, though. Didn't Melford commend you for closing the arrest?"

"Melford never has much good to say. He did share one pearl of wisdom – when superiors have to eat humble pie, they like to share it with their subordinates."

"Wow. That's really encouraging."

"Isn't it?" said Hogarth.

"But he said nothing aside from that?"

Hogarth shook his head. He wasn't going to share the rest – the part about James Hartigan MP was totally off-limits. As far as he was concerned it was off limits to Melford as well.

"Well, I'm sorry, we can't have that, guv. You need to be able to celebrate your success."

"You think so?" said Hogarth.

"Yes, I do."

Hogarth pondered an extra nip of whisky in front of News 24.

"Tell you what," said Palmer. "I've got a spare bottle of vino rosso. If you wanted, you could come round and I'd order a takeaway."

Hogarth looked at Palmer. The unreadable look in his eyes had her backtracking nervously.

"Just a glass of wine and some supper, that's all. Nothing really… or we could just grab a pint down the pub…?"

Palmer's cheeks tinged with the merest hint of pink. She looked away.

"It's just an idea, that's all."

"And a generous one, Palmer. But don't worry. I won't ever put on you again like I did before. I was out of order. It was unprofessional. You hardly need the hassle of having your boss hanging around your home after all these long hours."

"Unprofessional, sir? I thought it was funny, actually."

"Yes. Funny," said Hogarth. Funny was a part of the problem.

"Thanks, all the same. Drink one for me, Palmer and I'll drink one for you. How's that?"

"Spoilsport. But I suppose it'll have to do."

Hogarth grabbed his car keys from the desk. He gave Palmer a wink and slinked out of the door. "See ya. Make sure you have that drink," said Hogarth, and off he went.

Palmer watched the door clunk shut behind him and blew out a long breath.

"Well, that went well," she said. Then in a whisper, she added. "*Stupid, stupid, stupid.*"

Chapter Twenty-five

Hogarth's big feet were sprawled on his scratched coffee table beside three mostly empty foil takeaway cartons with traces of neon coloured sauce left at the bottom. He picked a few flecks of egg-fried rice from his shirt, and stuffed them into his mouth. On TV, a stern-faced reporter concluded his dispatches from a blighted middle-eastern war zone. Hopefully Igor and Borev were out of all that for good. These days it wasn't just the Yanks and the Ruskies on manoeuvres. The Iranians and the Saudis were at it too, playing war games in someone else's back yard. Same old crap, different decade. Hogarth changed the channel and found an image of a brightly coloured vista filmed from a helicopter. There were snow-capped mountains and crisp blue skies. Cyclists in wraparound shades hunched over their bicycles and gritted their teeth as they staggered up a mountain climb. It was easy bubble-gum viewing – until it reminded him of Trevor Goodwell. "Bastard," he said, and finished his glass.

He was about to pour himself another drink when his phone buzzed and bounced on the table.

He guessed it would be a comradely text from Palmer saying she'd drunk the wine she'd promised him. He grinned at the thought. It was banter, and he would reply in kind. She was a good egg, Palmer, and he wouldn't risk spoiling their working relationship by being a prat ever again. He needed her too much for that.

Hogarth lifted his phone to his eyes and lost his smile. He blinked and stiffened in his seat.

He put the whisky bottle down and read the text over again.

J This is Ali. I'm using a different number because I have to be very careful now. I think James knows something. I need to see you. Urgently. Meet me at the car park by Uncle Ron's.

"Uncle Bloody Ron's?" said Hogarth out loud. He frowned and scratched his head. Uncle Ron's was the run-down ice cream parlour at the Shoebury/Thorpe Bay end of town, where the beach and beach huts ended and the Ministry of Defence area took over the seafront. It was late. Uncle Ron's would be closed and the car park would be dark. Hogarth knew the car park had been synonymous with dogging, and other dubious sexual practices in recent years. But these days he was less au fait with it. Surely, Ali had more in mind than a bit of seafront nookie? All the same, with two whiskies in his system if Ali did want a kiss and cuddle, he wasn't going to complain. He hoped she didn't mind her kisses tasting of sweet 'n' sour with a hint of whisky. Then he thought about it again.

A new phone.

An urgent meeting.

Ali was in trouble.

What if Hartigan had turned against her? Then there was the stalker to consider…

Hogarth grabbed his jacket and car keys and stormed out of his house. He only remembered the alcohol swimming around his system after his Vauxhall had pulled out onto the busy London Road. But it was too late to worry about that now.

The seafront was busy along the flashing lights and party music of the golden mile. But beyond that, the seafront road was a long expanse of moonlight darkness occupied by a few late-night runners and cyclists. A few random drunks weaved their paths among them. He tapped the steering wheel and tried to keep his breathing calm as he drove.

Hogarth pulled into the wide dark car park behind the octagonal shape of Uncle Ron's, looking for any sign of other parked cars. There was a black van parked on one side by the public lavatories. He saw a kite-surfing logo on its side. Hogarth ignored it and drove around the car park in a loop. He looked into the area beyond, into the triangular field behind the last beach huts. In summertime the field was full of cars. It was used as an overflow car park. Deep into the triangular field, he saw a car. A saloon parked among the beach hut shadows. It didn't look like Ali's car. So maybe she hadn't turned up. Maybe Ali had got stuck – or worse – stopped by her suspicious husband. Hogarth considered his options then started to type a rapid text.
"Ali. I'm at Uncle Ron's. Where are you?"
He sent it to the new number. But there was no instant reply. Impatient and taking a risk Ali wouldn't like, he sent it to her usual number too. Just in case. If he'd still smoked, Hogarth would have happily reached for a fag. Instead he got out of the car and paced around in the cold. A freezing sea breeze rushed through his jacket and rattled the flagpole on the top of Uncle Ron's.
His phone buzzed. He lifted the phone and scanned it.
"Uncle Ron's? I don't understand. What are you doing there?"

Hogarth checked the sender. It was from A. The text had been sent by Ali's original number. Confused, he went back to the first text and now he saw the errors. The inconsistencies. She had called him J. When had she ever shortened his name like that before? Never.

Hogarth stopped pacing and stood stock still. His breath turned to ice.

"Oh shit!"

He started to type out a rapid text, to warn her they'd been rumbled. He mumbled the words as he typed them, concentrating to say just the right thing. He only heard the footsteps thudding close behind him when it was already too late. Hogarth spun around and put his arm up to block the attack, but the shadow launched at him with a flurry of punches. There was another shadow too. The second one was bigger and came at him from the side, lashing blows at his back and kidneys, and then his jaw with hard, solid punches. On his best days, Hogarth might have withstood it. But it was late at night. He was shocked with cold, and the food and whisky made him slow. The man in front of him sank a deep blow drilling into his gut. It doubled him over and filled his body with pain. Hogarth leaned down as the blows rained in, nausea filling his whole body. He heaved and vomited, but the pain carried on. The vomit sent the first attacker staggering back. Hogarth had enough energy left to laugh as he wiped his mouth.

"Scared of a little puke on your shoes… are you?" Hogarth worked hard to stand up as the first man backed away, and watched as he stepped into a pool of light from a street lamp. He was an aggressive looking man with a face like a London brick. Strong. Nothing like the stalker. But the other man was still at his side. Hogarth turned to face him, to try and fight back, but he didn't have the energy or the time.

Hogarth saw the fist coming a half-second before it struck him clean in the face. He went down. He hit the deck, narrowly avoiding the vomit, and then the kicks came again, and plenty of them.

"That'll do," said one, when Hogarth was groaning with pain. Most of it was feigned. If they thought he could take more, he knew they would have gladly given it to him.

"Time to get the message, copper. Stay the fuck away from her or this gets worse."

"Hartigan sent you," said Hogarth, in a croaky voice.

"Just stay away. Yeah?"

"Tell him…" said Hogarth.

"We ain't telling nobody anything!" said the bigger man.

"Tell the bastard that he's just lost my vote," said Hogarth. The big man landed one more kick as Hogarth let out a long wheezing laugh. Then he watched them turn their backs to leave. They jogged along the grass and dived into the car in the shadows. The headlights came on and the car shot away around the bend towards Shoebury. They were too far away for him to read their plates.

***

Hogarth had always hated being told what to do. He had been that way ever since he was a child. It was the reason why he'd seen so much of the headmasters office and had spent a lot of time standing alone, facing the wall. In the more than thirty years since, little had changed.

He saw Hartigan's Jag parked on the driveway, turned at a fancy diagonal angle as if it was still in the showroom window. Hogarth pressed the doorbell long and hard, then stepped down from the doorstep and waited. There was a movement of shadows behind the front room curtains, then a light came on in the hallway. A larger, male shadow led the way, followed by a female one. When the door opened, he saw it wasn't the secretary. It was Ali. He didn't look at her directly, but he saw the sudden shock on her face. He still didn't make eye contact. Instead he looked up at the smarmy James Hartigan, with his fashionable beard and his open-necked shirt collar. The man looked back at him in pure disgust.

"What the hell do you want now? Stay back, Ali. The man's disgusting. Look at him. He's a disgrace to the police."

"You've already had your say, Mr Hartigan. Tonight, you've had a free hit. But that's it. That's your last one."

"Are you threatening me?"

"I wouldn't dream of it, sir."

"Piss off," said the MP. He started to close the door but Hogarth slammed a flat palm against it and held it open.

"I know your game. I know scumbags when I see them, and you, my friend, are a scumbag of the highest order. What happened in that car park just now proves it."

"I don't know what you're talking about," said Hartigan.

"You wish you didn't," said Hogarth.

"Go away before I call the police."

"I'm going. But you gave me your message. And this is mine. I'll be watching you."

"Ali, is this the stalker you've been complaining about?" said Hartigan. He floundered away from the door, letting Ali get a clear view, before he blocked the door again.

"What do you think, Ali? Is this the man you saw?" Hogarth saw the arrogant duplicity in the man's eyes.

"No, that's not him. I've told you what he looks like," she said, her voice shaking.

"But how can you be sure? Now get off my driveway, officer, or I'll have your job before the morning."

"I'm going," said Hogarth. But he couldn't resist. He turned back. "Tell me, Mr Hartigan. Did you have any ambitions to be in government? Or even to get to number 10?"

Hartigan fell silent and stared at Hogarth.

"Because I now know enough to put the kibosh on that too, don't I? I don't care about losing my job. But I bet you care about yours. Good night, James," said Hogarth. "Sleep tight."

Hogarth ambled slowly back to his car. He heard the door shut behind him and the raised voices of a domestic argument commence.

He shouldn't have done it. But screw it. Maybe everyone involved needed a reality check, not just him. One way or another, here it was. Whatever happened next, he was in too much pain to give a toss. Whisky was calling. The morning would bring what it would bring.

Hogarth's phone buzzed through the darkness, buzzing louder than he thought possible. It cut through the black fog of his sleep, stabbing at his temples, announcing the pain which drunken sleep had hidden from him. Hogarth tried to stretch and he groaned out loud. His aching limbs finally woke him. It was dark, pitch black in fact. But it was still winter, and the mornings were not yet light. As he reached for his phone Hogarth's shoulders jerked with pain. His eyes snapped open and in hot shame he recalled what had taken place, the new enemies he had made, and the seismic shift his love life was about to take. None of it seemed possible. He hoped it wasn't. There were going to be consequences all round, and not many of them good. He grabbed his phone and the slits of his swollen eyes opened enough to see his LCD alarm clock. 11:57pm. He hadn't been asleep for more than forty minutes and now the pain had started over again.

A familiar sense of alarm gripped him. *Ali?!* But when he saw the name on screen all that changed.
Vic Norton. Norton was calling.
Legendary scoundrel, greedy little snitch and all-round waste of space.
Hogarth threw his phone far away from the bed and left it ringing. He rolled over, grunted and covered his head with the pillow. A storm of racing heartbeats and regrets gave way to a final, dead-bodied sleep.

Hogarth drank two coffees with his Ibuprofen and looked in the living room mirror for as long as he could bear it. His left eye was puffy and there was a dark gash by his temple. There were bruises all over his body. He could only imagine how the gossip machine at the nick would react to this.
A list of excuses whizzed around his head like a Catherine wheel but none of them seemed good enough.
It was ten to eight – time to leave for work. But first off, he wanted to get even with Vic Norton for the late-night interruption. In Norton's world, eight am was the equivalent of three in the morning. Hogarth picked up his phone from the floor and dialled Norton's number directly.
Norton didn't pick up, so Hogarth got ready to leave a snarky voicemail. But just as he was working up a decent insult, the nasal whine of Vic Norton's voice came on the line.
"I wondered when you'd call."
"Vic. I'm surprised you're awake this early," said Hogarth.
"And I'm surprised you didn't call back sooner. Unless you didn't check your voicemail."
"I thought I'd save myself that little joy."
"There's little joy involved, Inspector," said Norton, hamming it up.

"Spit it out. I've got work to do."

"Right you are... I've got some new facts about that girl of yours, Inspector."

Hogarth blinked at his reflection. He narrowed his eyes and his heart started thudding faster.

"What girl?" said Hogarth.

"You know the one. The one you haven't got..."

Hogarth growled and cut the call. But as the seconds passed, his rage turned into a morbid curiosity.

He turned for the front door, but he stopped at the threshold, and walked back into the living room. He looked at his phone and re-dialled the last number.

Norton answered before Hogarth had time to speak.

"I didn't think it would be long," said Norton.

"Whatever you have to tell me, tell me now, and tell me everything, or so help me I'll..."

"Ah-ah-ah. No threats," said Norton. "Or I won't tell you a thing."

Hogarth fell silent and blinked at his battered reflection in the living room mirror.

"Good," said Norton. "But there's one more thing, Inspector."

Hogarth listened. "Go on."

"This is going to cost you..."

Hogarth gritted his teeth and got ready to listen.

Get the final boxed set in this series now!

Thank you for reading The Darkest series books 1 and 2 the first double bill boxed set of the DI Hogarth Darkest series. I hope you enjoyed it!

I'd be honoured if you could leave a review. Thanks so much!

If you would like to get some more highly rated novels - for free - simply join the Readers' Group at SolomonCarter.net. It's free to join and once you're in I'll send you links to lots of cool stuff. Rest assured, I won't spam you and yo can quickly and easily unsubscribe at any time. There is a list of my other book below.
All the very best,
Solomon:)

The DI Hogarth Darkest series
1. The Darkest Lies
2. The Darkest Grave
3. The Darkest Deed
4. The Darkest Truth

More thrilling books by Solomon Carter

Long Time Dying

The first thrilling adventures featuring Eva Roberts & Dan Bradley, private detectives

1. Out with A Bang
2. One Mile Deep
3. Long Time Dying
4. Never Back Down
5. Crossing The Line
6. Divide and Rule

7. Better The Devil
8. On Borrowed Time
9. The Dirty Game
10. Only Live Once
11. Behind the Mask
12. The Dark Tide
13. Lucky For Some

Luck & Judgment

featuring Eva Roberts & Dan Bradley, private detectives

1. Luck & Judgment
2. Truth Be Damned
3. The Sharp End
4. Don't Go Gently

London Calling

featuring Eva Roberts & Dan Bradley, private detectives

1. Rite To Silence
2. London Calling
3. Promise To Pay
4. The Pressure Zone

The Final Trick

featuring Eva Roberts & Dan Bradley, private detectives

1. The Final Trick
2. Taste of Death
3. The Danger Room

4. Killers and Kings

Also available by Solomon Carter

The Last Line thriller series – espionage, international adventure and all out action with Jenny Royal and The Company

Black and Gold – Vigilante Justice short read series featuring Simon 'The Man in the Mask' and Jess. Crosses over with the adventures of Eva Roberts and Dan Bradley, private detectives.

Roberts and Bradley Casebook – segmented short read series available in novel format as 'complete box sets'. Continues the PI storyline from Long Time Dying.

1. Flesh and Blood
2. Rack and Ruin
3. Two Wrongs

THE DARKEST Boxed set 1

The Darkest Lies and The Darkest Grave

DI Hogarth Darkest Series Books 1 and 2

First published in Great Britain in 2018 by Great Leap

Copyright © Solomon Carter 2018

Solomon Carter has asserted his moral right under the Copyright, Designs and Patents Act 1988, to be identified as the author of this work.

This book is a work of fiction and except in the case of historical fact, any resemblance to actual persons living or dead, is purely coincidental.

All rights reserved. No part of this e-book publication may be reproduced, stored in a retrieval system, or transmitted in any form or by any means, electronic, mechanical, photocopying, recording or otherwise, except by a reviewer who may quote brief passages in a review, without the prior written permission of the author.

Printed in Great Britain
by Amazon